The Iron Ark

Ryan Loup-Glissant

The Iron Ark

Production copyright FurPlanet Productions © 2025

Text Copyright © Ryan Loup-Glissant 2025

Cover Artwork © Slate 2025

Published by FurPlanet Productions
Dallas, Texas
www.FurPlanet.com

Print ISBN 978-1-61450-686-7
Electronic ISBN 978-1-61450-687-4
First Edition Trade Paperback

...because largely, about all a human being is anyway is just a hoping machine.

—Woody Guthrie*

*He's a marmot in this mess if anybody needs to know

Table of Contents

Prologue

   Six Days Earlier   9

Chapter 1

   Fate's Auction   11

Chapter 2

   Assets   26

Chapter 3

   Suffered for What   35

Chapter 4

   Sturdy Boughs   50

Chapter 5

   Rat Food Runs and Rallied Rage   63

Chapter 6

   The Lie Rains Down   83

Chapter 7

   Things in Silly Boxes   102

Chapter 8

   The Mirror's True Curse   118

Chapter 9

   Nails for Names   135

Chapter 10

    Cops, Feds, and Lawyers   151

Chapter 11

    ...Care of Lost Equity   166

Chapter 12

    Connections   178

Chapter 13

    Closing In   195

Chapter 14

    Many Spokes   209

Chapter 15

    Licked Wounds   223

Chapter 16

    Directions Given   238

Chapter 17

    Snag or Two   253

Chapter 18

    No Sides   274

Chapter 19

    Intersections   290

Chapter 20

    Corks   308

Chapter 21

    The Iron Ark   324

Chapter 22

    Choices   338

Chapter 23

    Du bist ein Werwolf!   353

Chapter 24

    Reckonings to Come   366

Chapter 25

    Swears   377

Epilogue

    "Then I Heard the Judge Make His Decision…"   400

Acknowledgments   402

About the Author   403

Also by Ryan Loup-Glissant   404

PROLOGUE

SIX DAYS EARLIER

Cars huddled on the unkempt lawn and the summer chalet's dark doors were propped open to banish the smell. Nobody wanted to go in there.

The Ford Tudor crunched gravel as it rolled to a stop amongst oily New York State Police Chryslers. The weasel in the driver's seat stared over the wheel at the dark wide windows, mortar-stone chimney, and warped, neglected shingles for some time. He glanced briefly at the silvery photograph tacked near the glove box knob. A supple black-furred visage with a thin white stripe between her eyes smiled warmly at him before he put on his studious indifference, straightened his tie, and got out.

Cigarette butts were in a ring around four officers a good way from the structure. They watched the brown-pelted, tan-suited weasel approach, hitch up the wire frame lenses on his nose, and produce a badge. "Tomlinson, Bureau of Investigation."

"Thought you were the Federal Bureau now," muttered a mutt around his smoke's curl.

"It's in the works," the weasel muttered. "Have you been through?"

A cougar took a tobacco-tarred breath. "Eight bodies, shots fired. Something's off about it. Everything really."

The weasel looked back at the house. "Who called you?"

"Anonymous," said an orange tabby, scratching his neck. "Only found ID on one of them in there."

Minutes later Tomlinson was inside, blood stink crowding his nostrils and flies already seeking real estate. Crimson slashes painted the couch next to the crumpled corpse of one of the slain mammals. Others, mostly carnivores with one female possum, were dotted around the place. Near the couch, the lion Tomlinson studied was late middle age, stately, bespoke suit. He rifled through pockets where they'd already found the lion's iden-

9

tification and diplomatic documents. There was a torn slip with a hotel monogram for the Waldorf Astoria in New York. Big cat had money. A name scrawled on the business card's back stood out: Crawford Cain. Lupine.

Others would come to take photographs before anything else was moved but Tomlinson had what he needed. He passed an open, empty crate with winding chains lying snake-like around it and gave it a worried glance. There was no indication of what it had contained.

Four more corpses were spread out back behind the chalet, holes through their chests. A feeling crept up his hide then, like he was being watched. The rolling hillside trees were pleasantly anonymous in all directions but the sensation tailed him all the way back to where the police waited.

He ran into the sheriff, a bloodhound who arrived late and chewed discontent in tobacco form. "We know whose place this is?" the hound asked Tomlinson without preamble.

"I do." The weasel pushed up his glasses. He had sources the sheriff would never see. "Turns out it belongs to Donovan Calvert, the rabbit steelman who went missing in twenty-three."

Chapter I

Fate's Auction

The tarnished brass of last sun slipped away from Ohio, painting the lone pale farmhouse and clapboard auction sign swaying on its porch. Those present flicked their ears and twitched impatient tails, ignoring the two threadbare cats outside their circle.

Foreclosure auctions used to be held by day, but evicted farmers and 'steaders had banded together of late to shut them down, so most were held in near secrecy now for speculators who paid to be in the know.

The evictees stood at a distance, tails limp, the only eyes on them belonging to a State-badged Doberman whose flinty gaze held them back with promises of consequence. Behind the cats an old Ford bore a tower of tin pots, rusty tools, and dusty blankets, possessions to be pawned off on a westward crawl.

Polished sedans were arrayed around an inner ring of vulture-like mammals, hungry eyes to the home's porch where a capped squirrel waved for attention and squinted against the dusty air. "Lot seventy-two, item one and only, this farmhouse, adjacent barn foundation, and surrounding eight acres will start at four hundred dollars. As is."

Bidders ignored the disdainful spit of one of the evicted cats. Light waned. The bidding began. The opener was met by a stern cougar, upped by twenty dollars care of an impatient wolf. The cougar and a fox both went five-fifty at once.

Then came the call for six hundred.

All eyes turned to one of the sedans, a black Packard with its salon door ajar and its occupant sequestered in darkness. The voice was feminine, emotionless, unassuming.

An ermine before the auctioneer coughed. "Six-ten," she called.

A dog of mixed breed looked sourly at the rickety house, having not yet bid. The wolf growled out for six-twenty.

"Eight hundred," came the voice from the car, unwavering and certain.

Every gaze fixed on the dark maw within the sedan, breath was drawn, and eyes blinked.

The land and assets were projected to be valued at seven hundred and required extensive work to maximize any agricultural yield after the home was bulldozed. Another farm three lots over had sold at seven-forty with fixtures in better condition than this one.

Frugality doused greed quickly.

The auctioneer kept his practiced demeanor, not raising a brow. Away from the throng, the felines who'd not seen more than one hundred dollars at once in their entire lives fumed. They knew they should have hit the road after their eviction, but they wanted to see the face of whoever plucked the last ten years of their lives away, search for one iota of mammalian feeling in their eyes.

Silence fell. The horizon was now a strip of pale gold. "Going once," the squirrel called, eyes darting around. "Going twice…"

The scavengers grumbled. It was late. Other foreclosed farms waited to be swallowed, with dozens more to come.

"Sold." The gavel closed it and one of the cats hissed a low curse past the cop's unyielding shoulder.

The day's last ember died. Then springs shifted almost imperceptibly under the Packard. One hoof and then another touched hard soil and the doe stood, a mere silhouette in the porch's lamplight, no scent spreading. She wore nondescript black that kept slight to her sinewy frame and yet was cut almost matronly, flaunting no sign of wealth. Confident strides told every glance that demonstrations of affluence were, to her at least, irrelevant.

Thwarted bidder's sedans filled. Engines turned over. The squirrel met her gaze, deed rolled up and the key with it. "There will be signatures required, ma'am."

"Of course." She drew a leather-bound cheque book and filled the slip quickly. Her nose lifted to the worn home beyond. "May I?"

The squirrel shrugged. "You own it, ma'am, once your payment clears."

"Take the officer with you."

The squirrel made agreeable noises as he accepted the cheque. "Once he moves the squatters away—"

"No." She studied the house and ignored all else, her white throat still as though she held her breath. "Send them in to see me."

The cats were still in earshot and traded wary glances. "Somethin's off 'bout her," the male muttered bitterly. "Doe all alone wit' no husband."

His wife's tail curled in agitation. "It's more than that."

"Quiet you two," the cop growled, angry that he couldn't turn and check the doe out more thoroughly.

On the porch the auctioneer squirrel's tail touched the back of his own head and his gaze narrowed in the cat's direction. "Even if you've brought a chaperone, ma'am, that's not…advisable."

The doe's ears cocked. Her gaze met his. "I needn't fear them. Perhaps you might."

The procession of cars was filing out and only the lamps of the cop car and the oil burning on the porch kept night at bay.

The squirrel looked to the Doberman to confirm that he and the doe wouldn't be left alone with the evicted.

The cop glanced from squirrel to doe, and then back to the cats. "I'll wait a little longer. Don't you go causing trouble for upstanding folk." The Doberman scuffed trespassed dirt with his claws as the cats passed him by.

"I'll need you to wait another few minutes," the doe called to the squirrel as he took down the auction sign. "I need to check the condition of the purchase."

"It's as is, ma'am." The rodent stayed clear of the advancing cats.

"Please indulge me. I'll be quick and you can be on your way." Then to the cats, "Please come with me."

"What's this?" The female feline rubbed dusty hands on her last good blouse for the road. "You gonna taunt us with what we no longer own? This some rooter's game?"

Her husband had jammed hands in his worn pockets and was keeping them there. Shame bleeding into anger wouldn't serve either of them.

The doe stepped onto the porch. "Nothing of the sort, Marjorie. I'll need your help and will compensate you and Samuel both."

That gave them pause, not the least bit because Marjorie hadn't given her name. What meager scratch the cats had was in a tin box under the driver's seat and wouldn't last long.

"How much?" Marjorie's husband asked.

"You'll see."

The doe and cats alone together left the doe in a bad position to lie to them. "Alright," the female muttered.

The doe slid the key into the door and opened it into echoing darkness. "Please take the lamp. After you."

In they went, footfalls groaning naked planks. Bare walls climbed high, the emptiness of the house's main floor broken only by rickety ascending stairs and a cast-iron stove squatting in repose. Scents of burnt corn husk sweetened the air. When the last of the crops had gone, what little remained made for cheaper fuel than coal.

The doe closed the door behind them and lamplight was all there was. "I need you to remember, this is extremely important. Many years ago a rabbit came to you. His name was Calvert. Do you two recall?"

The cats traded glances, lamplight flickering in their eyes as the ghosts of more than a decade in this space hung heavy. Meals, plans, kisses, arguments, and ultimately despair.

Samuel nodded. "I...remember. But it was a possum feller as I recall, worked for somebody with that name."

The doe nodded. "That possum gave you something for safekeeping. Something that seemed unimportant at the time. You were well paid to speak to no one."

Samuel had all but forgotten the felt drawstring bag. "I made him show me to make sure we weren't hiding somethin'...wrong. It was nails. Black crooked nails."

"Large, like the nails that hold this house together?"

Ghosts of their own making crowded the shadows. So much taken from them... "Yeah. Bent like they wouldn't hold a flyer wagon together. We'd thought the possum was nuts. Then the rabbit with that steel company went under like all the other big shots and we just forgotten 'bout the whole thing. We had his money, didn't hurt nobody." In the closed space with the doe, Samuel realized he couldn't hear a sound or smell a scent from her. "Who are you?"

"I'll pay you if you bring those nails. It's important. Can you find them for me?" Oil light danced over the deer's golden features and the black dress that drank every ounce of illumination.

Still no figure given, but desperation forwent bargaining. "I can."

"I will wait here." For the first time, an emotion from the doe, an inexplicable anxiety.

"I remember," Marjorie said. "The board behind the closet on the cross beam."

"Please bring it down," the doe said.

The cats ascended the staircase for the last time. It was a torturously earned payout, assuming the doe wasn't lying. A faint square betrayed where the framed photograph had hung of Marjorie's passed sister. At the landing they felt the absence of the small table that had held a lamp sentry between the two rooms. Within their vacant bedroom, moonlight licked the closet's brass knob and within the dark Samuel felt the loose plank. The bag in the small space was dusty, silvered by cobwebs. They both held the bag between them, pain, love, and loss dangling before they descended again to the landing.

The doe wasn't there and for a moment they thought she'd fled. "The trunk of my car is open," came her voice from the dark, sounding strained. "Place the bag in there."

They went out, passed the squirrel auctioneer, his tail twitching, gaze directed pointedly away.

The car trunk was open and Marjorie set the nails within. The Doberman cop in his Ford watched suspiciously.

"Thank you," the doe spoke from far behind with a thin, labored voice. Something discomforted her. "Now come back to the house."

The squirrel auctioneer was indignant and impatient as he was beckoned back, eyes on the dark road back to Youngstown. The doe held the deed out. "You'll need your pen."

The oil lamp remained within the house, making its windows wink like tired eyes. "What for, ma'am?" the auctioneer asked.

"You have my check. If it clears the deed is thus approved and the home is turned over to the original owners. Write their names on the deed and meet them in town tomorrow. Again, this is pending the clearance of my check, which will occur without issue."

Marjorie gasped and Samuel's eyes widened as they approached the light.

"What's your game, ma'am?" the squirrel said as he took the unrolled deed back from her and turned in confusion to the cats.

"I have what I came for. Fill the deed in their names. Then leave. I doubt they'll want you skulking about their property too long after." She released the document and slipped back from the lantern's light. Shadows collected close behind the doe, beckoning in the corner of every eye.

The cats drew closer to one another, terrified at once by the slippery thread of hope. The world had ground them down over years. And now...

"Why?" Samuel croaked as he approached the waiting squirrel. "You took it. You took it all. Why would you give it back?"

He turned back to the house's dark porch where the doe's voice had emanated and found it empty. Marjorie's hand was clasped in his and their claws dug into one another.

Samuel felt the cold presence at his shoulder at the same time Marjorie did, as she turned toward the voice on the wind.

"I have what I need. So do you. You'll forget me soon enough as the end of a bad dream." The voice in Samuel's ear had no breath and his heart nearly seized. "The bank will offer you another loan. The few that didn't close down stayed in business by tempting the desperate. A better tractor, a sturdier roof, things you want before you need. That's the first drop of your blood they'll get. They'll keep drinking." Her voice receded into the night. "Don't invite them in again."

The doe's car started but no doors opened or closed. Driver unseen, it slowly rolled off the cat's reclaimed lot.

Hearts beginning to pound, the cats took the contract for their second chance and ushered the bank's lackey off their land with all haste. The cop left soon after.

The wind picked up and dust chased the cats back inside. Giddy feet stamped echoes as they ascended their stairs, entered the ghostly vacancy of their bedroom, and filled it with tears and laughter again. They'd unload the car in the morning.

Against the wind's whispers they made frantic love on the floor.

***

Burgers sizzled on the griddle, yellow sheafs of cheese nestling down. Lil could eat both, but with another two hours on foot, she barely had time for a few cold fries and the rank earthiness of hot coffee dashed with cream. The rush was over, but customers kept drifting in.

Furdy's Diner was a staple of Hancock, Maryland, a small town crammed into the puzzle-piece intersection of Maryland, West Virginia, and Pennsylvania. For all the ravages of the Depression, the knotted cross-road still saw soda wagons, ore trucks, ice vans, and slack-tied salesmen ruminating on their unsold vacuum uprights. They parked, gassed, scarfed down nickel burgers and two-cent red-eye coffees before hustling off to scrounge what they could.

Among the typical clientele of the sleepy and the harried, Lil's latest customers stood out. A scruffy weasel, a gangly wolf, and a stout-trunked German shepherd sat over coffee steam, the ruins of their dinner long since collected. The German shepherd held court and was likely collecting the cheque, his alabaster double-breasted suit boasting a tight, high ivory necktie. An indistinct gold pin shone on his lapel and a Stetson covered the hat hook by the boarded weekday specials. Next to him, the weasel's cap was pushed back, suspenders loose over a striped shirt. Across the wooden laminate table, the wolf in a powder blue shirt with rolled-up sleeves was tired but attentive.

"Purity." The shepherd's accent sounded middle South to Lil's ear— Arkansas, maybe Missouri. "That's what America lacks. Everything we say on every stage comes back to that. No compromises."

This at the wolf, who fidgeted and sipped more coffee. Lil saw as the mug tipped that it was getting low.

"You ready?" the shepherd asked as Lil approached, her ursine frame making the floorboards creak.

The wolf didn't answer this important question and Lil filled the silence as she towered over them. She was a big bear who kept customers at ease with contagious charm. The pot in her lace-draped hand sloshed gently. "Coffee's brewed fresh. Can I get you fellas some pie?"

The shepherd and the weasel were facing her, and the weasel sniggered. She felt the cold front of his disposition before he spoke, eyes down then up. "Yours wouldn't be my first choice."

The shepherd busted out a laugh, gaze finding the wolf's across from him. She didn't see the lupine's reaction.

Lil turned, feeling hurt well up with shame's heat. Her size always brought the rudest daggers. She stalked back to the griddle where Frank was setting burgers on plates and felt tears threaten. A familiar sensation drew something up from the earth under her claws like a tremor that made her want to stamp her feet. She didn't remember where her mother heard the phrase, but it stuck like a skipped record. "Can't bottle up when cork's been lost."

She wanted to get some air, but the next order was ready, and the bell rang. Lil found composure and bore the burgers over to a waiting couple of fossas who silently sensed her discomfort.

Back at the register, the wolf waited, the others already gone. Lil rang up the trio's order without a word and her brown eyes met his blue ones only for a moment.

"I'm sorry about…" he said. "That was…rude."

The hurt had settled down and the apology was almost a salve. Almost. "Anything else?"

The wolf swallowed, clearly uncomfortable as he counted out bills, grey-white fur moving up and down his throat. "May I ask…do you know if there's a bar around here?"

Lil blinked as she realized he'd tipped well enough. Perhaps he was sorry after all. "O'Holler's is two blocks south, further into town." She looked into the young wolf's eyes to find what lurked behind his trepidation, but his gaze moved off to his compatriots out the front window.

"Thanks, Lil," he said with a glance at her name tag. "I'm Luke. You have a good night."

He left like a sleepwalker and Lil watched him go.

***

"Want a cigarette?"

"Sure."

A pack of Rothman's was shaken and one came loose. Crawford Cain's lips barely touched it before the bulldog's blow rocked his jaw. The chair he was bound to shuddered and his claws scrabbled to keep him upright.

The dog that struck him rolled back his lips from grubby teeth. "Sorry 'bout that. But you deserved it for the trouble you've put us through."

Crawford licked upward to confirm his lupine nose wasn't bleeding. "That's fair, I suppose."

"Drink to calm your nerves?" Rank whiskey sprinkled from a flask into a tin cup on the rickety table, the dusty brick room's only other stick of furniture.

"Why not?"

The bulldog threw it in the wolf's face and Crawford sputtered.

"Sit tight," the dog told him and stalked out, kicking the wooden door shut behind him and throwing Crawford into near darkness.

Crawford dripped shame from his whiskers and listened for the mammal's receding footfalls. He smelled sea salt off the Boston wharf just beyond the small shack and wondered if he'd ever smell anything else.

"Gotta deal with the fucker," growled a voice that should have been out of earshot. The fucker under discussion listened.

"How. Nearest bar's a hop away. They'll hear gunshots in every dive in port."

"Nobody will care. They'll think it's a tug backfiring."

The ropes binding Crawford's hands were tight enough to hurt. They'd hurt worse if he got mad and the change came.

"The wolf saw us do the night clerk so we can't let him go. We need to know what he knows, like how he got the box key, first off. We weren't s'posed to have competition on this job." From the sibilant spitting Crawford guessed that was the ferret in the crew.

A third voice rumbled, a hound whom Crawford had barely seen but smelled more strongly than anyone. "You shot the clerk so handling that's on you, isn't it?"

Crawford could still see the light gone out of the rabbit's eyes when they popped him, right before they'd found out that the box Crawford had that clerk fetch was the one they'd come to nab. Horrible timing for everybody, worst for the clerk of course.

And now, so many questions.

Crawford's confidential hire had informed him that he'd be paid handsomely to obtain safety deposit box two-six-two from the National First Bank on State Street and he'd been provided with both a key and a legal document to do so. He'd been told the paying client couldn't appear them-selves without being told why, only promised nothing dangerous was in that box besides some nails which Crawford was welcome to check for himself.

What bullshit.

Crawford was coming to hate the private investigator racket. He should have stuck with selling cars after leaving Chicago.

His vision was starting to grey over a bit and he fought it. He needed to keep it together, think his way out of this rather than…

"All this for a goddamn box of rusty nails," the ferret complained.

"You sure they aren't silver or something?" the hound asked.

"Naw, they smell like, I dunno, iron. Good pay means it don't matter. We gotta dump the body and get out of town yesterday."

The bulldog who'd thrown whiskey in Crawford's face growled. "I wanna know who sent him. I mean, same time as us? Was he there in case we didn't do the job? Or to take it and finish us off? If I gotta yank out every claw I'm finding out. Then we pack it in, not before. Get to it, Lonnie."

"Why me?" The ferret whined. "I don't wanna get to Cape Cod with blood on my shirt."

"Because you boast at how good at this stuff you are," the hound insist-ed. "Make 'em feel the first few, really feel it, and he'll sing to make it stop."

Crawford's gorge started to rise; the things they could do with just a nail file or some utility scissors. He wouldn't be lucky enough to black out, not with what he battled inside.

And nobody was coming for him.

That did it. Fight or flight with no chance of the latter gripped his hammering heart and all at once his teeth began to ache: the first stage.

"Get a rag from the jalopy. Keep the mess off the floor," the bulldog told somebody, but the words were already muddy. Crawford's bonds hurt like hell, and he fought to keep calm, extend his senses, focus! It was a busy night on the verge of a crowded city, just like that night twelve years ago when he'd chased a scofflaw weasel into that midtown Chicago cemetery.

The bonds at his limbs started to throb as they shrunk around dis-tending limbs. The room grew smaller, the single dying bulb a ghostly star in a grey void.

He smelled prey as pain spread and the chair broke like a collection of twigs.

Silent! He shouted inside his shrinking cage of agency. Keep quiet! They have guns!

The memory of gunpowder stink was the last deliberate thing recalled before he rose and the door opened.

The ferret was still wearing the union denim coveralls of the janitor's garb he'd wandered into the bank with before jamming a gun in the clerk's face. Now he had a blade in his hand and he froze as his eyes roved up the torn shirt, broad wicked shoulders and slavering, distended jaws at eyes that were barely Crawford's anymore.

"Fugg," the weasel muttered.

Clawed hands like spread rakes cupped the weasel's head in a flash, cutting off a screech as the creature was lifted bodily off the ground.

A twist and a bite and the weasel's throat gurgled copper. Shaken like a ragdoll, Crawford bit him again, tearing cloth, pelt, and flesh from ribs. What he dropped to the floor of the storage room shuddered and bucked for a few seconds more.

Nose licked clean, Crawford smelled canine scent above ocean stink, oil, and grease. Round a corner, where the night's cooler air ruffled his fur, he smelled wetmark.

"Whatcha doing?" the bulldog asked.

"What?" the hound answered, irritated.

"Why are you doing that? Why you gotta piss where I'm pissing?"

"I'm just goin' same as you."

"Right on top of where I'm marking? What are you, a cub?"

Crawford found them bickering against a brick wall, tiny, smelly, amusing. He licked his jaws and his tail wagged. Clothes were heavy, constricting. He wanted to piss where they pissed, howl, find the moon, drag it down.

The dogs sensed something and both sniffed. The bulldog turned first and his eyes widened as his urination ebbed and stopped.

Challenge!

Crawford swiped playfully. The bulldog made wet, confused sounds as his lower jaw vanished in a mist of red and he fell twitching. The sounds from his turning companion were angry and the piss smell was encroaching, so Crawford chuffed his annoyance and put a meaty paw backed by a pillar of muscle against the other's skull and shoved. Everything under Crawford's hand spread on the brick with a red spatter and that scent made him hungry.

No! He couldn't eat even though he wanted to. Roll in his fun, maybe.

No! Thoughts swam up, deliberative, insistent. There was a box that stunk that he was supposed to want and he wandered around and sniffed until he found it. The part of him that wanted it took control again and he sulked as the world's colors resolved once more. The rent fabric that bound him hurt less as he stumbled towards things he put names to. The table held the deposit box, a revolver, a flask, and a car key. The box's proximity hurt.

Crawford Cain, whole and capable of deliberation and guilt, swigged the whisky flask and grabbed the long deposit box. It was hot under his arm, its very presence uncomfortable in a way he couldn't put words to.

As he stumbled towards the scent of engine oil out on the docks he forced himself to survey the two corpses, one still twitching, mired in the collective stink of blood and piss. He had to get scarce, so he dealt with what mess he could quickly.

Ten minutes and three splashes later, the thieves' car turned over with difficulty in the dark. Moonlight glinted off ripples of water beyond the dock where the dead were already floating out. He took the south route out of Boston before swinging east, looking for the right place where the General Motors could be abandoned and burned.

***

Fred Astaire and Ginger Rogers clicked claws under spats and spun to the swell of the orchestra as Samson watched, breathlessly mouthing the words. "Heaven…I'm in heaven…"

The silvery movement of lithe feline bodies in their finery entranced the goat, yet his gaze was frequently dragged downward to the spill of light upon the glinting fur of heads, pressed cheek to cheek in pairs throughout the auditorium. Their closeness and warmth were as indescribably magical as the celluloid courtship they followed. Samson drank it all in without understanding, curiosity boundless and his cares banished. In the here and now he was as much a part of the lives he imagined as he was a part of the affair on screen.

Soon enough, the RKO picture ended, velvet curtains squeaked closed. Samson waited while the silhouettes became mammals, rising and chattering over the buttery-scented concoctions in their paper bags as they filed out, himself last of all.

He picked a couple out in the Globe Theatre's lobby. The demure rodent pair were discreet in their isolation from the carnivores who'd left first. Their attentions were fixed closely on one another as they turned outside the movie house, momentarily rescued from the shadows of nighttime Scranton by the banks of lightbulbs under the deco marquee. It boldly advertised the premiere of *Top Hat* and a second run of *Scarface* on alternate nights with *Dracula*.

The female had short brown fur between her rounded ears, and for a moment Samson could believe it was Clara, his capybara friend from Noah's Plank School for Wayward Youth a whole lifetime ago. Reminiscence was inevitable even though it hurt.

He'd been a naive kid then, ignorant of any of the world's pains not heaped on orphans. Then a lion from a faraway place came to Chicago and trapped him in amber. In every sense that a physician would understand today, he'd ceased to be alive.

Now anonymity blanketed him. The downtown was busy enough on a Monday night that he felt no need to bind himself in shadow. Children wandered these streets all day and night, urchins invisible in a time when most pockets were presumed empty even as some declared the Depression was ending while others insisted it would persist. He passed his reflection in a store window, ignored the morose adolescent goat kid within it, horns barely stubs, beard a fleck, a still image that nevertheless moved.

He hadn't fed in two days, and yet with Celeste and Crawford gone for the past two nights, he hunted for understanding instead. Samson followed the rodents, listened, studied.

The female he'd almost thought a capybara was actually of marmot stock, arm in arm with a squirrel. Mixed relationships were less derided than they'd been even ten years ago, far less than the decade or two before his mortal birth. The country had other things to fret about.

The pair turned a corner and the thinning of automotive coughs let the tinkle of their chatter float back. The squirrel said something about cat hair floating against the closeups and the marmot said something about dancing lessons as she tightened her grip on his arm, claws crinkling the fabric just a bit. What that would feel like, Samson didn't know.

Shadows were long ahead, and he knew he could discreetly skip ahead to hear better, see their expressions, divine what they were thinking or feeling. Smell the popcorn on their breath. He didn't even know why it was important.

But the shadows he saw were already full, clumsily so, and they spilled their cargo.

The cat that slipped in front of the rodents was almost comically out of step with his counterpart on the screen back at the Globe blockily heavyset, claws scuffing pavement, shoulders indifferently shrugged. The other cat that sauntered from the alley was even more dishevelled, cap tussled forward as he coughed.

The rodents froze, then deviated their course only to be intercepted on the shrinking sidewalk. The first cat's words were terse, narrowed gaze roving from one rodent to the other. Down on his luck. Veggies out of place. Always, Samson had learned, always his kind were out of place. Religious hierarchy hot-branding anthropological myth, the meat-eater over the vegetarian. Natural law.

Instinctively, Samson bound a shadow before he could be seen, stealing the shapeless void in one pool of darkness between a step rise and a door frame. From within, he could see all four, rodents retreating, felines stalking. The cats knew they might be seen, careful to scatter if needed, the cowardly streak that soaks through most bullies. The cats weren't starving, but they felt the desire to feed.

With his own hunger burgeoning, Samson understood them better than the rodents they tried to corner. He hated that.

The marmot asked the cats to leave them be, the squirrel more forcefully, tail twitching. The cats asked for money, grins hitching lips high, teeth showing. Any moment now.

Samson knew he should depart, remembering Celeste's strict instructions during the years they'd kept here undetected.

Shadow to shadow, alongside, smelling aggression and fear. No gun oil. Thanks to Crawford he knew that well. Then he was past them.

Celeste would have minded her own business. He wasn't Celeste.

When he entered the pool of the streetlight behind the thugs, he had a rock with him that had held a trash-lid down. He puffed himself up like Tony Camonte in the *Scarface* picture he'd already seen twice. "Hey!"

The cats turned and the rodents froze.

"I get you a hunk a soap, you take a bath in it!" His aim was good even when he was mortal and the lead cat howled as the rock took him in the temple. Samson laughed theatrically and made a show of running as though his stubby kid's legs could barely carry him. The cats were at his heels with hisses. He gave them a half block before picking up speed, using his natural goat's affinity for heights to leap a staircase and then bound the endless shadows of an alley. The cats hunted for him for an hour, the smell of blood trickling ever upward.

He wanted it more than anything. The singing urge to taste rose with a fever pitch that he wrestled with all his will, and he nearly lost his hidden perch above it all. The couple had fled to live and love another day, the cats tired of searching. Soon enough Samson decided he needed to return home.

He could not drink. He would not drink, not of the thugs, not of the feral rats they kept. He knew what his willpower could earn him, ever fixing the image of his old teacher Ms. Mallory in his head when willpower threatened to wane.

At once Samson felt lingering despair settle down on his shoulders once more. For all his power, there were things in this world that he simply couldn't understand as a twenty-one-year-old mind trapped in a nine-year-old kid's body. But time would not freeze, not anymore. His body would move forward as blood's hooks grew weaker. He would age himself free.

He thought of Fred and Roger dancing and the cares that had hung around him through the week seemed to vanish like a gambler's lucky streak.

CHAPTER 2

ASSETS

Celeste had a choice to make: a night's drive of slow suffering from the cargo in the rented Packard's trunk or the burn from early sun that would heal in a few hours. She had little knowledge about what the nails in that bag represented, but she had memories. The sword cane Donovan Calvert threatened her with in Chicago over a decade ago brought that same nausea, that same grating pain down to her very bones.

She'd give anything to escape that discomfort as she vainly tried to focus on the drive back to Pennsylvania, holding the Packard on its furrowed course. Soon enough, Celeste chose the latter option, ensuring that the post office in Youngstown was open before binding herself in a heavy, thick shawl, kept for daytime emergencies, and hurrying in to mail the fiery bag of nails in her hand. Even through cover the sun was like scalding water, and the nails heaped on more agony through the bundle in her grasp. The twenty minutes spent mailing them were the most agonizing she could remember. The mail clerk, working her fox's nose to discern what was burning, politely said nothing as Celeste stood back from the counter through the whole transaction.

Postage paid, she hurried from shadow to shadow with fur sizzling under the shawl back to the car where shades had already been drawn. She drove a short distance west before parking for the day and fitfully sought oblivion in the cramped back seat.

When the sun set thirteen hours later, she needed the whole night to drive the three hundred miles to her current home just south of Scranton, Pennsylvania, resolving as the pain's memory faded that she'd never travel this far again on her own if she could help it.

Home was a comforting if mundane shape. Even in the dark, the heady perfume of bleeding hearts among boxwood shrubs accumulated near the wide porch where meager light drifted out over the pink-laced greenery. The house was dirty white by day, two stories of stout clapboard indistinguishable from the other homes peeking at hers through a dense copse of trees. Celeste didn't know their neighbors and their neighbors didn't seem to want to know them either, thankfully.

Crawford had returned from Boston. Unfamiliar blood scents from his aging Chevy told her things had not gone smoothly. He was in the kitchen in trousers without a shirt over his pale chest, fur scented liberally with peltsoap. The remains of a grilled rat and potatoes messed a plate in front of him. "Welcome back, honey," he muttered tiredly.

Celeste cocked an ear. "It's four in the morning, my dinnertime, not yours. I smell blood on your car."

He looked baleful. "Yeah," he sniffed. "Is that burnt fur?"

Celeste glanced over the veneer of domesticity kept for the singular mammal who'd only need it on occasion, a greasy coal-fed Crescent stove, Shelvador icebox, cupboards in faded duck-egg blue. Crawford wasn't as messy as most wolves, but dishes in the sink indicated room for improvement. "I'm fine now." She sat on a rickety chair. "The rental has to go back tomorrow and there's mail set to arrive in a few days that you'll need to collect. Those nails hurt to be near just like the last batch. Were you successful?"

Crawford looked at his plate and pushed it away. "There were some nits to pick."

Celeste waited.

Crawford sighed. "I took the long way back from Boston to make sure I wasn't followed, after going back to get my own automobile I mean. We, uh, aren't the only ones looking for those shards." He reached for a glass and knocked back what she smelled was whiskey. He had that distant look he wore when trying to feel nothing. "They didn't like competition, either."

Celeste felt anxiety rise. The anonymous party who'd hired them through an intermediary had never given assurances to make Celeste trust them, only much-needed funds, confirmation that assets of the presumed-deceased Donovan Calvert of Chicago were involved, and directions. The cash was a lifesaver, so to speak, but suspicion deepened when direct exposure to the nails proved to actually hurt.

Donovan would know where his own damn trinkets were hidden so he wasn't the client, and it wasn't his partners in the Martyres of the Black Well. Agents of Donovan's former order would have brought stakes and torches and a torture rack or two rather than send some muskrat with a check book. That left Sandy Mallory as a distant possibility, who knew enough of Donovan's organization to try gathering his most potent assets once the dust had long settled.

But the last to speak to her had been Crawford, who'd seen her run through with a sword in Donovan's steel mill before dropping to her likely death.

Crawford followed her silent train of thought. "I know we only took this job because whoever hired us knows we'd have the shards in hand and we'd call the shots, but I can't help wondering if they've been holding out on us about things, regardless."

"Did you kill them all?"

"Sorry."

She could see why he'd hit the giggle water hard. "Did you get anything from them first?"

"They had me tied to a chair and were going to torture me. My moonlit pal objected to that." He took another drink and shuddered. "Lot of mess to clean, so I floated them. Hope the fish are hungry."

Living with a were, even one learning to manage phases of the curse, was always going to be problematic. Celeste couldn't hide her annoyance despite herself. "Did you at least get something from them that indicated who they were?"

Crawford stared into a cupboard as though hoping it hid answers among the glassware. "I didn't even think about it until two were tossed into the harbour, head spinning where they'd clobbered me, post-change fog, all of that. The third one, a hound, had no ID when I rifled through his pockets. Nothing in their car either. They slipped into the bank and killed a clerk to get the deposit box which I'd already had brought out. I doubt that our client was theirs too since they didn't have a second key for it."

"So, you have the shards?"

"Dozen or so, already hid them. Made me queasy touching them, just like last time."

Celeste couldn't feel tired in body but could in so many other ways. "We have dinner?"

"Six rats left, I fed them," he indicated his plate. "This is one that Samson had, except…"

"What?"

"There was something off about it when he handed it over. It wasn't drained all the way and I, well, I smelled rat blood around back when I went to the outhouse."

Celeste turned that over for a moment and set it aside. She was too weary to really think. "Let's eliminate one uncertainty first." She rose and went to the telephone, dialing the exchange she'd written down. They put her through right away and she recognized the muskrat's voice. "It's me. We have two more of the caches. That's four now, and we have a complication."

She felt her fangs slipping free as he spoke. "No," she cut in. "No answers and no more expeditions until we talk to the boss. The real boss. We've run into problems that we need to work out. Send them here, otherwise you aren't getting this metal no matter how much you'll pay."

She waited for protest and heard only a sigh. "Very well. Tonight." They hung up.

Crawford wandered into the living room from the kitchen, taking a seat on the far end of the worn sofa he'd bought cheap from a liquidated furniture store downtown. He crossed his pleated trouser legs over the frayed oval area rug and flexed his claws. On the nearby mantle framing a vacant fireplace an old Victorian clock ticked away. She knew that he'd heard. "Tonight? So the big cheese is local. That was surprisingly easy," he muttered, worried.

**

Washington, DC at dusk buzzed like Washington at noon, only with a lowered pitch that Charlie Rothscub could feel. Wheels never stopped turning here. "Okay," he said to the quiet speaker on the other end of the line. "Today is October eighth, check in with me in the next forty-eight hours. Just stay observant and keep your ears up. Report back when you're clear. Good luck."

He ended the call, pondered pouring himself a drink as he smoothed brown fur on his brow, and went empty handed from the small bureau by his desk to the narrow window overlooking Ninth Avenue instead. Gazing east, he dimly made out the dome of the United States Capitol over the roof of the new National Archives building, fixtures of a bureaucratic machine that dreamed worried dreams at all hours.

He could relate.

Even after three months working in the modest office granted him by the Bureau, Charlie's lupine nose still wasn't yet used to smells drifting in from the crime lab where they analyzed scents, writing, and fingerprints down the hall. He'd witnessed the obsolete Prohibition department become folded into J. Edgar Hoover's Bureau of Investigation as war against organized crime intensified and the United States' investigative empire expanded to meet challenges from anarchist groups and agitators. Somebody had bought Charlie a glass of beer on the day they'd shot John Dillinger's thieving hide back in Chicago even though Charlie was one of dozens of fresh G-men who'd had nothing whatsoever to do with it.

His own special project was just a little wider in scope and was the reason he stayed in the office so long after his compatriots had put their hats on and shuffled out of their cubbies down the hall.

A knock came at the door, and Charlie shook out his tail before beckoning entry.

The ringtail who opened the door brought in efficient scents of printer's ink and plaster dust, restraining a sneeze with his slender free hand as he closed it behind him. Michael, as Charlie used first names with all his equals and subordinates, was an efficient investigator hired into the unit as a liaison with interstate law enforcement. Charlie caught the reflection of the ringtail's namesake drifting high over his desk on approach and briefly imagined the hips that bore it. Michael just might have been a fellow horticultural lad. Something in how he carried himself.

"News, Michael?"

"Some, Charlie. We've leads that rallies are underway, agitprop against Roosevelt's relief measures. Money's changed hands and a few transfers were traced out of country. Trails end fast. Here are the details." He set a manila folder down in the tray on Charlie's desk.

"Anarchist? Commie? Fascist?" The Bureau had eyes everywhere but Charlie knew Hoover wanted to put the screws to Reds primarily.

Michael leaned against the desk and his tail wrapped round his own leg. Charlie tried not to wonder if the fur of it was warm or cool. "The vast majority of rallies we're watching are moving against Roosevelt's New Deal. There's an ample supply of angry, destitute people without pots to pee in who either don't think things are moving fast enough or think that inclusion of vegetarians in the program is part of a nefarious socialist plot."

Being an omnivore and not really mentioned at all in Noah's parable, Michael put up appearances in a few more traditional holdouts, but Charlie was mostly enamoured with how the agent just couldn't ever bring himself to swear. Being so wholesome was endearing.

"I've just gotten off the phone with somebody keeping eyes on this Colonel character. Things are indeed in motion."

Michael's brows rose. "Colonel Rutland Blake? The segregationist?"

"That's a mild term for him, yeah."

"FDR's neutrality act is muzzling us, isn't it?"

Charlie closed his eyes and found himself thinking of grey wolf fur and just how soon he'd be able to scrub his mind of cares, if only for a little while. Cute as Michael was, Charlie had made a commitment. He composed himself as he went to the decanter on the bureau and poured a whiskey. "We catch any of these guys moving anything back to the German or Italian fascists, even one dime, and we've got our way to get Hoover's attention. Till then our budgetary and discretionary leashes are staying tight."

Michael nodded, crossing his legs, then uncrossing them as a thought came to him. "Another matter: the new cat we added to payroll, you want to meet her, see if she's departmental material? She's in DC right now."

Charlie offered a glass and put it back when Michael declined. Outside, dusk was setting fast. "Short lunch meet tomorrow should do the trick."

"She goes back to Virginia tomorrow."

"Then I'll drive to meet her."

"Really..."

Charlie met his gaze. "Yes?"

"It's just...the department's added three new people reporting to you, set meets with representatives, press, informants even, but for some reason, you just don't ever accept dinner invitations."

Charlie raised a brow, took a drink to forestall an answer. He'd long ago set the rule for himself that he'd never meet people for the first time after dark, never walk alone after sunset, never stop his car on an unlit road. Chicago was over a decade ago, but the raid that changed everything still kept his lights on and his closets closed. "I turn in early because I'm up even earlier. It's Edgar who has to give the nod anyway."

"Alright, sir. I'll pass the word along and bid you good evening."

"You as well."

Michael slipped out.

Outside the dark wasn't far off. Ivory flanks of edifices were gaining dusk's glow. Charlie had too many calls to make. The last one, to his oldest, closest friend, would be from home.

***

Celeste rose from the dreamless unbeing that was rest and sensed something was off. She had her own room in the basement of their Scranton home, cool with earthy scents of clay and brick. The upper floor windows could be covered over efficiently but the house was just within view of their nearest squinting neighbors. Windowless houses were cause for suspicion in Roosevelt's America.

She rose and slipped on a housedress that she tied over her slender white-chested frame before unlocking her door. Across the small hallway, Samson's door was already open and he'd already risen.

Remembering what Crawford had mentioned the prior night, she ascended to the main floor. The goat kid sat alone at the round kitchen table, a newspaper arrayed before him that he wasn't really reading. The weak kitchen lightbulb illuminated a muzzle that seemed…different.

"Crawford fetched it," he ruffled the paper without turning as he spoke in the Scottish brogue he'd lost little of in the last twelve years. Grey fur a shade lighter than Crawford's ruffled as he shrugged. "He's into the change and went out for a bit, hunting probably." A thick nailed finger pointed to the nearby window where unseen moonlight glinted over the countertop. "Seemed like something was bothering him."

Celeste took a step towards him. "Are you alright, Samson? I didn't see you at all last night. Were you in town seeing a picture?"

He didn't turn to her. "Yeah, a song and dance thing with Ginger Rogers and Freddy somebody."

"Fred Stairs I think." She sensed storming thoughts under guard. They were hard to hide in a body less than half the age his mind was. Samson had accepted the capriciousness of his existence over time, but the self-isolation which he'd slowly settled into of late concerned Celeste even as she'd recognized the tendency in herself.

Before saying another word she crossed to the rat room, the designated sitting room they'd boarded up to hold the livestock that she and Samson lived on in lieu of draining townspeople or neighbors.

In that room, squeaks and scratches came from the half dozen critters who'd remained feral by the standards upon which societies were assumed: clothes, culture, conscious desire. Nor did they suffer ambition, avarice, or guilt.

And there were still six of them. She closed the door and returned to Samson's back. "You haven't fed tonight."

The extra moment of silence spoke volumes. "I'm not hungry." He kept his muzzle in the paper.

"Samson…"

The front door opened onto darkness and Crawford slipped in, still shirtless, chest fur dishevelled. "We have company," he said, breathless. "Sedan coming up the drive, headlamps off. That was fast."

Their benefactor. Somewhere out in the woods were the shards Crawford had hidden, insurance that hurt to have. "You should be elsewhere," Celeste said. "Samson, you too. Take the paper upstairs with you."

Both males protested at once and Celeste raised her voice. "Crawford, you can be made to give up the shards they know we have, and Samson, I'll need you to keep watch from the roof to ensure they just have one car."

Crawford stepped in to close the door. "Why should I hide? Both our names are on the detective agency listing, Celeste. Even if you're the only one who's spoken to them—"

"I'm counting on that. If you're not here, you can be off making those shards disappear in their imagination. They'll be giving me the answers I want faster."

Outside gravel crunched under an engine's growl.

Celeste stood taller. "Now, everybody."

Crawford sighed, stalking past Celeste to the back. "You know what noises to make if things get unfriendly," he growled.

Samson rose and passed by, looking away. Something was different about him. "Don't hurt anybody," he said, sounding amused.

"This is a client, Samson."

His hooves clicked upstairs to the second floor without another word.

The ragged sound of an engine stopped. Only night fauna muttered beyond the hedgerows. Celeste waited.

The knock on the door came a moment later, no footfalls heard. Celeste opened it and had to look down. Had she a mortal heart it would have stopped.

Sandy Mallory ruffled her massive tail behind her, smiling a toothy smile above the loose collar of a black dress accented by red-checked knit stole made to mimic her own red fur. "Hello, Celeste. I can imagine you might be somewhat surprised to see me."

Celeste's shock broke in that instant and she beamed back, feeling the last twelve years and its worst fears melt away in an instant. Sandy was here in the flesh, flush with life. Celeste reached out to the diminutive Irish lily standing radiantly upon her porch and smacked her hard on the face.

Chapter 3

Suffered for What

"I didn't deserve that." Sandy rubbed her jaw with a red-furred hand.

Celeste showed teeth but kept her fangs recessed. "Deserve? Sandy, I thought you were dead!"

The sound echoed onto the long drive and the kept lawn past the three cars.

"I'm not." Sandy grimaced. "I have a driver, but he'll stay with the car if you'll—"

"Go to hell."

"Let me in."

Celeste's nails pressed into the door frame hard enough to leave depressions. She had Sandy's money and she had the nails too. She could slam the door in the squirrel's red face and make her wait twelve years or so.

"I know that you're angry, 'Leste. After all that's happened you've a right to be, but you have to understand, I didn't know where you went after that night in Donovan's steel mill. You packed and left with nary a word."

"I don't want to have this conversation here." Celeste avoided her gaze and wondered if any skulking neighbors could hear a word of this.

Sandy sighed with exaggerated patience. "Then shall we walk in the woods or go back to my car? I'll have us chauffeured around the outskirts of town or…"

Celeste wanted to smack her again. "Just come inside."

Out by the property line a wolf's head and bare shoulders poked up from brush. Ears fanned curiously forward as eyes glittered. She gave Crawford an exasperated shrug as she stepped aside and smelled that faint but familiar, indolent tree-rodent smell, overpowering the bleeding heart vines off her porch.

Sandy, either the rebellious lover who'd fled Ireland with her or the head-shrunk slave made by that steel baron bastard rabbit, found her way past the kitchen into the sitting room. She stopped to study the small clock on the mantle. "Is this a Japy Frères?"

"It is. Sit."

Sandy shook her tail out and took one end of the old sofa. "Where to start?"

Celeste took a spot across the rug from her in the high wing-backed chair, searching for signs of guilt. "Samson. We've company."

"I know," Samson said from a shadow over her shoulder.

Sandy looked up and her gaze widened in a fresh smile. "Samson! I'm so glad to see you. How—" her voice choked off as she studied him.

He was no doubt glaring over Celeste's shoulder at her. Good.

"I've been well," Samson said, a slight creak in his voice.

"He's done alright in the dozen years since we fled Chicago for our very lives. How about you?" Celeste broke in sarcastically.

"I told you I looked for you."

"And when you finally found us..."

"It wasn't the right time."

"How long?" Samson asked. He was pointedly keeping any emotions he felt buried.

Sandy's tail twitched. "I found you nearly two years ago, Celeste and Crawford first. It seemed you'd all moved on."

"Two years," Celeste replied bitterly. "You must have known we thought you were dead. But after both the rabbit and that mobster fox, you play easy with grief, don't you?"

Sandy met her gaze stubbornly. "You seemed content when I found you, if a bit short on cash to keep the investigations business going..." Sandy trailed off.

Celeste kept her tone in check, fanned her cinders of anger quietly. "Content? You and Donovan Calvert both disappeared at the same time. I couldn't go near his mansion, the world moved on, and a year later it burnt down. Disgruntled staff, the papers said."

"Yes," Sandy nodded gravely. "Disgruntled staff. That was it."

"And?"

"I suppose it was going to come up before I could tell you why I hired you and the wolf to go after the shards. I used money that Donovan left me and used intermediaries to hire you for reasons of safety."

Samson, far from struggling with any emotions, demurred into the background among the next room's shadows. "Safety for who," he asked flatly.

Celeste could see Sandy hurt at that and couldn't feel bad for her. She leaned back in her chair. "We're all ears, Sandy. I want to know what happened after that night in the mill with Crawford and the rabbit."

***

Seven hundred miles away, a confession booth was entered with care. "Sacristy." The word was a formality. Even though drink was now legal, the place kept its outlaw affectations like sacraments. The small door at the back of the chapel's confession booth swung back and the sparsely packed bar's latest patron entered, hat pulled low as the raccoon on the door nodded primly.

The place had changed hands, the fixtures updated, the bar better stocked. The energy here seemed to have dulled a bit. But the same ferret was at the bar, slight strips of grey darting his cheeks. "Do I know you, sir?"

"That's doubtful," he lied.

"What can I get you?" The bartender ran a cloth across the varnished oak top.

Donovan Calvert's grey-tinged white ears dipped back as the rabbit watched the ferret's dark-furred throat rise and dip in a swallow. Donovan straightened the tie on his nondescript grey suit and doffed his worn homburg. "The sisters left something for me." He dropped a ten-dollar bill on the counter.

Recognition dawned as the money disappeared. Customers were too far between to keep the list long, even over thirteen years. "Sir, if you are who I think you are—"

"I'm who nobody thinks I am." The ferret's pulse got louder and Donovan was annoyed by it. He'd drunk already, yet was ever thirsty. The bar was slick under his hands as though he were sweating. "Please, you know what I want and I know the rules to take it."

The ferret met his gaze, felt uncomfortable with what he saw and turned. "Of course." From below, the bottle appeared.

The ferret set a rocks glass down and poured a generous measure. The glint within the poured libation was as Donovan remembered and he dreaded to recall what it had cost him last time he'd sought the sisters out and paid their price—the memory of his father's soaked, frozen fingers slipping through his own on the deck of a sinking ship, a cry of terror as the sea bore him away. And after all that, the weeping awakening on the floor of his Rolls Royce when the drink's hooks finally let go.

Donovan wanted to hate the sisters for opening those wounds, but he'd made his choices, then as he did now.

"Won't be long, sir," the ferret said and Donovan realized he'd already drunk it, the first thing to pass his lips in years that didn't taste of hot copper.

He'd no car to return to this time. "I'll need a booth."

Following directions, he got settled. A drape was drawn and useless water set down.

He waited.

He had to close his eyes as blinding pain suddenly shot through them. Even sitting upon the varnished wood of the booth he could still feel the furrows of dirt dragged underneath his ankles as his burning, naked body was dragged out of the garden under a merciless Chicago sky into the grace of darkness. Sandy Mallory loomed like a crow. "Was it worth it? Are you learning as we did, Donovan?"

Agony allowed no answer.

Sandy was ever present. "You need only suffer enough to understand. I know you don't yet understand, Donovan."

He understood nothing. Time slowed, pain receded all too gradually over what could have been days or weeks, perhaps a month, awareness of the depths of his mansion transitioning from a pit in hell to a holding cell in purgatory.

Then they came. Far overhead, footfalls through his mansion, mortal and clumsy. Sandy and the clutch of his chosen huddled around him in the bunker system built below his mansion's already-expansive cellar. At all times, Sandy's warning crooned in his ear. "It's them…or agents sent by them. You know what will happen if they find you, Donovan? They hated you enough as a mortal, didn't they?"

Even in the cloud of confusion that was ebbing pain, Donovan knew.

Whatever the searchers found, they eventually went away. And still naked in the dark with nothing but regrets and recriminations to turn in himself like knives, Donovan remembered. Kitchen staff and mechanics and couriers, all gone. Edmond had fallen to his own fangs, and as for the others…

It occurred to him in the slow gathering of reason that the Martyres or their agents couldn't sense the teeming Nosfurs huddled from their prying eyes behind hidden hatches and stairways. That could only be if their reliquary blades failed to detect them.

And that would mean…

Sandy and the others had starved themselves anew. Damn them. So much composure in their suffering, so little complaint as their veins howled for relief as his did. Sandy and the other supplicants had learned to bear it as his mortal self had commanded them while he, their former progenitor and savior, cried like a leveret as he begged for a drop.

Their silent disappointment was collectively palpable.

Time passed. Sandy held him, coaxing him to redirect his mind from his starvation, the very torture he'd groomed her to accept as salvation. Her contempt for him had given way to pity.

As time crept on, the walls grown cold from the fleeing of autumn's last breath, Sandy at last brought him a brandy snifter, the very kind that he'd shared with the Austrian countess in his study a lifetime ago. In it was a sweet warm nectar deeper red than the most full-bodied Italian wine. He wept, dry-eyed, thanked her graciously for the gift he could not extract himself, his burns long healed but his new fangs mere buds. Down relief went in six gulps without a thought, and he licked spilled drops from his own arm like a feral. Sensation revived his corpselike body and he came to in ecstasy.

Sandy watched him with sad and yet sympathetic eyes as hunger's delirium receded from the rabbit at last. He knew what she wanted of him, and he would grant it. Donovan willingly discarded the last vestiges of resistance at Sandy's silent but methodical behest.

And so, their truce was sealed. He was shocked to learn when his bindings were finally removed and he was allowed to move, to stand, to dress himself, that nearly a year had passed in the dark, an eternity of fugues and terrors, death's spectre occasionally padding in mortal form through the abandoned mansion overhead. The Martyres still sought him out.

Now he was allowed to roam, and provided more blood to drink, its source unseen. In the dark his stately home took on aspects blind to the mortal eye, shadows of labyrinthine depth and slivers of moonlight tangible enough to dance upon. Earthly things on the drink carts and pantries and mantels were like fossilized bones, anthropological curiosities now, props for a pointless illusion.

One room in the servant's wing made him feel a familiar agony to approach and Sandy dissuaded him. "That's where the last mortal resides, our conduit to the curious who come seeking leads to where you've gone. They've got your reliquary cane in there in the event you or one of the others get too hungry."

Donovan left the door be, hating whoever had sold him out even as he knew that he'd depend on them as all of Sandy's coterie would. With a steel empire leaderless, the Martyres weren't the only ones to come calling after all. Sandy confirmed that Donovan Calvert was said to have taken abroad, whereabouts unknown, a waning trail laid for the overly curious to follow.

At last Sandy brought him to his own room, sheets freshly laundered, windows barred of all light. Never again would he see morning's rays rise above the boughs or the lake beyond in this new spring of nineteen twenty-four. Sensing unspoken sorrow, Sandy took his face in gentle hands and promised him, "We've much to learn from one another now that you're like me. Rest now, I'll have questions later."

She undressed him, then herself and they slipped into bed together. Donovan could feel that the shadows had eyes as Sandy coaxed him to relax, then awakened other latent parts of himself that pain had rendered dormant. He smelled what she wanted before she brought it from him and as they coupled frantically, a part of his mind sealed away despite the blissful shedding of anxiety that eased him. From agony to ecstasy Sandy had broken and carried him, slipped from the net of his designs to ensnare him, mind and fang and cock, to hers. He watched her breasts rise and fall, gaze finding his and letting it roam, her cold hips burned against his with an electricity belying the very definition of vitality. They finished in silence, not a useless breath wasted.

Donovan's last thought before restorative darkness was that he'd taught Sandy Mallory far too well.

When awareness returned a night later and he felt the Irish squirrel's pelt against his own rather than the cold grip of manacles, he took a deep sigh his lungs had no use for and felt her lips on his ear. "Donovan."

"Sandy."

"We need to talk about something of critical importance to you and I."

"Commitment so soon, Sandy?" His returning sense of humor belied his need to sift for her motives.

She faced him in the dark, their noses almost touching. "I mean something important to all of us in this house, as well as those who have left…"

It was the first she'd mentioned of some of his own former flock leaving. That was of concern. "Yes?"

"Donovan, I need to know about the nails."

"The nails…" But of course he knew. Ever since the Martyres had sent Countess Von Haften to undermine his work, he'd been compelled to make assurances. Edmond had secured caches of the "ark nails" that he used to make his reliquary steel at various locations throughout the country, some known and guarded, some completely unexpected.

"The nails at the mill were taken and the Martyres suspect you have more. The forged steel, Donovan, they took all of it that you still had."

Much of it was already shipped for use on various projects in and out of Chicago, test cases for the detection net that he himself couldn't slip. Something nagged at him, a detail he couldn't call upon on at that moment.

Her claws on his cheek brought his attention to the present. He'd all but forgotten her bite, her taunts, all that followed in his deadly garden. Her claws roved up and down his bare flank and he found he wasn't angry with her. How could he be? She had given him a gift with her bite, hadn't she? She only wanted him to understand the pains she'd undergone for him.

Even so, it was his instinct to be wary. "I can't say I recall where most of them are. I had to be very careful. With Evelyn turned against me you knew they would seek them out."

"There's a safe in the hidden rooms below the cellar, near the room where we…had you. We've searched the entire house from shingles to cellar dirt. I know you kept records far out of sight. And where you worked with Nosfurs captured."

He locked eyes with her and smiled sadly. "They were your experiments too, Sandy. Those who returned with you know full well it was your face above that slab along with mine. Don't let yourself forget."

Despite keeping her expression neutral her claws stopped tracing his frame and clenched, just a bit.

Donovan squirmed. "We agree it was the best course of action at the time. The Martyres wanted you dead and I wanted…"

"Slaves," she released her grip and turned the russet shape of her back to him.

"I never saw you that way," Donovan sat up behind her. "I did my best to keep you safe."

"And would you now?" Still with her back to him, thick tail behind her and still. "When it's more than essential to do so?"

"Yes."

"Then give me the combination to the safe downstairs. You triple reinforced it, I assume for very good reason."

"Sandy…"

"Donovan, I know you think that the last knowledge you hold that I don't helps you cling on to some scrap of power, but you have to realise, that trail we left for the press and police and the Martyres to follow will end. They took your mill and its caverns below, they took your overseas accounts. They'll stop searching different corners of the world for you, and when they do, they'll all come right back here. They already left a spy in the city who we've quietly dealt with. You've been drinking him."

Donovan turned his eyes to the distant ceiling as he finally realized. After all his labours, his empire had been parcelled and carried away and he didn't know how to feel. "I don't remember it."

Sandy loomed over, pushed him back down with a hand on the rabbit's chest, tail twitching above. Her shoulders and breasts were graceful temptations, but her expression was hard. "What do you think they'll do if they have you, Donovan? You were already in hot water with your order when you fell out with that lioness who wanted me dead. Good lay no doubt but she'd have killed you if I hadn't killed her first."

"You?" Donovan blinked and sat up on his elbows. "I had that Prohee wolf..."

"Don't get distracted," Sandy snapped. "She came after someone important to me and I sent her to perdition for it."

She really did care, Donovan thought, and couldn't resist a smile.

"I'm serious, Donovan. You broke from the Martyres, made servants of Nosfurs, and were connected with offing Von Haften. They'll take so long to kill you their grandchildren will finish the job. We need to thwart them obtaining those nails first."

"I...remember where the caches are. It's not in any safe. Do you have a pen?"

From the dark recesses of his room a slim hare emerged, startling Donovan alone. The hare crossed to the disused desk, wiped away dust and obtained a fountain pen and paper before approaching the bed, ignoring their nakedness.

Collecting himself, Donovan rattled off four locations that he knew were lies. He'd hundreds of bank boxes, dozens of tracts of land, and even with all those holding places available to him he'd still paid intermediaries to guard his secret, chosen carefully by Edmond and hidden under cover of other errands. Those nails were leverage. Without them, he'd nothing left against Sandy or the Martyres.

Until he figured out a plan.

"Satisfied?" he asked when the hare, Cedric, he remembered, had left. Donovan noted that the hare still looked emaciated even as his fangs had grown back. Keeping the Martyres from finding them had cost them much in discipline.

Sandy pushed him back down, gently but insistently. "For now."

Those two words told Donovan that now wouldn't be long enough.

He had free run of his opulent home, save the single room where they sequestered their kept mortal, who was their calm face to any who'd knock by daytime on the front door.

Donovan and that turncoat were separated by a door but little else. Donovan wasn't master of his own home anymore, much less any of his industrial instruments beyond it, and had to find out what had become of all he'd been sequestered away from. Sandy had no papers delivered and the wireless, telephone, and even the parlor radio were all disconnected.

The electricity bill was still being paid, with only one mortal remaining needing it. So isolation had to be deliberate.

To ask too many questions about the outside world would raise suspicion. He made his choice to escape and waited on the next night's stirring to act.

She rose before him, acquiescing to his sluggishness as she left the bedroom to check on his former disciples, now hers. Donovan slipped from the bed, got dressed frantically, and stole to the window. It was securely nailed down and wouldn't budge.

A presence at the door outside prompted him to dodge for a shadow. In his panic he settled deep into its recesses.

Strange. The world beyond remained clear and yet he felt muffled, as though under a layer of lace. He forced himself from the vicinity of that shadow when the presence moved on, countless creatures who didn't draw breath now haunting his mansion. He slipped out into the hallway, hurrying from alcove to alcove until he reached the all-but-abandoned servant's quarters with its single strip of light across the carpet under a sealed door. That wasn't important now.

He took the servant's narrow stairwell to the ground floor, then tried the servant's exit to the outside, also locked, before wandering in the pale light past a few other skulking members of his former steel-working apprentices, all of whom bowed respectfully without saying a word. At the front doors, he casually tried the latch and found it unlocked. The front door where he'd found the Countess from Austria waiting impatiently on his stoop, where he'd waited countless times for Edmond to bring the car around for trips to Steelworks Association meetings, the opera, picture shows, and one or two clandestine meetings with madams whose impeccable discretion was the least of their skills. This portal admitted the outside air, the drone of freezing waves off the lake, and the groans of winter-naked trees.

He glanced over his shoulder once and saw Sandy standing there, smiling coldly, disappointed, her flinty gaze promising…consequences.

He'd no beating heart to seize and that made the stab of fear worse. Donovan bolted.

With preternatural speed he cleared the snow-dusted lawn and the winding drive, leaping one hedge, eviscerating another. At the border of the Calvert estate, a tall wrought fence was his only barrier to freedom.

If Sandy followed, he didn't see her. Neither did he see any of his wayward Nosfur flock. He hurtled towards those gates, knowing even as an itch became profound discomfort that he could scale it with his lapine strength and a little momentum.

By the time the pain struck, he had no chance of stopping. He felt as though he passed a membrane of barbed wire and collided with pure pain.

The fence burned him like hellfire, and he bounced back from it with a scream that would carry for miles. Sense memory took him back in that white-hot instance to that very moment after he'd killed Edmond over a year ago. Sandy had offered him his reliquary cane sword and without thought he'd tried to take it.

He was brought full circle in shame.

"The work was done a week after you came to stay with us," Sandy said as she stood above where he rolled on the cold ground. She was wearing the nightclothes she rarely bothered with, and her feet crunched the thin layer of snow. With no breath to see she resembled one of the statues that lined the gardens, a playful nymph bestowing mischievous cruelty. "You were distracted when you signed the work order, such an important mammal you were. We could have had the fence stopped, but that would have aroused serious suspicion. The barrier forged from your steel went up around us and we knew..."

Sandy stepped forward and winced as she ran her claws across those bars, first one way, then back. She stepped back with her fangs out, squinting through pain. "Discipline would have to save us once again. Not providence, certainly not you, Donovan. You've seen so much and learned so little, after all the pain we've traded."

"Fuck you."

Her smile was beatific. "There's the part of you that won't ever die, no matter what box you find yourself in."

Donovan didn't see the others but knew they had gathered.

Realization that his bindings hadn't been truly removed, only loosened, deepened his despair at first, but over the next several nights, anger began to fill the empty spaces between the books he didn't want to read and the dwindling number of his captors who would speak with him. Sandy still stayed with him, danced around his recalcitrance. She wanted to confirm he'd given up where the nails were.

Donovan knew that he was in a cage of his own making as much as hers. He hated this mansion, all the failed endeavors it represented, a life of leisure to disguise a deep-seated fear of failure in sight of all those he'd felt contempt for. If he spent even the smallest sliver of eternity haunting these halls he'd truly be in Hell.

Every exit from here was pain. He'd surrender to it every time.

Unless.

He bedded Sandy several nights later, worked with the shape of her, made her feel truly special. He wanted to love her the way he knew she'd want him to. She'd hate him soon enough.

He'd collected his books in the right place and filled his pockets with all he needed. He wandered the home he had built and passed the servant's quarters where Sandy's last mortal pet was kept. They'd be a priority, he was sure.

Satisfied that there was no turning back, he went to the study where two of his children, now Sandy's, read Milton and Fitzgerald with tails curled around them.

He'd be sorry for the interruption later. He lit a candle, wandered over to the window to regard the snow gently falling outside, and touched that candle to each hanging drapery for just long enough before pulling corks on the dust-covered drinks cart, overturning it onto the waiting stack of books and letting the candle fall.

That gave him a head start.

He heard his name called as he left the mansion for the last time, Sandy's Irish lilt lending a menace as the six or seven of their brethren stirred within the glow of eviction along with her.

What came next would hurt like hell, and as he hurtled towards the iron crucible's clutches, legs flexing for a leap, Donovan Calvert was eager to face it.

"Is that all there is?" whispered a voice at his snow-flecked heels.

"I said is that all, sir?" The weasel stood over him in the Sacristy bar, righting the glass he'd toppled. Donovan's grey-pleated thigh was wet.

He shook off the sensation of hurtling through the dark, spared the total recollection of his hands and feet burning unbearably as he tumbled down the hillock on the fence's other side, through muck and cold and filth.

"I wish to meet you," he muttered and felt the world below him imperceptibly shift, guiding him forward. He knew at once where he had to go. "How very sadistic of you."

Yet in their own way the sisters had been considerate. They'd long departed Chicago but would be returning just for him. The night was young.

An hour later he'd crossed half of Chicago, minding the pratfalls he'd placed for himself in elevated train and bridge repairs over a three-year period in the twenties. He'd been so proud when he first refined and expanded the influence of the Ark nails that had increased the utility of the Nosfur-burning iron beyond the simple knives, axes, and rapiers his former colleagues fetishized.

An American Empire would have joined the coasts together under his absolute authority and now, over a decade later he had to avoid taking the night train in Chicago north, not just to avoid sections of reliquary-steel track repairs, but to keep clear of the massive pillar of nausea and pain that was the Chicago Board of Trade Building. Its entire core was composed of his defunct company's steel, most of it reliquary. It stood as the last major project for Calvert Steel before the company went belly-up in the twenty-nine crash.

He hadn't wanted to return to Chicago again under any circumstances, but it held the only known place where the sisters maintained one of their conduits for contact. With the Martyres certain to kill him if they knew what he'd become and other Nosfurs certain to kill him if they knew who he'd been, he was fast running out of options to stop what he'd personally set in motion: the turning of the entire civilized mammalian world into one of unrelenting pain.

His fury with Sandy was well renewed at the memory of what transpired eleven years ago, but as the money he'd managed to retain was running out and his feeding patterns threatened to expose his refuge, Donovan had only one course of action available.

The Martyres of the Black Well in America had to all be killed before they killed him and he needed to know where they were.

Simple, really.

Even following the lakeshore on foot, the Trade Building was merely in sight and gave him a headache.

A short time later, one facet of his shame gave way to another one and he was in the vicinity of cursed ground. The fence that had caused him agony on the night he'd fled his home was now gone. The remains of his mansion had been swept away with it. High-class but unimaginatively uniform townhomes were stamped into the earth about where his garden had flourished. The pit where his cellar was had become a stretch of lawn.

His gaze roved across the wooded lot demarking where his old property line terminated. There he saw, on the ruined trace of his front drive, a rusting General Motors sedan. Leaning against it, a young wolf and an elderly otter in musty bohemian dress watched him intently.

"Thank you for seeing me." Donovan's gaze darted between the two of them as he approached. "Somebody's missing."

The sisters said nothing at first, then the otter sighed. "That would be Leguna," she said in thick Creole as she and the wolf traded looks. "It's been six years now, guess your ear isn't close to the ground."

Donovan shook off anxiety from the memories he'd surrendered for this meeting. Likely the bottle that now held them was in their automobile. "Six years? Where is she?"

The young wolf was beatific in sad patience. "In the ground, rabbit. Cancer. Same that took her eye."

Silence carried the sounds of late-night automobiles crawling the coast and the rustle of autumn wind through trees starting to shed. "I'm sorry," Donovan said at last. "You all did such great work together."

The otter, Grisand he remembered, huffed. "Our election-fixin' days are o'er, bunny. We have a higher calling, or had, at any rate."

"I don't need you for that. I need Sandy Mallory, my prior...accomplice. We've been somewhat estranged, and I need to find her. We have a common goal, and I can't use my network to find her. Second, I'll need to know the travel plans for one Christof Von—"

"I'm sorry, but our circle is broken," the wolf said primly.

"What do you mean your circle is broken?"

"A red-furred lass seeks legacy's pricks," the wolf, Baliosi was her name, intoned.

"But danger beckons with ancient tricks…" Grisand added and trailed off.

Silence.

"What else?" Donovan asked.

"Ain't n'er else. Circle's broken, Bali said. What do ye think that means?" The otter bit her lower lip.

Donovan waited for the punchline, and a sinking feeling set in as nothing came. "This is preposterous! I paid the price and called you!"

"Yes." Baliosi nodded tiredly. "That's why we came."

"But you can't help me!"

"We know," Grisand said, patiently. "We just told you that."

"But I paid the price! I called you!"

"We know!" they both said at once. Annoyance made the reply a bite.

"Damn you! You're telling me I suffered for nothing?"

Grisand grinned, showing sharp teeth under her curling whiskers. "Every fool's last question. But there are no final questions for you anymore, are there? You became what you wanted to shackle all those years ago. Ironies aplenty here."

Donovan didn't know what to say. Night sounds of the town he'd come to hate rushed into the silence and he bit back a scream.

CHAPTER 4

STURDY BOUGHS

"Particulars aren't important but suffice it to say that Donovan and I had a wee falling out."

Celeste glared at Sandy across the sitting room. The Japy Frères mantle clock ticked and a whisper of wind made it past the empty chimney flue. "Twelve years may have passed but I distinctly recall discouraging you from ever seeing him again." Celeste had also suggested Sandy help Samson handle his new existence as a Nosfur instead. He'd overcome that hurt and Celeste didn't want to dredge it up for him again. "Is the rabbit alive?"

Sandy's expression and the way her thick tail flicked suggested a significant detail was being sequestered. "Well…"

Samson came around Celeste's chair and sat at the couch's other end from Sandy, sitting up straight with an off-putting formality that Celeste felt was a slight.

Celeste held Sandy's gaze. "Stop being coy. He's either dead or he's not."

The way her whiskers dipped and rose…

"No." Celeste glared at her.

"I had my reasons."

"You didn't."

"Didn't what?" Samson said.

The front door opened at that moment and Crawford sauntered into the short front foyer, buttoning up a checkered shirt. "Startled the Caddy driver but he was swell about it." He held his tail and planted himself on the couch between Sandy and Samson with a huff, glancing either way at both of them with an extra squint at Samson.

"Sandy…" Celeste gripped the chair arm and had to keep herself from snapping it off.

"He wouldn't stop, and he had to learn."

"Learn what, Sandy?" Celeste was exasperated. "You actually made him into one of us?"

Sandy glared back and ignored the wolf and goat whose muzzles snapped her way. "He would never have stopped, and the bastards who sent him here wouldn't have stopped, so I ensured that he'd lean to our side."

"You're talking about Donovan?" Crawford was confused.

"The rabbit who wanted me dead, yes." Samson muttered to his right. "I hate that louse."

Crawford put an arm around him and patted the far shoulder. "Turns out everybody does." He nodded his chin at Sandy. "I suppose if he meets more of his crusty lion friends, they'll grease him."

Sandy grinned, trading a proud grin with Celeste's sour ear-lowed glare. "The Martyres aren't all lions, Mister G-mammal, but they will indeed sort him out."

He raised a brow. "I'm retired from prohibition work."

"Liquor was federally legalized in thirty-three so just about everyone is," Celeste added flatly. "Do you know where he is?"

"I'm afraid not. At this point he's running from his order if they haven't caught him already which is why I was able to take my time investigating things he hid while we were…together."

Celeste sensed a great deal unsaid. "I would suppose that's more than just the nails you've hired us to chase. I'd expect all his money didn't go up with the house his servants burnt down."

"Well, I needed to hire you both with that money."

"Both?" Samson's practiced indifference slipped. "Not all three of us?"

Sandy steepled her hands, elbows on knees. "I'm so sorry, Samson. I didn't know you were still with these two until just before I had the job offer put together."

Samson huffed. "I'm no fool. They can't put a kid on a detective agency's payroll," he muttered.

"Right," Sandy said uncomfortably. "That brings me back to why I've come this evening."

"I demanded it." Celeste said.

"It was only a matter of time before I chose to come anyway," Sandy said wearily, folding one thick leg over the other.

"Such as when others after the same nails tried to kill one of us?" Celeste asked.

Sandy was taken aback. "What?"

"My turn," Crawford rumbled. "The bank in Boston had another crew after the deposit box. It was open late and four jokers came in while I was waiting, beat up a guard, and killed a clerk before stealing the specific box the clerk had already pulled for me. They knew I was after it and clobbered me before I could force a change."

"Force…you mean you can control—never mind, that doesn't matter now. I certainly didn't hire a second crew."

"Well, whoever knew about your nails knew about these ones but not about Celeste and me. They tested my key in the deposit box, found out it worked, and were going to beat more details out of me down by the docks."

Sandy was on the edge of her seat. "Did you find out who hired them when you escaped?" Sandy asked evenly.

Crawford's hackles didn't rise all the way but didn't stay smooth either. "'Fraid not. They and my more…rustic self didn't get along too swell."

"You killed them." Sandy's chide was as disappointed as Celeste's and Crawford's ears went flat.

"I'm not pleased about it, but they were going to start yanking things off of me."

Sandy stood up. Despite eighty years divorced from most of the mortal ticks of being a squirrel the nervous energy still returned when anxiety summoned. She paced from the wall back to the chair, studying the paisley wallpaper and Sears-Roebuck calendar by the telephone, tail and whiskers twitching as she went back to the fireplace clock. "I've long suspected that Donovan might do something more about the nails he'd hidden even though he couldn't go after them himself for all the pain they'd cause him now. And he'd be extremely reluctant to hire proxies. The Martyres might still be hunting after him care of the missing lioness cunt who hurt Samson before disappearing."

Sandy stopped abruptly and faced Samson, clasping her diminutive, red-furred hands. "Apologies for the language, Samson."

"It's okay, Ms. Mallory. They let me in on a word or two in my early twenties. I'm growing up one way or another."

Sandy kept looking at him, brow furrowing. "On that subject, you were bitten less than two days after I taught you decimals for the first time. You're looking…quite different, I've noticed."

Celeste turned back to Samson and looked at him, really looked at him, now that he wasn't turned away or lurking in shadow. He did in fact look older, years older in fact.

All the information she'd shared with Crawford about the un-drank rats and Samson's even more aloof nature clicked. Doe and wolf traded ear-lifted looks before settling on Samson again, who'd stood up himself and was wandering towards a darker corner of the room.

"Samson," Celeste said, "Have you been—"

He turned back and jutted his chin out, that of a young but mature stranger, and gritted his teeth. His Scottish brogue had softened over the last decade but came back with biting frost. "Ms. Mallory was explaining she's turned the fella who wanted to capture us all into a Nosfur and Crawford was nearly killed by nail thieves who Ms. Mallory didn't even know about so that's not important right now, is it?"

The silence dropped the room's temperature, all eyes on Samson. The clock ticked as he fumed. "I'm not even really part of all this since I'm too young, aren't I? I should just take a long walk."

Crawford reached out a hand but the goat kid skipped out of reach, went round Sandy with a click of his hooves. A moment later the front door opened and slammed shut.

"Poor kid," Sandy muttered. "He's starving himself old, isn't he?"

Celeste ground her teeth. "You showed him the way that's done, didn't you? That was before abandoning him."

Sandy glared back. "I had to fix certain problems, Celeste. I thought you'd understand."

"I don't. Of all the things I don't understand, what I really want to know is why you even hired us to risk our lives going after these nails of yours instead of just chasing them down yourself. You're rich enough to buy and throw away farmhouses and already have your own people."

Sandy looked like she wanted to chase after Samson but sat still, looking cornered.

"We didn't get you here to get half the answers," Crawford growled. "So, tell us." He furrowed his brow as he glanced at the empty foyer. "To hell with it, tell Celeste." The wolf rose and hurried after Samson, tail stiff.

Sandy and Celeste were alone as the front door opened and closed. Sandy met her glare. "I'm truly sorry. I didn't know your lives were being risked, just that closeness to the nails would hurt some."

"Some."

Sandy looked away. "I'd been chasing down clues that Donovan left after his mansion burned down and the authorities crawled through it. I had to obtain as much money as I could from the accounts I had signatures on in Chicago before they seized everything." Sandy was getting flustered again. "Donovan kept very many warrens: the steel mill, his New York flat, and even a Louisiana shipping company. The process was agonizingly slow, especially since he'd hidden many of the caches where his brood couldn't find them. The last few Nosfurs that he'd turned drifted away at that point. They wanted to be free of Donovan's legacy when his mansion burned down but I knew I was just as responsible for losing them."

Celeste wanted to say she was grateful Sandy took responsibility for something but didn't interrupt.

Sandy composed herself. "I found several of his concealments for the nails but not nearly all. So much of my digging was useless and the Martyres of the Black Well were already hard on my tail, having bought out Donovan's steel mill using proxies."

"Must have lost a lot of money when it folded in twenty-nine."

"They didn't give a fig about his mill, just the physical assets. That was why I had to move so quickly. The rabbit had something like thirty safety deposit boxes in America alone. We couldn't do this slowly a single destination at a time, which is why we needed you working in tandem. Securing the shards quickly is vitally important."

"And we made ideal searchers, having the unique ability to feel immediately if the nails were real or counterfeit and not being sought specifically by those bastards."

"That indeed."

"But why are they so important? What do they even do, other than make weapons for these Martyres to hurt us with?"

"That's what it's for, but in a more refined sense. You've no doubt felt instances of pain while prowling Chicago, strange bits of discomfort here and there."

"I assumed it had to do with slow aging. Forgot about it after I left for good."

"No, and you've not aged a day my dear."

Celeste curled her legs up on the chair. "I'm not quite ready for flattery from you."

Sandy wrapped her own tail around and held it gingerly. "Well, Donovan improved the potency of the shards to the point where he could melt it into girders for construction projects and have a much more expanded detection and punishment range."

"Detection?"

"The metal doesn't just cause you pain and wouldn't just cause you a lot more if near a cast beam. With the right refinement the steel also serves to find our kind when we're near one and notify the holder of a bound object, like a pendant or a bracelet."

"You did mention some of this before we parted."

"Chicago was a wild time," Sandy said and Celeste knew well what she implied.

"This steel then can both find us and hurt us."

Sandy nodded. "When on a blood high the effect is increased. Only a long abstinence lets us bear being near it or hide from it, though it's still incredibly uncomfortable after years dry. Cover a city with enough of this steel and you can force a Nosfur population to abstain from blood to avoid the agonies of Hell itself."

Celeste let silence carry as she put her thoughts together. "That's what Donovan did to you. That's why you starved yourself...for him."

Sandy let her tail go, her fidgeting done. Ghostly quiet was only broken by the click of the mantle's clock and light fuzz of electric light. With animosity faded, the squirrel had gone from pensive to reflective. "As bad as Donovan was, we both know I made even worse mistakes with that mobster fox you turned after that. I've not seen him in years."

Celeste realized that Sandy didn't know what had become of Bucky and didn't want to broach that topic. "I never heard another word about speakeasies for blood drinkers after Chicago and assumed you learned from that mistake." She kept her tone sympathetic to push towards closure. "I didn't want to make that fox into progeny, and I've managed to forget him."

Sandy met her gaze and nodded. "It's the shards we have to worry about, and the rabbit who hid them all. Donovan is out there, isolated, hunted by his peers, and after so many years, growing desperate. I can find a new job when my money someday runs out. As I understand it, this last job provided me with a house in Ohio to sell."

"No, it didn't," Celeste corrected. "I gave it back to the owners. You never told us to retain it. The nails were all that mattered, we were told."

Sandy's whiskers twitched. "Oh."

Celeste shrugged. "But we took the nails and you're still rich, you were saying."

"Yes, well, the missing rabbit whose face filled papers and fortune periodicals for years is going to have a hard time staying incognito and I don't have things that much better. Martyres know of me and no doubt have one of Donovan's many photographs in whatever might not have burned down. I'm starting to run out of his money, and I've been long worried that I was being tracked. The fear is justified, let me tell you."

Celeste nodded. "And that, I take it, is the real reason you stayed anonymous and apart from us."

"Yes. Much as it pained me to do so, yes. I'm just sorry that I couldn't tip my hand as to who I was when I had you hired beyond warning you not to touch them. We have air to clear, you and I, and I was also worried we'd have been sidetracked by our mutual concerns."

"Yes," Celeste said, trying to sort the whirlwind of emotions she juggled as memories of Chicago turned over in her head. "We've a lot to pick at."

***

Samson wasn't hard to find. The driver of Sandy's Cadillac sat quietly, a paperback in their paws held outside the driver's window so meager moonlight could illuminate pages. Crawford traded a nod with the silhouette in the car as he passed.

Crawford followed the faint goat smell round back of the greying house's clapboard side and saw the goat kid's own dark outline high off the ground in the basswood tree he liked to scale. He sat on a long, thick branch, legs dangling, arms folded.

Crawford came to the base of the tree, pondered calling out, thought better of that. He started climbing, cursing just once as his toe claw snagged and splintered a thinner branch. A minute or so later, he'd made it twice his own height off the ground and hauled himself to a branch adjacent Samson's that bowed under him, just a bit. "You like it up high, huh?"

"Celeste told me Nosfurs are drawn to heights. Goes double when you're a goat," he said indifferently.

Crawford looked out across the moon-swept roll of canopies, a light wind disturbing their glimmering surfaces. The roof of the nearest house to theirs was a dark shingled square less than two acres to the east. "I'm sorry that you've been kept outside of most of this. It's not fair to you—"

"But if clients looking to catch their husbands or wives cheating or their partners embezzling funds find a kid working out of a detective's office you and Celeste have set up, those already uneasy with a veggie-carnie pair will turn right around. I get it. From the very start, I got it," he replied. "That's why I took the steps I took," he added bitterly.

"But this…" Crawford adjusted his weight on the branch to avoid falling off and chose his words carefully. "This isn't you, Samson. Starving yourself to make yourself age isn't any solution. It's going to hurt more and more to make that happen. Celeste told me that she was only able to hold out for a few months after she was turned. I don't know the full skinny behind that; she said it almost made her go feral."

"Like you get," Samson said evenly, with no recrimination. "You're learning to manage it."

"But I can't stop changing, just as you can't stop needing what you need. Eventually, you'll have to drink again and—"

"Did I remind you of your son?"

Crawford fell silent. Insects chirped and boughs groaned. "My son?"

"That night in the superintendent's office when the rabbit wanted you to kill me. It would have been the easiest thing in the world. I was confused, terrified of the wrong I'd done. I'd never done more than hit somebody in the schoolyard over a stolen toy and I was standing over a man I'd made dead and cold and feeling so, so horrible for how strong it made me feel. You could have shot me and I wouldn't have felt everything you'd need to do after that. So easy."

"Don't think like that, Sam. You know full well that was done to you against your will and I can't…do that."

Samson turned to Crawford with his young adult face, devoid of physical scars but with veteran, wounded eyes. "But in that office, you were thinking of him, your son who you left in Virginia. That was why you couldn't kill me even though I was just a vicious, bloody problem. You were reminded of him, somehow."

A weight that settled was uncomfortable but infinitely familiar. "I do think of Lucas and Kamila. Often."

"And yet, you let them go, to protect them from…" Samson curled his hands into claws.

Crawford found his eyes stinging. "I told myself at the time I'd see them again, one day when I could control it." He remembered red-stained brick on a Boston storage room's floor and knew the truth. "But I can only negotiate with it, give it enough of what it wants to avoid taking more—"

"That's why you had to let them go." There were no tears on the goat's face. A Nosfur had none to give.

"Yes, I did." His own wet eyes were catching moonlight but he didn't care. "Getting back into their affairs and leaving again without warning is the most horrible thing I can do. They deserve full lives with their pain behind them. I can't give them hope and take it away again."

"Lost hope is cruel," Samson said with a swallow and turned back to the moon-brushed forest. "But to never have any is worse. All my friends in my short life have grown up and moved on. I can't go with them and barely have any memory of my real parents. There's nothing to let go of. And with a twenty-five-year-old mind I have to know what I'm missing of adult life. Even if it's just for a short time, Crawford, I have to feel and I have to know. You understand, right?"

Crawford was silent a long time before he gingerly slid towards the trunk on the bough that precariously held him. He couldn't draw Samson into a hug but he could wrap his right arm round the trunk to rest his hand, the one less one finger, on Samson's shoulder. "There's a lot of my life I haven't told you about that I wish I could forget, but even the worst of it did make me who I am. I'm sorry, Samson. There's no easy way out of what you're feeling." He tightened his grip as Samson looked down at the ground below. "Just know that you're important to us. Celeste won't leave you and for as long as I've got, neither will I."

"That could be a long time. You're pretty agile for somebody who turns forty-three this year."

Crawford shrugged. "Haven't met any others like me to ask, but limber or not I'm pretty sure I'm not immortal." He grinned sheepishly.

"Yeah," Samson said. "Lucky you."

***

Tired and still fuming, Donovan Calvert arranged for a stay on the outskirts of Cleveland, halfway back to the refuge he'd guarded for over ten years. The hotel's proprietor hadn't wanted to have a rabbit in his more expensive rooms and Donovan could actually see the end of his finite cashflow for the first time in his life. He accepted placement in the last room at the end of the row on the hotel's second floor when the sun began to rise and he considered his next steps. Fucking sisters. He hoped the dead coyote was getting drowned in Hell and that the otter and wolf would follow soon after. They'd taken his time and his pain for nothing.

Mallory could be anywhere, assuming she'd not been rounded up and destroyed. As for the Martyres, Donovan only had one lead. The newly opened Waldorf Astoria in New York had a guest, someone who'd come on business and who'd been photographed for the society papers. The New York Times article only mentioned Christof Von Haften once, and Donovan had no idea how long he'd be in America before the old leonine bastard would return to Austria. Time was short.

Taking the Martyres on in Europe was a foolhardy, insurmountable effort. Therefore, drawing them out in America as they continued to settle affairs here was the only viable move.

Obviously, rather than follow Von Haften, Donovan would have to decide where he'd be for himself.

He didn't want to call from where he wanted to lay his trap, the last hidden refuge he had from the mortal world and the predators he'd once worked with, but it was the only place where he could sufficiently control the outcome and hide his hand. He'd have to draw Von Haften in, obtain the information he needed and kill the bastard.

Donovan covered the windows, blocked the door with a chair and planned until tiredness took over. He'd call from elsewhere, outside of town, split some of his support off to investigate.

Seeing the look on the lion's face when he realized Donovan had turned would be equal parts thrilling and shameful. But if his gambit worked, the bastard wouldn't die alone.

A plan formed and followed Donovan down into the dark.

***

Crawford and Samson came back inside. "She's close," Samson muttered.

"Oh?" Crawford followed him inside with a glance to the silhouette of whoever had waited in the car. The form was slumped back on the seat, shoulders rising and falling in sleep. Mortal.

"Sandy. She's staying somewhere close by. It's three hours till sun-up and she's still here, assuming she hasn't had Celeste promise her a spare room."

"Celeste and Sandy do go back a bit but not entirely in a good way."

"Oh?" Samson didn't seem to be intentionally mimicking Crawford and the wolf wondered how many of his mannerisms had imprinted on the kid over twelve years.

"Long story."

Samson's look said he had time.

Crawford glanced into the living room as he entered and saw that they still sat across from one another, a little less formally, but guarded enough. Appeared to be talking shop.

"We'll have to move fast for that next cache, assuming it isn't too late," Sandy said, leaning forward with palms pressed together. "It's in a deposit box in Allentown, just an hour or so from here where I've rented temporary accommodations. And…if Samson wants to help."

Samson stepped around Crawford and into view. "What can I do?"

Celeste glanced to where Samson entered and back to the squirrel with eyes narrowed and ears lowered. "Sandy…"

"If there were other unknown parties on your heels then they would recognize you and possibly Crawford as well. Samson has three advantages. First, any competition for the remaining shards, assuming they've obtained the same information, wouldn't recognize him. Second, he has certain advantages required for this plan that my valet can't manage as he's mortal."

Crawford didn't like where this was going. He put a hand on Samson's shoulder which the goat kid shied away from. The kid wanted to help, be involved. Crawford couldn't fault that, even as he recognized the danger he'd already been in. "And the third?" Crawford rumbled.

Sandy looked straight at Samson and Crawford felt discomfort at the sadness in her eyes. "If he's starved himself, then he'll feel far less pain than Celeste or I would in the shards' presence, possibly less discomfort than even you would, Mister Cain."

"What do we do and when do we do it?" Samson asked without hesitation. His nub of a tail shook behind him. The look that Celeste traded with Crawford told the wolf that the doe was ready to slap the squirrel again.

"Tomorrow night," Sandy said. "We'll take my car."

"Lemme know what I have to do," Samson said, decided.

The plan that Sandy outlined involved everybody and was both straightforward and brief. The vault would be accessed by bank attendants and a decoy box brought out that Sandy had the key for. In the distraction, Calvert's box for which they didn't have the key would be obtained. They'd force that open later, elsewhere.

Samson was grinning when she was done, and Crawford couldn't help feel the kid's mood lifting. "This is gonna be grand," Samson said proudly. "A bank heist with three Nosfurs and a werewolf." He beamed back at Crawford. "If they made a talkie picture out of it, which of us would Bela Legosi play?"

Celeste was stone faced. "He's a Hungarian cat, so nobody."

A short while later Sandy took her leave, sensing that she was near to overstaying her welcome. "The bank closes at 8 p.m. and we'll only have two hours of darkness. We'll need to be there as early as possible. My car's passenger compartment is well sealed so we can leave at dusk."

"Very well," Celeste replied evenly.

The valet was coaxed awake and Sandy's car chugged away. Celeste and Crawford traded wearied glares. "The kid is happy to be on board," Crawford reasoned. "It's not for us to speak for him. We owe him that."

Celeste was direct. "I know he means well, but I can't be sure of Sandy. She'll do things to get what she wants…" She looked after the open door to the basement, where Samson had already descended. "I need to be fully rested. You should get some sleep before you run your errands today."

She went down and he went up and they took their rest.

CHAPTER 5

RAT FOOD RUNS AND RALLIED RAGE

The few hours of shut-eye Crawford stole did him good. No nightmares about the Boston docks followed him into the waking world. He rose to a quiet house, feeling from first stirring that the change was getting more insistent despite its respite on the coast.

The next full moon was in two days on October 11th and even by day the cold lunar eye coaxed him between every tree branch and from behind each ghost of cloud, whispering of racing prey, muzzle-warming blood, and baying in moon rays. How many snatches of that experience would he remember this time?

His Nosfur companions were vital in ensuring he had the chance. When first roaming for a roost outside Chicago they'd restrained him in a basement at costly damage to rented property.

They'd since spent the twenties seeking more remote places to haunt with yards backed up against wide natural expanses. Celeste's dwindling mob money and his own last government paycheck bought rickety houses in sparse counties, always two properties at a time. One stayed empty providing a place to decamp to if need be and they always sold the former home within a few years. Sadly, even when it was good for private investigating, they could not afford to put down community roots.

Then the crash of twenty-nine cut business to nil and the slow trickle of funds they had left became a gushing bleed as income all but froze. They did manage to find business. The world never ran out of cheats. Sadly, few could pay to fight them.

Fortunately, they were a hunting family in every sense of the term.

Water boiled on the kitchen stove and Crawford gathered invigorating earthy bitterness off the coffee grinder, one of the rare few aromas his conscious self truly cherished.

Accumulating the discipline to keep closer to home when he transitioned had been trial and error, marking the boundaries with more meaningful spoor than the feral staples of urine or musk rubbings. Strategically employed scents included gun oil on posts, whiskey dashed on shrubs, fur cream on rocks: stinks to stir his self-aware, refined mammalian personhood. But they weren't enough. The Nosfurs spent full moons on alert, coaxing Crawford back home after a romp with small balls of fried ground-chuck hung out back to beckon him home. Kind work for ex-vegetarians whose meals already came warm.

In the end, who came home carrying whom, Crawford or the beast? Ten years after the Scopes mammal trial, debate still raged whether the clothed, combed modern mammal was Noah and Christ's one-step nautical project or natural selection's slow stew. If they found Crawford dead in his were state, the whole debacle would probably start again, giving Crawford another reason not to be seen or heard. He rolled his eyes at Bible-thumpers but really, really hated lawyers.

There was only a little cream in the ice box. A dash was enough to tame the coffee's bitterness and he sipped it slowly on his front porch, laying out the day in his head. In return for Celeste's and Samson's shepherding, he'd once again fulfill his end of their arrangement and see to errands daylight denied them. Crawford finished his coffee, pumped full a wash bucket and scrubbed out the car to remove the last traces of blood scent from Boston before towelling the cracking diamond-stitched leather down. Once that was done, he phoned the rental company to collect the Packard Celeste used for the Ohio job. An hour later two sprightly fennec attendants arrived. One took the key, had Crawford sign documentation, and then followed the company coupe in the Packard away. Another expense for Sandy to settle.

Two cranks sputtered Crawford's Chevy to life. He ground the aging car's first gear up and was on his way.

The road into Scranton wound peacefully. Sparse fencelines became further spread across acres and the air thickened. Chained-up textile mills routed by weed-choked train tracks surrendered to sparser machine shops and gas stations rousing back to life. This was followed by clusters of New England style residences, apartment rows, then smaller house lots. Upon distant hills, the peaks of older estates looked down, some showing signs of life.

The year 1935 was gradually splitting America into two worlds, one in which farmers and shopkeeps scraped out any existence they could while larger companies and banks rallied by absorbing bankrupt kills. They said Christmas under Roosevelt's initiatives would see people spend again. Others said the managed economy would lead to disastrous inflation. Crawford wasn't much into economics on the larger scale. No casework in that.

He took the main artery of Birney Avenue, forking right onto Pittston. The feral livestock and pet supply store was a clapboard affair and one of two small places in town where he could buy feed for Celeste and Samson's rat colony. As advertising the keeping of multiple rats would have one wondering, Crawford went to a different store each time to seem like his cub only had one of the critters for amusement.

He entered the musty shop, thick with cured leather and bagged grains for cows, horses, and any number of ferals including lizards, mice or— "I'll need some rat feed, 'bout two pounds," Crawford told the proprietor, a squat brown-haired cat who scooped a barrel with a clicked tongue.

"Only beast I sell feed for right next to their poison, which I sell a lot more of in this city, lemme tell you."

Crawford hated small talk. "Well young Sammy loves his rodent. Thing eats more than he does." For any of the rats in Celeste and Samson's clutch that was true enough.

"Too many rats flooding this goddamn city since the mills started bellying up. Beggar trash clogging the alleys."

Post-war pessimism crested back when the bacchanal twenties were still roaring. Six years after the markets had folded, the slow sinking of the common mammal into destitution was the first topic of conversation in any business that kept afloat. On every soup kitchen line, all he ever saw were blank faces and bared teeth. Desperation was dangerous.

The cat hissed. "Damned veggies started flooding this town in the late twenties, mouths to feed without end, bringing their backward ways. Should go back where they came from."

The gripe was idiocy. Most carnivores were also from somewhere else, but Crawford demurred and counted his money low on his side of the counter. He slid over a couple dollars.

The cat squinted. "Lost that finger in the war?"

"Factory accident." True enough.

"Keep it if you can. Goddamn herbies took all the jobs away with their vote and started ruining all the good neighborhoods. Carnies are fed up with it, oh you damn well bet."

There was a pale stack of pamphlets by the cash register that Crawford had ignored. The cat fed Crawford's money to the open drawer and slid the top pamphlet over next to the bag of rat food. Crawford didn't want to read it but didn't want to be rude either. "Thanks," he said evenly and took both as the bell above the door rang. An elderly goat wandered in and Crawford couldn't help but turn back to see what the cat would do after his snarling diatribe.

The cat's expression went from sour to whisker-drooping blank and the pamphlets by his register were dragged out of sight. "What do you want?" he asked in a voice that conveyed nothing at all.

Crawford went out into autumn cold he hadn't registered before, senses tuning for the impending change. He put the bag on Chevy's passenger-side floor and glanced at the pamphlet. It was new enough to smell the ink.

"COMING TO A CITY NEAR YOU, RESCUE OUR COUNTRY'S PURITY AND TAKE AMERICA BACK."

A quick glance inside revealed a list of cities stretching from states west to east and ending in Boston. Under this was a sketched illustration of mammals, all carnivorous species, standing at the bow of a boat under an indistinct giant whose arms spread wide, encompassing them all. The creatures below waved American flags, arms raised in triumph, palm-flat as though cleaving the waves before the boat's prow.

Under that was a list of names, the top of which was bolded "COLONEL RUTLAND BLAKE". Crawford had heard the name before but quickly scanned the rest of the retinue of jokers before crumbling it up to throw it away. His claws were already curling the paper's corners when the last name crossed his eye.

He froze and read it again.

He'd not spoken to his wife in years, their parting as amicable as they could manage with the truth of his sexuality aired at last. He knew she and Lucas had stayed in Virginia, expanded the farm, and she'd remarried another carnivore, a dog of some sort.

She'd changed her last name along with that.

So had Lucas.

Cain became Marsten for both of them. And at the bottom of this pamphlet of speakers for the American Purity Party was one Lucas Marsten.

Crawford dropped the pamphlet to the seat next to him and felt a well of worry start digging itself. It couldn't be him. Lucas was just over twenty-one now, a few years younger than Samson would be if the goat kid aged as mortals do. Why would a wolf barely trimming his chin be a speaker at a rally railing against—he checked the pamphlet—communism and immigration?

As he sat at the wheel of his car he realized that he himself had entered his twenties fighting Germans and Austrians across the Atlantic, grinding his soul into something dark and self-recriminating. The crash of twenty-nine had done other kinds of damage to those coming after. His mind began to race with worry. Plans for the rest of the day fell out of importance.

He was set to meet Charlie Rothscub again a couple days after the change cycle was past, but Crawford couldn't wait. There was a Western Union telegraph office just a few blocks down.

***

Charlie heard nothing he didn't already know and realized quickly that the section-heads meeting was a farce.

"Homosexuals," Edgar said.

Charlie nearly choked on the coffee he was lapping. "I beg your pardon, sir?"

Edgar's bobcat whiskers creased along with his dark blue suit. "They have communist ties, don't they? The Russians like to recruit homosexuals, that's what our eyes and ears into pro-Stalin groups has been saying."

Charlie set his coffee down and coughed. "Well, no sir. It simply confirmed that the German Bund and other far right groups weren't allowing them."

"But they are more susceptible?"

"Homosexuals, well…aren't more likely to betray their country. They're more likely to be blackmailed for being homosexuals." Charlie watched his tone. "Real enemies of America try to take advantage of that."

Edgar was nonplussed. "They turn to God if they know what's good for 'em. And how about the vegetarians. They wanted the vote but can they be happy with that?"

How goddamn often did they have to go over this? "Well, Director, I obviously can't speak from experience but those who work to get representation tend to respect the institutions that vote affects more than anybody simply granted that privilege. So, I don't think vegetarians are any kind of—"

"Then, it's a good thing they had to work for it." Edgar grunted.

Hearty laughs went around the pale wooden table. Charlie joined in weakly, hollow as a bell without a clapper. He spoke into the trailing silence. "I've compared details with all the other teams and we've proven that there are no vegetarian-centered rabble rousers or dissident groups operating and—"

"Not yet," Agent Krint muttered over a smouldering cigar. Every strand of Doberman fur and cotton thread on her smelled of those cigars and Charlie hated her worse than any among Edgar's circle of ass-licks. Her comment got a few snickers.

Charlie coughed. "If anything, it's resistance to depression measures which is driving most of the activity we're seeing. Anti-communist and anti-immigrant."

The office doors parted and a muzzle poked in.

"Come in," Edgar sighed, giving Krint a look to blow her smoke in another direction.

Charlie's assistant Michael entered, his long ringtail barely making it in the room before he slid an envelope over to Charlie and smiled. "Apologies, all." He turned and was gone, tail shortly after.

The other agents eyed Charlie who tapped the envelope on the table. "I've asked to have any activity-related telegrams sent to me directly. We've got three agents in play right now following the activity of a group of interest closely."

Edgar sighed. "Well even if your leads aren't in the right place at least you've got some. Let's talk about organized crime folding into the trade unions. Agent MacDonnell, you have an update?"

The meeting didn't go on for much longer, just enough time for Edgar to see if his hunches, and by extension the administration's as well, were being proven or not.

Twenty minutes later Charlie had banished himself to his office and locked the door. He unfolded the telegram. "Charlie meet three days earlier. Will holler from Chicago."

"Holler" and "Chicago" were two of several combined word pairs that Crawford used to confirm it was him and not one of Charlie's active agents in the field. They were supposed to reacquaint this weekend after three months apart, just a few days after the worst of Crawford's unspoken "bout" had passed. Charlie had almost forgotten the smell of him.

The night before the full moon just might be cut short if Crawford didn't have better control of his affliction. Charlie wasn't worried. Yet.

He worked for another hour then heard the lunch-time rumble in his empty lupine stomach which override other sensations that came with pondering Crawford's fractured smile. "Taking a short walk, Michael," he called into the next office. "Want anything from the deli?"

"All good, sir."

Five minutes later he was at street level, taking a right onto Pennsylvania. He found the phone booth inside the vestibule of a barber's shop and called Crawford's exchange. He answered suspiciously fast. "Been missing you too," Charlie whistled high enough that passing dog's ears raised.

"Charlie." Crawford sounded a bit distracted. "Real glad to hear your voice. Tomorrow night okay?"

Charlie walked his mind through tomorrow's schedule. "I can make it work. Dinner first?"

"Dinner will be late as I've got an evening errand with the wife and kid, won't take more than an hour. I'll drive to you right after."

So curt. "You alright, Craw?"

A moment passed. "Yes. I've really missed you."

Charlie instinctively checked to make sure nobody was standing close to the booth's glass panes. His tail wagged and thumped them. "Same here, can't tell you how much. Some details…" The details were for the hotel room outside the city that Charlie would book under an assumed name. Charlie would be there before dark.

"Swell, Charlie. That's swell." They traded goodbyes and Charlie ended the call knowing something really wasn't.

***

Dozens of faces, muzzles closed, eyes dark and fixed. Determination supplanted confusion as the Colonel made his promise to the masses in the darkened pool hall. "God as witness, we'll drive them all out. The communists, vegetarians, atheists, and their demon agents in the unions. We'll defeat the "New Deal" that Roosevelt wishes to force down our throats! We've had enough of lesser mammals usurping upstanding carnivores who sweat to build this nation and I and my partners in countries across the Atlantic will lead the charge against all that robs us of our birthright."

A few more nods and whoops of agreement among the observant throng, just a few. There'd been back and forth at the hotel as to whether "usurp" was too complicated a word for the rabble to understand, but the Colonel stuck with it anyway. The cadence of authority was enough to draw them in. Lucas studied the German shepherd from the front row, watching how the white-suited Colonel worked the crowd. His muzzle always jutted, defiant and stubborn. His raised arms deflected the objectionable and claws grasped the unseen future at the right moments for emphasis. A hot, furious breath carried through the air, moving the restless tips of tails all around. Of all those who entered this saloon, more than half would leave armed with indignation and grievance at the unseen forces conspiring to crush their livelihoods and steal their freedom. The right enemies simply had to be drawn from nebulous uncertainty, given names, shown for their nefarious designs. Lucas didn't even realize he'd sat up straighter as an army was recruited around him.

The Colonel brought a wide palm downward, gently, cushioning the growing jeers and growls that threatened to drown him out. Fury was palpable enough to put in one's pocket as the voices stilled and silence was granted him once again.

The Colonel then glanced down to his protégé in the front row, the young wolf who was his newest convert to the cause.

"We are now a fatherless nation, abandoned by those we expected to care for us." The Colonel spoke these words into the quiet, his eyes holding Lucas's before lifting to the crowd, carnivorous orphans of a new revolution. "We must find strength in each other in hatred for our enemies: this government and the meek whose votes they seek. We will forge our own path, and I will be here to help you take this country back!"

The applause was thunderous and Lucas rose to his feet with them, his long-empty heart filling with something cold and validating that he felt through every stamp of hundreds of dusty feet. The Colonel's arms raised once more, his lips curved in a smile that was cold and pitiless.

***

Dusk arrived. Crawford roused Celeste first, then Samson. They both came to consciousness with that eerie, preternatural immediacy that he still found unnerving. No yawns, no stretching, corpses in perfect repose before their eyes opened and they came to be.

Celeste stayed dressed in light of the fact that Crawford would be bringing her about early. Despite his preference for males, the female anatomy could still arouse something in him. They'd long mutually decided that physical connections, even with no emotional attachments intended, would complicate things.

Samson, who settled and rose in the same clothes for days at a time, had no symptoms of puberty to worry about, blood-flush or starving. His preoccupations with maturity settled in other areas as his mind passed two decades in a body holding time all but still. "Can I drive?" was his first question when they all assembled upstairs, and the headlamps of Sandy's Cadillac turned into the drive, illuminating their front porch right on schedule.

"I don't know how Sandy will feel about you at the wheel of her Caddy but you can drive my car," Crawford said with a shrug. Samson's gangly limbs were just long enough for the Chevy's pedals. Interestingly, the aging he'd brought on by holding back from the vein hadn't made Samson noticably taller.

"I wonder if we should take just one car," Celeste cautioned. "A procession heading to the bank might turn heads."

"Two cars at the only late-open bank in town won't mean anything." Crawford scratched his neck. "Plus, if we leave early, you'll need more space in that Caddy to bunker down against the dusk."

That settled it. Sandy leaned out the Caddy's back window as the car pulled into the shadow of a copse of trees, the tip of her thick tail poking out with her as though a second head. Even in the dusk the tiniest thread of sunlight made her wince. "Bank closes in two hours, we need to hurry."

Celeste was at Sandy's car in a mere moment as though darting through a shower of volcanic ash and entered the car's passenger compartment with small French curses.

"Sam's with me," Crawford called out as he went to his car and drew his own jerry-rigged curtains against the fading light. He'd be able to pull them back before they even made town, keep both cars from looking like hearses. "Go."

With a nod from Sandy to the ever silent and attentive driver, they did.

Moments later, Samson bounded to the driver's seat of Crawford's car and settled in with nary a wince. The light was weak enough to barely smart him at this point with his depleted veins. Crawford took the passenger seat, waited patiently while Samson started the old beast up and they were off with a lurch.

Samson worked to second gear, brow furrowing and small tail lashing once on the seat behind him. They both braced as they bounced over a divot at the property's edge. Samson straightened the old machine out and kept on.

"Back in action, huh?" Crawford said, wondering when the last time any action had been. Then he remembered four months ago when they had to fix the leaky roof, keeping low to avoid glimpses by neighbors who'd question a wolf and goat tarring shingles three stories up in the dead of night.

"Yes," Samson said, guardedly.

Didn't want to talk about it. Crawford fidgeted as he wondered what to do about the starvation-aged teenager driving the car. "You want to go over the plan again?"

Eyes ahead, headlamps bobbed as they met the main road. "I'm fetching that box. Simple enough for me." He afforded himself a small smile. "As long as the ladies aren't late."

"Celeste won't be," Crawford assured him. "She got those other shards back from Ohio."

"Not yet. The mail comes in a day or two she said."

"Well…" Crawford juggled whether he should raise the issue and demurred to talking around it. "We are grateful for your help. Youth has its benefits and a click in my elbow tells me I'll be envious of that immortality of yours sooner than later."

"No, you won't," Samson kept his voice even, guarding something volatile. "You had a wife and a kid and a job and a salary. Even if it all didn't work out grandly there's a lot you won't regret never having. You also have your friend in Washington. Lots to live for."

Complaining about his curse would be a pathetic deflection so Crawford thought hard as the car sped up and followed the dim shape of the Caddy ahead. "Only for a little while, Samson. When it's gone…"

"I really don't want to talk about it," Samson said. "My being older and less hurt by those nails is helping this work. That's how I put myself here. It's the whole reason I'm useful." He sped a bit too much and then slowed a bit.

"But it's hurting you. Don't try telling me it isn't. Samson, please don't think that your usefulness to any jobs we take is what's important to us. Celeste and I both care deeply about you. You know that, don't you?"

He nodded curtly and said nothing further as he chased a shape to a distant town.

**

Ahead on the road, Celeste and Sandy settled into the darkness but kept the window drapes closed. "How long?" Sandy asked.

The driver looked over his shoulder and Celeste saw light glint in his mortal eyes. The scent of muskrat carried back. "Half hour to town," he said primly.

"Thank you, Bruno," she said softly. The white of a smile flashed back before both eyes returned to the road.

"New friend?" Celeste asked.

"Old one, worked for Calvert for years."

"Didn't know they'd be looking for alternate employment, but I'd assume these times are difficult for everyone."

"It's complicated." Sandy's shrug was felt where their shoulders touched.

"I'm surprised you didn't keep the rabbit's Rolls Royce. Or did he keep that in the divorce?"

Sandy smiled. "The Rolls stayed but I had to part with it. It was too familiar around Chicago and honestly with the world gone the way it has it would be vandalized in every town we stabled it in. Lots of resentment against the wealthy since twenty-nine."

"Only since then?"

They were quiet as the car moved on, headlamps fighting night and Allentown drawing close.

Sandy was curt when she spoke again. "You have your reasons for being angry with me and I have my reasons for doing what I did. I can only apologize so many times for steps taken to protect us all."

"I worried about you."

"You departed. I could have been resentful too, but I had to stop Donovan's plan from coming to fruition. Chicago is just a wide pit of pain now. That one damn trade building, all those trestles and bridges…be glad if you haven't gone back there."

Celeste shifted her position and crouched in the wide seat so she would be eye to eye with the squirrel. "And when all this is done, when you have these shards and we've done whatever we need to do with them, what then? Are you moving on?"

Sandy turned back to her. "I was going to ask you the same question. Domesticity has done a fair bit of damage. Your house smells mildly of goat kid and strongly of wolf musk. It's…awful." Sandy laughed.

Celeste found it impossible not to smile. "You get used to it and I like having them around. They've both been trampled by the world in ways that make me remember myself."

"From France, back before we met?"

"Chicago. We were all trapped in ways we couldn't recognize at the time. No steel required."

Sandy nodded. "What it would be like to be free from the worst of ourselves..."

Pale illumination coalesced outside the drapes—the passing constellations of a town at first dark. Celeste pulled back the curtain. Allentown wasn't a swarm of activity like Chicago, but it buzzed in its own way, much like Scranton.

"We're close, Ms. Mallory," said Bruno, making a right turn.

Celeste opened the curtain on her side and saw the Allentown National Bank, Corinthian columns recessed in Beaux Arts masonry rising high out of sight.

Bruno slowed and checked his mirrors. "The Chevrolet is behind us."

"Take us around-side. We'll be meeting Samson near there when he has the package."

Around the building's grey flank, the deer and red squirrel disembarked and sent the Cadillac onward to slowly circle. "Up there," Celeste angled her muzzle high and Sandy followed. The power junction joined the bank building at the third corner, hissing faintly with the current it fed to the building.

"I can climb that quicker than you," Sandy said assuredly.

"Skipping shadows, speed won't matter," Celeste countered. "Let me do it as I know which line to cut without frying myself." She met Sandy's glance. "You're not shorting Crawford and I our payment for this job."

Sandy's tail bobbed with amusement as she stepped aside and found a shadow that oversaw the street. "I wouldn't dream of it."

Celeste bound a shadow, then another higher. The hum of electric light crackled the shadow's boundaries as she came face to face with a junction box that she worked deftly.

***

Crawford entered first, fedora in hand, and got in line with his decoy's key. After sundown the bank was sleepier in disposition, just two tellers tiredly holding the fort and a security guard in snappy dress with hip revolver standing in a bleary-eyed interpretation of attention near the arch to the wicket. Every bank that kept solvent through the first half of the thirties had a gun on the door, not just to prevent robberies, but the creeping fear of a bank run and violent demands for full withdrawal by panicked mobs who tried to clear it all out in the first couple years. Banks bled out fast when the panics came in waves after twenty-nine. Crawford wouldn't have given a damn if he didn't know that when the banks died, whole towns weren't far behind.

The man on the door would be the hardest for Samson to avoid completely and Crawford had the sneaking suspicion that the bear was vaguely familiar in some way.

The goat kid in question would make his entrance soon to wait for the signal.

"Box withdrawal," Crawford told the fox at the wicket and waved the key. The fox eyed it and sighed. "I'll need the manager. A moment, sir." He tottered off while Crawford waited.

Time passed and he glanced to the door through which Samson would be coming. Celeste, and likely her immortal squirrel friend too, should be around the other side ready to make their move. Would the security guard dreaming of his first pint after clocking out have his blood quickened if he only knew that Nosfurs existed like the vampires in the picture shows? How about no less than three of them surrounding this bank? All too likely he'd piss himself and run as soon as start shooting.

Fortunately, no blood was getting drunk tonight.

According to plan, at least.

A shadow fell over Crawford as the wolf turned over the key in his hand and he looked up into an impossibly broad chest trying to escape a cable-knit cardigan. "You wish to access a box in our vault?" The bear above it rumbled.

"Sorry to ask so late but yes. It's quite important." Crawford put his key down on the counter in front of him to brook no argument. Sandy had a box registered in his name with a few dollars in it, a prop, nothing more.

Silence.

"Good man," Crawford tried to sound impatient without rudeness as his eyes trailed up. "I know this bank is closing soon and I…"

The bear that peered down at him hardened his chiselled gaze to a cold glare. Crawford felt his heart in his throat as recognition took hold, fedora nearly dropping from his other hand.

"Cain," the bear managing the bank rumbled.

"Uh…Beatie?" Crawford's heart thudded. His old boss, head of the Prohibition Unit in Chicago, loomed over him.

The unit that Crawford had abruptly departed from.

Memory came with a stink. Beatie had labelled him a rotten coward and chewed him out before the whole team in absentia. Charlie had reluctantly told Crawford about it, unable to explain to anybody on Crawford's behalf that their former co-worker had been turned into a moon-primed time-bomb of primordial violence.

At that moment the bank's door opened and Crawford heard Samson saunter in, hooves clicking.

With his tail ready to curl up inside himself, Crawford had to bury the emotions that bubbled up and he swallowed. Five minutes left, maybe less. "Been a long time, Beatie. I'm sorry we don't have time to catch up…"

"Shut up," the bear said, a deep breath stretched the cardigan impossibly tight. "You think I don't remember you, you yellow back-stabbing—"

"Uh, that's not fair."

"—cowardly, post-deserting—"

"I had to leave."

"Leave?" The bear spat and Crawford felt moisture hit his nose. "Leave? We had a goddamn mob war with cannibals burning speaks down and aldermen getting assassinated and who the fuck do you think you are to walk into this bank and tell me that—" Beatie caught something out of the corner of his eye at the next wicket and his demeanor changed, voice dropping to an appeasing whisper. "Ms. Grafton, I'm so sorry for my composure just now, just a teensy problem that came up. Please accept my sincere apology and we'll waive that fee for the wire payment to your nephew in Sicily. Would that help?"

The ermine at the next wicket nodded with bruised indignation as the fox serving her shrank back.

"Handle that, would you, Tracey?" Beatie's demeanor returned to ice as he turned back to Crawford. "I should shove you in a deposit bag and mail your cowardly ass to Siberia."

A hoof scuffed behind Crawford. Any second, the next phase of the plan would happen and he wasn't ready. All the arguments he'd long ago composed to defend himself came to the fore and were swept away by sheer necessity. "Okay, fine. I'm horrible. I'm a louse. I was cowardly and I ran and I begged Charlie to forgive me which he did because he's the outstanding officer that I could never be. I see that now."

Beatie's glare very much doubted that he did.

Three minutes. "You've said your piece. Let me have box two-one-six and I'll complete my business and get out of your fur, forever if need be. I'll wait right here."

Beatie stood and seethed and the large clock above the vault ticked forward.

The bear turned, storming for the vault. The other bear working security joined him as they worked the keys and massive latch to open the vault wide enough for Beatie to wedge himself through. Moments passed. Any second now.

Beatie reappeared with the box Crawford called for, setting it down just loudly enough to demonstrate contempt but not enough to disturb Ms. Grafton who was having her account information confirmed.

"Get out whatever you're getting and then take your stinking hide—"

At that moment the lights went out, casting the whole bank into near-total darkness. Lamplight from the street bled in through the front window, providing the wicket frames and vault door with long menacing shadows.

Darkness conquered the vast majority of the place. For Samson that was more than enough.

Crawford didn't hear him pass, didn't feel a thing as the goat Nosfur bound the nearest shadow to himself and followed it to the next and the next, transgressing the physical laws binding mammals to the earth. Crawford barely registered a slight distension of a shadow in the vault door's wake, the barest disturbance of perception even though he'd been actively seeking it.

Now it was his turn. He lifted the deposit box that Beatie had set down and dropped it to the marble floor between his toes, screaming bloody murder as the box struck an inch from calamity. "Aww Gaawd! It broke my damn toe!"

A beat passed. Then Beatie responded indifferently as though a soup had obtained a fly. "Right. Tom, flashlight."

Crawford took deep cursing breaths that echoed through the bank's vaulted space.

Samson didn't need a lot of time and with the world being nothing but shadow, his passage to the exit should be clear and all but immediate.

And Samson should not at all bump into the bear security guard coming back around the long counter's hinged exit and be momentarily visible in the flashlight's beam, a compact metal object held against his small shivering frame.

However... "The hell?" Tom the security bear said.

Samson hurled himself towards the door, shadow-binding impossible as the bear's flashlight instinctively followed him. "Does that kid have a deposit box? Hey, stop!"

For a mortal, there wasn't enough time to get into the vault and out again after the two bears came out, even at full sprint in perfect light. Crawford immediately realized this and hollered. "That goddamn rabbit or what the Sam-hell-ever doesn't have the box. It dropped on my foot!" He hopped in place on one foot like a Rockette line dancer. "Shine the light here, you numbskull!"

The light went to Crawford, then down, then returned to the blue collared shirt on the kid's fleeing back. Samson was at the door already and wresting it open. The bear guard decided that he'd taken something and gave chase, but even mortal, a light-hooved youngster kid was an easy match for an ursine nearly twenty stone in weight. He'd scuttled off past the lamplight outside before the bear nearly collided with the heavy swinging door.

"What kinda operation are you running here, Beatie?" Crawford let his growl out, hopefully coaxing the other bear back before he got outside and hooked a scent. "Yer a bank! Think you could try not to injure your customers by paying the electrical bill?"

The growl that came back from the silhouette across the wicket was two octaves lower in register. "Don't get started with me, Crawford. It's not my fault you're as clumsy as you are cowardly." The voice receded to a distant corner of the room where a chair scraped and a flashlight was dug out of a drawer. That light bobbed out of sight. "You just wait." The flashlight found the startled ermine down the counter and his voice turned to treacle. "And you as well Ms. Grafton. I won't be but a moment and I offer my heartfelt apologies."

The front door opened and was filled with a back-lit silhouette of panting ursine dejection. Samson had gotten away.

There was a snap and light blinded everybody. Beatie returned to Crawford who fought the stars in his eyes with blinks. "Do you have what you need, sir?" The last word was like the jab of a rusty nail as Beatie looked down to the box Crawford had lifted.

"I don't yet have an apology for the way I've been treated today." Crawford wanted to leave, but had to vent the indignation he'd put on as he did so. When Beatie eventually found two gaping slots in a vault he'd taken one box from…

"I apologize for not stripping you of your Bureau badge before tossing you out on your tail in twenty-three." Beatie snarled. "So you can hit the bricks."

A memory flooded in from the bear's tight, smokestunk office. "You stole the decanter!"

"What?" The other bear had stopped panting and joined his boss.

Crawford had a clear path to the door now and he figured that if a bridge had to burn, well… "On my second to last day with the detail, you took a whiskey decanter from my car and brought it in to file as evidence. But you didn't! I saw it in your office, half-drank the next day while you were chewing me out over going to the wrong speak!"

Confusion was pushed away by dawning memory and bank manager Beatie glanced around to assess how may pairs of eyes were on him. "Time for you to go, Cain." Contempt remained, but much less indignation.

"You did have a tipple, didn't you? Did any of that whiskey ever even make it to evidence? Is that one of the reasons you left the Bureau and now push pencils at a bank here in—"

"I said *get out*, Crawford! I don't know what the hell you're talking about. I won't charge the fee for your box access but I don't want to see you again."

"Fine by me! I know where I'm not wanted!" Feeling hustled out, there was nothing suspicious in obliging. Crawford stuffed on his fedora and almost forgot to theatrically limp a bit on the way out. Beatie's humble apologies to the elderly ermine for the beastly interaction were muttered behind him as the bank's door closed.

Outside and down the street he saw his car but no kid. As he approached a nearby shadow spoke with a hiss. "I couldn't get it there," Samson's voice was reedy with pain. "It's shoved under a mailbox behind you. I had to kick it and run."

Crawford turned, crouched, saw a glint of metal under the four legs of a red cast-iron postal box. He scurried back and pulled down his fedora as he dragged the deposit box out, hustled to his car and tossed it in the trunk, feeling that familiar, inescapable discomfort. He returned to the shadowy corner of the closed furniture store and saw a stretch of dark expel a goat kid. He was clearly disturbed, trying to shake pain off. "We need to get going, Samson."

"I couldn't do it," the kid moaned. "Even starved, it hurt. The second I pulled that box out, it hurt and I lost my shadow!" The goat kid's blood-starved body seemed to have aged even more.

"It's okay, I'll take it from here. Remember that box is full of things intended to hurt you. You did good, kid."

"But I didn't." Samson was looking away so Crawford couldn't see him fight anguish. "I nearly let us all down."

Crawford looked around. One couple passed on the street's other side and two cars chugged by. No eyes on them. Right now they'd be putting Crawford's box back. When they noticed the missing box they'd be back out here coming for the kid.

There was more than doubt buried under the kid's stubborn exterior, but there wasn't time. "You didn't let down anybody. Don't let yourself feel otherwise. Come on," Crawford said. "I'll take these away and get them hid. You have to meet Sandy and Celeste. They'll get you home." He wanted to take more time, get the kid alone and talk him down. There wasn't time with the danger of the bank so close and that hurt to know.

"Where are you going?"

"I have to meet Charlie, catch up. I don't have much time." Crawford was loath to leave even though time was moving against him. "I'll keep the nails safe."

Samson recognized his anxiety. "Okay, Crawford. Don't nibble on anybody who doesn't earn it."

A shadow at the corner stirred just a bit. He knew that Celeste and perhaps Sandy were watching as he went round to the driver's side. "I'll see how it goes."

Samson took the dark and Crawford took the driver's seat of his old Chevy. It was late, but he could still make it to the diner outside Baltimore before midnight.

CHAPTER 6

THE LIE RAINS DOWN

With the sun down, Donovan Calvert was on the move. He found a public phone and whispered a phrase to the front desk attendant at the Waldorf in New York when he was finally connected. "Tell Von Haften's attendant that true hearts cannot be forged, only forever beaten with perfection's aim."

Donovan waited. Christof Von Haften would recognize one of the first lines of the supplicant's oath when the message was relayed. The night was still as he waited. "Who is this?" the Austrian lion rumbled with something that wasn't contempt or impatience. Was it hope?

"Been a very long time, Christof. Evelyn told me so much about you before we parted."

The silence was leaden, the intake of breath that followed was ragged. "Calvert. You're alive."

"I am."

An automobile passed. An owl hooted deep within a distant copse of trees. Even in surprise Von Haften would have presence of mind to have his people call back the phone company to discover where Donovan's exchange was.

"What happened to my wife?" Christof kept his voice level, unrushed. He'd sent her to America, or at least hadn't resisted the assignment. Donovan could only imagine how much guilt found Christof over the last decade as the inevitable conclusion set in.

In spite of all the Martyres had done to betray him, Donovan felt he was due closure at least. "As you've no doubt surmised, Evelyn is dead. I'm sorry."

Christof took a deep breath, said nothing.

"I didn't kill her, Christof. Regardless of our disagreements, we did get along rather well." Christof would know exactly what that meant, but couldn't be given time to dwell. Time to really sell the last twelve years. "It was an officer of the law who murdered your wife, a wolf who gained my trust, squandered, and betrayed it. I had to go underground, flee Chicago. I didn't know who to trust."

"You fled from us, Donovan? My wife was…" Christof's voice caught. "And you didn't reach out to us or send so much as a telegram?"

"For good reason. I've survived at least five attempts on my life in the last three years, Christof. What's afoot here is far worse than anyone ever feared or thought possible, and yet I honestly don't know if those who tried to kill me weren't working at your behest. You were already scheming to seize all I had." Donovan's bitter distrust felt good to lay plain.

Christof didn't care to address his suspicions. "Who was it then who killed Evelyn?"

Donovan could taste the bitterness…and the doubt. Let him have the closest answer to truth he'd ever need. "An agent formerly with the Federal Prohibition Bureau named Crawford Cain. He's out there somewhere. I'm his loose end."

"You are everyone's loose end, Mister Calvert." Germanic frankness made that even colder.

"Then let's discuss this," Donovan said, realizing his next words passed a point of no return. "I've much to show you and it's all at a chalet in the Catskills I've kept under an assumed name for years. I'm tired of running."

Christof had a long moment to stew. "Where?"

Donovan provided a township, a junction, and the name of a winding road. "Come alone," Donovan added, knowing he wouldn't. When the call ended, the location of this booth would be reported back to Von Haften within minutes. They would all be on the move.

He hurried, melting himself into the forest's endless supply of shadows, moving at a pace the wind itself would envy as he traversed forests and rocky gulleys. The last vestiges of privilege afforded by his former life meant nothing here in the wilderness where a million creatures teemed. Yet he was safer in nature's bosom than he'd ever been in his soft Gold Coast bed. Sandy's bite made him a slave to certain wants, yes, but freed him of restraint and inhibition. Someday they'd meet again and he'd thank her or kill her. He'd know then which was appropriate.

A sallow-hided heifer wandering a dark pasture on the outskirts of the Allegheny Forest was an appetizer, its painful lowing drawing a mangy hound, shotgun loaded. Donovan disarmed him and opened his windpipe greedily. There were no screams from the canine. He was as thin as his few cattle. No ring on his finger. And so, no second course.

Donovan dragged the meal deep into the dark to drink his fill, plans wheeling within his invigorated mind under a scattering of winking stars. He left the dilapidated farm behind with a single light awaiting no one's return.

He was ready for Christof, one of countless loose ends he'd relish seeing to. Donovan had shown Evelyn a better world and she'd scorned it. They all had.

What would have to pass now wasn't really revenge, simply survival of the fittest.

He hurtled through the dark to a rendezvous long prepared and a shadow followed.

***

"You did very well, Samson," Sandy put a hesitant but reassuring arm around him. "I'm sorry for how much that must have hurt."

Celeste watched Samson's aged face for clues as to how the goat was faring, but he'd grown withdrawn. If anybody could help Samson see the folly in what he was doing to himself, Sandy was the perfect candidate.

Samson screwed up a pained expression and looked to the car's fabric roof. "It hurts, just like the starving hurts. I thought the nails wouldn't hurt me if I didn't drink."

Sandy shook her head. "I'm sorry. They always hurt, just less than if you'd fed. The Martyres, and the rabbit I used to be with, well, they use alchemy to make it worse. The pain fades fast, I promise."

"But not drinking, to stay my real age," Samson lowered his muzzle and met Sandy's gaze. The car was rocking now as the muskrat at the wheel turned it back onto the drive at Celeste, Crawford, and Samson's home. "I can smell…" He glanced at the driver and back again. Worry welled up as he sought Sandy's gaze for truth. "When do the urges get better?"

Celeste watched Sandy struggle to say what needed be said.

"They won't. I'm sorry but it will always be hard, even if you make the pain your very best friend the way I tried to."

He didn't answer, lips pursed in anger.

Sandy slid her palm up and down the goat's arm. "I'm sorry."

"No." His voice was gaining a growl.

"We've arrived," the muskrat said curtly, exited, and opened the rear door next to Celeste. She didn't step out, so the muskrat stepped away, sensing the tension.

Celeste put her own hand on Samson's back. "We can help you, but you have to understand that you can only hurt yourself if you persist in doing this any longer."

"I want to be alone for a while."

The doe and the squirrel looked at one another.

Sandy pursed her lips over her thick teeth. "I don't know if that's—"

"Of course, Samson." Celeste stepped out of the car and the goat was out right after her. He stormed up to the house and went inside.

Celeste and Sandy watched him go.

"I can imagine how hard it's been."

The contrition seemed genuine, but Celeste wasn't sure how to feel. "Let me catch you up. Assuming you can stay?" She glanced from Sandy to her muskrat driver and back again and made a decision. Crawford wouldn't be back tonight. She'd seen his demeanor outside the bank and was certain of it. He was keeping his own counsel about something and as with Samson, she had to respect accommodations that helped their odd family thrive.

She wasn't Crawford's mother any more than she was Samson's. "I have a guest room"—Celeste indicated the dark house—"for your driver on the second floor. Samson spends much of his time listening to the phonograph when he wants solitude."

The muskrat nodded with thanks, prim as a rich man's valet. He reminded Celeste of someone she couldn't place.

"Where will I rest?" Sandy asked.

They had hours till dawn. "Come with me," Celeste said.

In they went, turning on one porch light that Samson hadn't bothered with. Like the planted flowerbeds and kept lawn, it only served for appearances.

As though reading her mind, Sandy's voice piped up behind Celeste's as she followed her in. "Do you often keep it somewhat bright in here?"

"Till about ten or so," Celeste led her to the stairs and up again. Down below the floorboards a ragtime band played up thin and tinny from Samson's phonograph. "We've had close calls with neighbors and need to be visibly invisible if that makes any sense. The last dozen years have been more exciting than I would have expected."

"For us as well. I live in Atlantic City now."

"Swanky."

"In the summers to be sure."

Celeste listened to the horns drifting up from below and fought her first impulse. Samson would only retreat further if he felt cajoled or coddled. The rat room was ready when the urge for nourishment grew too great. He'd come around when he was ready.

"Let's go up a bit further."

One of the two rooms on the top floor had a Juliet balcony just outside the neighbors' view which gazed out over the dark carpet of forest past the house's rear yard. This was where Celeste hopped over the rail onto shingle. Squirrel feet landed behind her with immediate purchase.

In the silvery light night fauna muttered while wheeling insects sought dance partners. The doe and squirrel crouched together on the slanted roof and drank in the peace of it all.

"Reminds me of Dublin out over the bay," Sandy muttered.

Dublin, where they'd first seen one another, had been long before Donovan in Chicago ended everything. That loss was as much Sandy's fault as the steel baron's and Celeste wondered how she'd make Sandy accept that. In the moment, in that stillness, her last bite of acrimony fled completely. "Have you been alone?"

Sandy met her gaze with a surprising coyness and drew out her answer. "I have help where I am now. You mean…in that way?"

Celeste looked away, then met her gaze again. "Yes."

Sandy's lush red tail shivered and stilled. "I don't have what we had."

Celeste nodded. "That's a sort of answer. Is it…money that keeps him around?"

"Bruno provides things for me that I can't provide myself. I provide in return. Like your wolf I suspect. I hope he hasn't hurt you."

Celeste could see that Sandy didn't want to necessarily dance around questions of companionship, but she felt on more precarious footing than this roof. "Crawford has always been mostly in danger of hurting himself. Let him be a moment. Why are you here?"

"You know…"

"You rationalized it well. We are the best you can find to get the rabbit's nails. But you needed to find us first and I know that took time."

Sandy nodded. "You migrated quite a lot."

"For good reason. As comfortable as this may seem, we're always watching the horizon for trouble. Anxieties are easy to hide under touch-up coats of paint."

Sandy opened her mouth and closed it again, sucking at the back of her teeth in trepidation before speaking again. "I hadn't stopped thinking about you for a single day, Celeste. I know I chased you away. I helped chase you all away."

"Feeling guilt?"

"That and want." Sandy looked away over the trees. "Something drink never fills. I'd loved before you, you know, the kind that feels true and endless. But it was spurned when I was sent to the convent in Newry. Piety made my chosen impious, time took her away. You know much of the rest. How does a convent cure a sapphic after all?"

When she glanced back, Celeste saw a flash of regret.

"That was before I was bitten. Life's pages turned, took those I loved and hated away." Sandy flashed a smile. "Then I met you."

"And…" Celeste said evenly, but with no malice.

Sandy's lip trembled and she was in the larger doe's arms whispering bitterly into her chest. "Oh Celeste, I'm so sorry. The guilt I was sired on never left me. 'Twas only buried. When Donovan took me and my life was laid bare, it was waiting for him to exploit. And I let the bastard do it."

Celeste's own pain bubbled up, anger tamped down. "I thought you'd been killed when you disappeared. But I searched. I even prayed once. And when I found you, saw what he'd done to you, I'd never known such fury.

At him, Sandy. Even when you tried to betray me, even in the heaviest weight of that, I only ever truly hated him."

Sandy sobbed, face unseen, into Celeste's shoulder, an undammed river of purgation at last. "I thought I was saving you. I thought I could save both of us. I was so wrong, Celeste, so stupidly, naively wrong. What we had was the purest thing in my life and I ruined it for us both. I don't know if it's possible for you to truly forgive that."

Celeste put a hand under the squirrel's chin and turned her gaze upward to meet hers. Her answer was met readily enough with the softest press of their lips. The night went still and Sandy let out a sob into Celeste's mouth as she rocked in the doe's arms. They had no breath to trade but for the sounds they made, and Sandy was plaintive as sorrow was overtaken by wants that were heady but insistent, approaching desperation. "What about..." Sandy spoke in the space between kisses. "They'll hear."

Sandy of course meant Samson far below. And her man who was mere shingles away.

Celeste didn't care about how Bruno reacted, but her worry for Samson's dilemma warred with primal needs she'd suppressed for far too long. Celeste drew Sandy to her, leaned back towards the shadow of the home's unused chimney. The shadow slipped round them both with gossamer, blanketing dark as they bound the space beyond nature's frail membrane together.

Their tongues entwined, hands went round throats, slipping to spread fabric of their respective garments down from their shoulders, to their breasts, hands moving quickly lower on one another, hiking up the simple dark ensembles chosen for their role in the bank heist. Sandy's underthings were teased down delicately at first, the dark lace like slick webbing in the moon. The Irish squirrel huffed and tore them off before revealing her sex to the night. Celeste, for her part, turned briefly sideways, slipped her own underthings away smoothly to settle beyond the dark.

Sandy straddled Celeste. They were not flush with blood, but recently enough fed that their hearts beat in slow, measured rhythm, the processes of mortal life all but stopped and yet the spark connected them. Legs spread, joined in silence, their sexes touched and lightly brushed across one another. Hands found one another's backs while their other fingers entwined, came down between them together. Weightless in the spell of their immortality they did not slip on the roof's rough surface as they found one another's essence. Celeste had long been adept with teasing the clitoral crown while Sandy worked the doe's folds with insistent strokes. Their fingers worked high and low, Celeste circling Sandy's labia while Sandy tickled Celeste from within.

The sensation made Celeste laugh, giddy while the squirrel moaned into the doe's ministrations. They took their time, breasts licked by moon's dewy light as they departed from their shadow, found one another's gaze, and came back to one another at last. As Celeste was the more practiced Sandy found orgasm first, long tail bunching and curling. As the hiss passed her teeth, she bade Celeste lie back, eyes to the distant stars and leaned in. Sandy's tongue was patient but insistent and Celeste released herself with parted jaws and peeking fangs.

They lay and listened. Far below them, Samson's record kept on. "Oh, 'Leste, we shouldn't have…"

Celeste clasped Sandy's hand and held it firm. "I'd hear if he ascended. He's nimble but hasn't managed stealth well at all. I'm glad he's never had to sneak up on another like us."

Celeste let the night air steal her last heat as she gathered her thoughts. "You'll have to help me with him. You'll need his trust and he'll need yours if he's to truly contend with all he's going through. He has learned well how to evade my questions, Crawford's too." She sat up and restored her clothes to modesty, watching Sandy do the same. "It's important for you to know, getting back into my life will involve helping him navigate his. Even with an aging mind…"

Sandy met her gaze and Celeste felt relief that Sandy didn't hesitate. "I understand. I'll do that."

They composed themselves and went down. Sandy stopped by the room offered to Bruno and the muskrat obligingly withdrew an atomizer of subtle perfume that he applied to her throat in a single puff, his expression implacable. Celeste didn't know if she could readily trust him but returned his curt nod amicably enough.

They descended to Samson's private lair where he'd spent many a night brooding and the slight disturbance of air from under his closed door told Celeste that something was off. She knocked and then peeked in. The record was now skipping on the phonograph under the open basement window, dried leaves skittered across his neatly made bed. The kid was gone.

***

Crawford made the rendezvous in Maryland at about five to midnight by the lounge's ornate clock. A familiar brown wolf waited in a round-benched booth behind a half-drank Singapore Sling. If the low light of the crushed velvet and brass-railed place bothered Charlie his warm toothy smile hid it well. The vantage kept everything where the brown wolf could see it.

He rose as Crawford approached and they clasped hands warmly, eyes trading all they couldn't say before the limp-tailed salesmen crowding the nearby bar. "Nice place you picked." Crawford nodded his muzzle at the dated deco décor. "Reminds me of places we rolled over in the bad old days."

Charlie shrugged as they sat. "I prefer to remember better places I visited in my off hours," he sighed, "those that didn't get rolled over for their own reasons."

The problem with reminiscing about Chicago was that every good memory battened down against a bad one.

"You coping well with the joint problem?" Charlie raised a brow.

Joint problem in their breezy offhand also covered jaw problem, textile problem, and meat sweats. Crawford sighed and summoned a shuffling marmot who took his order for an old fashioned on the rocks. "My physician found a restorative for me. Rare-cooked ground chuck in a lunchbox, or hanging from the porch. Reduces excesses when I get too hungry as the night goes by." Celeste and Samson also enjoyed fewer feral hog guts in the bathtub but that story could stay untold. "I'm starving. You eat?"

Charlie wagged and the booth padding thumped. "They brought bread already. The steak here is six ounces of heaven and the kitchen hasn't quite closed yet." They ordered two with fingerling potatoes and morsels of heaven went down.

They caught up on as much of Charlie's work with the Bureau that they could talk about, which wasn't much, and of Crawford's nomadic movements across Pennsylvania as they could cover, which was even less. Crawford thought of mentioning their old Prohibition boss now manning the desk of a bank one state over but didn't want to sour a vastly improved mood.

All the while the urge to slide round the booth and get shoulder to shoulder was palpable as the rumble of an earthquake fault line. Charlie was turning forty in a few months and Crawford was three months ahead of him and the fire that had caught them both by surprise twelve years ago hadn't ebbed. They knew where they were, felt every passing pair of eyes and the urgency building off the last three months. So much was on Crawford's mind, the impending change he'd need to manage, the pamphlet bearing the name of his son, but the warmth of so much more than comradery kept him in better spirits as the bone and gristle were borne away and Charlie got the cheque. He slid over the address of the hotel, two miles away. "I'll leave first," he said with a smile and a twinkle in his eye Crawford felt down to his loins. Charlie put on a brown fedora a shade darker than his own fur.

"What happened to the porkpie?"

Charlie's eyes darted up to the brim which he adjusted above them. "In the words of my esteemed director, that hat made me look like a 'faggot, pool-hall communist.'"

In spite of the threat threading between Charlie's job and his true nature, Crawford had to laugh. "You're the most charming pool-hall commie anybody will ever get to know."

Charlie gave a Chaplinesque wag of brows and ears as he lit a cigarette, offered one that Crawford declined. He gave Charlie a two-minute head start, doffed his own cream-colored hat to the slinky cat waitress and slipped out.

An hour later, their cars were a lot apart and they were behind blinds. Charlie's shirt was off and his pale-pelted chest rose and fell as he settled on the bed, curling his clawed toes. "You're close to the change, aren't you?"

"I'll have to fight hard to stop it tomorrow, night after that the moon's full and it'll be impossible." Crawford slipped his jacket off, loosening his tie slowly. Wolf sweat was loading the room, heady, lip-curling. "I've been working on controlling parts of it."

Charlie stubbed his smoke out on the bedside ashtray, watched Crawford slip off his suspenders. "You mean you, uh, can you just turn halfway?"

"Kind of like that. I can get only parts of my body to change, fangs, claws on one hand or the other. Once I made my legs long and kept my arms short, but I could only hold that for a minute.

Charlie sat on the bed and looked curiously at Crawford. "So. You can get any part of your body to grow monstrous and feral on command."

"I'd need a lot more practice before we mess with that."

Slacks were undone and slipped away. "Very well."

Their clothes accumulated in a tangled mess. They drank deeper scents, nostrils flaring.

Charlie had long loved the mingling of a bitch's perfume—the kind used to smooth the edge on a female lupine or canine's sharp arousal that they sold with every winking metaphor in the book—with the rank undertone of maleness. Charlie had on occasion tried to hint that Crawford would look fabulous in a dress and in the right time and place he'd be game to accommodate, just for the kick of seeing how Charlie enjoyed it.

Crawford, for his own part, loved the distinct touches of masculine or feminine odors, the subtle mix of rank and sweet sweat that traditionally found the opposite sex's nose. He knew he was drawn by both and on the rare occasion of witnessing public courtship his nose caught the telltale arousal of female and male bodies entwining with intent. He'd pick their essences apart like the finest wines.

Perhaps Charlie was a more traditional homosexual, as the pathologists liked to call them now. With the other wolf's cock in his hand, taxonomy didn't amount to bunk.

Amusingly, he'd removed his shirt and left on his own fedora. Its wide brim cast a shadow over Charlie's stiff member. "Let's see if I remember what to do with this thing."

"No tips for you, sailor," Charlie giggled and thrust his hips. His own hands were tracing shapes in Crawford's chest fur, then moving to the flanks.

Crawford slipped low, tongue darting through black lips as Charlie's cock released a bead of anticipation over his knuckles. He shivered around Charlie's side-probing fingers. "That tickles," he laughed and shook his stiff prize. "This is delicate work here."

Charlie showed all his teeth. "No, it isn't."

Every part of Crawford was on fire. "If you say so." Teeth nibbled the brown wolf's tip, just a tiny, wincing bit. Then he took it into his mouth, clawing at Charlie's hips.

Charlie lost his grip on Crawford's sides, settling back on the bed. He sighed once as his hips bucked, took Crawford's hat off and flung it at the closed hotel blinds. "Oh God drown me."

"Stay on deck," Crawford tried to playfully order around Charlie's cock, but it sounded like nonsense. His mouth slipped away and he nuzzled hazel-furred testicles. He knew Charlie didn't want to finish in his mouth. His claws worked the reclining G-man's hips, then went inside and invited Charlie to spread his thighs. Above his tail and below the balls hid the delicate pucker of his ass. A claw parted the fur and he pondered giving it a shine, rolling his tongue around his own teeth. In the moment he didn't feel like he was ready for that, so he wet a claw with his tongue instead.

His finger was an inch deep when Charlie grunted. "Crawford. I want to..."

Crawford glanced at the underside of Charlie's muzzle from around his masted cock. "Yes?"

"This time...can I...drive?"

Crawford always fucked Charlie when things got that far, which was almost every time they met, save the one instance where Charlie's brother had stopped in from Spokane and had no idea about them. They'd had to steal a mutual fondle during the twenty minutes alone when the sibling went out for a pack of Camels. Shortly after, Charlie had been promoted to the new bureau and caution became outright clandestine between them.

Neither of them noticed any more that they whispered during sex. Crawford whispered back. "Sure, Charlie. I'm game."

Crawford had brought KY Surgical Jelly in the smallest package pharmacies carried, said it was for removing jewelry from his wife's finger that had swollen, an ironic lie. He opened it and dipped a claw. "Just let me—"

"I've got this, Craw." Charlie rubbed his finger against Crawford's as he sat up, taking most of what he'd applied and then transferred that to his still engorged member as he sat up. "Maybe you should lie down and relax."

The hotel bed was a bit stiff, but Crawford helped that by shoving a pillow under his own muzzle, handing back the tin of jelly as he did so. Exploratory fingers transferred cold smoothness to the space under his own tail and began working around. Something about seeing nothing, not even a reflection of Charlie in the blind-concealed hotel room window, made the sensations of his mate's ministrations much more pronounced. He faced the uniform slats of the room's blinds and closed his eyes as claws dipped in and out of him, stretching slightly. Then contact came from something else.

"Ready?" Charlie asked, breath bated with excitement.

"Show me what you've got," could be famous enough last words.

Charlie moved into him. What resulted wasn't pain exactly. Nor true discomfort. He clenched instinctively as he was invaded and a sore shock receded as Charlie withdrew like a tide.

"Too much? Want me to stop?"

He didn't. What he felt was strange, but something in him wanted to take it further. "Don't stop, Charlie. Just, go…slow."

Claws settled into Crawford's bare haunches as Charlie pressed again, this time going deeper. Flush heat parted him, spreading waves of nervous confusing energy through his loins from back to front. His lover was inside him, truly inside, and he wondered if in some way if this was what female mammals felt when that connection was made and everything latently feral yet presently self-aware drew into a welcome pleasure that felt just right.

Because when Charlie pulled out again halfway and slid home once more it felt just as welcome as it did strange, a whole new realm of experience Crawford had simply been reluctant to try with Charlie always seeming so satisfied, the groove of routine so well dug. His own cock was hard and stabbed the hotel mattress, just one conduit of carnality. As the brown wolf picked up speed with engine-piston urgency Crawford's rear end flushed warm and blissful.

Heat's friction sweetened the release as Crawford messed the comforter with his issue. There wasn't any sensation of a pop or a stretch, but Charlie's action slowed with a faint hissing between his teeth and Crawford knew he was taking Charlie's ejaculate deep within. Slippery slickness spread down low where Crawford's nerves were most sensitive and he felt pearl collecting on the underside of his balls. Charlie was ready with a handkerchief.

"How'd that feel," Charlie asked through pants as he dabbed at Crawford's soft parts, already knowing from experience.

Crawford blinked his eyes through stars. "Heavenly. I always thought I had the best end of things."

"Now you know every end is the best one." The chuckle in Charlie's voice was comforting.

Crawford didn't want to lift his muzzle from the pillow. He'd have to do something about the top sheet on this bed but his limbs were rubber. His next words were carefully chosen, casual as he tried to be. "Some other friends of yours only like the taking or the giving?"

Charlie lay on the bed next to Crawford and rolled to face him, dabbing at Crawford's slick cock with the hanky and the messed bed underneath. "Old haunts had pansies like me who were often set in one way or another. The more flexible, the less lonely. Even in the biggest cities, a lot of us worried about being lonely, never more so than in a crowd. But you know what that's about."

"I've had you since I've known I liked this," Crawford sighed. "There hasn't been anybody else. Too complicated with all the moving. We can't have company save the occasional plumber. You?"

Charlie said nothing for a time. "I notice tails swish about…once in a while, but government work…"

"Yeah. I can imagine." Crawford felt his arousal fade and remembered something else. "I was wondering if I could ask you for a favor."

"This about those martyrs again? I've had my ear to the ground for the sake of your thirsty friends but if there are stake-wielding Europeans traipsing through America they're lying low now. Can't do any kind of official inquiry without…"

He trailed off as Crawford's hand rested on his.

"Not those goons. You mentioned you're after fascists, right? Agitators and rabble rousers and such?"

Charlie sighed. "Commies too." He rolled away and fished for his jacket. Crawford watched Charlie's cock soften low as the wolf turned back. "Smoke?"

"Yeah."

Charlie put one in his lips, sliding his fingers gingerly along the roll before he lit, puffed once, and passed it to Crawford who pushed up on his elbows. Charlie repeated the ritual for himself and they sent smoke up to the yellowing stucco.

Charlie took a puff or two to collect his thoughts. "It's a mess. All the unemployment and resentment. Even with the recovery initiatives rolling every fool with a manifesto is whittling grievances into something they can hook the downtrodden on." He raised a brow. "You're not thinking of finding one to join, I hope?"

Crawford fumbled the smoke against his lips. He was going to remain composed when this came up. He'd promised himself.

"Craw?"

To hell with it. "I never said a proper goodbye, Charlie. When I parted from Kamila and we, sort of patched things up as much as an end can be patched, I didn't say anything to my son, just left him a note, some hasty rambling thing like I tried to write back when I was in the war."

Charlie said nothing for a minute. He'd never married, never wanted to. Still, he had the wherewithal to understand what that could still mean to one who'd lost all that. "Are they okay, Crawford?"

Crawford swallowed, set his cigarette on the nightstand ashtray. "My jacket is by the door, pass it would you?"

The naked brown wolf rose again, and in the post-coital haze, Charlie seemed hesitant. Or maybe he was just tired. Charlie passed Crawford's coat and he rifled through the pockets. "Read this," Crawford handed the pamphlet he'd taken from the pet shop to Charlie who studied it.

Charlie swallowed. "We know this group. Not as prominent as the American Bund, but…"

"Read the name on the front of the pamphlet. Not the Colonel whatsizname, down lower."

Charlie did so, and Crawford sensed tension. Charlie didn't always enjoy talking about work. On some rendezvous he hated it. Still, he pursed his lips and his whiskers shivered. "Would this be…your son's…"

"Kamila remarried. Marsten is his new name. I'm worried that's him."

Charlie looked at the pamphlet and then away. "It may be," he muttered.

"I need to know anything you know about this group."

Charlie's smoke was reduced to a nub but kept burning. "Okay."

"I need to make sure my son is okay."

"Crawford…"

"If he's in with a crowd like this, God, Charlie, these people are the worst news. I still read papers. They find vegetarians in soup kitchen lines and beat them to a pulp. If they think they're commies…"

"Yeah, they are some nasty customers," Charlie muttered as ash fell on the pamphlet, then on the carpet. "Look, I'd stay out of this if I were you. These people are more than bad news. In fact, I'm already keeping an eye on the Colonel's people." Charlie looked up, met Crawford's insistent gaze evenly. "Keep it mum but we've had people slipping into a few of their rallies. I'm going to ask you not to go to any of these."

"If my son is at one of these—"

Charlie sighed. "Then for his own sake, and yours, you shouldn't let him see you. If something ever goes down, I can try to make sure he's not hurt in any way." Charlie gritted his teeth.

Crawford did the same. "Try? Try not to hurt him? Goddammit we did, what, twenty speak hauls together in the Windy? How many of those ever finished tidy? Heads were always busted. These people don't want a drink." Crawford snatched the pamphlet back and waved it under Charlie's nose. "They want a revolution. They want to kick people like Celeste and Samson out of the goddamn country."

Charlie turned away, snorting. "Not people like your friends exactly."

Crawford felt his temperature rising. The glow was faded now. Charlie's disposition was, he couldn't put his finger on it, but Crawford found him almost dismissive, like this topic was spoiling his night.

"You know what the hell I mean, Charlie. Don't be cute. If these people have their hooks in my son, they'll make him like one of them. A reactionary, hell, maybe violent ignoramus. Tell me they won't."

"That would be a bad choice, Crawford, I agree with you. But your son, is, what, in his early twenties now? He's an adult. That means making choices you won't like"—he grit his teeth—"or me either."

Crawford stood up and paced to the other side of the room. His teeth ground. "I need to wake him up, get him to realize that he's going the wrong way fast."

Charlie glared back at his partner. "Stop and think, Craw. How will you drag him away to listen? Are you going to force him to follow a father he doesn't know out for a drink to reminisce? Remember that you got out of his life to protect him. I've tried to help you accept that. It was hard enough to do it the first time."

Crawford glared at the tangle of their clothes through a red hue. "It might have been my worst mistake."

"And what happens if you show up? Do you re-enter his life with that condition you can't talk about and barely control? Fake a reason for being out of his life for over ten years? Worse, since you can't, will you just give him a pep talk about how nasty fascists are and then fade away again?"

"No. Charlie, if this is my son, he's a speaker at this thing."

"I'm…shocked as you are. But you have to let me handle this. Remember why you left. He'll be back under that tent with fury in his heart a flat second after you absolutely break his heart again. I'm sorry but—"

"No!" Crawford snarled and swiped. Claws that sprouted like rake tines shredded the mauve-papered wall, skipping plaster bits across the room.

Charlie stood up quickly, raised his hands, open, appeasing. "Crawford, you're on the verge. Please, have a seat. Let me say my piece."

The grey wolf's other hand was sprouting claws, and his very bones were on fire. He crouched and set a hand on the dresser, trying to piece words together from the vice of his mouth.

His son was in a vice. A cruel, calculating vice. Grifters and charlatans looking for boots to put on poor, unsuspecting necks.

"Please, Crawford. I get why you're worked up. I do." Charlie approached and put a hand on his shoulder, gentle but firm.

For his part Crawford took deep breaths. What bristled just under the surface couldn't be made to reason, but it could be led in reason's direction. Crawford had no plan. What could he do for his son with no plan? He needed a plan.

"Sit down, Craw. Just breathe."

Crawford teetered as he was steered back to the bed. Charlie's eyes roved his naked, rippling body up and down. "Let's take a second and understand a couple things."

"Okay." The voice wasn't entirely Crawford's.

"Firstly…" Charlie said, visibly tensed in case he had to bolt for his very life, out of the room, nudity be damned. "You still don't know for sure if it's your son there. The Bureau has local agents in areas this clown troupe is visiting. Let them get more information. That's what they're there for, right?"

"Right." His mind was soupy but at least Crawford could resist tearing a door off its hinges.

"Second. If they're agitating, hurting anybody, causing any kind of public nuisance, we can deal with that. If we have to arrest the speaker who may be your son, then we'll be gentle as we can."

"As we can…" Teeth receded, but only a little. Possibilities reeled in his head.

"Understand that the Bureau doesn't have a lot of restrictions in fighting dangers to the country, but there are areas where my hands are tied."

If it was Charlie's son, Crawford thought, would he find a way around them? "Can't you explain to your boss just how dangerous they are? Hell, pretend they're Capone and see if they skipped taxes."

Charlie laughed nervously. "I want to grab my director's lapels and do all that. But it doesn't work that way. Not in Washington. You know the fights I'm already in, and they're one step forward, almost always one back."

Crawford felt the room get smaller. "You know these bastards are our threat too?"

Charlie traded glares with him and in the space of a moment the brown wolf seemed to have aged many years. Charlie broke the tension by taking two more cigarettes and flicking them to life with a tarnished nickel lighter. Crawford had full control back, took his smoke with a shaky hand.

"I won't forget that," Charlie replied. "I can't. But you know what really gets me, Crawford, the one thing that takes hold in every moment in every one of those meetings I sit in? It's that compassion as a basis for any change is seen as the worst liability by those above me. If I show any evidence at all that my aims are towards making anybody's life better, or providing a fair deal to those underfoot, I've lost. Everything is about order, a quiet, rigid status quo. That's what I'm expected to protect. Every argument I put forth has to be coldly pragmatic or rationalized in terms of a cost-savings analysis for law enforcement or protecting this corner of the nation's productivity or that one. Because the second empathy or genuine care or love comes into anything I do at all, that's it. I've pinned myself as a sucker activist and the smoke-filled rooms where the real decisions are made close their doors with me firmly on the outside of them. I've got procedures, I've got regs. And I've got means. To a point."

Crawford smoked slowly, sore bliss fading into a buzz of anxiety. "But you don't quit."

"You know I can't." He took a deep breath. "I'm still going to try to help your son, within all the means I have. I will do that."

They were silent for a few moments, embers cooling within them both. Crawford watched Charlie grasp for a measure of calm.

"Have you put it behind you now?" Crawford asked. "Chicago, I mean. I'm hoping it was long enough ago."

Charlie was quiet for a long time. "I've only had one nightmare, sometime in the last year. I'm at a party, city hall, or a really a swanky speak, I don't know. Leslie is there, agent Spettle, who was… Anyway, we're laughing about how silly everything is and she says to me, 'The thing that surprises me the most about all that comes before us and after, is where things really are in the grand scheme of things.'"

Charlie took a deep drag and stared into the jaundiced roof above. "She sees that I'm confused and then says, 'Who'd have known that Hell was actually above us the whole time.' She smiles through a hole in her face and just out of the corner of my eye I see the limbs dangling down from the darkness above and I pour another drink. That's all I do." Charlie sighed. "Just pour the next round. I didn't even wake up that upset."

The silence hurt as the tobacco burned out. Crawford cleared his throat, not knowing what to say. "Did you bring it?" Always the last question.

Charlie nodded, rose and went to his things, brought out the pink-bulbed atomizer. They'd leave smelling like sex, but atop that, they had to don the scent of the only acceptable costume. They lay back on the bed side by side. Charlie held the female-canine's-musk-imbued, store-bought perfume high and with three quick squeezes the lie gently rained down upon them both.

When Crawford left soon after, the sky was cloudy and thunder muttered in from somewhere that he didn't want to look.

Chapter 7

Things in Silly Boxes

The chalet's vaulted roof loomed over as Donovan dragged the crate in through the propped craftsman-style doors. In the dark his oldest remaining abode was a grey spectre of neglect. Back parlour windows glanced out on the ashen smudge of a decayed garden, vegetables long pilfered by feral ruminants and claimed by brambles. Inside the ghosts of mortal life were sketched out, the bar dusty, the iceboxes and stove rusting, the cigar stand's thoughtful scents faded. Bookshelves teemed with dusty tomes of worlds no longer cared about.

Once the crate was placed near the stacked stone fireplace, he carefully set the assembled contents inside, an insurance policy to end all policies. The line from within ran underneath a hearthside carpet to the expansive kitchen's swinging door. Through there the line terminated near the carefully prepared pantry. He then placed down the crate's lid and fetched the chains, working fast. Presentation was everything.

The blood high kept him moving. Outside cicadas droned the passage of time as he approached the front doors to close them both.

He froze when he heard a sound.

In the twenty years that Donovan had held the deed to the place, standing long before the first beam had been erected on his folly in Chicago, he'd had no real neighbors, the closest being a retired trapper half a mile away whose path remained uncrossed. Down the winding furrowed dirt road that nature was reclaiming, he heard trees groan devoid of wind, vegetation parting roughly.

It was doubtful Christof's people could be on his doorstep now, even if they ignored the booth he'd phoned from. The last of his own traps was now in place, but impatience won a very short war within his still chest.

Fleeting down one of the now overgrown back paths, he sought its source. Every sound in every direction was intimately familiar to him and he sunk through shadows, scanning the road where his quarry would pass.

At a junction in that road, naked pale wood was visible on a fractured branch, dangling low enough to brush the road. He let the stillness speak. No other sounds, not the whisper of a creature's crawl nor the drone of any distant motor. The bough break appeared fresh, no rot in the limb. He picked his way back to the house carefully, eyes on the road the whole way. As he approached the chalet's peaked roof, he saw glints of light on the rolling hump of the Catskills beyond. Dawn was an hour away or less. He sequestered himself in his chalet, checked the points of egress one last time, testing the air for a scent. Was there the trace of feline?

These mountains were stalked by predators without sense for centuries, avoiding the spark and spoor of sapients who wore clothes and fussed over worldly things. Donovan fussed once more. He could have tried to keep this place safe, gone back to New York where he'd started, confronted Christof there.

But no, he was merely rotting here, watching the decay of all he no longer cared about. And he needed the advantage of a place where he controlled all if he'd be successful.

So, he waited behind drawn curtains that kept the glow of dawn at bay, resisting the urge to rest in one of the expansive private bedrooms down the hall from the living salon. He'd perfected lengthy wakefulness every few days over months, always resting fully on days before. Rest of some nature would come after this ordeal, however it played out.

***

Samson turned the dime in his hand and considered carefully before seating it home and bringing Ma Bell on the line. He gave the exchange for their house and Celeste answered. "I'm alright," Samson said. "I'm somewhere safe, a hotel. I just needed to get away for a bit, clear my head."

Samson looked at his reflection in the telephone booth's glass window. His features had certainly aged, his nose broader and cheeks further defined, but frustratingly his horns were still barely adolescent stubs. His stomach churned and limbs ached when he moved them but he could conquer that. Sandy had done this for years before teaching him math and history. The curse wouldn't beat him.

"Samson, Sandy and I want to help you. Which hotel did you go to?"

That doting concern irked him immediately. Celeste always warred with her own need to be independent and respect the same in her housemates, but he'd no doubt he still seemed a child to her and would always be. "No need to worry. I'm old enough now to get a room on my own, no funny questions asked. I still have that money Crawford gave me."

"So you won't tell me." Celeste paused a moment. "Samson, really, are you worried I'm going to scurry over there and force feed a rat to you?" She let the humor creep in at the very idea and Samson felt his resistance waver, only for a moment.

"I'll need at least a day or two. I won't get into any trouble, won't expose us."

"I know that, Samson. But we do need to talk about this. What you're doing…it's not healthy. Don't make Sandy's mistakes."

They were both silent for a time. Outside the hotel's lone phone booth, a pine marten in a patchy suit pointedly looked at the battered clock on the hotel lobby wall and back at the closed phone booth with dusty fedora in hand, claws working the carpet impatiently.

"I've thought a long time about it and the only mistake made was… one I didn't choose. I'm going to a movie when the sun sets and I'm already stuck in here for the day."

"Samson…"

"I'm really tired. I need to put my head down."

"What movie are you going to see?" Genuine interest.

She'd never stop trying. If Celeste only had less care for others than she wanted to admit. "Does it matter? It's never really the movie that's interesting." He laughed nervously and his voice didn't sound any different. Not yet. "It's at the Globe movie house in South Scranton. I'm seeing a picture that gets us all wrong."

"Alright, Samson. Please come back so we can talk. I promise I'll listen."

"I will." There was a knock on the glass now. The marten was close enough to smell, his pulse fast. "I'm perfectly fine." He forced his mouth closed to keep his fangs in, ending the call with a smile.

Twenty minutes later he was in his room, door closed, shades drawn. The "Do Not Disturb" sign dangled outside. Samson slept with his fangs out, hunger thwarted once more.

***

The car came to Donovan's chalet at around noon. No, two of them, large displacement cars travelling close together. The front door was the only one unlocked and heavy footfalls shifted the cobbles that Donovan had purposely unbalanced, behaving in the manner of nightingale-wood palace floors in Japan, thwarting silent approach. One of the stones was shifted by heavy feet, others by lighter, defter touches, some of which spread out.

The knock was loud and insistent.

Fighting the urge to find a shadow, Donovan made himself draw air in and out. "Please come in, Christof."

The doors parted and were filled with the broad shape of a thick-maned lion, dark golden fur bunching over the Viennese coat, Kinze by the tailoring. A burgundy Windsor knot bobbed under his jaws and a silvery watch chain led to a checked vest pocket, the same red piped checker pattern of his slacks.

His hands were joined pensively behind him and Donovan wondered momentarily if one held the reliquary axe that would even now be projecting a warning to its master, that a Nosfur was present. He'd prepared for that.

Or perhaps the axe was tucked away and the burden of detection was passed on to his entourage. The two cats at Von Haften's flanks were unfamiliar faces, bearing the blank detachment of professional muscle, well armed but futilely trying to avoid appearing so.

The sun was directly over the chalet's roof, fortunately. Nevertheless, the glint of light was like a molten steel pit stared into for too long. He winced and fought the urge to step back.

The useless scotch in Donovan's hand bobbed as he raised it from behind the chained crate where he stood and indicated a half-full decanter on a table at the room's center. "It's been a long time, Baron Von Haften, please do come in."

The lion and his shadows did so, eyes instinctively to the corners before Christof's returned to his. "Why now, Donovan? Twelve years you waited, knowing that my wife's last whereabouts were unknown to me." Christof stopped before the whiskey decanter and glasses, staring into the objects there as though they were pieces of some unwelcome game. Donovan noted that the lion's English was now almost perfect, the barest Germanic traces brushing his consonants. "All this time, you had telephones, you had"—his stormy eyes rose to the rafters—"sanctuary."

Donovan brought all his indignation to bear. "Sanctuary? This little scrap of real estate? Evelyn was taking steps to seize my company, my whole bloody empire, and you helped her do it! I showed her such incredible things and for that, she tried to lay me low. Had the agent who broke my faith in him not killed her—"

"I don't believe you," Christof rumbled, hands still concealed, henchmen looming. "You tell me some Prohibition agent killed my wife and simply expect me to accept that? I was already certain you'd betrayed our faith even before my late wife acquired a single share in Donovan Steel. That's why Evelyn took action."

Donovan ground his teeth as he stepped round the crate, denying Christof direct line of sight but close enough to offer a challenge. "I'd given you a means of getting ahead in this war, of laying the Martyres' enemies low. Instead of giving me the credit I deserved or even hearing me out you had Evelyn ruin years of progress and had her try to kill me!" Here it came. "Or that's what the Prohee in my pocket told me when she was laid out with a bullet in her back, that she'd come to my mill to finish me off. I dismissed him from employ after that overzealous gaffe and shortly after dismissed myself from your circle. And why not! You wouldn't have believed me then any more than now. Under your direction the Martyres have made misstep after misstep for over a decade and you sought any scapegoat that you could!"

Another angry step round the box, another inch closer to the cord leading back to the kitchen. The two cats at his vision's periphery were statuesque in detachment.

Donovan heard more cobbles disturbed outside. A moment later the locked door latch lifted at the back of his kitchen exit, fiddled, and then stilled. His chalet was surrounded.

Christof's fury curled lips from teeth and he unclasped his hands at last. The left held his ornate axe, black-forest oak mated with a scarred wedge of iron. One thumb rested on the head's back, meaning it was singing to him now. "Where is her body, Donovan?" There was pain behind the menace in his eyes and that made Donovan's decades-long nemesis even more frightening in stature.

Donovan took the deep breath he'd practiced and spoke the truth as he knew it. "She was discarded in the molten steel, Christof, and that left me no body to bring to you. It was not according to my will, I assure you."

The axe wavered in the old lion's hand and Donovan saw grief take him hold.

Another creak at another outer wall—another interloper testing his tiny kingdom's boundaries. He'd have to move faster...

Christof found his voice at last. "And all this for your stupid fantasy of Nosfur suffrage, her life wasted so your squirrel could play her tricks on you."

Donovan should have expected her to come up and found it simple to improvise. "Oh, there are no more tricks to play, Christof. That endeavor to bring the Nosfur to grace has indeed died." Donovan took a step back to the left and placed his hand on the crate. "I've been working to further perfect what little of my steel remains on my former acolyte. She tried to betray me as the crooked Prohee wolf did."

The lion's thumb worked the back of the reliquary axe and his gaze fluttered over the chained box, logically connecting sense of Nosfur proximity to the crate before him. His gaze transferred to Donovan's suddenly, holding the rabbit down with that old familiar disdain. "Where are the Ark nails, Calvert? If you are to even have a chance at forgiveness for the endless miseries you've caused us both over the past twelve years..."

Donovan was confused. "Both of you?"

The front door had almost closed against the daylight glare, but a diminutive form even slighter than Donovan's own lean frame slipped through into the low light. Her fur was white, whiskers low and ears back. The naked tail brushed the door in a way that Donovan found familiar. A belt around her denim-wrapped waist bore a small dagger that she fingered.

"Care to introduce yourself," Von Haften said, a polite order rather than a request.

The possum spoke in crisp mid-Atlantic. "My name is Elenore. My brother, Edmond, was your manservant for over eight years. I need to know what became of him."

Donovan remembered his first act upon returning home the night Sandy turned him; Edmond's struggles had been punctuated by futile beats on Donovan's chest that brought him to embrace the lifeline vein like a lover, Calvert suckling as the possum weakened.

"I don't know where he is now," Donovan lied and saw she immediately knew it.

Glass broke from the vicinity of the kitchen back door and the latch worked. Christof, the possum, and the cats all ignored it.

"You'll pay for that," Donovan chided, glad he no longer contended with the urge to swallow.

"What's yours is ours, Donovan, such as it is for all members of the Martyres of the Black Well. As loath as I ever was to put any faith in you, I could at least assume that you'd hold to a few of our mutual principles." Contempt dripped cold.

Donovan set his drink on the crate as a hound crept in from the kitchen and circled to his right, nose working.

He pared his anger back. "Faith, Christof? I'm not convinced that you haven't tried to kill me. I'm not sure now, either."

Edmond's sibling glared at him. Had his former manservant ever told his master of a sister? Too many complications filled his chalet and he was starting to regret this gambit.

Donovan evaded the possum's gaze and met Von Haften's cryptic one. His barbs hadn't ruffled the lion even slightly. That was disappointing. "Why don't you and I bring the temperature down somewhat. I'm sure I can help you put your mind at ease"—Donovan tapped the crate—"and turn over my gift to you all, a peace offering. You've no doubt felt her presence."

Leonine eyes drifted downward, then up. "My wife told us you'd made a détente with the vermin, that your steel was supposed to keep them alive, but in some form of control."

A dream had already died and Donovan didn't want Christof to enjoy the satisfaction he was now forced to grant him. "I've reconsidered. Call it a question of liability."

"Liability. Do you hear that, Elenore?"

The possum's gaze was hard, her prehensile tail curling and lashing.

"Yes, the inconveniences of keeping Nosfurs alive on this world versus the inconveniences of having to rid the world of them. Tell me about an inconvenience, Elenore."

The possum was diminutive next to Christof but rage inflated her. "My brother called me on the night Mrs. Von Haften went to your factory, told me little but I knew enough. You'd disappeared, your factory was locked down for an emergency. He said he'd call me back once he spoke to you, that your car had just arrived…"

Donovan knew the rest but had no lie prepared for Edmond's end. The fate of his servants, which had fled, which had died, and which had turned on him when Sandy took over, was all a blood-intoxicated blur he'd presumed irrelevant.

Christof studied the crate. "Elenore came to me much later, of course. Her brother's disappearance troubled her and her family had made many sacrifices on our behalf, within their limited means. Together we made many deductions."

Donovan's ears drooped as he felt the metaphorical light of day drifting in to find him. How could this have gone any way but terribly?

His last resort was a mere foot away, provided he could get to cover in the instant he'd have.

Christof swung his axe effortlessly, letting it balance head-up erect upon his open palm before slipping down into his closing fingers. He'd been an expert hunter in his day, with the ability to strike a target with his reliquary from a thirty-yard fling. "You disappeared without a trace and left no word where you'd gone. Your mansion, once searched, proved you'd left everything behind that was important to you, including your recent scent. If you weren't dead, why hide from us as we dismantled your company? We were on your jealously guarded turf, after all."

Donovan didn't answer, stock still, counting paces from mammal to mammal.

Christof spun the axe, admired its sheen. "We observed from afar, biding time while we searched amongst all your other property holdings, presuming maybe you'd furnished a hideaway of the cozy sort you'd made under your steel mill. Alas, you neither came nor went. Then one day after we moved on the mansion inexplicably burnt down. And contact was detected at its outskirts. Yes, Donovan, Evelyn told me about how your little talismans work and we made one for your reliquary steel gate with an excised fragment of it after searching the grounds. I kept it on my person for quite some time. Many Nosfur passed that gate when the fire took your home down. Far too many weaker contacts, very shortly after the passage of a strong contact, a recently fed one." Christof showed his array of natural leonine teeth. "And years later, at a chalet under an assumed name, here you are." He glanced to Elenore "My dear, if you wouldn't mind."

The possum twisted her tail around and took hold of it with one hand. Her other drew a dagger.

Donovan couldn't stop her, couldn't flee even as he knew it was coming. She nicked her tail tip and dots of crimson escaped the point of contact, filling the air, distributing scent as she raised her prehensile member above her head and daintily swung it around.

A hunger which Donovan had never fully learned to restrain began to flex under his gums and he forced his mouth to remain locked shut. If they saw fangs sprout it would all be over.

All three present henchmen stepped back. The short possum before him held fast, her own sharp front teeth bared in a cruel smile. Christof for his part took a deep breath. "Go ahead and sow more lies. I can already see what I need to see in those dark, dark eyes of yours…vermin."

Every mortal took a single breath. Donovan took aim instead. He threw the scotch glass as hard as he could. The dog closest to him yelped as glass and nose broke. The rapier Donovan had hidden, a close copy of his former reliquary that would burn him upon contact, was kicked up into the rabbit's hand and he rushed to close ranks with one of the cats who raised his own sword. Their blades connected, parried, slid past one another. A twist of bodies put the cat between Donovan and the cat's counterpart who was drawing a pistol, all too likely Ark-nail chambered.

Donovan cut low and got a nick past the hilt, putting his cat's grip off guard. He'd practiced his forms over the years, letting nothing dull, combining his own training by the best swordsmen in the Martyres' ranks with the preternatural speed his Nosfur affliction granted. He worked over the downward parry of the cat with a twist of his blade and thrust for the acolyte's throat, connecting lower and to the left of where intended but finding pliant space just above the collar bone of his sword arm, punctur-ing the trapezius. The cat howled and was laid low by two bangs of his partner's gun, one through the ribs and the other grazing him high, stamp-ing Donovan through his ear, flashing pain through him. A frantic cut took the cat down.

The possum of all people was the next on him, stabbing clumsily as she leapt over the chained crate, murderous rage in her eyes. "You killed my brother!" Her swipe almost took his other ear as Donovan ducked and her tail whipped round to smear blood on his sword-arm sleeve. Christof rum-bled something angry behind her; she was acting out of turn for a properly coordinated attack. The cat with the gun tracked them both, angling for another shot.

Christof paced slowly, feeling no urgency, attentive as he allowed his lessers to expend themselves in tiring the monster out. One of those less-ers had at one point been Donovan himself, thrown into a skirmish to prove himself, results derided as sloppy rather than congratulated for his deftness.

Elenore's flat blade had the same reach as his, but Donovan intercepted her downward swing easily. She was quick, but her skills too unpracticed, untested, desperate.

His reflexes from dozens of pitched battles allowed no room for pity. In four matched thrusts and two steps, his superior speed worked against her slashing jabs and his blade opened her throat. Rather than let her body drop, he drew her close, letting blood and tears splash him equally. The cat had spread his stance, braced and fired again. The bullet for Donovan's head struck hers.

He had a possum-shaped shield before him and released his own slippery sword to grab the one dangling from a limp, furless hand. Pain exploded as he realized that Edmond's sister had a reliquary blade. Acting instinctively in the instant he had, Donovan threw the brimstone-hot blade end over end with a scream. The hilt appeared in the cat's chest and he was full of surprise as the pistol waved left, stamping loud holes through leather book spines and an oil rendering of the HMS Victory. The cat toppled, curling fetal as he died.

His moment chosen, Christof was on him. Donovan pedaled back-wards at incredible speed, but the lion had calculated his retreat, swinging the axe as he rushed and nearly cleaved through Donovan's fanged muzzle. He stood astride the massive crate and Donovan shouted in desperation at it, "He's here, get him!"

Expecting something from the crate, Christof feinted from the object, granting Donovan just enough time to hurl himself through the swinging saloon door to his derelict kitchen. The dark cable from the crate's true contents ran around the cast-iron stove and Donovan grabbed it. He launched himself into the darkened pantry where a hole to the cellar had been cut, a quick descent to the momentary safety of darkness and the fate prepared for all his enemies above.

The line grew taut as he found the drop through the cellar hatch. He pulled it as he flexed to leap.

There was resistance, then a give within the unseen crate as the line came free with a snap.

Nothing else happened. Donovan froze.

Christof entered the space, eyes covering corners. The kitchen had shadows but Donovan hadn't bound any of them. The axe in Christof's thick fingers rendered escape into any pocket of darkness moot. The gleam in the lion's eye carried malicious glee that needed no smile.

Donovan flashed through a memory, his very last mortal experience from the position of power that Christof now held over him. Sitting in his Rolls Royce back in Chicago, his still-living possum chauffeur in the driver's seat. Donovan's own reliquary sang in his still living hands, the doe called Celeste clinging to the useless protection of her thicket of darkness, the thrill of the chase that followed.

She'd escaped into the dark in what the rabbit hadn't known was his last chase as a Martyre.

Outside of his chalet, there was no escape at all, just the pitiless knives of the morning sun.

Christof smiled. "You're prolonging something that should have happened on the very night the rabbit's true life ended. It was a sworn duty for Donovan Calvert to destroy himself before he was fully corrupted." Christof was cold with disappointment. "His own molten steel would have granted a merciful ending that the vermin before me will not be granted. He was, as I always suspected, truly a coward."

Donovan's shame was scalding, contempt boiling over for the imperious fool who'd stymied his every step in the Order. His own sword was in the next room, which may as well be across the Atlantic for all the good it would do him. He would not go without a fight.

Christof Von Haften stalked only as close as he needed, axe raised above his mane for the killing strike. Donovan wouldn't dive into the cellar. There were no weapons down there, only old port bottles and a thick tarp which had been vital to a plan now thwarted. The only way out was through light's agony. He braced himself to lunge. Christof wouldn't finish him with any triumph. He'd cripple the old lion if he could.

Outside a scream pierced the air. Nosfur rabbit and Martyre lion perked their ears, both confused. The first scream was followed by the pounding of heavy mammalian claws across patio shale followed by another yelp. A body struck the ground.

With his axe still raised, Christof took a step back and swung to the right, not at Donovan, but rather at curtains pulled tight against French doors to the patio where the dog had slipped through. Light flooded the kitchen and Donovan hissed. No beams struck directly, but the brightness hurt his eyes and he ducked back to the doorframe of the pantry.

Christof glimpsed something outside and the lion's eyes went wide. Glass broke and Christof's chest grew a long bolt, six inches of dull steel. He made a noise of surprise and his axe clattered to the mustard-tiled floor. Blood spattered between his feet as he staggered back against dusty cupboards, scrabbling for purchase. A cabinet door was nearly torn off as Christof fell on his backside, tail curling about him. He gave Donovan a single glance of surprised contempt, as though the Nosfur had brought this about himself, and slowly dragged himself away.

Adapting to the proximity of the light, blinking through the pain, Donovan studied the path between them. The butcher's block of a food preparation island where servants had long ago shaved carrots and grated cilantro provided low cover to creep beyond the light's direct stabs. The sun through the windows brushed a shoulder and he felt the fire like spit sparks, ducking lower. Whatever had brought this turn of fortune was only discernible with a direct stare into agony, so he rushed round to the thin trail of smeared life the lion left as he pulled himself away from whatever force beyond the window made the dark seem instinctively safer.

Donovan followed Christof back to the main salon, slipping between the useless prop of the crate and the long leather sofa upon which Donovan had plotted this very moment, he triumphant and his first nemesis of many laid low.

"You killed…" Christof huffed and a mist of blood coated his chin. The first tug of the thirst was pulling at Donovan already, his fangs sliding free with insistence.

"You killed my Evelyn. Didn't you?"

Should he toy with him? A bane to his existence was inexplicably on death's doorstep and yet here, in the moment, Donovan was little more than hungry. There was too little satisfaction to be had in Christof's fall. "I had her killed, yes. The Prohee wolf was a pawn. I learned that well enough from you." The hiss the fangs made of his words sounded more natural, Donovan realized. This was always his true self. Sandy merely released him. "I wanted Evelyn to see a better future as I wanted it for all of you. Had she not worked against me, you and I would be toasting a new empire together, Christof."

The lion grimaced through pain and the bolt bobbed and Donovan saw the blood mist accumulating on his jaws, knew the lion couldn't see him as dark collected. "I didn't want…an empire of vermin!" The word hurt to say but Christof was glad he said it.

"That's alright, you old sod." Donovan watched Christof's hands seize at his sides as the rabbit leaned in for the feast's kiss. "That empire would have been mine."

He bit at the jugular and tasted lion's blood. Copper sang around his fangs and tongue and drew in like sweetest fire. Christof's arms enwrapped him, a last attempt to fight becoming an embrace. When they fell away, Donovan kept drinking and rose to the heights of keenest awareness.

And with awareness, questions.

The mystery of his imperative aid would have to remain unsolved for now. He went to the crate first and found that the nails parted too easily. The lid lifted, he studied the coiled roll of dynamite sticks, deliberately separated from their fuses. The cellar below was meager protection from the obliteration of his chalet and all within and without but would have sufficed until the rubble settled and he was able to scuttle to tree cover under the meager protection of a tarp to rest and recoup.

His telephone rang, breaking the silence. Then it rang again.

Donovan froze, feeling a sense of complete isolation among his ene-mies' corpses. His exchange had been provided to no one in many years, certainly no one who knew who he'd been in life. Another ring.

He wanted to drink further, take every drop of Christof into his veins, but he instead lifted the handle-set to his ear and mouth, his heart flush and pounding again. "To whom am I speaking?"

The voice that replied was not quite reedy, not quite raspy, bundled with a frenetic energy. "I needed a minute or two to return to my guest house. So sorry if I kept you waiting. That certainly was exciting, wasn't it?"

"Who is this?"

"I've watched you. Well, rather your neighbor, the trapper with the broad shoulders and the baritone singing voice he thought no one ever heard. He was delightful to get to know." There was a wistful sigh. "Your guests are gone now. Four outside, and your lion friend, he looked extreme-ly disappointed, didn't he? Have you any guests left? Are we speaking alone?" The accent was indeterminate, something mid-Atlantic, with a slight lengthening of the vowels.

Donovan felt as though a presence were at his shoulder, but it was the blood singing its usual song. "Yes."

"That's splendid. Really so sorry about the scare I gave you, but hon-estly the explosives in that silly box of yours wouldn't have helped. Far too much yield. Would have been lion, cat, possum, and rabbit stew all over the valley."

Donovan didn't know what to say, nonplussed.

"So good of things to work out for us both," the voice added primly.

"I still don't know whom I have to thank."

"Me, obviously. And the man that your lion sent to cover the house with a bolt launcher from within the woods. Kind of him to provide, made things a bit easier. What's important is that more stooges of the Martyres will be coming if that lion, whoever he was, doesn't report back. But I'm sure you know that."

Donovan looked back to the crate, pushing back countless questions the interlocutor wouldn't answer. "I did intend to make sure there was nothing for them to find."

"Oh, really?" The mood shifted and the caller bordered amusement with annoyance. "Well then, Donovan Calvert, light a lamp and tip it over." The sigh was theatrical. "No need to wipe your ass anymore so you forget how to do everything." There was a pause. "Actually, no, don't do that."

"Don't destroy this house?"

"No. Here's the thing, erase all traces of any other hiding holes you may have and otherwise leave it as is. Pull the bolts from their chests, get rid of the stupid guns they brought and leave it all behind. You aren't ever going back there so give them a mystery they'll be tied up solving."

Donovan gripped the phone as invigorated wheels turned. "I suppose you'll want me to go next door to the trapper's house once the sun goes down?"

"No. It's starting to smell in here and we'd best both be going as soon as the dusk permits. You and I need to meet, Donovan, at the Royal York Hotel in Toronto, up in the Dominion of Canada. But first—and this is very important, Donovan—you need to visit another friend of yours living in Atlantic City, New Jersey. She should return from business shortly."

"Who would I need to meet in New Jersey before coming to Canada?"

"A very old friend of yours, Alisandre Mallory. You need to make amends with her before you make amends with me."

His flooded heart actually skipped a beat. "You know Sandy..."

"So many do, many mutual acquaintances, Donovan. But try to keep up, because the 'amends' part of things is the whole reason why you're talking to me in your parlour right now over the cooling corpses of your old bridge game buddies and not dragged outside to enjoy some sunshine while still kicking. I don't want to upset you, Donovan, but you're very short on friends at this juncture, aren't you? I'd say about zero."

"Yes," he felt cold as implications settled. He was in thrall at the moment, and seeing Sandy again on more even terms was an exciting prospect. "Yes, I see."

"When you kiss and reacquaint, you'll trade information. She wants to know where the last of the coffin nails are for your stupid daggers and Lincoln Log cabins or whatever your steel became"—the voice became momentarily raspier and a snarl was checked—"or at least more of the places you cached the damn things. I, in turn, need a name from her. An alias often used by a very old friend of mine for certain transactions that would never have been done in her own name. Her true name, as Sandy well knows, is Celeste Val De Mot. Get that alias, bring it to Toronto. Then the real work begins."

"An alias that will help with what work exactly?"

"We're doing it right now, Donovan. We're destroying that stupid, decrepit order of yours. That is what you want, isn't it? I'll help you, you'll help me, and we'll both have the most important thing to us both in the process."

"Revenge?"

"No, my boy," The laughter was infectious. "Fun."

Chapter 8

The Mirror's True Curse

Celeste knew where Samson would be after the next sunset and tried not to worry as the sun cracked the unseen horizon and began painting the clapboard home's flank. She wasn't his mother, as she'd said.

Sandy had volunteered to have Bruno check the hotels in downtown Scranton and that offer had touched Celeste, but she reluctantly decided to respect Samson's desire for time to reflect. Sandy's next words had chilled her: "When the veins go completely dry it's going to be more than aches and pains for him. Madness can beckon. I've seen it. Know that and be ready."

Sandy had business back in Atlantic City, leads as to the whereabouts of another cache of Calvert's nails that needed confirmation. The end of that horrible chapter was close now. Sandy promised to return and sealed that offer with a kiss. She folded into Celeste's arms in an embrace quickened by the rising light and then retired to the sealed cabin of her Cadillac, windows shaded tight against the day. Celeste traded a single cryptic stare with the muskrat at the wheel, his expression blank and yet scrutinizing the doe carefully, judging her in some fashion.

The car receded down the long drive, silhouetted against the crowding greenery and Celeste found a moment of stillness surround her as she was alone with the creeping dawn, studying the slow flood of details only natural light granted. So many mornings over the decades had been spent seeking that precise moment when the curse's price became too much, to recall her last days under wide blue skies above, see how the clouds commingled with light to split the rays coming through.

She had lost much to the Nosfur condition, but Samson had been denied so much more, his life frozen in time.

And what could Celeste do? She had ruminated so long on lives and destinies stolen by cruelty and circumstance. It had taken decades to accept how she'd failed her own younger sister in Paris so long ago. After paying the sisters' price of the dram in Chicago Lavert's memory returned to haunt Celeste every so often.

When they'd moved to this aging house a row of spikes by the fence line were all that remained of a barbed barrier for cattle made long obsolete. They'd stood erect at first, ghosts on sentry. Celeste had gone out after they'd settled and pulled each of them up from the ground. Crawford and Samson had asked no questions, merely piled them behind the back of the house to rust.

Unlike Lavert, Samson was no distant regret to be reminded of. Nor would she ever let him be.

Light touched one of the porch posts and the glare became too much, Celeste's flesh feeling the itch that heralded the burn.

Celeste shut the dawn away and wondered as she descended when Crawford would return. She lay down. Hours passed in a blink that put a tired-looking wolf at her basement door.

"Did you get sleep? The drive back from Maryland must have taken time."

Crawford shrugged. "I got in a few hours rest since getting back around noon. I've got lots on my mind, change aches are back something fierce. Samson get off to rest okay?" He had ham and oatmeal on his breath. It had taken Celeste years to accept that the lupine ate meat of some sort with literally every meal when he could afford it.

"I would hope so. He called me from whatever hotel he slipped away to last night while I was talking to Sandy."

"He—hold your horses, the kid isn't here?" Crawford's ears folded and he jabbed a thumb over his shoulder at the opposite door. "What's he doing at a hotel?"

"Taking stock of his life. We've anticipated that this day was coming."

Crawford pulled at the suspenders on his ostentatiously perfumed dress shirt, letting them settle over his worn slacks. "I never assumed he'd just…go. Did Sandy chase after him?" His tail lashed.

Celeste shook her head. "Sandy was ready to seek him out. Samson told me not to worry, that he was going to a movie. I gave him his space for that reason and Sandy went back east to follow up on another lead."

"I should go after him."

"I think we shouldn't."

Crawford opened his mouth to retort and Celeste spoke over him. "Crawford, he's not my son or yours, much as we may occasionally pretend for appearances. We can help him to a point, but he has to come into his own as best he can. We promised him that."

"You worry about him for good reason. You once told me he's like the little brother you never had, remember?"

"He is. We talked." Celeste slipped past Crawford and ascended the stairs with a side-eyed glare. "And you weren't too worried when you left right after the bank debacle that clearly upset him."

Crawford followed her up, bristling a bit. "I had to see Charlie about something—"

"My nose works just fine. You don't need to be provincial about the details."

"It was about something else…" Crawford trailed off and tossed something under his arm on the salon table. "Let's change the subject. Did you and Sandy make up?" Crawford asked evenly.

Celeste crossed the salon and checked the time on the ticking Japy Frères clock. Just after eight p.m. No light bled past the curtain's borders. "Make up what?"

"My nose works even better than yours and I can smell her on you," he said with a grunt. "Sandy is still technically our client. The only one not dragging tail on billing, I might add. We still haven't been paid for the Wainright case and we've a faucet upstairs, needs fixing at some point."

"Sandy thinks the last of the nails will be in hand soon if a lead she's chasing proves useful. With the nails at the bottom of the deepest abandoned mine or body of water we'll have no more of the rabbit's steel made. And we'll get paid."

She turned to see that Crawford had thrown down the newspaper. She opened it past Frankin Roosevelt's war against unemployment and the Scranton board's decision to hold off road repairs. Towards the back among adverts for washtubs and fishing rods, she found what she needed. "He'll be at the Globe Theatre."

"Seeing what?" Crawford rummaged noisily in a kitchen cupboard for something to nibble.

Dracula was in repertory at the Globe. "The film that gets him and I all wrong," Celeste remembered. "It starts about now so we'll need to be there in the next hour or so if we're going to speak with him." She glanced up to meet his gaze. "We can talk to him, but if he needs more time and decides to be left alone…"

"Okay. We'll give him that." Crawford gingerly sat in the highbacked chair. He tended to flop down into furniture in that typically lupine space-possessive way, but his demeanor betrayed concerns he was keeping checked. "On the reason I left quickly, I had other things to talk to Charlie about that were within his…territory, career-wise."

"Was it about our case with Sandy? Or the Calvert estate, whatever is left of it?"

"Neither. Even knowing what I am I've kept him out of our affairs as much as I can for good reason. He has assurances that you aren't killing anyone and as for myself, well, I didn't bring up Boston since I didn't start that mess. The less he knows the less he needs to lie to anybody who could cause us grief."

Celeste sat on the couch, smoothing down her faded blue dress. "What matters did you two discuss while your clothes were still on?"

"Nothing that could cause us harm. Well, not directly."

She set her ears and held his gaze. "No secrets, Crawford."

"It relates to my family, my son specifically. We've not spoken in a long time and…" The wolf sniffed, unsure what to say or not say. "He's fallen in with a tough crowd that wouldn't take kindly to our kind, well, mingling."

"Nosfurs and weres?"

Crawford raised a brow and a lip to show a carnivorous fang.

"Oh."

"I don't know what to do. I was out of his life rather abruptly. He's sure as hell confused and angry about…things."

"I don't want to be a broken record, Crawford, but as far as you've come in managing your were aspect, you left him and your ex-wife to save both their lives. Your son in particular will never know what sacrifice you had to make."

"I'm still his father. Time and distance don't change that. The regret is less hard to deal with than what would have come to pass if I'd tried to stay. Knowing that keeps me going. That and..."

Celeste cocked an ear.

Crawford smiled sadly. "Things just might be getting better. I hope."

"What do you mean?"

Crawford sighed wistfully. "Sometimes...what I have isn't a curse. I feel a connection with things when I'm turned and there's nothing between my fur and the world, a peace with losing myself, a grounded kind of certainness, if that makes any bit of sense. I think sometimes that self-awareness takes that away from us all."

Celeste chuckled, unable to help herself.

"What?"

Celeste's lidded eyes stood in for lungs that never sighed. "I don't want to make light of what you're saying, Crawford, but as miraculous and transcending of the mammalian experience as being a were is, Samson and I literally had to stop you from chasing a train when we rented in Connecticut."

Crawford grunted and then shrugged, his tail crossing his legs. "Almost caught it."

***

"I'm sure Count Dracula will excuse you." Gasps spread through the Globe as Mina looked up and regarded no one in a cigar box's reflection. "You must go to your room as Professor Van Helsing suggests."

Samson watched the silhouettes of other patrons before him, many seeing this picture show for the first time. Dracula was nearly four years in circulation but too few could afford the quarter a new picture cost. The repertory's dime admission provided a window into a film that was so diverting and yet so...wrong.

A world in which Nosfurs had no reflection would have suited Samson just fine. The screen's impression of Samson's world only truly reflected the anxieties of its audience, terror of the unknown and exaltation of civilized mammalian society.

The feline count Dracula stood imposingly over the otter playing Mina, a member of carnivore stock holding court over another. A trade-paper rumor had it that Mina was originally cast with an unknown lapine actress, but studio heads had balked at the idea of a rabbit being courted by the otter actor David Manners playing Johnathan Harker, so they'd hired Chandler instead to reduce any chance of scandal, keeping it in the species and in good omnivorous mammalian graces.

And this picture had been put together before the Hayes code clamped down on anything even remotely immoral seeming or untoward. What a world.

Samson watched the watchers and felt that telltale jolt as dozens of pulses jumped when Dracula knocked the mirrored cigar case from Van Helsing's hand. The old hound scratched his chin as the Hungarian-accented cat told of his dislike for mirrors and Samson moved his gaze across the backs of each head before him, watching ears cup forward, arms cross shoulders, fingers clasp protectively, amiably…lovingly. Vigor throbbed in their veins.

Every day for the past twelve years the same mirrors that hid Bela Lugosi's elegant feline visage from the austere count revealed the clumsy goat kid to Samson, perpetually snared in gangly adolescence. Resentment took misery's shape, and then one day he'd looked at the rat squirming in his grip, told Celeste he'd drink in private, and released it into the woods.

Two months later, hunger ebbed and abated and returned, gaining in force as he clung to the memory of elderly Sandy Mallory's lessons at Noah's Plank School, her secret safe in her own counsel and his own life as yet unmolested by a lion's. For what seemed such a small cost, Sandy had beaten the curse of time's rejection.

The closest couple to him made cooing noises between munches of the white popped corn that sold for two pennies a bag outside. To fit in, Samson had bought some of the substanceless snack for himself, wondering idly if it had any nourishment even for the living and unwillingly imagining coppery essence soaking upward through the fluff. He'd set it aside before he felt sick, but around him pulses taunted relentlessly.

The couple, so close he could smell the crackle of their attraction, nuzzled one another in turn before the silvery shadows of the picture play, paying little attention, finding a sensation in one another's company that Samson felt beckon without understanding. His young adult body fidgeted, and he blinked away confusion as hunger mounted, their pulses quicker than other, solitary viewers, their lips giddy with breath that they swirled together as lips briefly touched.

"Did you see the look on his face, like a wild animal!" John Harker exclaimed on screen. Samson could barely hear the line delivered through the pounding.

"Wild animal? Like a madman," admonished the whippet playing Dr. Seward. Samson couldn't remember the actor's name and didn't care. The theatre was drowned out by beating hearts, fluttering sighs, gasps at actors muttering of feral dogs and bats. And all the while the mysterious alchemy of connectedness circulated before him like a foreign language, to savor, to consume.

There was another half-hour of run time to go but Samson couldn't stand any more. He was on his feet, the stage prop of his popcorn left behind. He stumbled to the exit and out of the theatre.

He needed to get back to the solitude of the hotel, out of the city, he didn't know. Hunger hammered every hoofstep past the bored liveried weasel usher who was pulling down the ticket booth shutters while chiding about no refunds.

He needed a telephone. He was dizzy, famished, and confused. The booth down the street from the Globe was illuminated by a single lamp around which countless shadows beckoned with the promise of safety. He ignored the stares of a small gaggle of roving dogs whose ears pricked at the sight of a young goat on the town at night all alone and traversed the road, ignoring the husky honk of a motorcar that chugged nearly to a stall as it braked.

He was at the phone in a moment and a few coins danced from his pockets into the street that he avoided. He rang the house's exchange and heard living breath on the line. "Who's this?"

"Crawford, it's me," Samson croaked. The booth felt as though it was tipping around him.

"Sam? You alright? Are you still in Scranton?"

"Yes."

"Okay. We're leaving now to come see you. Is the picture over already? Are you near the Globe where that Nos-vampire thing is playing?"

"I am, yes."

"Okay, hold on."

Celeste came on the line. "Samson, do you feel alright?"

She knew. To his shame, she knew. "I'm not," he fought for control. "The hearts around me are too loud. I'm trying to stay away but they're too loud." It was just like the bank again, trying to be strong, reliable, an adult in control, and he was failing pitifully. He shrunk within himself and felt the ravenous urge to feed all that much closer. It was a surge cracking a dam.

"It's alright, Samson, we get that on occasion, all of us do. You'll be alright."

"Sandy…"

"Sandy succumbed, Samson. She drank. We all succumb in the end." She lowered her voice. "You need to get somewhere quiet, find a shadow up high, away from everyone there." He heard a high-pitched feral screech. "I'm bringing nourishment. Stay hidden till we arrive."

"How will you find me?"

"Go up high near the theatre. I'll find you."

A squealing rat, a tincture of relief, a shrinking, adolescent body pulled back outside of time. He felt the sinking realization of ultimate defeat and wanted mortal tears back so he could cry. He was so close to knowing. His voice was the reedy voice of the child he was trapped within. "Alright. Please hurry."

They disconnected. Miles away, Crawford would be cranking his old Chevy to life.

In the stillness Samson's refrain made its ineffectual return. He could not drink. He would not drink.

But the words felt hollow. It was inevitable now.

Dogs passed in the pool of light outside of the booth, giving him the barest glance. The smell that came to Samson's nose then was familiar and from a different stock entirely.

There was a thud on the booth's dirty glazed glass pane and a blunter muzzle and nose fogged it between two splayed clawed hands. The cat's bare forehead bore a winding, dirty bandage from a rock thrown a few nights ago less than two blocks from here.

Two other two cats prowled around the booth, tails high in dominance, snickering, hissing.

A fragment of Tony Camonte's line from *Scarface* was resurrected from a cruel, sharp mouth that muffled through the booth's door. "Got that bar of soap for us, stinking little goat?"

A rock was thrown, not at the booth itself but up high, breaking the only light bulb that kept them all in view of Scranton's denizens in the cooling October night.

The hearts beat like war drums and Samson saw his own reflection gaze sallowly back as the light above went out. In the dark his fangs slid low and free where they belonged.

***

Dozens of speak raids, several tails of untrustworthy spouses, and four liquor stores hitting closing time had helped Crawford perfect the Grand Prix entrance to countless American townships over the years, or as fast as one could accomplish with a neglected thirteen-year-old Chevrolet barely holding its oil.

Celeste would survive a crash but couldn't spare the time to let her bones knit. She patted the rat cage behind them as the car bounced through a left bank, her form-fitting slacks and blouse sliding over the Chevy's cracked-leather seats. "Unless you intend to have Samson get relief from your vein, which I'd be worried about even trying, you'll want to slow down and get to the Globe upright."

Crawford made a noise of agreement and slowed a bit, breathing hard. He was approaching his needed change and Celeste would worry about that later. "Pull over there and let me out. Then proceed slowly into town. I can find him faster."

She wanted to kick herself. She'd been starved on occasion over the past hundred and sixty years, desperation shredding inhibition to near-feral status. She'd assumed Samson would come around long before that but realized she could have seriously underestimated how long he'd been fasting through the aloof calm he projected. The consequences of that mistake could be disastrous.

Crawford pulled the car over and Celeste leapt into the alley's ample well of shadows. In moments she was up high under the meager moon's glint and skipping herself through shadows like stones towards the art deco ziggurat façade of the Globe Theatre's crown. She reached the movie house in a mere minute, high-wattage light drifting up from the canyon of activity below. Theatregoers disgorged into the street in pairs and trios. With an abundance of caution she kept low, knowing the shadows even up high were too meager to properly bind above the marquee's brightness. There had been a brief thin rain and claws below picked across the cobbled road carefully, avoiding puddles that would wet their toes. Samson was not among them.

There. She saw a phone booth, ensconced in comparative darkness. The streetlamp nearest to it had either burnt out or been extinguished. In Samson's plain distress, he wouldn't have gone far.

The winds changed.

Celeste smelled blood.

***

Thirteen hundred miles away, just outside of Wichita, Kansas, the earth's essence heaved, grains of sand shifted, and amphorae, jars, and bottles clinked in disturbance in racks spreading through the dark.

"A house of blood in hill's blunt teeth,"

"An alley soaked in youth bequeathed…"

Something dripped far off, punctuating the silence in the antechamber where the nexus of tunnels converged.

"Sunovabich." Grisand tugged a whisker and her sigh nearly blew out the candle before her. "Like try'na catch radio ditties with a bent spoon."

Baliosi shifted the ratty pillow she sat cross-legged on, kicking up a smidgeon of dust. "Something's tugging fate's tail really hard but it's just a snarl."

Grisand grunted. "We lookin' positively coullion to the powers be. I say mourning period's long over. We need the next third to find us." Grisand turned to a twisting stretch of racks fading back into interminable dark. Drums were beating louder out in the world. Some were distant and ponderous, some like the frantic heartbeats of critters round the corner.

A head poked from a pocket of dark. "Sisters?"

Baliosi started, slapping the dirt floor with her thick tail. "Dammit Joachim, how many times I gotta tell you to stop sneakin' up on deah? My heart ain't got many ticks left."

The beaver winced, bucked teeth and Nosfur fangs a fence of contrition. "I'm truly sorry Gris'. It's just…"

"You can tell us." Baliosi smiled, her wart sending one whisker high. "Are your brothers and sisters faring well? They don't talk to us as often as they used to. They behavin'?"

"We're all doing well tending our charges, thank you." The beaver completely slipped free from the shadow and bowed slightly. "It's just that, deeper in the caverns, where the older jugs and pots are sealed shut, well, the shadows there…"

"They whisper?" Grisand asked carefully. The otter traded a glance with her lupine sister.

"I think, yes, they do. Some even louder than the bottles themselves."

The sisters pondered a moment. "Okay," Grisand licked her dry lips. "Gonna make you a suggestion that you pass on, mon ami de crocs."

The beaver's flat-iron tail brushed the floor. Now that he was settling back into drinking from the vermin caught down here, he'd regained some of the vigor he'd lost working iron for the millionaire rabbit back in Illinois. "Certainement."

Baliosi shifted the robe she wore, ruffling her neck fur a bit. "Should any shadow whisper louder than any vessel you tend to, maybe don't play within it. Just leave it be the same way you leave what's within the bottles be. There's things adjacent to other things down here and, well…"

Joachim blinked and clicked his teeth, sharp and bucked. "Are they dangerous?"

Otter and wolf traded looks again. Grisand sighed. "Oh I don't think it's so, gris-gris of sorts unknown. But we've questions nagging and noise be coming to the fore wit' little sense just now." The otter stared into the bottles resting on the nearest rack, tempests at the ready. "Time we get answers, and they ain't here."

"You mean?" Baliosi raised her brow.

"Yep. Road trip."

Baliosi's tail wagged up a storm. "We need a fix for the Gee Emm outside. Cranker's broken, needs a horse hitch into town."

Grisand scratched her chin, nose wiggling in thought. "I've a better proposition. The neighbor weasel down a piece from the gas bar and haircutters, you know de one I mean, he's got a wrenched-up Model Ayy fitted for shine-runnin' outa the hills."

Baliosi cocked her head. "What, Jesse? He still racing that?"

"Not so much anymore, meanin' we can get it as a loaner if you…"

Baliosi soured. "Oh no, Gris'…"

"What you don't need to marry de fool, he's jus' a red-blooded American boy who knows a nice-looking keester when he catches a tail go high. He don' need much more'n a smile and the right tone of voice." Grisand smoothed her more ample otter frame under her thick caftan. "I only wish I still had your sway to turn as many muzzles my way."

Baliosi stood and stretched. "Fine, we need what we need. I'll see the weasel at first light."

Grisand turned to Joachim. "We'll need to be movin' fast. Joachim, fetch my special crate for me would'ya? Ye know the one I mean, has all our fixin's for de road."

Joachim knew the crate and wriggled with anticipation as he turned and darted down a tunnel past the dim liquid embers in the endless array of bottles. The two remaining sisters watched him go, happy that the diligent Nosfur beaver couldn't feel the knot of anxiety hanging heavy between them.

***

Crawford parked the Chevy and reached into the deep recess inside himself where his companion denned. Instincts spoke, deep extensions of the same awareness every evolved mammal had, but more attuned to what they spoke of. Fear peppered the wind, heralded by the recent shedding of blood.

The night denizens of Scranton smelled it too, though unconsciously. Small groups and individual travellers hastened their pace, kept to wells of light seemingly without knowing why. Downtown core marquees and lit windows battled the dark, but even there he could see every other nose quivering against the faint, untraceable miasma that Crawford's refined tools sorted. More than one source of blood pulled him along. Sweating terror tinged it savagely.

At the Globe, he parked, picked a direction, stalked quickly. There would be bloodhounds in blue here soon, half the police force right behind. Whether or not Samson was connected with that scent, he'd best be elsewhere.

An alley breathed death and Crawford's memories gave him bright, horrid flashes of things he wished he could forget. At a left junction of brick just a few dozen yards down he found a broken baseball bat. A foot past that were the empty feline claws that had held it. Crawford's night vision easily made out the sightless eyes on a head canted at an unnatural angle against the wall and the bib of crimson painting his shirt collar, spotted on the high brown trousers of his bent legs.

A little further the dark gave up another shape, feline also, still and cooling. His blood scent could be picked apart from the other and as Crawford's nose worked, he thought he could detect a third.

His belly rumbled. "Dammit, not now. Where are you, Samson?" He fought the urge to holler for him and tried to follow the third blood trail, which seemed to point everywhere.

He turned slowly, muzzle twisting as his nose built a case. No evidence of the goat kid that he could see. He rounded a corner, foot coming into brief wet contact with feline blood, and came face to face with a ferret behind the shiny badge of the Scranton police department.

Crawford fought a moment of confusion, frozen to the spot, then collected himself. "Officer!" he stammered. "Thank God you're here! There's dead cats in this alley!"

The cop's nose had already been working hard. Now he drew his gun and Crawford stepped aside, hands darting for sky and then dropping as the ferret's gun pointed past him.

The officer saw the closest dead cat and called over his shoulder. "Vic! Neddie! Over here!" He eyed Crawford up and down, then slipped past, staying apart from the wolf as he roved.

"I..." Should Crawford say more? Say less? "I followed the smell down here, thought somebody was hurt and found those two."

Other officers huffed down the alley from an adjacent street, both wheezing a bit. Guns were in all three mitts as soon as they saw bodies. Two fanned out as Crawford stood stock still, a sound drifting down to him that was so high in register that only his elevated senses could hear it. It was a sound he'd heard only once before in a superintendent's office over a decade ago. When he recalled what it was, he knew for sure what had happened and his heart broke for the kid.

The ferret who'd seen him first met his gaze with hard eyes. "You're going nowhere."

***

Celeste found the cat up high, throat opened like a crimson feed bag and Samson huddled nearby, eyes dark pools that stared at nothing, bloody lip quivering.

Celeste left the last shadow and approached gingerly to sit next to him, recognizing anguish in the set of his shoulders and the scrabble of his hooves on the roof. Samson searched feebly for words as Celeste waited patiently.

Samson swallowed. "They followed me, forced their way into the telephone booth...I wanted to run. It was dark everywhere down there." He took a moment to settle himself. "I stood my ground. And when they came, I was hungry." He gazed at the feline corpse with its second wide crimson smile. "Nothing but hungry."

She reached a ginger hand out and he flinched at the contact on his shoulder. Celeste's question held no judgement. "How many chased you, Samson?"

"Three."

"Did you...?"

He grit his teeth and hissed through the fangs she knew he hated. "I cut them all. They'd seen me and tried to hit me with their bats. I was quick, and when the blood was out in the air..."

Pragmatism came to the fore and Celeste hated how easily it came. "You had to," Celeste ignored the shoulder that tried to shrug her off, holding tight. "If you'd killed one of them, the others would know. And they would tell others. The whole city—"

"I killed three people." The anguish in his voice was more palpable absent the deep breaths that signaled panic.

"You've been starving and they attacked you." Celeste corrected him.

"Sandy was starving." His voice was small and wavering. "She resisted."

"She couldn't sustain it. Nobody can."

"It was all for nothing." Samson raised his hands and Celeste saw they were bloody as a butcher's. Soon they would become more slender, more gangly, the digits of a child. "I ended their lives and it was all for nothing. None of us are going to grow older, not ever!" He cried out and hammered the tarred roof hard enough to scatter pebbles under his knuckles. "This was all I wanted."

His eyes met hers, pitch-black pools of despair. She rose again, took his hands in hers and brought him into an embrace that he struggled against. But she was firm and held him as he sobbed.

"Why couldn't Crawford end me? It would have been so quick."

"It wouldn't, and he couldn't." She responded rationally, even as she felt the tears, she couldn't shed for him any more than Samson could shed them for himself.

He hissed into her shoulder. "I'm gonna be trapped as a wee whining tike for all of eternity, a circus freak, even among Nosfurs. And another murderer to boot."

Night sounds echoed upward and Celeste found a thread back to her own grief. Long before Crawford and Samson, before even Sandy, Celeste had pondered what would have become of her sister Lavert if she'd saved her from the guillotine. Watch her fade away, year by year until she succumbed to time? Or would Celeste have made her sister like herself if she knew how? The question had been abandoned. It had to. Celeste would have gone mad with rumination otherwise.

When Celeste spoke her words they were cautious in their honesty. "That's the price of this, Samson. The old Nosfur who misses youth will never reclaim it. The young Nosfur wants to experience maturity can only spy it through others." She glanced down at the corpse of the cat beneath them, eyes empty of the last truth he'd learned. "We're spectators, Samson, you and I. We're tourists through the world's fickle changes in fashion and faith. Everyone I ever loved before the bite is dead and gone forever. It'll be the same for you soon enough."

Samson kicked gravel with his hoof, teeth grinding. "Are you trying to make me feel worse?"

Celeste shook her head. "I'm saying that you feel one kind of pain instead of another. If puberty's urges never touch you, you'll never have to pick a flower to see it wilt before you. I've done that. It hurt, Samson. Love will be stolen from all like us who seek it among the living. You suffer in this moment, but you could be suffering so much worse. I can't expect you to understand that now."

Samson pushed away, nearly putting a hoof on the dead cat's hand. "That's easy for you to say when you have Sandy, isn't it." There was venom in the words.

"You wouldn't understand…"

"Oh, go to hell, Celeste, I'm not twelve anymore! I'm an adult even if I'm stuck in this. I can't be what you lost, Celeste, not ever. I'm not your goddamn dead sister!"

Grief flared and Celeste had to stop herself from striking him. "I told you my sorrows in confidence, Samson, you and Crawford. Some wounds won't fully heal in any lifetime. I'm truly sorry that the cat who did this to you didn't care about that, but I care about you even though you cut me very deeply just now."

Samson closed his eyes and shuddered. The blood had brought him fully to life, vibrant and yet pitiful. "I'm scared. I thought this could be a gift if I could only control it." He was already looking younger, paradoxically shedding age as misery accumulated. It wouldn't be long. A night, two at most until he'd again be the kid from Noah's Plank School.

Celeste held his gaze when it rose again. "I don't believe this is a gift or a curse, merely what we are. We've only one another to get through it and I've learned that solitude doesn't help." She reached out with a hand. "So let us help you. This wasn't the way, Samson, I'm sorry."

He looked down at the cat. "They wanted to hurt me," he said distantly as he raised his hand.

Celeste took it and helped him up. "They wanted to be dominant. Were you mortal, you know they might have killed you."

His reply faded to whisper. "I barely remember bringing him up here."

Training had taken hold. Feed up high. It was inappropriate to compliment him on keeping that lesson. "We need to find Crawford." Celeste studied the corpse before her carefully. "And we'll need to make this problem disappear."

The lake was a few miles west. Celeste had moved bodies that far before, difficult though it may be. "Are the others close by?"

Samson collected himself. "A block in that direction," he pointed dejectedly.

"Crawford was searching around the theatre. With his nose he may have found them and with a little luck, we can handle this discreetly."

A short while later they found shadows perched well above a harried throng and knew any chance of discretion was long past.

CHAPTER 9

NAILS FOR NAMES

Half a day's travel passed in a blink and Sandy was brought out of repose by Bruno with the gentlest of pokes. They were in a dark garage. The squirrel rose from the car feeling no need to stretch but delighting in the sensation regardless. She felt that night had fallen in Atlantic City and heard waves rolling far past the beachside strand and the boardwalk.

Access to her well-appointed but modest apartment was facilitated by a narrow staircase from the garage, where Bruno saw to her things. Within the apartment, Sandy's living space was a mix of utility and scant but luxurious furniture. The salon was wood-panelled and tidily stocked with a small number of personal effects accumulated over the past ten years. Joyce, Fitzgerald, and the King James Bible dotted shelves along with keepsakes from Chicago and New York, traces of calamitous life spanning ninety years, nearly sixty-five after being turned.

For both habitants, the greatest jewel in the Atlantic City apartment waited beyond the curtains Sandy drew wide. Out on the northeastern reaches of the city the hum of revelry was muted but ever present. The bright lights of the Steel Pier glimmered out from the fainter glow of the boardwalk from which jazz and the tinkle of mammalian merriment drifted faintly over the hush of the rolling waves, constant and calming. The Depression hadn't sunk its hooks into this place, not fully. It was the last scent of the roaring twenties, fighting time's tide. Sandy felt a tincture of shame in loving it.

"Are you tired, Bruno?" she called down the hall.

"Never too tired for you," Bruno answered warmly as he put her valise away and joined her. "Do you need invigorating?"

He looked tired. The drive from Celeste's rickety house with its quaint wolf smell had no doubt been long. "Perhaps later, Bruno, thank you.

135

Please collect my letters and notations. We'll need to arrange pickup of the nails from Scranton in the next few days." She wondered then if Celeste had made progress with Samson's dilemma, picked up the telephone and got a connection to Celeste's exchange. No answer after several rings. A small nudge of worry intruded but Sandy knew the kid was in good hands. She'd be sure to speak to him once the unfortunate affair of the Ark nails was finally over.

Bruno brought the letters and retired with a quick kiss on Sandy's cheek. As he stood up slowly, she saw that his collar was open, the small scars at his ruff almost hidden by pelt. "So polite of you to offer but I really want you to get some rest. Don't worry." She ran her claws gently up his collar and round his chin in a caress. "What Celeste and I have won't take away from you and me. This remains special, Bruno."

He bowed as her touch fled and went to rest on a cloud. She knew that his slumber would be as deep and untroubled as her own.

Quite unlike her waking state. Sandy sorted the mail quickly. It was mostly penned discourses with contacts from old affiliates of Calvert's steel distributors all over the Midwest and Pacific Coast that she'd written as an interested party. Excess forged steel from Calvert's mill had long been liquidated, the reliquary-cast among them. Polite inquiries chillingly confirmed they were snapped up by European buyers, likely Calvert's ex-patriots among the Martyres. It was the Ark nails that had Sandy truly worried, however. With what Celeste and Crawford had managed to secure already they could have tainted the frames of half the buildings in any major city. One replaced girder could be felt several floors and a block away.

And she'd helped Calvert set this in motion. So it was her own mess to sort.

More mail, more dead ends from all her inquiries as night settled, leads dried up. She should take some time, walk the boardwalk, sample the salty night air. But she knew that the next hiding place for Calvert's remaining stash was close at hand, clues in something an associate said or wouldn't say. Hours later, she resigned herself to the fact that two dozen inquiries answered left nothing to go on.

She was ready to visit with Bruno, take him up on his offer, when she felt a presence and glanced upwards.

The silhouetted figure on her balcony lounge chair outside wore a disheveled white suit, worn but familiar. Tall ears were erect and cupped in her general direction. He saw her see him.

"What?" Sandy hissed.

Donovan Calvert rose, the moonlight catching the silver on his ear tips and let himself in. "I'd have brought a housewarming gift but"—he closed the French door behind him—"the sheep are too tightly packed down where the noise is and I spent the entire night driving here from the mountains of New York State. Most importantly, my money bought this place, so it's technically my house, isn't it?"

"No, it is not. You burnt down all you ever had when you ran." Her fangs were cold when slipped free. "I only took what would have been mine were I in your employ and not your slave."

Donovan's eyes narrowed with sardonic amusement and his ears dropped. "Were there chains on you, Sandy? He crossed her threshold and took a seat on the long couch. "After that first week or two?" he added with a shrug.

"You counted on invisible chains never breaking. Arrogance cost you just fine."

"Oh, Sandy, if you only knew. I had such high hopes for…" The rabbit was upright and out of his seat in an instant, ears stabbing back. "You!"

Sandy's glare darted from Donovan to the vestibule by the sparse kitchen where Bruno stood stock still in his night clothes, mouth open in shock at the sight of his old master. The muskrat hunted for words and nothing came out.

Donovan's muzzle hung low, fangs pushing free with a hiss. "All that time, and you were the one."

"Sandy?" Bruno's tail wound round himself as his eyes darted from Sandy to Donovan and back again.

Sandy was to her own feet and between them immediately, tail and head low for a charge.

Donovan ignored her. "The better part of a year chained naked in my own cellar, waiting vainly for rescue from somebody, anybody who would wonder what happened and come for me, and you were the bloody one Sandy convinced to betray me."

Sandy reared back, fangs fencing her bucked teeth, eyes black and merciless as she went nose to nose with the rabbit. "Bruno was the only one of your own staff you couldn't get fangs in to drink dry. You betrayed him, Donovan, all of them. Don't you remember? All your hangers-on and sycophants. We had to kill most of those in the house still loyal to the Martyres when they saw I'd turned back to the vein, and not only did you not try to stop me, you were picking off the slowest of them."

Donovan attempted to slip round her but she was quicker. The rabbit hissed with ears pinned. "You signed a pact, Bruno. You were supposed to be loyal to me!"

The muskrat stammered, holding his ground with extreme effort, tail coiling painfully. "I was loyal to our cause, Dono—Mister Calvert. You returned from your mill and without a word of warning you murdered Edmond on the doorstep." His eyes were wet but the muskrat held tears back. "Sandy offered me protection."

"You fucking moron," Donovan's voice rose to a shout. "Sandy did this to me!"

Sandy cuffed him, nearly knocking Calvert off his feet. He stared at her in shock and she met his glare furiously.

After all she'd done, he somehow imagined she'd not resist him? "You feckin' bastard, I showed you who you truly were, tried to show you some inkling of the incredible restraint it takes to be one of us even without your forge-making metal nannies. What did you learn for all that? Nothing."

She pointed back at Bruno, who was ready to bolt but to his credit hadn't succumbed to the fear wafting off him. "Bruno was put in an impossible plight between those he'd sworn to consider his enemies and his former master turned gluttonous killer, but he survived. He saw we could be merciful, let his foolish inclinations go, and survived."

Donovan held perfectly still but for shaking fists. "You all tortured me with his help."

Sandy smiled coldly. "I scolded you with your own vanity and lack of restraint, Donovan. Bruno didn't do that. He was handling tasks we couldn't while we hid from the Martyres."

Donovan held fast, not advancing but not backing down either. "Fetching mail and changing the lightbulbs just as he was fit for, no doubt." He gritted flat teeth between fangs as though grinding something distasteful. "When the police and Martyres came you, you lied, sat, and enjoyed the luxuries of my home while I was writhing in pain below."

"As Sandy would no doubt tell you, sir"—Bruno fidgeted for composure and stood his ground—"I did what needed to be done. The police were easy enough to deal with, but had the Martyres of the Black Well learned what you'd become…"

Silence fell. Only the surf and the muttered merriment of America's dwindling hedonist ranks drifted in. Donovan narrowed his gaze as his eyes fell to the muskrat's collar. "You serve Sandy in other capacities as well…"

A self-conscious hand went up to push Bruno's collar back in place, and Sandy decided to break that tension. "We help one another, Donovan, in ways that clearly haven't crossed your mind. I suppose you've been alone."

Donovan didn't answer, turning instead to study Sandy's sparse shelves. "It took me some time to find you, Sandy, and I can say I'm somewhat surprised. I'd have thought you'd have sequestered yourself in a monastery or convent once the guilt set in. I'd have never expected you to park yourself on the doorstep of one of America's last seedy dodges from the Depression."

"A convent. Really? That part of my life will never be mourned. You were the last demonstration that piety is worthless when given to the faithless. How did you find me?"

"A friend pointed the way." Donovan turned a leather-bound copy of *The Tempest* in his hand and sniffed it before putting it back. "What's important is why I'm here."

"You caused me great harm and I returned that favor, Donovan. You'll bring a lot of woe down upon yourself if you don't watch your step."

Bruno stood stock still, unsure whether to stay or go while Sandy stayed between them.

Donovan waved a hand airily. "You can dismiss your pet for now, Sandy. I've not come to start any fires. Quite to the contrary, I bring a peace offering in the form of a trade. I know what you've been looking for, and from the return addresses on some of those torn envelopes, you're running out of places to look."

Sandy looked to the mess she'd been ready to discard. "Bruno, we'll be fine. Let me speak with Donovan alone for now."

The muskrat looked to Donovan who gave Bruno a flat glare in return. Bruno wandered back to his quarters warily.

"You've obviously used some of my techniques. You have Bruno ever so obsequious and willing to please, don't you?"

Sandy rolled her eyes. "I've used nothing of your methods, Donovan. Otherwise, he'd hate me too."

He sneered. "You're telling me he lends his vein out of, what, love?"

"There are kinds of devotion you wouldn't understand, try though I would to teach you."

"I once thought you had true devotion for me."

If he wanted some form of pity… "I did. I woke up."

Whatever he had expected upon crashing her party wasn't coming to fruition and he seemed pained. "I know it's well behind us now, but it was more than devotion, wasn't it?"

Sandy wished Celeste were here. She had so little difficulty cutting the cords of false sentimentality and would be glad to help Sandy toss the rabbit over the balcony onto the sands below. "You were a rabbit who succeeded in a world that didn't want you to. That had an initial attraction, yes. I thought I loved you for defying what they tried to make of you. In the end I hated you for what you made of yourself."

Donovan sighed with worthless lungs. "Well then. Thanks to you I've had to make myself something else entirely. And I've had success. One of the inner council of the Martyres is dead. Von Haften, the husband of a certain lioness you don't miss."

Sandy was intrigued if not impressed. "Cleaning up the mess you helped create, are you? Well, if so, tell me where your shards are so I can ensure that they go to someplace where they can't be used against us."

"I came to do just that, several caches worth. I've realized they aren't the leverage I thought they would be and they're just as good in your hands as mine. That life is behind me."

"I've note paper…"

"Just one thing."

Sandy cocked her head. "We both want the nails gone, Donovan. What more is there to discuss?"

"I found you through someone who helped me, though we haven't met yet. He told me where to find you."

"Who?"

"I don't know him. I don't even have a name. But we'll be meeting in Canada and he wants something in return for helping me find you. Something completely inconsequential, but I need it nonetheless. He's already demonstrated he can help me cull the Martyres of the Black Well. We can't do it alone."

Sandy's tail twitched. There were some assumptions made here... "There is no 'we', Donovan. I don't trust you and my only aim is to be rid of your nails."

He was silent for a long time, stewing in the way she'd seen so often when he schemed and lined up all the obstacles to what he wanted, things to manipulate or destroy. It frightened her that in her ignorance she'd loved that about him too.

"A name then. I have to bring him a name."

"What name?"

"One used by a friend of yours, Celeste Val De Mort."

Sandy's pelt crawled. "It's De Mot. This person knows Celeste?"

"Or knows of her. Again, we've not met, only spoken over a telephone."

"And he wants a name."

"Yes, an alias of hers. One she used to cross the Atlantic with you."

Sandy remembered. The voyage, the rolling dark of her cabin, a broken vessel of blood and a friendship first formed over a wriggling rodent's pulse. Then that first caress... "Why does he need this? She's never used that name again."

"Proof that I can be trusted with a task? A demonstration of commitment? He seemed a bit eccentric, if proficient with a crossbow."

"Proficient with—You could just tell me where the nails are," Sandy rose and began circling the room. "You've no obligation."

In an instant Donovan was in her path. "But then I would break his trust and be alone again." He hesitated for only a moment, exasperated. "I can't be alone anymore, Sandy. My money has all but run out and my last refuge discarded. I know you're through with me, you've made that plain." He couldn't keep the hurt out of his voice. "However, it's the name for the nails, no negotiating. You've not seen your doe in years so it shouldn't matter to you."

Sandy turned the name over in her mind. In finding Celeste's current home she knew the name hadn't been used there. It was possible Celeste had forgotten it herself. To refuse and risk losing Donovan's nails, the very bane of her existence for over a decade, was unthinkable.

She didn't doubt that some part of the rabbit still wanted revenge for what Sandy had forced on him, current détente notwithstanding. Donovan deserved to be alone, but what harm could she avoid by just giving him the worthless thing he wanted. "Marie Laquoix," Sandy said. Marie had been Celeste's instructor of letters when she was a fawn in Versailles before the Revolution. But Donovan didn't need to know that.

"Marie Laquoix," Donovan repeated, glancing to the window. Sandy glanced with him and saw the Atlantic's distant slit in the peek of a new dawn.

"You should get to a hotel while you still have time," Sandy said. "After you give me the location of the nails."

Donovan said nothing, watching day's threat burgeon. "It's more than just addresses. There are directions. In one instance a combination."

"Then you should hurry," Sandy approached the curtains and drew them tight.

Donovan approached her secretary and withdrew paper. She had a typewriter under a cover there, a Remington that Bruno used to take her dictation. He fed it and then began clicking away methodically. All the while the glow increased under the drape's feet.

"You're running out of time," Sandy said with some annoyance, trying to avoid peering over his shoulder. He could easily draw the sheet, tear it up, demand more from her in trade.

But the simplest thing for him to do would be to simply make something up. Fortunately, she'd given up nothing important, and he needed the nails gone just as badly as she did.

"I am out of time." He concluded as he stopped typing. "I've the stolen car of a dead aristocrat six blocks away where it's likely being ransacked and stripped by luckless gamblers." He laughed at the image and set his ears back. "It appears I'll need to stay here for the day."

He turned to her, his gaze placid and revealing nothing. "After that I've a place to be."

The sun rose outside as Sandy and her uninvited guest stared at one another until tiredness pulled stronger than mutual distrust.

It was late in the morning when Sandy relinquished awareness, Donovan's eyes closed and the rabbit was still. She thought once of stakes through the hearts and decapitations, of the furnace that claimed all the failures in Chicago she'd been charged with trying to save.

She wondered if Donovan could be saved and let awareness go.

***

The house was empty when they returned as always, but between every tick of the clock was an unspoken worry. Samson finally gave it a voice. "There were two dead cats down there with Crawford. What if they arrested him?"

"I appreciate that you want to help him, Samson, but stop and think." Celeste felt the same tug of worry even as she reasoned. "His scent was not on those bodies. You and I both know that. He's just a concerned citizen who found them. That's all."

"It's my fault." Samson paced in the kitchen, blood high making him younger by the second. Celeste knew that he'd be back to an adolescent frame when they sought safety from the sun in the basement.

"No, it isn't. You told me they attacked you, Samson. Would they have killed you?"

"Well..."

"Could they?"

He stopped and grabbed his own horns in worry. "No."

"Anyone who tries to do so will have a story to tell others when they learn they can't. There were no options."

"But I—"

"Samson, listen to me. The nails buried at the border of our property are one kind of threat but the worst that can ever befall us comes if the world knows we exist. Let Bela Legosi turn into a cardboard bat on a string and have the world gasp at that. Killing three violent cats in order to prevent a whole world panicking is the kind of trade we have to make. You only mourn them because you're more morally inclined than most mortals and that's—"

They both heard the crunch of gravel and light that wasn't part of any coming dawn flooded the living room before turning away.

"Lights!"

Samson flicked off the kitchen switch and Celeste leapt atop a chair, unscrewing the hanging shaded bulb while ignoring the burn of her fingers. They both bound shadows within the kitchen's corners immediately.

There was a moment before the key turned in the lock and labored breathing filled the front hall. A trace of dawn bled in and was shut away. A moment passed while the intruder remembered what to say in this instance. "It's Walter Privens. Want to buy a Chevrolet?"

They both slipped free. "Crawford, you don't sound well. What happened?" Celeste could smell his anxiety when he leaned against the kitchen's door jamb.

"Cops asked me a few questions, got my name, address, the usual. Told me not to leave town."

"Did they hurt you?" Samson was aghast. Crawford blinked, recognizing the goat's return to a kid's physical aspect. To the wolf's credit he didn't comment on that.

"No," Crawford said. "The moon did. I didn't change and it really hurt. Tomorrow night is the night. It's going to be a hard one, I can feel it."

Samson's lower lip curled as he looked from Celeste to the wolf and back again. "I'm so sorry, Crawford, this is all my fault."

"No, Samson, no. I was in the wrong place at the wrong time. So were you."

Samson looked at the floor and Celeste was at his side. "You had no alternative. It's that simple."

"Celeste is right. The police knew them and they were no angels. They found junk in their pockets they'd mugged that very night."

Samson accepted Celeste's embrace and felt his numbness as though it was her own. "It's gonna be alright, Samson," she said and hoped he was convinced.

***

"So, this was all phoned in anonymously. Strange that they wouldn't just walk away and keep it quiet." Special Agent Tomlinson stood behind the Catskills chalet and glanced down at the fourth dead body on this side of the place, a hole near his heart. The dog had bled out the mouth and his lips were painted with surprise.

"Strange for sure." A spell passed. "Mob hit?" The local sheriff bloodhound tailing him round the outside felt compelled to throw out theories because that's what cops did with silences. Tomlinson was annoyed.

"The dead lion in there is an Austrian foreign national with various financial interests throughout Europe. Too early for theories but the perfect time for containment. Any of your boys and girls who make a little on the side calling the press are strongly advised to not do that. I'll know if they do." Tomlinson looked at the hound straight through his spectacles and let the reflected Catskill pines hide what he was thinking. "I need this name circulated as a potential material witness as soon as possible." He handed over torn paper.

The name was hastily scrawled. "Who's Crawford Cain?"

"We'll know soon enough if he's anything at all. In any case, I'll need any neighbors within gunshot hearing range of this place canvassed and interviewed."

"Just one, trapper lives up the hill. We know of him, domestic with an ex a few years ago. She beat him senseless."

Tomlinson nodded distantly as he passed the back of the house. Faded lawn furniture clustered a disused firepit. Framed hedges had long gone wild. "I'm going to go through a few more things inside before I call Washington and start notification processes for next of kin overseas."

The hound's face went sour and he painted a small part of the crime scene with tobacco spittle. "Dealing with foreigners ain't ever fun."

Tomlinson glared at him. "I've gotten rather good at it. Maybe I'm just less judgemental."

The hound cleared his throat. "One question irks me."

Tomlinson raised a brow. "Just one?"

"Our guys went through this place quickly and got a little spooked but weren't in there any less time than you were. How'd you know this place belongs to that rabbit from Illinois, the steel guy who went missing? Ain't no Calvert on the deed."

Tomlinson sighed. "We were notified that Von Haften was coming here and who he was meeting by somebody we keep in touch with at the Waldorf Astoria."

"The hotel in Manhattan…you're spying on this guy?"

"No comment. I'm going to stress again that nobody on your team talks to the press. I mean it. Uncle Sam really means it." He let that sink in.

The hound understood readily enough. "Was this lion and his posse some kind of threat to the country?"

"No. Not the lion."

***

Lucas felt the shadow at his shoulder and knew his time was up. He growled low in his throat through the telephone. "Mom, just because you didn't take up with some sub-mammalian reprobate doesn't mean I'm gonna love that fish-breathed yowler you shacked with. I'm fixing to shove his tail in the stove if he talks down to me ever again."

Kamila Marsten sighed on her end of the line. "I'm worried about you, Lucas. This isn't like you."

"It is just like me and you just don't know it. I've found a real calling and don't need anybody pretending he's my father. I'm glad I'm without one."

A hand rested on his shoulder, heavy, reassuring. The message through the grip was plain. He didn't need her. "I've got to go. It's an important day and I've a speech to prepare for tonight." He turned and was nose to nose with the Colonel. "We've got a nation to save. I have to go, Mother."

If Mom believed him when he hung up he didn't know. The Colonel needed him and Lucas needed to be ever present.

"It's official, you're on, cub." The colonel put a cigarette in his mouth, ignoring the general store advisory not to smoke near the salamis and cheese wheels just outside the booth. "Tomorrow is our time, right here in Hancock. We'll be on stage at the biggest venue yet and everybody here for me will be here for you if you win 'em over."

Butterflies danced in Lucas's stomach and he could already count the sea of shining, smiling canines he'd gaze into soon enough. "You…think I'm ready?"

The Colonel guided him over to a counter where cold-cut sandwiches were being prepared. "You know you are," he said as he looked up at the shopkeep. "Two clubs. Generous on the mustard with mine."

The raccoon behind the counter dipped his head, wiped off on his apron, and set to work.

The colonel watched meat slice. "You had a chance to donate to the cause, friend? You know what we're all about?"

There were two others from the Colonel's entourage wandering the small store where Lucas had entered to use the telephone. Benny the weasel and a cat named Lucile poked at hanging sausages and smelled the recently ground bags of coffee, all priced down to account for scant business.

The raccoon arrayed the slices of rye bread out on the butcher block, eyes avoiding the German shepherd's cold gaze.

"Well, sir, I do regret that times being what they are I'm short on spare funds to—"

"And why," the Colonel asked, cocking his head back thoughtfully, "do you suppose that is, friend? I see you're alone in here. Can't afford to employ anybody I would suppose."

"Well, sir, no. That is, not really." Whiskers fidgeted and the sandwich bread nearly slipped off the block.

Lucas watched the Colonel give that a space. "Not really means somebody. I'm seeing you alone, right?"

"I have a girl who does the cutting and the stocking. On some days."

Neatly arrayed stock was rifled behind the Colonel and Lucas. Curious, indifferent claws moved and sniffed. The German shepherd and wolf both ignored it.

"She get a good discount on the wonderful cured meats and cheeses you sell here?" The Colonel leaned forward and held his gaze, forcing the raccoon to slow his progress and stop. "Or maybe just the cheese? You know we didn't pick this town at random. We've been very particular as to where we'd carry the truth of our national plight and the dark road we have to follow. Left pamphlets last time in fact." His nose roved left and right. "They all gone?"

"They, uh…" The raccoon stopped talking to avoid stammering. "I still have a few."

"But I don't see them. Do you see them, Lucas?"

Lucas looked about, shook his head. Tension smothered the store with silence.

"Any by the door, friends?"

Twin negatives from Benny and Lucy.

"Did she take them?"

"No!" The raccoon all but shouted. "Why would anybody…"

"We saw somebody putting your shingle out last time. Sweet leggy little bunny rabbit. Saw her again when we came back. That who's got your extra cash, friend? In a town positively full of unemployed, desperate carnivores who would literally kill to put meat on their tables. You're going to waste that precious money on somebody who can't even appreciate most of the bounty that you offer? I said more mustard, didn't I?"

The raccoon's pulse was clearly racing as the mechanical assembly of the Colonel's and Lucas's sandwiches nearly finished up. "You know what, good sir?" The raccoon applied extra mustard to one pile of sliced turkey and ham, hastily scraped up plates, set the sandwiches upon them before lifting them to the top of the deli counter. "These two are on the house. I don't want any trouble."

"How much you pay her?"

"Sir, that's really not—"

The Colonel showed all his teeth and despite himself Lucas began to feel the raccoon's discomfort as his own. "How much, in the middle of this blasted world of desperation, do you pay that long-eared lettuce muncher to work a carnie's due job? Son, make as good a sandwich as God can allow but we're all gonna know if you lie."

"Forty cents per hour." The raccoon closed his eyes, hands together as though in prayer. Mustard smeared one finger. "Probably ten hours a week. Her father helped me when times were tough and I owe—"

"Four dollars then?"

"Yes. I would suppose so."

"Well then," The Colonel took his plate, then side-eyed Lucas until he gingerly lifted his. The raccoon looked on the verge of a heart attack and the Colonel met his eyes with fiery judgement. "We just need to come to a little understanding about your hiring practices." Laughter flanking the Colonel told Lucas without turning that both the Colonel's bruisers were close.

The raccoon glanced from glare to glare, meeting Lucas's eyes for just an instant. He opened his mouth to speak but the Colonel cut him off. "Kid, step outside. Wait for me."

Lucas didn't know whether to hold his ground or follow the Colonel's orders. The raccoon saw something in his eyes and his own begged. "Lucas." The Colonel's voice dropped low. "Wait for me."

Out Lucas went, feeling eyes on his back. He stood in the flow of bodies, no sound escaping from the deli as he stared at the phone booth he'd been in mere minutes ago, now occupied.

Less than a minute passed before he was joined. In the street the Colonel ate his sandwich at hurricane speed and used a thin sheaf of cash to brush crumbs off his immaculate suit. He separated a five and three ones as Lucas tried to meet his gaze. "Didn't take too much to convince 'im." The Colonel sighed. "We're meeting the mayor tonight and ensuring he knows what's what. Take this to the drug store down the street and get something top shelf. Whiskey. Not wine. Use whatever's left to buy yourself a decent tie."

Lucas looked at the money in his claws and all that it implied made him a bit queasy. The hand returned to his shoulder. "You just might have potential, Lucas, to learn what's important from what's not. Friends on further shores are rising to restore their destiny as this world's masters. If we let any of ours sink into the mire with the commie and the veggie degenerates then they'll take us with them. Remember that."

The hand fell away and the Colonel departed. The man could never afford to appear weak through expressions of sentiment. Not for one second.

***

Sandy came to early, instinctively. Her eyes darted around the apartment which was empty of any movement but her own. Two pieces of paper sat by the typewriter on her secretary desk and she approached warily. To her relief the typed sheet with the last locations of the nails remained.

Next to it lay another note, hand scrawled. Sandy twitched her tail nervously as she read.

As I take my leave of you, accept the last truth you ever need to learn, the one you taught me with fervour. Eventually, anyone and everyone you deign to love or trust will betray you. You don't deserve that pain.

Love, Donovan

Sandy let the paper drop, panic rising as she followed the well of silence that dominated her apartment to the room at the end of the hall.

She found Bruno splayed, eyes sightless, twin blossoms of crimson at his starched collar and cold as a cruel promise. She quietly closed his empty eyes as fury pushed grief aside.

CHAPER 10

COPS, FEDS, AND LAWYERS

Crawford saw Celeste and Samson off to rest. One minute they were present and alert and the next minute their eyes were closed and they were both stone-dead enough for the cold ground. It was disturbing just how little of anything their bodies actually did when they weren't speaking, walking, or interacting with things.

He closed Celeste's door carefully even though he knew it wouldn't wake her and crossed the hall feeling the shiver of his own unique preternatural itches. A whole night with no changes had him on fire and he regretted not just parking the car on the way back by the roadside and loping off to get back to his true nature's nature.

Of course, that was a dangerous prospect. Scranton proper was just one wrong turn away and without the Nosfurs at least keeping an eye out things could have gone horribly wrong.

He confirmed that Samson was also relaxed, flat on his thin mattress and already younger, the effects of his dangerous gambit passing as quickly as a day-cold. Looking in on the still goat kid Crawford realized glumly that there was at least one mammal's childhood that he'd not had to run out on.

That got him thinking about Lucas again and whether Charlie's people could keep him safe if Feds raided the outfit he'd fallen in with. Communist and anarchist groups got busted up all the time and jail time for resisters was punitively long, care of anarchist bombings back in the twenties that few forgot about.

Fat lot of good Crawford could do about that now with his were aspect itching to toss the icebox like a shotput into the neighbor's yard. He wouldn't be much use to anybody for days at least.

He tried to stay busy with work for a bit. Even with Sandy Mallory's nails being a top priority, not to mention well paying, they did have the Wainright and Tuxley cases ongoing. Celeste had developed photos in her curtained-off darkroom upstairs. Several pictures revealed a shipping clerk bundling something out the backdoor of a warehouse whose owner, Mister Tuxley, suspected theft. Ms. Wainright, whose husband was caught with a wandering eye wanted to pay them to follow him around some more, convinced the old cat had a third mistress. This town wasn't big enough for that but they'd happily run the meter if her payment ever arrived.

Crawford studied the Tuxley case pictures. The weasel from the warehouse job was hunched like a second-string receiver hustling the ball over the line but the photo was too blurry to confirm exactly what he had.

"Getting that camera inside a shadow is a hell of a trick," Crawford muttered enviously. Much of what Celeste could do was much more useful to their current profession. Crawford's main preternatural contribution was picking apart scents forensically, biting through the occasional lock and, well, being awake during the daytime.

Try as he might to keep his mind on task, he couldn't stop worrying about Lucas. Options started creeping in past the aches and joint pains. Calling Kamila was right out. He'd promised her a life of her own and they'd moved on. She wouldn't have encouraged Lucas to do this and all Crawford could do with a call was remind her that Lucas's estrangement was at least partially his fault. Calling Charlie wouldn't help either. He'd only just passed on word and Charlie was going on constantly about how damn slow everything was. Law enforcement took forever to find anybody in this day and age.

The door buzzer sounded as Crawford was stirring a little whiskey into his morning coffee. Salespeople weren't supposed to knock this early, a bylaw he'd looked up. Crawford growled as he got the front door and found a quartet on his front step.

He hadn't heard cars come up over the kettle whistling on the stove because both of them had stopped just at the tip of his driveway. A bear, a wolf, and two cats in trench coats and beaten homburgs and fedoras all stared him down. One cat's hand was up and a badge was brandished. "Crawford Ellis Cain?"

Crawford's tail went limp. "Good morning officers. That's me. Uh…I answered questions in an alley last night for over an hour and told them everything I saw. How can I help?"

Glares were most of the answer. "We're here to place you under arrest."

"For what?"

The wolf, black furred, licked his own nose. "Two counts suspected murder, one count abetting a bank robbery in another municipal jurisdiction. You're coming back to town with us."

Crawford felt cold as multiple hands on hips on his porch itched for him to make a move. He succumbed to his primal nature, raised the coffee mug with its Irish-bonded kiss, and downed relief for his aching body in five hot swallows.

***

Coincidences didn't happen with fieldwork as widely scattered as the Bureau handled, so what Charlie heard made him uncomfortable. "Tell me about the source of the funds. A holding company where?"

Michael's long tail swished round as he turned pages. "A prominent National Socialist organization, funny how they apply that term, is getting financial backing from a holding company in Schenectady, New York that appears to have folded. Vast sums of money were used for acquisition of industrial assets from a defunct company out of Chicago that went into receivership shortly after the twenty-nine bust."

Charlie's mind worked furiously. "Some military contractor? Every other government stoking discontent in our backyard wants an eyeball into Uncle Sam's shiny new tanks and planes."

Michael set the pages down on the desk between them. "That's just it. It's nothing of the sort. It was the material holdings of a steel company, Calvert Steel specifically. The one with the rabbit who went missing eight years before it shuttered."

Charlie nodded. "Read about the estate burning down. Eccentric millionaires going off the rocker since the crash are becoming old hat. So, what's important about this steel?"

"Nothing. Steel companies are all over America and Europe, but multiple payments were processed for ingots and girders well above market value from depots all over the country, many that were designated for construction projects underway. It must be a front for something else, somebody's bananas means of making financial transfers look somehow legitimate." The lemur laughed. "It's failing miserably at doing that."

Charlie never met the rabbit who ran Calvert Steel, but he'd seen him at the election of Mayor Deever the night before his life and understanding of everything in it changed for the worse.

And of course, Crawford had worked for Calvert in an investigative capacity immediately before being forced to leave Chicago. Charlie had never pressed him too hard on that affair. Soon enough, Chicago was as behind both of them as it could ever be and Charlie hadn't wanted to ask any more questions.

Now a lapine ghost was risen. "Alright. Nobody ever found Calvert, but somebody is chasing down his company's steel who also likes supporting far-right causes that disparage vegetarians making headway in American life, much less becoming millionaires in it. That seem a little... ideologically contradictory to you?"

Michael laughed. "Screwy to say the least, sir."

Charlie sighed. He needed answers and he knew somebody else who wanted the same. Hopefully a certain lupine would be calling him very soon.

***

Celeste's eyes opened and she could see the milky threat of daylight making the shades glow. The feeling came that something was very wrong.

She was up in an instant, counted meager shadows, bound one instinctually and listened.

"I don't have time for this." Crawford was incensed with somebody on their porch above. "I found those dead cats in that alley. If I killed the bastards I would have scrammed, wouldn't I?"

"There's a third cat missing," an interested voice tried to sound disinterested. A cop.

Celeste and Samson had put that cat in the lake with some difficulty, but she'd not told Crawford that.

"We'd like to have a quick look around while you talk to some friends downtown."

The lupine barked in laugher. "You think that, what, I killed a couple cats and took one home?"

Celeste unbound the shadow and opened her door quietly, hearing the sneer in the reply clear as a bell.

"People do get lonely this far out of town. We're gonna check the premises to be sure while you're back at the station. We've somebody coming in who wants to talk to you."

"The hell is this? There's a pesky thing called the Fourth Constitutional Amendment and I'm busy…"

Celeste heard them move in. Crawford could have resisted, could have even given into the change that wanted him at every second. Smart calculation got him off that porch without any of that. This happened amongst claw scrapes of Celeste couldn't tell how many other mammals.

She crossed the hall quickly and let herself into Samson's room where the childlike body lay. One touch to his shoulder brought him alive.

"What?"

"It's not noon yet. Keep away from the window. Police are here. They're taking Crawford away."

Samson's young eyes hardened. "We have to—"

"No." Celeste was firm but her voice didn't raise. "With the sun up, we're both in serious danger. We'll have to hide until after dusk, at which point we can go after him."

There was the sound of a floorboard creaking above, tentative and purposeful, alien to their abode. Crawford's indistinct Virginian chatter could be heard from outside, squabbling verbally with others, loudly. "They're inside the house," Celeste muttered.

Samson's fangs showed in stress. "He needs to turn tonight. If he's in a police station…"

"We'll figure that out. Root cellar. Now."

The root cellar was barely a few feet wide but it was deep, with recesses dug where shadows would always be for the casual searcher who shined a flashlight in. They were in it in moments, backs tight to the wall and shadows selected for binding. Down here the bones of the house transmitted every step and the baritone of two carnivore voices, heavy and breathy.

"You wanna go top down? Or split up?"

"Top down. Listing for the business here says he works with a partner, a doe according to records, though the business cards don't say that."

"A progressive, huh. He a pinko too, you think?"

A snicker came back. "Commie private dicks, that'd be a gas. Don't turn anything over yet. Paperwork isn't through for the warrant and we could get in hock if the place looks ransacked."

Celeste could confront them, demand they leave, but only if they came down here. If they insisted she follow them up there where rays of sun penetrated… "No matter what you hear them do, Samson, stay hidden. I mean it."

Samson did what she told him. Things moved above. Things moved back, playing safe for the moment. They were noisiest in the kitchen, the oven opening and closing, utensils rummaged. The Nosfurs nestled into the recessed shadows, close enough to hear one another when speaking.

"Will they find the nails we've been collecting?"

Above, the couch groaned as it moved. Celeste was glad that Samson was being pragmatic. "Crawford buried them well past the old outhouse and the hideaway creche we built. They will be fine."

But would they? If Samson, Crawford, and herself were forced to flee this place, would they be able to return and recover the shards again?

The claw scratches moved together and apart around the main floor where the majority of their meager possessions were collected. Much time was spent in the office where confidential materials relating to cases Crawford and Celeste shared were spread out.

"So many closed shutters in this place. I mean, I get seclusion but—" Something scraped on the desk. "This cat the one we're looking for?"

They were no doubt looking at photos of the philanderer that Celeste had photographed over a week ago.

"No," came the bored response. "Missing one's years younger."

The door opened next to the space Celeste was most worried about. "The hell?"

Screeches that drifted down suggested they'd opened the rat room, where five critters currently remained.

"Are they working to cure the plague? God, even with all the herbs hung it stinks in here."

"Perfect the plague maybe. We picked the wolf up first in an alley, didn't we?"

The replied voice had a shudder. "Dirty little bastards. They'll want to know about this downtown, I'm sure."

"Yeah."

They finished in there and then came the groan of feet on the stairs down to the basement. Neither Celeste nor Samson had breath to hold.

"Lookit this. A room with a small bed, single indent." Wood groaned. "I smell, what is that, a deer? It's barely there. Female's clothes, few nice things. Is this the wolf's partner's room?"

"Maybe she's a secretary. Hang on, there's another room across."

Footfalls approached and faded into Samson's room. "Another one, clothes folded in here look like a cub's." That cop had a loud-working sniffer. "Faint, but I'm thinking goat."

"The wolf they took downtown keeps…two veggies in his basement?"

"Tenants he doesn't want house guests to see? Neighbors won't like it? If the doe works for him then maybe she gets her pay skimmed for rent." The other cop's pause bore the tenor of a shrug. "Or maybe he's a pervert. I mean, even by wolf standards the guy's scent is pretty rank. Probably gets into all kinds of ungodly interspecies strange."

The other chuckled. "Looks too tidy down here for that kinda business."

"Probably has them clean up. Smells carry right? I mean look at this," Something shifted in Samson's room. "This is a Lucille Bogan record? "Shave 'Em Dry", in a kid's room? They let him listen to this?"

Samson shifted uncomfortably and Celeste kept her groan inward. Samson had lied to her and Crawford about the kind of "special-order" blues he'd asked Crawford to pick up on a run in the city. When they'd heard it, the snicker and wink Crawford had gotten from the record store clerk now made uncomfortable sense.

"Noah, drown it. Nobody's here. If you're right, damn cur should keep that sick bunk back in the coastal cities where it belongs."

Samson's things were quickly rifled through and Celeste realized that Samson had crept from his shadow. His eyes had black-pooled and his fangs were at full sprout.

Feet scuffed near the door and Celeste hastily moved from her shadow to the one behind Samson, pulling him bodily into cover. "Don't," she whispered in his ear as the two cops noisily shuffled out, shined a flashlight into the dank cellar space that illuminated all but their deep recesses.

"Empty cellar. Boring host," one cop muttered and the other chuckled again.

They ascended the stairs and Celeste and Samson slipped free.

"They're going through all our things," Samson muttered worriedly. "They'll know."

She knew what he meant and sighed. "There are no clues in this house to what we are."

"Don't you have records in your office—"

"Nothing pertaining to us, Samson. I'm careful and so is Crawford."

"If they find us, will we have to kill them?"

The question caught Celeste off guard, not because she hadn't pondered that exact question a handful of times over the past dozen years. Most often it was those they lived near who posed the greatest risk. Celeste, and to a lesser extent Crawford, had impressed upon Samson the most important lesson for their mutual kinds: a neighbor, no matter how friendly, is a stranger who can see too much.

It was the tone of Samson's voice when asking the question that chilled her, like he was weighing an undesirable chore.

Samson's ears were forward, attentive for the answer.

"No, Samson. These cops go missing and we'll be the center of something larger, you know that."

"If they discover us, they'll want us to come up. They may want us to go outside."

Celeste shook her head, holding his gaze with her own as footfalls moved above. "We can't let them discover us. It's that simple."

Even returned to an adolescent's frame, a cold pragmatist met Celeste's gaze. "Okay."

Drawers were opened over their heads and casefiles were spread out by nosy cops and Celeste prepared herself for the worst.

***

"You know, usually when we get a name that circulates through inter-state jurisdictions it's the start of a really long mammalhunt that'll go weeks, even months before we hit jackpot. You, Mister Cain, are some kinda record."

After sweating in an interrogation room alone with two cigarettes, a jerky slice, and a burned cup of coffee, Crawford found himself under the direct scrutiny of no less than three brass-hard carnivores with dissecting eyes. The bloodhound—every police force had at least one—leaned against the door with his blue coat unbuttoned and clutching a stovepipe hat. He looked old enough to be Civil War surplus.

Across the wooden table and perched on one chair, a red fox in dress shirt and a tie so paisley it apologized for itself smoked a fat Camel and stared him down. The companion interrogator chair sat empty, the brown weasel in tan suit and spectacles opting to shed his nervous energy standing. He wore a trench coat despite the heat pounding down from the light above and had no badge in sight. He could have been a detective, but Crawford found his air more overbearing than he'd expect.

Crawford swallowed. It was late in the day, but he had no idea how late, and the moon, while out of sight, still stoked the fire inside. "So," he croaked. "What do I win?"

"Time to reflect," the weasel took over from the fox. So far, the fox and the weasel were doing all the talking. The hound on the door was just a hard glare promising consequences were close by.

"Here's the skinny. You gave your details at the scene of a double murder last night whose investigating officer found your name in state-wide search bulletins wired in that very morning when he went to type up his report. Since I'm on that case, it got back to me."

Crawford studied the weasel. "You're not based in Scranton I take it?"

"We're from all the way up your ass if you don't tell us what a lot of important people want to know," the fox growled.

"I'm with the Federal Bureau of Investigation," the weasel answered levelly. "And I just got off a three-hour drive from the Catskills in New York. Can you guess why?"

"Good fishing?" Crawford guessed with a shrug. Acting casual at this point almost hurt but he felt three noses sifting for fear, agitation, blood.

The weasel smiled. "For my type of catch, you can assume so."

"Well, if this is about that alley last night, I didn't kill anyone," Crawford muttered. He wondered if asking for a phone call and getting Charlie on the line was a good idea and figured it wasn't. "So, what happened in the next state over that I'm supposed to know about?"

The fox and the weasel traded looks and the weasel shook his head. The fox burned down his Camel. The bloodhound was still a gargoyle at the door.

"I had friends back in Washington look into your history, which you might be surprised to know was already being looked into before you earned my interest. You've got a file it turns out. You were a Prohibition Agent with the Revenue Bureau until the summer of twenty-three when you abruptly left Chicago during the most violent month of the whole war against Al Capone."

The fox shook his head. "Al Capone wasn't boss yet in twenty-three. It was his mentor, Johnny what's-his-name."

"Of course," the weasel smiled. "A lot happened during what the newspapers called the Summer of Blood. Several officers killed in the line of duty, one torn to pieces in the most violent feral attack in an American city in decades. A speakeasy burned down where ample evidence was recovered of torture and cannibalism, an Alderman assassinated, and in the middle of all that…was you."

Crawford felt his heart speed up and took a deep breath. "Dozens of officers were in the mix that summer and I had my own problems."

"We know," the weasel nodded and light played on the round spectacles he wore. "All sorts of theories have swirled campfires and Legion Halls for years about that summer. Some say they saw the dead shuffling the streets at night, others say witches were seen worshipping the devil by moonlight by the bay."

"Witches?" The fox snickered and tugged his tie. "I went to Chicago to see the Phillies beat the Sox. Don't rightly recall any broomstick commuters or gingerbread houses in the North End."

The weasel shook his head. "The government actually had the city's water tested the next year to see if something was driving mammals crazy, but nothing came of that. I reached out to a few more reliable sources in higher positions. I spoke to your former boss on the old Prohibition Bureau over the phone during a lunch stop. Turns out he met you the day before yesterday in Allentown and you were accessing a safety deposit box while the place was getting robbed of another one. Interesting coincidence that helped match your whereabouts before you gave us more definitive clues in that alley last night. It's almost like you wanted us to find you."

"I didn't steal anything from any bank," Crawford growled. "I still don't know why I'm here other than having really bad luck at stumbling across other people's messes."

"Hackles down." The fox's expression hoped Crawford wouldn't drop them and provide an excuse.

Crawford stewed in his agony. The day was getting long and his time was running out and he still didn't know what he had to talk his way out of.

"Let's review. You killed a suspect fleeing a speak in twenty-three, had a dereliction charge, and then you full-on ran away when the team needed you most."

Did the weasel already know that his partner was Charlie Rothscub, who worked out of the same Bureau this weasel did? He might even be this weasel's boss, or the weasel his. As long as Crawford kept his mouth shut and didn't name-check Charlie he could pretend he was an old forgotten co-worker.

"Detective Latimer." The weasel looked the fox's way.

The fox swiveled an ear to the weasel without taking eyes off Crawford. He was haloed in tobacco smoke. "Agent Tomlinson?"

"I'd like a few minutes alone with Mister Cain if that's alright with you."

The fox and the hound at the door traded looks. The fox sighed and shrugged. "Alright, it's your show, Agent Tomlinson."

The door opened on slightly cooler air from a distant scent of stale coffee and the traces of city miasma, the faintest hints of freedom. Crawford gripped his chair as the cops slipped out and the door closed freedom away.

Agent Tomlinson took the seat the fox hadn't sat in and wrinkled his nose. "So, what did you do in Chicago? Seeing as you're suspected in a murder according to a source who has now, themselves, shuffled off."

"I didn't kill anybody in any alley!"

"Not the cats, nor any of the more colorful exits in twenty-three though many are still looking into that all these years later. Where were you on the night of June second of that year?"

Crawford itched and it was torture to sit still. He couldn't think straight. "Packing to leave Chicago."

The weasel folded claws on the table and smiled. "The now-deceased Christof Von Haften believed you were killing his late wife Evelyn Von Haften according to records left with his associates."

The name rang a bell he could barely hear and Crawford didn't give a damn. The crawling within him wanted out. "Von Have-'em? Is that a German actress or something?"

"She moved to Chicago on business in the early summer, disappeared a week later."

"Never met her."

"How about an associate of hers. She was staying at the residence of a steel magnate, Donovan Calvert."

Crawford took a deep breath, trying to look impatient rather than pained. Or scared. "Oh yeah, right, goddamn rabbit Rockefeller."

"He disappeared on the very same night."

Crawford had to make sure he gave this Fed nothing. "Good for him. Getting out of that damn city was certainly the best decision I ever made. Maybe he took the lion with him." His clothes were starting to itch and he could peel them all away in moments. The thin walls would be marzipan under his claws.

The weasel wasn't smiling any longer. "Who told you Von Haften was a lion?"

***

The door opened above and claws scuffed as the police departed. An engine started. Gravel was disturbed as a car chittered away.

"Stay here and don't move," Celeste said. "It's later in the day and the light will be on the west side of the house. If they didn't open the shutters, I'll be fine."

Samson didn't say anything, listening for any other sound at all. He kept his head about him. "They didn't have a key to lock the door,"

Which meant if a cop was still outside... "Good thinking. I'll be careful."

Celeste pondered her next move. If Crawford was held in a police station in the city and the sun went down, the change might be unavoidable, moon in sight or not.

They couldn't let that happen. Not there.

At the landing, Celeste pushed the door outward. They'd deliberately re-hinged it not only to open outward but to block the closest light source, which would be from the eastside sitting saloon where the Japy Frères ticked away on the salon mantle. Light was meager and indirect, the shutters only parted slightly by the roving claws of Scranton's finest. Past the scratching and hisses of the rat room, the office where Celeste and Crawford worked was still dark. The shutters in there had a latch to ensure they never parted unintentionally. She crept past it towards the kitchen and glanced at the desk to see the files there had more or less been closed as they were, two cases still on top.

The kitchen itself had an overhanging porch and a forward-facing bay window with direct sun blocked by the foliage of the trees up their drive: both desired features when Crawford had scouted the place. Outside the indirect light ached to look at but Crawford's worn Chevy stood alone, casting a longer eastward shadow. Night was just a few hours away.

She heard a noise then and peered out.

Round the last bend up their drive a sleek roadster with white-walled tires approached, definitely not a police vehicle. Celeste crept back into the office as the car came to a stop, the door opening and closing.

Claws crossed her porch. There was a knock followed by the creaking open of her front door and the meager light grew.

Idiot cops who left hadn't clicked it shut, Celeste realized with an inward curse. Whoever stood at her front door now had an unobstructed view down the main hall to the open basement door. "Hello?" The voice was feminine, species indeterminate.

Celeste was trapped in the office and ducked behind the desk, mind working furiously.

There was a step into her home. "Mister Cain? Ms. Mauve?"

Mauve was the name that Celeste went by on their business cards, position given as secretary for the more conservative clients they'd have to earn cheques from. If this was a prospective client…

"Mister Cain, I represent Martha Wainright, a current client of yours."

Celeste's glance went to the folder on the office desk where a sepia cat's ears poked out, photos from the shadows outside a seedy motel ten miles out of town. The ears belonged to the skulking shape of Bruce Wainright, Martha's amorously adventurous husband.

Perfect timing.

Another step. Celeste could make out scents now, a heap of floral perfume burying the slight rankness of some earthy discharge. Not a cat in her foyer.

Celeste would have to wrap this up fast. "I'm in the office past the kitchen," she called out clearly enough that Samson would hear. "I didn't get your name."

A skunk in a tweed suit with thin lapels over a high-collared shirt rounded the corner. "Samantha Perival. I'm an attorney for one of your clients, a Martha Wainright."

Celeste had seated herself behind the desk, Crawford's spare coat round her shoulders to hide that she was still wearing her day-sleep clothes. "Of course, please come in," Celeste beckoned to the opposing chair. "Mister Cain is out on an errand and indisposed."

The skunk's raised tail reminded Celeste of Sandy's: lush, yet ivory on black, a piano key in photo negative. She regarded Celeste with blue-grey eyes that were insistent, assessing as she stood in the doorway. Celeste felt something palpable above her immediate anxiety. For Crawford's sake she had to move this along quickly.

"I don't recall Martha having legal representation for this case."

Hands folded. "Until your most recent report, it sadly wasn't needed." The skunk nodded at the folder. "May I?" Without waiting, she took a few steps forward, slid the folder her way, opened it and started going through Celeste's pictures as she stepped back, stopping only to reach into her suit vest and feel around for a moment before extracting spectacles.

Inexplicably, the anxiety Celeste felt became a pronounced discomfort that flashed into an instance of physical pain that receded just as quickly.

Ms. Perival stood at the door and glanced at the pictures. "I was brought on when Mrs.—well, soon to be Miss Wainright decided to go ahead with divorce proceedings."

Celeste focused as the sudden discomfort resolved itself into recent memory and forced herself to think. Crawford hadn't shown the spurned wife the pictures yet, and she'd haggled for twenty minutes about the daily fifteen dollars and expenses that Wainright wanted to argue down to ten. She wouldn't spring for any lawyer. Not this soon.

"Shouldn't she see the photos first?" Celeste asked carefully, her voice nearly catching. "After she pays for them?" The office telephone was on the table by the shuttered windows and Celeste noticed a flinty glance over the reading spectacles as the skunk ignored the photos she held.

"I really ought to give her a call," Celeste suggested.

"Not necessary," the skunk said, smiling thinly. "I spoke with my client a few hours ago and she's ready to proceed. I can pay you the final day's retainer right now." Ms. Perival's hand went back into her vest and stayed there. Her tail twitched behind her.

Celeste's ears cocked as the discomfort rolled into nausea. "This was of course in person, at her home, correct? Mrs. Wainright never liked conducting business over the phone."

"But of course," Ms. Perival said. That smile widened on the lawyer's muzzle again. "Does Mr. Cain prefer cash or check?"

Celeste came to her feet and their eyes locked. Wainright never met Crawford by daylight. Her husband was always there sleeping off his last night's "shift work", and the wolf had been strictly warned from visiting.

Celeste swallowed in living fashion. "Has she confronted Victor, her husband?"

"She did indeed." The skunk's hand froze and the smile vanished. "But of course, his name isn't Victor, is it?" The blade the skunk drew from her jacket was silvery, seven inches long, and the mere sight of it brought Celeste a fresh flash of pain.

The skunk bared her teeth. "And you won't be cashing any checks in Hell."

Chapter 11

...Care of Lost Equity

Crawford wanted to pant buckets and knew the weasel Fed could see it. He also wanted to let the shift happen, swing the slinky bastard like a marching baton and see how solid the walls were.

"I knew..."

The weasel adjusted his glasses over dispassionate eyes. "Yes?"

"I knew the rabbit was in it with a lion. I saw her on his arm once." He couldn't even imagine the rabbit having a lion twice his size on his arm. Calvert's ego wouldn't have accepted that. But Crawford had to sell it.

"But you didn't know who she was."

Had the weasel mentioned she was in the papers? His claws were digging into the table so Crawford folded them in his lap. If he broke anything in here then he'd have to break everything in here. He could smell the angry carnivore musk stirring into the gun oil from who knew how many hip or underarm holsters.

"I could guess. Rabbit like him wouldn't date casually out of species. Had to be somebody important and I'd read or heard later that a society carnivore had gone missing. I don't recall where."

The weasel paced again and Crawford saw his hand dip into his suit jacket to grip what was likely the butt of his gun, eyes locked with Crawford's the whole time. Peacock-strutting always pissed him off.

The weasel sneered. "Would you like a cigarette, Cain? You don't look well."

No sense trying to look the stoic. "I don't feel well. I found dead bodies in an alley last night and it's brought back a lot of memories from the war and I'm not answering any other questions tonight. I've decided. If you aren't going to charge me with anything..."

"The police here don't have to let you go. Under suspicion we can keep you overnight and we have lots of potential charges on tap." The weasel laughed at Crawford's expression. "Oh, come on, Cain. You were a Prohibition agent. How many people who you thought held out on a stash or worked for the Outfit were fined or jailed for the mere suspicion of an Eighteenth Amendment violation while you and Chicago's pack figured out what else you could stick in their fur? I've got so much more to work you over with and endless federal tools to do it with."

"Lawyer. Now."

"A moment." The Fed stepped out and shut the door. Crawford's ears perked as his strained but efficient hearing caught the fox whispering about sweating him out based on what they found at the house. The weasel thought about this, asked where the most secluded phone was before stepping away.

The door opened again and it was the fox this time. "Gonna level with you, wolf. Scranton PD weren't at your house for very long, but wind is wind and there was doe and goat on it. Where are they?"

A nightmare was coming true. Crawford kept his hands low as the sting came from claw tips that were starting to distend. "You can't search my home."

"Probable cause. A suspect in at least one murder, well…"

Crawford's jaws ached and his limbs were starting to feel like liquid fire and his claws were already piercing the chair's wooden arms from underneath. The growl in his voice belonged to a vengeful demon as fury became a furnace. "You soulless bastard, you're every jackbooted thug that I used to work with, seeking someone to grind in the cogs for sadism's sake! I've done nothing! So let me call a lawyer or let me go!" The room was getting smaller and the fox needed to get out of it or become red paint.

The vulpine looked spoiling for a fight but kept the demeanor of a carnivore whose prey was cornered and showing hackles to look big. "Fine," he sneered. "It's getting late though, so you won't be making any calls tonight."

The window of the interrogation room was hammered on and the old hound leaned in. "You need to take this call," he said with a quick cutting glance to Crawford. The fox was out and the door closed once more, leaving Crawford in a wooden box that shrank by the second.

***

The blade-wielding skunk's eyes promised violence and Celeste didn't bother with questions.

She put her back against the wall of the small office and both hooves kicked. Full strength delivered, the desk left the parquet floor and slammed itself and its crowning folders against the opposing bookshelves, the skunk deftly sidestepping before lunging.

The sword nicked Celeste's forearm with a cattle-brand kiss and she shrieked, ducking low before hurtling herself into the hallway. The skunk backswept, missing Celeste again but striking the door jamb to the office and chipping wood away. "*Moirire, Satanae servus!*"

Celeste had but an instant to pick an escape route, upstairs or down. Either was a dead end, but the basement was at least free from stabs of late-day sunlight that the police may have already wrought by drawing curtains during their search. So, she hurled herself downward towards the basement, realizing at once that Samson was still in the shadows in the cellar. She pushed through her own door and hurried in to find a proper weapon of some sort. She was far stronger than the skunk, even wounded, but the skunk was obviously trained for that.

If she could get the skunk to follow her in, Samson could slip away, get higher and hidden. She might finish Celeste off but leave him.

Celeste didn't intend to be finished off. In her room she grabbed her own garb from yesterday, spun fabric round the arm not burning from the sword's contact. Arm wrapped, Celeste broke her body-length mirror and collected a shard before positioning herself behind the door, all in a few instants.

No sound came, not from the skunk pretending to be a lawyer nor the goat kid down here with her. Moments ticked by in torturous silence.

"Overconfident, arrogant Nosfurratu," Samantha called down from above. "Do you actually think I'm going to follow you down into your vermin warren in the dark? Where you have any number of traps waiting?" The skunk laughed pitilessly. "I've tracked your kind for years, bloodsucker, sent no less than four pairs of fangs home from these shores. Want to know what never tarnishes them?"

Celeste forced herself into the preternatural calm that only the dead could manage. She'd not be drawn out.

There was the snap of something small and a careful intake of breath. "Flames." The voice receded, footfalls softly fading. The next sound Celeste heard came from the kitchen where springs groaned at the dropping of the oven door.

"Looks like your pet dog isn't home," the skunk taunted. "I suppose if this house burns down, I should wait for him to arrive. You don't want to die alone."

Scents caught up with the snaps and crackles of things not intended to burn, spreading beyond the oven's shell. There was a five-yard upward charge to where the Martyre toiled and blades of daylight spread about everywhere past the top step. She'd torn every drapery free.

The cold calculus of risk had guided Celeste since the first hoof on America's shores. Smoke reached her nose, the kitchen curtains were burning and the stink was strangely calming, as though she'd smelled it before. Celeste centered herself and pushed away any urge to sentiment or sorrow as odds of survival slimmed to zero. She'd lived a long life after mortality's end.

She allowed herself a moment to wonder what Sandy would do when she learned what happened, then put her mind firmly to Samson.

He still had a chance.

"You know what to do if the house burns," she said, too low for the skunk above to hear. "Get through your window, use the tarp to escape. Ignore what you hear."

Celeste glanced into the mirror shard and grinned a cryptic French grin. She closed her eyes and made herself say the rest. "This was prepared for. Crawford needs you as you need him regardless of how many years his curse grants him. Never forget that."

Celeste took the stairs two at a time and hurled herself through beams of wicked sunlight at the skunk who stood poised with sword raised. Pain flayed Celeste under her thin house dress.

Having expected to see the doe dodge the rays rather than hurtle through, the skunk was caught off guard. Her downswing was a half second late, clipping the back of Celeste's shoulder blade rather than sinking though her collarbone as intended. Their bodies collided, twisting as they lost balance and Celeste rolled with her into the growing inferno of the kitchen where flames were already climbing the cabinets to lick along the ceiling. They grappled as they struck the table's legs, its chairs already toppled and separated.

The heat was uncomfortable, but not the speared agony carried through sunlight. Celeste pressed her best advantage as she found herself nearly under the table. Smoke was building fast.

Only one of them needed to breathe.

The skunk switched the blade in her hand and leapt to her feet. Celeste grabbed one table leg with a free hand while her hoof pressed the other. Quick opposing jerks snapped two legs away, taking support from one side of the table entirely. Celeste rolled underneath as the table toppled between skunk and doe. The reliquary blade sunk through to the hilt with a splintering thrust, a mere inch from Celeste's chest. She kicked out, pushing the table over completely with the blade hilted in it and Celeste rose with one broken table leg in her hand. The stove to her right was a tower of fire, stinking of burned grease and drape fabric. Celeste dipped the lacquered leg into it and brought it back up burning. To Celeste's back was the window to the outside.

The skunk kicked once, twice. The table was a sturdy piece of furniture Crawford bought near Niagara Falls six years ago, but the reliquary blade had been expertly sharpened and the table was discarded in two pieces. Flames licked up walls and cabinets, obscuring the top half of the room with smoke and Celeste heard a dull roar from somewhere she couldn't identify, perhaps water boiling in the pipes. The only wall not on fire was behind her, where an open window held the glare of light on the shadow-side of the house. Pain awaited on all sides and her body was already in agony, but Celeste crouched at the ready, bearing the jagged, flaming table leg as the skunk adjusted her stance.

"Nowhere to go, monster," the Martyre shouted and coughed, crouching low under smoke that made her eyes water. "Hold still and I'll end the misery for both of us."

Celeste felt the heat accumulate. "Come and kill me."

The skunk smiled, sniffing and squinting against the smoke. Behind her, through one of the rays of light, a shape moved, ghostlike, covered head to toe in a dark impenetrable tarp.

Something sailed in from the living room and the skunk was struck on the back of the head. She flopped forward as broken glass, gears, and other assorted clock parts danced throughout the kitchen.

Celeste didn't hesitate, swinging the improvised torch downward to the skunk's sword-arm, breaking it.

The skunk dropped her weapon with a scream and Celeste swung again, shattering her other arm near the shoulder. The ceiling above them both was fully engulfed, flames curling black on the stucco everywhere it slid. Celeste reached down through her own pain and fury and hoisted the skunk up by her armpits as she thrashed.

One strong heave would put her headfirst into the stove that was the heart of the conflagration, but Celeste resisted the urge.

She hurled the skunk in the opposite direction instead, where a collision with the wall would end the Martyre's life in an instant.

But that wall had been weakened by the spreading flame. The skunk arsonist's head, shoulders, and torso went right through it instead.

She kicked her legs feebly as Celeste looked on, blankly.

The tarped shape waddled its way quickly and muttered something indecipherable under the hiss and snap of burning plaster and wood.

"What?"

Samson took a tentative hoof over clock parts and spoke louder from under the tarp. "Why'd you shove that skunk into the rat room?"

All at once the skunk's legs began kicking as she thrashed free of the hole in the wall, screaming with no less than two rat's jaws grasping nose and cheek. The other critters skittered past through the makeshift escape. Blood spackled as the skunk leapt and span, furious ferals swinging like tassels. She made a blind left turn at the smoke-choked hall, unable to see the stairway into darkness where she'd taunted Celeste mere minutes ago until she was tumbling noisily down it.

"We need to get out of here!" Celeste slipped under the tarp that had been stowed under dry wrap outside of Samson's basement window, much as one lay outside hers. He'd known the plan.

And had followed at least part of it.

The hall was now full of smoke as the flames carried. The window of the kitchen on the eastern shadow-side of the house was their only means of egress. Celeste took one half of the table the skunk had cleaved and

171

heaved it, breaking glass. "Crawford's car is outside! We'll need to head south with the shades drawn. It's going to hurt, Samson, I'm sorry."

"Right," Samson replied, worried but resolved.

They shared the tarp as flames dipped the ceiling, their home and recent refuge sagging under fire's onslaught and charged at the broken window.

***

Well, shit.

Crawford could feel the distant pull of the moon and knew that if he saw a sliver of it out there all control would be lost immediately.

As it was, he was sure he had minutes at best.

He struggled to remember how he'd entered here. Big lobby, tight hallway with registration desk. Secondary waiting area, short hallway, holding cells, and drunk tank. Assuming he wasn't shot down, could he make his way out to Scranton's streets?

The fox left and Crawford took labored cement-lung breaths, rising to his feet as his ribs started to throbbingly distend. His mind sought to escape the here and now and his imagination took him on the worst possible trip: officers combing his farmhouse, noses sniffing as they rooted through his found family's things, finding Celeste and Samson in daytime repose, defenseless, helpless.

His teeth became fangs and his claws become scimitars as he felt the smallness of the wood and glass cage around him, growling furiously.

This was it. His clothes became a shackle to discard and his prison a thing to bite.

All at once the lights went out.

Cast in darkness, clothes rent and jaws flexed and limbs elongated to a loping span. Crawford heard sounds of police calling in confusion, then fading to nonsense, prey-hoots, and gasps.

What it meant didn't matter. Leaving mattered very much.

The clear barrier to outside the confined space was a ghost in his memory and Crawford attacked it with a leap.

It shattered and cut and he rolled with a roar that filled the cavern about him. Confused sounds became fearful hoots in bellows that he could still understand as words. "Someone pulled a fuse! Prisoner's loose!"

The meaning wasn't certain, but the instinct it fueled was clear. Run! Flee!

Crawford shook off the fabric that stiffened his limbs and hurtled past a chamber of sounds, mostly screams of other prey and predators that were startled with nowhere to run. He collided with one, smelling of vulpine, shoving it against an unseen obstruction that cracked with contact.

A loud snap of fire lit the space for an instant, revealing claws covering cowering faces in tableau against walls. Dust grit struck his fur.

A draft of air, a whisper of sound gave him direction and he leapt a barrier that scattered detritus and pulped leaves. He rolled to a stop as something swept the air above him, connecting with an obstruction just above his head with a wooden crunch.

He dashed towards escape from the dark tunnel of stinks and screams. Hunger bit as always but there was no time.

Another shout, another volcanic snap. A barking howl exhibited pain as two creatures in here with him collided in the darkness.

There, more wind, and scents. That shaped sound again, noises that made sense to another mind. "Flashlight, goddammit!"

There was fumbling and a beam of light behind him missed his flank as he darted round to cooler air and the distant hush of oil-stinking beasts, a smatter of nocturnal whispers, and on the periphery of it all, faint cicada song.

He headed straight for it, slamming through smooth bark and rank iron into the deep amber of dusk and pulling a shout from a mammal just outside. The ember of dropped fire under a surprised feline face rushed by, indistinct in the dark, and he crossed the gulf of dead mounds of iron to hit the soothing earthy pine scent of clustered trees ahead.

He had an instinct for safety, a direction, a mingling of scents that called him to den. But he was hungry now. He followed the slivered sun, angling to flank it, then south as it faded. He rooted out a feral thing that screamed as it died and rolled in what remained after he'd had his fill.

Light had faded completely now, and as he followed the trails and spoors of paths worn by other creatures travelling parallel to him, he came upon what could only be described as a second sun on the horizon, neither rising nor waning.

He approached slowly, passing other mammal's dens at the limits of their expansive borders, smelling the spoor of burnt meat, the decay of vegetation, stinks of oil and vulcanism. Every so often he'd creep into the shift of the wind and he'd smell the carrying scent of wood burning: rank, crisp, and undefinably unclean.

All in a familiar distant place, the place where he denned.

An animal call wound past at a distance, sustained and mournful, following the carved paths he avoided in the direction of his den. He felt a melancholy that was inexplicable as something barely recognizable was understood to be gone. As the calls accumulated to the pyre of distant, consuming light, he threw back his head among the thicket of tangled nature and howled in sorrow.

Ferals in the distant foothills, far and wide, teeming or alone, heard and picked up the cry. All the world carried a blanket of calls around the fiery star fallen among them. The wolf that had a name that knew not what it lost, thought of a doe and a goat and cried dirges of confusion.

Not prey, they were not prey. Their familiar if distorted scents lay dormant and he snuffled as he crept closer, sensing proximity of other creatures around the pyre of his den. Mammals with tobacco stink and labor sweat and many bearing thick rigid tendrils twisting rain in ropes down on his former habitat.

He was confused even as fury took purchase and he flexed his limbs. There were only fifty hard lopes to what he'd known as his sanctuary for so long, surrounded by so many squat barking creatures. He'd scatter them like leaves.

A sound drew his attention. To his right, a doe crouching low met his darted gaze and showed flat teeth in challenge before darting back.

Doe scent! Familiar!

He loped after around trees, over cropping rock and soil, far from the blaze of the place that no longer smelled of all he knew. He came to where an open pit of vegetation bore the gritty oil stink of something familiar and large and squat. Within it an ungulate regarded him with sad eyes that locked with his.

Prey-mate from prey-pack. The contrary impressions battled quickly and the wolf snuffled as he approached the black squat shelter and forgot in that moment the doe that he had given chase.

Vegetation was disturbed to his right.

He cocked his head and roved his eyes to a patch of dark that grew a shape fast as any wind. White numbness exploded in his jaw, his eyes rolled to the star-break between the boughs above and he fell, the dark taking confusion away with all else.

He didn't dream at first, not as a feral, not as a civilized wolf. A blanket of nothing swaddled him tight. Then sensations without shape crept through dormant awareness. The blue of a sky holding the perfect cool sphere of a moon that spoke to him in soothing assurances, glinting down upon shoulders that rolled as they loped, through places dark and light, muddy and dry, loud and busy with clangs of confusion. Yet under all of it was the whisper of a voice he'd long forgotten belonging to a scent he'd long lost.

"Why did you do it?" croaked a wolf in shuddering motion, cool leather at his bare back and buttocks.

A firm hand took his shoulder and steadied him from sliding downward. "He's waking up." The voice was young and pained.

"Crawford." The other voice was higher but more affected, weary. "Stay down, don't sit up. We're halfway there."

There?

He had a voice but only wanted to growl.

"How are his arms and legs? Still shrinking?"

"Yeah," the younger voice, he smelled ungulate, wasn't quite relieved. "He's back."

"We need a telephone."

Crawford knew what a telephone was. He shuddered as the vehicle he was in hit a bump. Something rattled next to him. Crawford's meaty fumbling hands lifted something cool and yet sharp edged that he raised and could barely make out in the dark of a road at night. It was flat, had stamped numbers on it and was bent in his hands.

"Celeste had to take the number plate off your car. They'll be looking for that when they finish putting out the fire. She also had to knock you out in the forest when you came up on us—"

"Fire?" He could say words. "What fire?"

Light filled the back seat as the car came to a stop. "No, thank you. I can fill the car up," Celeste told somebody.

"Have it as you have it," was the desultory reply from a stranger as gravel kicked away.

"Samson, see if there's any more clothes to buy in there."

"Keep down." Samson was the goat's name. Crawford was coming back to himself. He stayed low, staring at what he now knew to be his own Chevrolet's floorboards as the goat kid vaulted over and somewhere close a hinge complained over a small ringing bell.

Time passed while Celeste stopped pumping and muttered something to whoever took her money. They in turn talked to the goat kid who came out and asked about cost.

"I ain't no haberdasher root-boy. What you see's what you get," somebody grumbled.

Soon enough, the doe and goat kid had resumed their seats, chugged the car to life, and they were off. "Can I get up now?" Crawford finally had the strength to ask.

"We're twenty miles from the second home in Harrisburg," Celeste called back. "I would think it best you not be seen by any passing cars, even this late at night."

Their backup home in Harrisburg was a dump they'd put money on in the last four years, emergency shelter to be actually resided in only if forced to flee Scranton. He puzzled things together slowly as impressions formed from the moment the lights had gone out in the station.

"Cops all over our place no doubt."

"Maybe sifting through what's left. We were forced to hide until the sun was down so we can't be sure."

"What's left?" Crawford couldn't help but raise his ears and nose to collect the night air flowing in from outside the car. "What happened? And how'd you get to town so fast to bust me out? Cutting power to places is getting to be old hat, I suspect." He was trying to be wry but didn't feel it.

There was silence for a long few moments, only the grind of the engine. "Bust you out?" Celeste was confused. "We were trapped near the house after nearly being killed and seeing it lit aflame. We don't know how but the Martyres of the Black Well found us."

Crawford couldn't absorb all that in his state. Flames? The Martyres? The concepts themselves felt like abstractions under the weight of exhaustion. Foremost on his own mind was the question he needed answered most even if neither doe nor goat had any idea.

"Well...if you didn't kill the power in the station, then who the hell did?"

Chapter 12

Connections

Night fell in Atlantic City at just before seven, days lengthening into autumn. Donovan Calvert made his escape, flush with fresh blood's fire and weighing next moves.

He'd see his interlocutor from the Catskills of course, his only way forward now that he'd gained the trinket of information from Sandy and settled a score. Donovan had been turned against his will, and Sandy had reverted under circumstances that Donovan could only imagine. But Bruno, well, he'd simply betrayed Donovan for whatever graces Sandy plied and that was unforgivable. The muskrat had tasted of pipe smoke, and all too briefly Donovan wanted a smoke too. But that want fled and Donovan was left with nothing but resentment again.

The last of his cash was running low and he needed speed to keep his timetable, so he returned to Von Haften's as yet unmolested car, despite his initial intention to ditch it. Pedal to the floor hurried it most of the way to New York, the engine protesting the entire way and the honks of perturbed nocturnal motorists fading quickly. He abandoned the car just after the north side of the Passaic River bridge in Newark on a downslope with the car's brake disengaged. Watching Christof's last expensive possession slip with a splash into the murk was satisfying, but it was fast approaching ten p.m. and he had to hurry. He called a taxi from an empty diner, minding that he had a dot of blood on his worn lapel, and tipped the cabbie leopard another three dollars over the ten if he'd step on it to Penn Station in Manhattan.

A mix of emotions washed over him as he entered Manhattan, where his first home and office had been established before decamping to Chicago to open his mill and build his mansion. The city had grown taller in twenty-odd years, the deep night obscuring such recent titanic additions to the skyline as the Chrysler Building and the Empire State. Had Donovan maintained his empire, he'd have finagled contracts to feed steel to those hungry marvels.

And if his steel was in Manhattan in any significant concentration, he'd be suffering for that.

It occurred to him as he disembarked, completely devoid of luggage, that his acquired steel could have been used in projects throughout the region. Only the age of the station before him, finished a few years before his emigration to America, ensured no surprises here.

Unless there had been major repairs. No time to tread lightly.

He entered the vast vaulted hall, approached the ticket desk where a marten waited patiently under cushioned echoes from a dozen meters above. "Toronto, Ontario." Donovan said. "Soon as possible."

"Of course, sir," the marten said with more affected enthusiasm than was due this hour. The distant grumble of a fox waiting impatiently for some connection could be heard clearly.

The attendant's smile didn't waver. "Would you like a sleeper cabin on one of our Pullmans?"

"Yes."

"Bed berth or stateroom?"

It hurt to have to think about that. "Stateroom. I want total isolation for the trip. I'm too light a sleeper."

"Very good, sir. We do have a direct route that leaves after nine in the morning."

Donovan's ears went back as he counted the dark windows above him, blank wide eyes that would rain daylight upon every square inch of this place by eight a.m. "That won't do." He closed his eyes as panic started to encroach. "I need to be in Toronto before daybreak if possible."

"I highly doubt that's achievable, sir. A moment if you would." Maps and timetables were unfurled, scrutinized, discarded, replaced. Hope bled out of the space between them as time passed.

"I have a partial solution for you, sir," the marten said brightly. "We have an express train leaving for Albany in just over thirty minutes. That will arrive by approximately seven in the morning. At that point, a business sleeper Pullman carriage on the New York Central Line will have you in Hamilton by around noon. You can then switch to local fare to Toronto."

It didn't add up, he realized with dread. The fastest train on the New York Line couldn't have him where he was going before the sun rose. The vaulted halls of Penn Station crept a little closer. The marten's whiskers twitched as he waited.

"Is there a hotel with immediate access to the station in Albany? I have a condition that flares up and, well, I need frequent rest." Twelve years had taught him that fewer details led to fewer questions.

"As I recall there are no hotels immediately present."

"And how soon does the carriage for Hamilton leave?"

"Quite soon after arrival, sir. Your luggage will need to be portered over to the sleeper in 10 minutes by the schedule and you would have time for perhaps a cigarette. There are drinks and late-evening fare served on the train—"

"I'll take the ticket." It occurred to him that Hamilton, Ontario might not have an accommodation for him as the sun would most certainly be up. "Wait!"

The martin was scrounging for his ticket and inkpad stamp. He froze. "Yes, sir?"

With such a dangerous absence of knowledge in Canadian cities he should delay, figure out a way to do this more efficiently with shelter pin-pointed along the route.

"How frequent are trains from Hamilton to Toronto?"

"Very, sir. The east–west line is a major transit route."

Instinct made waiting a difficult prospect. The Martyres had found him and he was now without transportation in the hub of one of two cities in America where just about anybody might recognize him. Twelve years, not aged one day.

A train that could cover the distance he needed in the time he needed would not be built any time soon. His benefactor, whoever they were, would not wait forever.

"How soon does the express to Albany leave?"

An end to the marten's patience was deep in his eyes, glinting through. "Twenty-seven minutes."

"Sell me the tickets." Cash left, tickets came. Donovan boarded the train with its upright seats and somnambulant mammalian cargo, another half dozen souls. As the train began to pull away his reflection came back from the window against the ink of dark and rising city lights falling back. Once the city was gone the night of the country gave up nothing.

He often wondered how many like himself were out there now, navigating their fates with fear or predatory zeal. How many would know who he'd been before his pulse had stopped and what they would do to him if they did?

The refreshments cart attendant passed on when Donovan ignored him, pitching libations to a lanky canine, then a brown-furred rabbit whose seat faced his further down the car, her ears tipping left and right as his own were with the rhythmic clacking of the rails.

At the blood's apex Donovan wanted to celebrate existence, and at the lows of starvation he only wanted escape from pain. This moment, with veins neither flush nor famished, was when the ghosts of lost possibilities found him. He'd had a wife once, a childless marriage that failed due to differing wants. He'd cut her loose with a small fortune and a resolve to marry his ambitions first and foremost in America. The brown rabbit across from Donovan folded her slender legs, eyes never meeting his, blinking against exhaustion. With the blood still in his veins he watched her flank slide against the carriage seat's wooden rest and was bluntly aware that he wanted two things from her instead of just one.

When his current blood ran its full course within him, he'd want just the one.

So, he didn't approach, didn't even meet her glance when she nodded awake and looked up.

Self-pity reared itself once again at what Sandy had taken away. No nights by the fire watching winter's onset out frosted windows, sharing mulled wine, a look, a touch. Whoever was waiting in Canada had to understand what he was going through. There would be so many questions.

The New York Times Donovan had bought had nothing for him, going on about the exotic draw of non-carnivorous music, thousands of dollars found in a lost deposit box, and some incident in Ethiopia. His mind kept moving ahead on his timetable to the first debarkation in Albany. The tracks outside Union were well covered, and he could keep to the west side to avoid dawn's first peek as he hurried to his private cabin and drew the blinds shut. From there he'd have to secure telegraph dispatch to have the soonest train of the same sort to Toronto. And arrange for a place to reside until it arrived. He'd lock the door to his cabin and make them wait if he had to.

His thoughts were mired in what steps to take when something peculiar occurred to him. He'd never been to Albany that he could recall, yet he knew about the covered sheds that accommodated its trains. This was a common enough element in most stations wanting to protect passengers from the elements, but he distinctly knew there were three track-parallel porticoes, two of them freestanding.

How did he know that when he'd never seen the station with his own eyes?

Then he remembered. He'd seen the Albany Union station's renovation blueprints years ago, during his last year with a pulse.

Bruno's blood was waning in him following the exhilaration of racing Von Haften's stolen car and the scurry for passage to Canada. What little was left brought his dormant heart to beat uncomfortably quicker.

Albany's late-twenties update had been one of the contracts acquired by Calvert Steel Industries, three shed porticoes restored and reinforced. At least four of the stanchions on that track were reliquary steel. He'd not been on hand for installation, of course, so he had no idea which four pillars, but it didn't matter. He was heading into his own trap.

And he couldn't change course, couldn't abandon a train that wasn't stopping. He didn't even know where the hell it was. Countless small towns followed the Hudson River north to Albany. If he leapt out now he'd be nowhere, with no guarantee that he'd find shelter as the sun broke the horizon and sought him out.

Ten minutes between trains. Just enough time for a cigarette, the ticket agent had said. The conductor who shuffled by to confirm his fare saw his agitation. "Alright, sir?"

Why lie. "I could use a drink."

The cougar glanced back to the service compartment. "I sympathize." He swung his tail. "Sadly, we've no intoxicating libations on this train. Only coffee, tea, and a few seltzers we can provide syrup for if it strikes your mood."

By the time he reached Albany Donovan would have just enough blood left in his veins for the agony to start but not enough to feel the effects of any alcohol. "I'm in Hell."

The conductor's whiskers twitched. "No, sir, actually we're passing through Poughkeepsie."

"Leave me be."

Grumbling, the man did.

In a couple hours, he'd feel the sting, then the pain and nausea. He'd watched countless Nosfur captives go through it, Sandy included. How she'd delight in seeing him now.

***

Crawford sat up. He was naked, but in the back of the Chevrolet nobody else driving at night would see him waist down, even if he should be hiding. He folded his legs in Celeste and Samson's presence and tried to be casual as the car bounced along. The Chevy's beams cut the night ahead as they wound southwest toward Harrisburg. Two places to reside at all times. Tonight was the night it paid off.

"So how I got out is a mystery, huh?"

"What's important is, did you hurt anyone?" Celeste had her ears splayed back in worry and to catch the wolf's reply.

"I might have bumped a cop or two. But kill anybody, I don't think so."

Celeste muttered something French and disdainful.

To Crawford French often sounded disdainful. "Look, you know it isn't me when it happens, not the self that can recall things or make conscious decisions."

"That's everyone in their drunk tank. What I'm trying to get you to clarify, Crawford, is if anybody will be seeking you out as a confirmed murderer."

"I didn't kill anyone. Look at me. Not you, Samson."

"I'm not," Samson said disinterestedly, eyes ahead.

"I'm driving," Celeste sighed.

Crawford chuffed and smoothed the fur on his chest. "Even when the memories don't leave impressions, I know when I've…dined." He licked his lips. "I ate a critter out of town but I'm clean. Just have a headache."

"I apologized for that," Celeste said unapologetically. "If you'd howled again and drawn the attention of the fire brigade…"

"I'm not covered in blood so you know I've not killed anybody...our size. It's messier for me than for you."

"I've no doubt."

"And I don't burn houses down that have just about everything we own."

Celeste faced the road and Crawford could hear her teeth grind. "Just about, Crawford. Just about. The suitcase is still in the trunk with our emergency supplies so you don't have to hang about like a reprobate bohemian and can put some clothes on when we get where we're going. It isn't much, and I'd hoped that last gas station would have more."

"I'm sorry."

"Let's set tempers aside. The Martyres found us, possibly through our detective work or by following one of us home from either Boston, Ohio, or the bank in Allentown. We have to...*merde*."

Samson sat sideways on the passenger seat, arm slung over. The cabin was so cramped that his knees were brushing Celeste's hip. He glanced furtively between the doe driving and the wolf in back. "What?"

Celeste hissed, her fangs out. "The package I sent will be in the mailbox soon with the nails from the Ohio farm. The one Donovan's people used as a cache out West. The mail just might be the only part of the house not in ashes that they'll sift through."

"And the other nails are buried out back," Crawford winced.

Celeste's hands made leathery creaks as they squeezed the Chevy's wheel. "We have to get them. We can't go back but we'll have to get them." She rummaged through the door pocket. "Samson, there's a map on your side. Try to see how close to McAdoo we are using the next road marker. There's another gas station there and they had a telephone when last we passed, I need to make a call as soon as possible. We'll top up the tank again."

Twenty minutes or so later Samson passed up the suitcase in the trunk to Crawford who kept low as he slipped shirt and pants on. Samson worked the pump, nearly sloshing out some gasoline when he heard Celeste get agitated.

Crawford caught it too, and both of them waited while she finished the call and left the booth to return to the car. "We can't get Sandy's help." She kept her voice down with effort. The station attendant's eyes were down counting Celeste's coins behind the grimy general store window, even less interested in their affairs then the last station they'd visited a mere hour ago.

"What happened, Celeste?"

"Bruno was killed, her driver. It was Donovan Calvert."

"What?" Despite his own urgency to stay unnoticed, he nearly barked.

Samson's eyes roved to the gas attendant who still didn't look up, rustling a paper.

"He didn't look at any of us, Samson, please get in the car," Celeste assured him. Samson didn't meet her glance when he did as she asked.

She started the car, this time with Crawford up front and Samson settling nervously behind. "Calvert found out where she lives, came to her in Atlantic City, demanded some information in exchange for the last locations of the nails he's concealed. Day came, she rested and Donovan killed Bruno. Drained him."

"All those years making yours miserable for, well...that, and now he's just letting it all go," Crawford muttered.

"All his society friends think he's dead and many of our kind would oblige them for what he's done to us. He could very well be insane after so long alone. That happens quite often." They were on the move south again, headlamps feathering the winding dark. "What's a moral compulsion to someone like that? In any case, with Bruno dead, we've no one to get back to the house and dig up the nail caches for us."

"We'll figure out something. First, we'll need supplies to get hunkered down in Harrisburg, then figure out next moves. I'd go back myself but Scranton PD will be combing the whole state soon enough," Crawford growled. "I wish to God I had five minutes alone with that white bastard in order to make him suffer."

***

Albany announced itself with bleeds of electric light through the windows, the thread of dawn still a half hour away. They were ahead of schedule.

Union Station first announced itself in Donovan's bones. His teeth started to ache, his joints felt a swelling. Then his organs began to crawl. The train slowed and Donovan gasped as his stomach knotted and pains flared in his chest, something between deep muscular stress and heartburn, rendering the center of himself a raw sinew that drew too tight and was plucked with each clack of the wheels on the rails. When the first pillar of the station's end passed the window, he felt the first stabs of agony and he fought to keep himself from doubling over.

Seclusion was the only protection against making a scene. A fetched doctor, an applied stethoscope or a hunted pulse would damn him. So, he forced himself to stand on barbed-wire legs, hobble to the nearest carriage exit, and lean in the dark space near the door until the train came to a complete stop. He forced his way out onto the platform, nearly toppling muzzle down. His ears were back and limbs clenched in the boxer stance of a burning mammal as his pained gaze darted around. Signs were posted by the clock marking the time as six thirty-two. On the signs the sleeper bound for Hamilton was due to arrive by quarter to seven two tracks over. Thirteen minutes of agony till the train, another fifteen before it departed. God couldn't be begged for deliverance here, only that timetables were kept. Had he fed more recently then ten hours ago, he knew he'd be uncontrollably writhing and screaming right now.

Donovan found a bench and fell into it, eyes on the porter helping luggage be moved to the platform and a smattering of a half dozen mammals. "You'll be helped momentarily," the weasel said. His tone wasn't overly disrespectful of their respective carnivore and vegetarian natures, but then Donovan cynically assumed that was only because the man was paid not to be.

A second porter came out to help and passed Donovan with a wary glance.

"You there, good sir!" Donovan's teeth chattered percussively as his innards fought each other with hot coals. "I'm not well. Do you have a bath chair, or a…"

The second porter was a grey squirrel with a clipped tail for yard safety. "A wheelchair, sir. We do have one to assist the infirm. Do you need a doctor?"

"No!" Heads turned but nobody else stopped. An attendant on the train handed down a suitcase to the squirrel with a bark for attention. The squirrel hauled it over to a waiting fennec madame whose impatience with the vegetarian staff was unspoken but not disguised.

Donovan grunted. "I just need to get out of the weather, inside until the next train to Canada. I have a condition." His teeth chattering sold that he was cold even as his jaw was on fire with the rest of his skull. Donovan clamped his eyes shut and didn't see the squirrel's reaction.

"A few moments, sir."

An eternity passed. In the dark behind his eyelids Donovan felt his body's essences broiling, brands of agony and nausea winding their way through. Had his stomach any contents, they'd be on the stonework between his feet.

The creaking of wood and steel approached even as he throbbed and Donovan opened his eyes a crack to see the wooden upright shape of a wheelchair held in place for him. Moving him inside would lessen the agony only by a fraction but it was a fraction he'd greedily take. Lifting and throwing himself into the chair nearly toppled the squirrel behind it and the porter gruntingly rolled him across to the open station door. Just inside, Donovan bade he be pushed further back and into the dark and there he waited, counting down the infinity of seconds until the next churn of steam and howl of brakes brought the westbound Pullman carriages into sight.

Eternity went by, more regrets taunting him from the harping of his body's viscera, a prison of desiccation and decay that he'd as soon leave behind for any next world that waited. But he was grounded in this one with not a soul to commiserate with.

When the train slipped into its berth, Donovan saw the glint of first light on its hull. He called for the porter but he'd been pulled away on porter's business.

Twenty yards, across the Stygian river of four rails and a forest of poisoned steel trees.

The doors opened and a few mammals shuffled off.

To hell with it.

The wheelchair struck the wall as Donovan shoved himself upward, and before he could even lose his bearings he summoned the natural flight instinct of his species. He hurtled himself forward like a drunken madman over the station's threshold, into the cascading miasma and pain, through the whip-lick of first dawn's herald. across the first set of tracks, stumbling on the rails of the second. He lost balance and tripped in the acid bath of agony that revealed one of the reliquary girders to his immediate right. He stumbled towards the open carriage door and made it up two steps before landing on his knees. A canine attendant in the New York Line's livery stood there with his ears splayed and remarked in Bostonian brogue, "The train doesn't leave for another seven minutes, sir, though we do admire your punctuality."

"I've a condition, please help me up," Donovan croaked and he was helped up. "My ticket…"

He drew it with spasming fingers and an elk porter behind the canine sighed. "Next car, sir." The elk had his rack cut down to regulation and put the rabbit's arm over his shoulder. "We can get you a tall glass of water from the dining car and help you sleep it off."

Shuffling between cars took a few teetering minutes, and when the door to his private stateroom opened, Donovan braced himself for the crabwalk to the bed. "Close the shutters. Please." His eyes were closed as the porter did as bade and Donovan was incensed to smell the cervine's essence and hear his pulse and know that even in the throes of rawest pain, he still wanted the very essence to pass his lips that would make it unbearably worse.

"Thank you. Please let me rest."

He stared at the ceiling long after the door was closed. Not nearly soon enough the engines chugged to life and the carriage started to roll. Agony became throbbing pain became fading discomfort. Soon enough he could sit up and leave his cabin on raw legs.

He found another attendant in the dining car, ice rattling in a drink shaker, a morning-dawn mimosa by the smell. Donovan stayed back out of the sight of the car's one open window. "I need to send an urgent communique to Hamilton, Ontario before we arrive at the station there and need a response issued to me by whoever is in authority there." He put five dollars down. "Time is of the essence."

The message relayed was simple, the tickets furnished to be paid for once aboard. The response brought back to his private sleeper was straightforward in acknowledgement of his tight schedule. Daylight climbed outside his window, and when his carriage rolled into Canada, another porter came through with a customs form to confirm he'd nothing to declare.

The train to Toronto, another Pullman sleeper that was on its last stop from far out west, awaited. Donovan would bear no further agonies today and cared nothing for appearances. He took the heaviest of the bedrolls, wrapped it about himself in the manner that Sandy had used all those years ago with the matronly shawls she wore during school teaching. Donovan confirmed the distance to the next train before darting to it, fortunate that the track's position on the shadowed side of the building avoided the worst of the rising sun and provided only the most cursory flutter of scalding heat on his covered back. He was soon in the next train car, securing the shades, and they were on the move again.

Toronto Union Station, he'd confirmed, had underground access to the Royal York Hotel and the tracks were completely covered. As the crucible of Albany, New York faded and the slow trudge into Toronto completed, Donovan felt excitement rising hand in hand with trepidation. It occurred to him that he'd not been given a name to ask for at the hotel, nor a specific time to arrive by.

He'd enough money left in his pocket to room for a few days at best. When the train let him off, it was as though he were back in Manhattan again. Beyond the rail yard's beau arts architecture, climbing Doric columns vaulted over an open central esplanade. This he avoided as squares of light projected down from the high arrays of pebble-glass windows. Instead, he kept to the lower concourse, passing under the street fronting the station to arrive at a French door opened by a wolf in crushed red livery. A wide marble staircase was flanked by brass poles bearing the Red Ensign of Canada, a dangling crimson flag with the British Union Jack at its canton and a central coat of arms. The stairs ascended to the two-story lobby and the Royal York Hotel's ornate front desk.

There was the quiet, dignified bustle of wealth steadily on the move and the smell of the place confirmed how new it was. The Dominion of Canada was still a loyal subject of King George the Fifth and this edifice bore all the stately features of a crown holding.

Its comportment didn't impress him. He'd never been much of a monarchist during his upbringing in Enniscorthy, Ireland, where his expatriate father had operated a modest but tidily profitable brewery.

Donovan's enrollment at Oxford for the first four years of the new century had disillusioned him as to the stratifications of English life. His new-money wealth raised him only a few rungs above those who collected pennies to sweep the floors. He'd hated the place, opened his first steel mill following his father's death in Preston, far enough from his family's stake and far enough from the prigs who'd mocked his rejection to carnivore-centric fraternities.

Should be well enough that life was gone forever.

There had been at least two British Royal descendants ordained into the Order of the Martyres of the Black Well during his own tenure but Donovan hadn't sought their counsel. It had been his honor to leave for one of Britain's upstart escapees from colonial rule. Canada, charming as it might be, was barely its own country nearly seventy years after confederating and might never be.

He approached the slender whippet concierge who eyed him claw to ear tip with no emotion from behind his desk, and Donovan lamented he had no name to request.

But one to give. He waited for a room key to be provided by the whippet to a silver fox who drifted away with bellmammal-pushed trunk in tow. Then those eyes were on him entirely.

"Welcome to the Royal York," the dog told him adroitly.

"My name is Donovan," he answered. "I've a friend who asked me to meet him here."

An eyebrow rose and for just an instant Donovan felt a presence, close by, just over his shoulder. He glanced back to the stairs descending to street level and then up to the dark balcony that overlooked the main foyer, creeping round all sides.

When he turned back, a key rested on the marble before him. "You're awaited in the library," the whippet told him breathlessly. "Second floor, right up there." The dog glanced to the balcony above and met Donovan's eyes again. He'd been told to wait for the rabbit's arrival and was clearly pleased his task was finished.

Donovan said nothing for a time, then took the key. "Thank you."

The stairs to the second floor were stately, brassed, and came to crushed carpet that he followed around to two massive closed doors overlooking the lobby. The key turned in the lock, the great door opened outward.

Inside the room was high-ceilinged, oaked cornices and rosettes above, lined with shelves arrayed with countless leatherbound volumes. It was

dark and cool, the shades fully drawn. Many of the books were sequestered behind the faint gloss of glass cabinetry. He closed the door behind
himself and the low level of light dropped even further, casting the books
and high-backed leather chairs astride a fireplace into darkness. Shadows
filled every corner, from the cold fireplace on one side of the room to the
stand of newspapers hung like offerings of laundry at the other.

"Find Plutarch. A page is marked. Please read it." The voice was paradoxically ashen in timbre, yet silky with assurance. It came from everywhere all at once. The shadows gave no clue.

Hesitation hadn't served him all this way. Donovan crossed the cool
carpet to shelves on the left side of the room, searched out the letter and
found the single volume in jade-tinted leather behind a glass door already
cracked open. He slipped it free and opened it to a ribbon-marked page.
One remark had an underline. "Music, to create harmony, must investigate
discord," he read aloud.

The reply came from within the shelves themselves. All of them. "That
we must, indeed."

The voice was the same he'd heard on the telephone in the Catskills.
"What does that mean? How did you find where I was? More importantly,
how do you know me?" Donovan's eyes roved the open space, the chairs,
a low table, a cart bearing glassware, gins and whiskies. The presence he'd
sensed below was gone. It was as though he spoke to himself in the darkened library.

"Let's put the first inquiry to last. Your whereabouts were gleaned
carefully through one who owed me a particular favor, just as you now owe
me one for saving your life. As for knowing you, well, really Donovan, who
doesn't know who you are if their memory is jogged enough? You worked
so hard to cultivate your public image."

"You have me at a disadvantage."

"I found you that way." There was a shrug in the reply. "The name
Sandy Mallory gave you…"

Donovan slowly stalked to the end of the shelves on the one wall, eyes
scanning the shadows closest to him. Behind the streetfront south-facing
windows whose shutters were well drawn, pinpricks of sunlight made the
deepest shadows in the room even deeper.

Donovan moved slow and kept out of the light's miniscule lances. He thought back to how he'd left his former protégé in Atlantic City and a pit grew in his stomach. Had finishing Bruno been a mistake? "How do you know Ms. Mallory? Are you a new acquaintance of hers?"

"Neither of you know me, but I know both of you quite well. It was only a matter of paying attention."

"And who would you be? The name she gave me meant nothing to me, even if it was apparently important to her deer friend, Celeste. It caught Sandy off guard when I asked. Is she an old acquaintance of yours?"

"No," the voice was on the move, far out of sight, through a forest of literature and canyons of darkness in the relatively confined space. "But it will prove useful to us all as I've said. I take it you provided the location of your last shards in return?"

"Yes. If you wanted them yourself, we could have negotiated directly. You did go through the trouble of helping me with my problem after all."

The voice abruptly changed location again and a book left a shelf. "You would never have trusted a stranger with that information. You don't know me. Mallory, on the other hand, is doing the work we all need done." That labored and simultaneously silky voice almost seemed at Donovan's perked ear. "You left quite the mess for us to contend with, didn't you, Donovan?"

Donovan stopped at a leather-backed chair and wondered if he should sit. His joints still ached from the crucible at Albany. "It would seem so."

"It's a pity there are no ways to this hotel that don't junction through one of your little gifts to us all. The first time experiencing that pain is, I can say from experience, quite instructive."

And Donovan froze as it all made sense. "You bade me meet you here in Canada because…"

"They're a delightfully mixed sack of English stuff-tailed reserve brushed with French insouciance. Often just as pretentious as Americans although loath to admit it. More importantly, as I know you'd figure out with that smart lapin brain of yours, the route gave you a chance for a little direct enlightenment."

Just out of the corner of Donovan's eye, a book was thrust back onto the shelf and another taken, leafed through loudly in a shadow. Donovan set down the Plutarch on a table bearing a shaded lamp and hurried to the sound in five strides, finding only a narrow slot on a dark shelf where a volume was missing.

Donovan turned in the dark and wandered back towards the covered window again, its shades bearing the sun's onslaught. He stepped carefully over a thread of sunlight as the directionless voice followed him.

"Many of your acolytes got lost after you took your sabbatical, Don... and one of them talked, a rather old goat whose fangs you plucked personally. Funny that he didn't blame you for any of his pain through all that he recalled of his time in that little cottage you'd made. Not so soon after leaving you anyway. Time dulls things, thankfully."

Donovan slid past the window to a decorative mantle between the plush leather chairs. A brass clock ticked. Shadows were deeper than the Atlantic bosom on a moonless night.

"Not too many of us forgive you now." Claws seized Donovan's wrist in an iron grip and the rabbit hissed, his fangs erupting as he was dragged toward the slender form poured into the leather chair he'd leaned on not moments ago.

The dark recess of the high-backed leather revealed the milk of downy fur under tufted lynx's ears, piercing slit eyes over a round muzzle that grinned toothily. His white fur with just the barest of sandy patterns disappeared into the shirtless vee of a double-breasted jacket and a white orchid corsage over one breast. The leather tome of Plutarch was spread in his other hand. "All mammals whilst they are awake are in one common world: but each of them, when he is asleep, is in a world of his own." The lynx closed the book one-handed and set it down. When he released Donovan his gaze pinned the rabbit in place. "For years, you, Donovan Calvert, worked to deny any of us our very agency, deny us any world of our own and trap us in your designs, greed painted as suffrage. And for what?"

Donovan collected himself as recognition creeped in from years of study in the Martyres' sequestered libraries in Cologne. They'd honed the Nosfur-hunting craft and gathered the scholarship of centuries and Donovan had seen hints in triptych depictions, etches, fire-damaged oils, diaries, and scrawled prayers left by hands long dead. "Are you the one they call Ferriel?"

The lynx laughed and shrugged his jacketed shoulders. His gaze measured the rabbit almost possessively. "Really, what's in a name? What's important is that I offer a means to make overdue amends for all the considerable harm you've caused. You will know me as Ferrault."

CHAPTER 13

CLOSING IN

Friday night began in mourning but Sandy had to suspend sentiment. Bruno had to be attended to. She drove him north in the back seat of the car he'd chauffeured for years, fighting the urge to look back. Theirs had been a quiet intimacy, expressed on rare occasions when he'd voluntarily sustained her most essential needs. She'd never contemplated feeding him the herbs to bring the change, and he'd never asked.

He'd skirted the verge of death at the Calvert mansion for so long, outliving his Martyre loyalist cohorts by luck as much as anything else. But Calvert had wanted to sup him and she'd kept Bruno safe, and he'd accepted after danger passed that his own mortality and her perpetuation ensured they could never fully connect.

All left unsaid ended with sand on his closed eyes, in his slack mouth, his ears hidden last. Bruno's deepest desires and aspirations were now unknowable, anxious as he was to serve. He had family somewhere in America from which he'd been estranged. Sandy doubted his meager things provided clues to their whereabouts.

Sandy's only certainty after the final turn of Earth was that Donovan would suffer when she found him again.

She returned to an apartment of ghosts and telephoned Celeste. The operator couldn't get a connection. Celeste reached her instead in the early hours of the next morning from a gasoline fill station and Sandy's misery found a new low. "It was the Martyres." Celeste rarely panicked, but her veneer of reserve had chipped away. "They followed either Crawford or myself back from one of the caches and staked us out. I'm sure of it."

Sandy didn't doubt her. Finding Donovan's materials had been a relay race from the start. The relentlessness of his benefactors was something Sandy knew all too well.

"We'll have to bide our time before going back to get those nails, but that's another bushel to sort. Before he killed Bruno, Donovan told me where the other caches are. I'm going to set out tomorrow."

"If the Martyres know, Sandy..."

"They'd have them already. At least they don't know where I'm living yet. You can't go after them as you'll need to stay low."

Silence carried Celeste's attempts to find an objection. Despite her pains, Sandy put a smile on so Celeste would hear it in her voice. "Also, the Martyres and myself go way back. We'll sort this out over a pint of the first o' the bastards in line."

"Sandy, you're a fool. Don't go after them."

"Only room for one fool in our relationship. I'm practiced at lumping hubris with humor, Celeste. It's an Irish talent. In any case I can't go tonight. You let me know when you're all settled and safe."

They ended the call and the warmth at Celeste's voice faded quickly. The apartment's empty space weighed the world.

***

The Harrisburg single-story residence was a dilapidated flop, bought on bank foreclosure as most homes had been over the past three years. Its sagging roof and weed-choked porch were homely enough to discourage break-ins and hopefully squatters. It was one of six or seven sequestered residences in the western flank of Harrisburg's outskirts. Down the long rutted route, most houses were empty or dimly lit with only whisps of chimney smoke.

The forests of southern Harrisburg rolled towards the distant Susquehanna River far off in the dark and as the Chevrolet bounced to a stop Crawford put his claws on the dash, wincing. "I've got some bad news."

"You're turning," Celeste and Samson said together.

"Is it obvious?"

"There's a smell," Samson said. "Right before, every time."

Crawford cleared his throat. He felt his jaw getting swollen. "Good to know. I think I was changed back early because you knocked me out. I didn't know that worked."

Celeste stared ahead over the Chevy's steering wheel. "Good thing I've certainly never had to do that before," she said flatly. "If you're going to shift now you might want to remove those clothes. Counting the suitcase, you've only two outfits to your name."

The weight of all that the fire had taken hit Crawford at that moment, and that in turn pressed his need to have no weight at all. Breeze bade the forest to sigh in welcome. "Samson and I will…well, we've little luggage so we'll keep an eye out for you."

That fact didn't seem to trouble her as so much else clearly did.

Crawford brought his things into the closed mustiness of the house, leaving the key they'd kept in the car on the lone kitchen table that had just one chair in a vast, vacant space. Once naked, he bounded out on all fours, the grass and brambles a wealth of scents that beckoned him. Crawford forgot himself completely and let it happen. The freedom from all his worries was bliss and he loped and lived for a short while.

He regained himself in a fetal position under the home's table and found that dawn's encroach had Celeste and Samson take to the root cellar below. Crawford Cain put on his clothes and responsibilities and took the Chevy into Harrisburg proper, parking on the verge of a row of sparsely occupied storefronts to find provisions for himself and ask about pet stores.

"Trapper south of here sells live feral crits. What'cha need'm for?" the beagle asked around a plug of tobacco.

Crawford sighed. "Vermin are getting smarter. Teaching my cub to shoot."

"He have alla his fingers?"

Dammit. "He does."

A pharmacy stop for a pint of bourbon and nine miles south later, a muskrat held up a distant, naked feral cousin by the tail. The trapper turned the rat in the air out by a shed emitting clucks and screeches. "I've got eight to sell."

Crawford had realized on the way over that they'd set up no enclosure for the rats when they'd bought the place and swept it out. Would they be fine just milling around the second bedroom? Celeste at the very least would be disgusted by droppings.

"Four."

"Live?"

Crawford didn't want any more questions. Every crackling radio he passed in every corner shop could have bad news from law enforcement stuffed between Adventures of Ellery Queen and Duke Ellington's latest. "Yeah. Teaching my cub to shoot."

"Well then." He took a wood box lined with paper and started setting rodents in it. Watching them mill and bump Crawford saw headlines on print lining the bottom. A whisker straightener ad, something excoriating Roosevelt, a torn pamphlet with dates he'd seen before.

Ignoring a screech and a lunge to bite, Crawford plucked it up: the same list of cities he'd read before, winding across the nation and ending in Boston. The third to last was in Hancock, Maryland, eighty miles from here and a state line away, with today's date. Under the list of names with Rutland Blake on top was that of his son's.

"You don't go for that rat shit, do you?" The muskrat leveled a gaze that was beady and truth-seeking. "Cause I don't spit palms with fools that do."

"No," Crawford was grateful for an instance of easy truth. "I just… recognize a name."

"Everybody recognizes somebody they know when those bastards prance through town." The muskrat's jaw clenched hard. "Had a brother marched off to Washington in thirty-two who fought in the Great War, wanted Hoover to pay his due bonus out like thousands of others who bled in France for a promise, of, well…" The critter in his grip stopped struggling and dangled helplessly. "He came back a month later stinking of despair and tear gas. I haven't seen him in a long time, wonder if he'll turn up at this rally or that revival or what the hell. Fact is, his future got stolen by gamblers and hucksters in coattails with tickers. The rich can't get richer without cheatin'. And they can't keep cheatin' without pushing anger some other damn place." He added a rat to the box and Crawford saw the trapper had two of his own fingers missing. "Poor people is desperate people and when factories close and the crops dry out from rot, they feed blame like bad soup. Oldest fable, oldest lie. Happens again and again."

"I know what you mean," Crawford muttered, and dropped the pamphlet for the rats to shit on. He'd been promised that soldier's bonus like so many others, to be paid out on his birthdate in 1945. Starving stomachs and mounting bills wouldn't wait that long, not for anyone, so the Bonus Expeditionary Force had mustered. Under other circumstances, had he been starved of PI work, he'd have joined that march to Washington himself. "I wasn't surprised at how things turned out."

Ten minutes and four dollars later, his Chevy chugged at the long end of the muskrat's farm drive with a southern or northern turn to take. He pondered the pamphlet again. Lucas was with the rally moving to Hancock today, eighty miles south. Crawford had work to do at the second home up north, was on the run, couldn't get to him.

Couldn't warn him that no less than two separate divisions of law enforcement were on his heels for sins yet to be committed, eighty miles south of where he idled at that moment. The Chevy could do about fifty miles an hour with the pedal flat…

The rats screeched as he veered south.

***

The tuned Model A rolled northeastward and Baliosi kept the map from flapping with some difficulty. Gears ground as the car aimed for a corner and hung it hard.

"Shoulda just took a train," Grisand muttered at the wheel.

"But we both feel it, where we need to be. Will we even be there in time?" Baliosi was confused, feeling truth's spectre duck from sight.

"I dunno. I'm starting to think we'll never get this back,"

"It will when we assume it won't. You know how it goes. Leguna's laughing through the veil at us at this point," Baliosi snorted.

"I hope the kids are okay."

"'Course they are, sweet souls all of 'em. Clutch couldn't be in better hands."

"Glad we know somethin'. I hope we close this circle soon. I'm getting sick of seeing into the mist halfway."

A honk startled otter and wolf both, making Grisand swerve a bit. A scarred Oldsmobile plank-decker pulled alongside and a mangy dog leaned past an oily arm. The cigarillo in his lips tilted up fast as his teeth ground out a grin. "Goin' my way, darlin?"

Baliosi and Grisand traded looks and sighed, unsure which of them the cur was courting. The words were on their lips, but incomplete, cloudy. "Your rear right's goin' flat again," Grisand chided indifferently.

"How d'ya know?" The dog's eyes went wide with surprise as a pop sounded and he swerved as he fell behind. "Ah mai Gawd, fuggin' damn…!"

He was a memory soon enough. "That's all we can sus out now," Baliosi sighed. "Flat tires and pie that will be stale. We need to find 'er and quick."

"I got a sense, just a sense mind you…" Grisand concentrated.

"What?"

"A father seeks, a son conceals…"

"The lost dame fears what the heart, uh, reveals…"

The road bumped underneath and one thread weakened while the other was lost.

"Dammit, feels important," Grisand cursed and ruffled the map some more. They were far from the coast, far from Kansas. The middle of the middle, lost sailors without wind.

"They all do, child. If it pushes up from the center like that, you can bet it sure ain't 'bout the Mammal from Nantucket. We need a sign, a compass point, something to fix us on the path or fix the path onto us. Where are we anyway?"

They hit a bump in the road and glass and wood complained. "Near the Maryland-Pennsylvania border. I think that Hagerstown is to the east of us and to the west is—"

"Straighten out the crate back there, would you?" Grisand sighed. "We've got important stuff coming loose."

Baliosi crumped the road map and shoved it between her legs as she turned back to the wooden box behind them both in the narrow space. Corked bottles clinked and sloshed.

A silvery shape in the morning light was ahead on the road, growing quickly. It bounced like a tadpole in play and briefly crossed into the Model A's rumbling path.

"Merde!" Grisand hissed and swerved to the shoulder to avoid a hit.

A dark picketed fence post buttressing one shoulder caught the right fender, a nick just short of catastrophe that skipped both sisters' hearts. The ditch was slight but sufficient to bounce the car hard on already-tortured springs and deliver otter, wolf, and seven bottles into the air's momentary grace before thudding two mammals back down and six bottles all over the space behind them.

One dark red container, wax-corked, spun unseen by the frantic occupants before bouncing over the Model A's rear gunnel. It slipped through one of the long fence's many gaps and down a sheer slope of crabgrass and loose pebbles.

The collection of stones at the bottom, arrayed in rows with etched names and dates, stood silent as the glass-liquid missile bounced among them, guided by far more than inertia's unseen hand.

It struck one of the cemetery markers and shattered, spreading oak-aged tannins imbued with long spoken words of power and portent. They sunk and set something whispering between fate and chance.

A quarter mile up the road with the Model A straightened out, Grisand swore up a storm. "Idiot cubs, crash into any damn thing but sense. Nearly sent my fanny up to my throat."

A stirring in the air met a rumble from below. They both felt it. It wasn't the car.

Baliosi had spun around. "How many bottles did we pack in the excursion box?"

"Eight? Five? You packed it, I dunno what kind o' stuff you brought. Feel 'em all up, something's muttering pretty loud."

The otter kept her eyes on the road and all of its idiots while the wolf grabbed rolling bottles and put them back in the bed of strewn straw. One sent lightning up her arm. "Bali, a cork is gonna pop soon. We need to swap a vessel!"

"Where?"

"Ahead!"

The otter squinted at the wolf, but only for a moment. "You mean to tell me that the thread we're pulling on has a vessel about to get drank on the path we're already on? The gris-gris ain't playin' around if so."

"If so." Baliosi held one dark bottle that held fireflies of essence within, beckoning any and all. "You'd better step on it."

She kept her eyes back to the bottles every other moment, fighting wind and map and watching the collection juggle in the straw. "I could have sworn I packed more than this."

Two miles back, the earth was disturbed.

***

Tomlinson watched the frame of the house smoulder. "What could have been so important in here that they'd burn their own house down"—the weasel turned and regarded the cops left on watch over his spectacles—"or did you people cook a ham steak and lose track of a match?"

"We were in and out." The Irish Setter was indignant, but not sarcastic. They all knew better than to show lip to Hoover's people. "We didn't even touch anything. The place was empty when we went to get a coffee."

A car pulled in to join the others, siren off. The fox from the station got out and joined the weasel. "We went through the things our birthday-suited lupine friend dropped on the way out. This was in the pants he discarded." He handed Tomlinson a pamphlet. "Arresting officers smelled booze in the cup he downed. Must have had wormwood or rotgut gin or some damn feral-izer funk in it. That wolf went nuts."

"Went something…" Tomlinson muttered as he flipped through the distressed item. It had names and dates, one of them today. He knew the name at the top of the pamphlet. "We know that Crawford worked with a doe secretary. This outfit wants to kick vegetarians out of America."

"Are they communists or something?" somebody asked and was ignored.

Tomlinson studied the names. He'd obtained some information about Crawford Cain from a few extant sources when they'd brought him in. He had a dissolved marriage, co-workers who wouldn't piss on him if he were aflame, only one child…

He saw the name near the bottom and smiled a needle-toothed smile. "If he finds some clothes, I think I know where he might go next."

"You calling Washington about this guy?"

"You leave that to me, Lieutenant. Anything you find in that house, I want you to—"

"Officers!" The shout came from among the timbers, where a pickaxe was being used to shuffle things around the rough square that the melted shape of a file cabinet suggested had been an office.

A soot-blackened badger pointed his muzzle towards where a dog so black he was a scratch poked his head up from a canted doorframe in the very center of the mess. The dog coughed a cloud. "Get a doctor! We've a survivor in the cellar!"

***

How stupid was he? The question came and went as Crawford found a place along the dirt road's cluster of cars to squeeze in the Chevy. He then merged with hat tipped into the wandering herd. Fortunately he'd had a shorter-brimmed black fedora amongst the packed check-shirt and low-hemmed, wrinkle-pleated trousers that dragged around his toe claws. The ensemble in most places would have him sticking out like a sore thumb that sang hymns but the threadbare comportment of the mammals trudging to the town's center kept him in good enough company.

There was a grumble amongst those he followed, indignant and anxious. The jobless in America easily topped twenty percent amongst the papers favoring Roosevelt's policies but was declared to be at least half the country by the president's detractors. Crawford wasn't meeting any glances but knew well and truly that if he asked around, he'd find assumptions leaned the detractor's way.

He noticed that every single one of the marchers were carnivores like himself. Further on, at the cusp of a massive circus-style pole tent, he caught brief glimpse of a limp red flag with something black and angular creeping at its center. It was lost amongst the marchers, gravel crunching under claws and hot breath muttering discontent. Crawford moved silently in their stale wake.

The dark of the tent yawned wide and he didn't attempt to step out of the rough line that was forming. A second portal further to the right yawned and disgorged canines, felines, and mustelids, nervously energized in the way of those who have not been fed, but rather pointed to sustenance.

Within, a voice was nearly bellowing.

Crawford asked no questions of the brown bear smoking a pipe over folded arms, eyes meeting his for the barest instant. Next to the looming bear, a box rested with a carved slot atop it. The cursory sign above it was painted in capitals: "DONATE TO THE CAUSE TAKE THE NATION BACK!" A thin hand on a passing rail thin mutt dropped a coin to hit others down in the dark.

Crawford wondered what Beatie back at his Allentown Bank would think of this place and realized with a start that he could possibly be in this crowd. Too late, the dark took him and shoulders to left, right, and behind packed him in tight, facing a spotlit stage whose occupant was just visible over the peaks of bobbing ear tips and more than a few hackles.

"We were lied to," the voice said, young, hot, and defiant. "A nation that would keep us all safe, they said. We were lied to. Those who fought the wars to set our place in the world would be fed the best morsels of victory's flesh. We were lied to."

The speaker took a step. His greyish muzzle had a moonish glint in the klieg light. The wolf's ears were back, guarded and ready to fight. Blue eyes glittered. "And as our jobs are stolen and another worthless president passes out scraps to the unworthy, we count ribs on our cubs and watch tractors rust out, the dust choke our crops, our livestock thin out. Even my mother's chicken coup, the pride of our family for generations, can barely afford grain to keep the eggs laid that bless the breakfast tables in our corner of Virginia."

Crawford's heart skipped a beat as those blue eyes turned defiant indignation in his general direction, the cheekbones behind the young muzzle familiar from a thousand looks in grooming mirrors.

"Lucas," Crawford breathed and a weasel at his shoulder shushed him.

"We have a great test ahead of us," Lucas Marsten, formerly Lucas Cain, insisted. "The weak have been given licence to take that which is ours by God's own law. We supped the flesh of the Almighty and at his behest we will fulfill our manifest destiny to take this country back!"

Hollers and whoops snarled up around Crawford, some hands raising fists straight up, more than a few directed to the stage with claws flattened vertically to represent the cleaving prow of the Ark as Crawford had seen on the pamphlet's scrawled illo. Lucas's eyes roved the throng to receive their blessing, his eyes stopping momentarily on the singular gap in the crowd where paws should be raised. Lucas's gaze trailed down and met Crawford's mournful gaze, confusion giving way to suspicion.

Was there recognition?

A German shepherd suited in white took the stage with him and startled the wolf by clapping him on the back. "Lucas Marsten, everybody. Give this warrior for our nation a hand."

They did and Crawford drifted back as the wolf on the stage slipped out of the shepherd's loose contact. Both headed for an exit and Crawford was immediately moved by a crush of bodies in an opposing tide for the exit.

"We're going to take a respite," Crawford heard from the stage. "While we do, Sisters Abagail and Tangine will come out and play us a song on the six-string and spoons."

The crowd shifted just enough and Crawford slid through the gap almost lapine-like. He followed his son out of the tent's flap into the light and round a left turn between the tent and a flaked-painted wood building, directly into the growling muzzle of his own younger reflection.

Two wolves caught each other's scent and teeth peeked through lips and closed again, almost simultaneously.

Crawford's last words from Lucas had been heard on the verge of a change, days after being recruited for his first investigative work back in Chicago. That young, frightened voice had haunted him through that phone booth in the West End: "When are you coming home? Nothing here smells like you anymore."

"What the hell are you doing here?" The wolf with the fuller voice before him was furious. "It is you, isn't it?"

Crawford grasped for words. Twelve years since he'd heard this voice. "Yes. It's me."

Silence couldn't hang because of the bustle around them, the flapping of the tent wall in an errant breeze, and the click and clack of spoons under strings plucking hard with a whoop or two over indistinct, yowling lyrics.

"Why are you here? Now?" Lucas guarded something bubbling deep behind his glare. "You aren't a part of my life. You don't get to just walk in here—"

Crawford stepped close enough to feel the heat of the anger off him. He took a deep breath, realizing that he'd just about forgotten all he wanted to say. What came out was a stammer. "Lucas, listen. This is important. You're going in a dangerous direction. I've been around angry people my whole life who look for others to blame for all that seems wrong in the—"

Lucas struck him. Crawford's lips were parted by the muzzle blow and his teeth rocked behind them. The sound was like a gunshot in the tight space between the tent's outer burlap and the wooden frame of the storehouse behind it.

"Lucky I found you then, isn't it, Pa?"

Crawford tasted blood. Shame numbed it hotter as he met his son's hurt gaze.

"Lucky in what way?" A gravelly voice inserted itself like a blade.

The German shepherd's muzzle poked from a Stetson brim's shadow as he came round the tent's curve, white double-breasted suit hanging on him with the sparkling blankness of a dinner place setting. The left breast bore a golden pin that drew Crawford's attention like a fishhook. A three-spoked wheel, each thick arm with a sharp left joint.

Both wolves turned muzzles the shepherd's way, one supplicant and one suspicious. Crawford realized his own son was looking to this dog for guidance.

"I don't know you," the shepherd idly muttered, his Midwest drawl long and suspicious as his eyes found Crawford's.

"No, sir, you don't," Crawford said and was surprised to hear his Virginian slip back into his strained voice like a tailored glove.

"Mister Marsten?" The inquiry was a patient demand for explanation, eyes still locked with Crawford's.

The younger wolf looked to the older one, then back to the shepherd, his standoffish stance unabating. "Nobody important Colonel. He's just leaving." Emphasis made that a suggestion.

"Like hell," Crawford growled.

The three of them stood there and the shepherd raised a hand and waved back someone outside Crawford's peripheral vision. His ears turned back and he realized other bodies were blocking the mutterings of mammals still meandering in and out of the tent. All at once, he felt a tug deep within that he recognized and didn't like.

No. Not here.

"What the hell do you want then?" Lucas was annoyed, clearly feeling the Colonel's glare as heavily as Crawford did.

"We're talking," Crawford said. "In private." The scents of bodies starting to crowd in fluttered his nostrils and at once he felt territorial. The change he accommodated last night hadn't been fully satisfied.

"Yeah?" Lucas swallowed. "There's one bar in this part of town I hear. All that Prohee nonsense I heard about you from Mom never fooled me. Won't be surprised if I see you drowning in it." The tail behind him suddenly lashed as hurt surfaced and was forced back down. "Meantime, I don't wanna talk to you."

A rank weasel, the musky bear that had been watching the tent entrance, and another lanky dog crowded in. Crawford didn't let himself turn around, fought his hackles fruitlessly.

"Sounds like my boy's pretty clear on his desires. Let's have us a little understanding, you and I." A claw airily reeled shep and elder wolf together even as eyes told a harder story. "Lucas, go take a walk. I'll talk to you shortly, son."

Crawford's eyes met Lucas's and saw something in there that hurt both of them even more. He'd made a mistake but that was just the start. A lurch within himself told him that the change wanted to manifest desperately. "Lucas, please."

The young wolf's eyes were wet, then closed, then open and hard. "Stay the fuck away from me, you deadbeat louse." He turned, tail lashing, and stormed round the tent's flank.

Scents, all hostile, closed in. And just like that the desire to change suddenly and inexplicably fled. Sinewy arms wrapped around his as the German shepherd stalked forward, nose testing the air.

"So, you're the deadbeat," the Colonel said through licked teeth. "I've not heard much about you but what little came up told me enough. My boy's early life was ruined by you."

"You don't know what the hell you're talking about."

"No?" The shep was quick. His fist was back and forward in a breath and caught Crawford under his ribs. A blinding white flare of pain made everything grey as Crawford doubled over. Mustelid and ursine hands drew him up, dragged his muzzle back up by the tightening of his scruff.

"Too many eyes. Further round back."

Crawford couldn't speak, wheezing hard. The desire to change was damnably absent now.

He'd never shifted during the daylight, the moon's gaze weakened. But here, in this moment, he surrendered, needing it. He wanted to tear these bastards apart, bathe in their blood, rip out the tongue of the dog who'd dare call Lucas "son". But the change was nowhere to be found, almost as though the curse had lifted itself away.

He was dragged, mud scuffing the knuckles of his feet and claws as he was manhandled round the tent to the weeds and ditch. All sounds of the camp were reduced to mutters. He rose his head into a dark-furred fist that nearly broke his nose, so recently healed from the docks of Boston.

The back of his knee was kicked, his other ankle swept out by a claw swipe and he was lowered to the mud but not dropped, arms still locked in an iron grip.

"You delivered a force of vengeance to me that I intend to wield by your abject failure as a father." A punch nearly fractured his cheek as the Colonel drawled. "You're a reprobate." Someone kicked a rib, making him buck. "A traitor to your one responsibility as a patriarch." His ear was boxed and Crawford cried out.

The Colonel's taunts would not relent. "You dare to come here and try to bask in your son's light after kicking him out from your paltry shadow? You're nothing. You're nobody."

Crawford was let go and he fell and went fetal. The will to change returned, but not strong enough to take hold. The world was spinning as he bled and hurt and kicks rained on his back and flank.

A short eternity passed before the Colonel laughed. "This bastard got mud on my pant leg. Least we can leave him where he belongs."

Crawford winced as hot breath came to his back-folded ear. He could sense the leer of Colonel Blake even though his eyes were shut tight and couldn't see him.

"Don't come round here ever again," the Colonel growled. "The new world we're building has no room for trash who've fallen so far. Nibble some grass."

The last kick sent Crawford tumbling down the ditch to the reeds and stinking sewage water. He choked and sputtered as he lifted himself just enough to settle on the opposite embankment, pain pinning him down while the gibbering laughter of the Colonel and his men faded back to their hateful pageant under the big top.

Crawford moaned his son's name and clutched wet grass as consciousness spun and slipped away.

Chapter 14

Many Spokes

Lucas settled into the diner seat at Furdy's feeling cold. The bear was back on shift again and he couldn't remember her name. Didn't matter. Nothing mattered at the moment.

Anxiety raged as a ragged menu slid in front of him. He wanted something but he didn't know what. Steak and eggs without the eggs? A life without the spectre of failure in his own blood?

"Lucas."

Twelve years had put nothing behind him and he had run so far and so hard, climbed the ranks to escape—

"Marsten!" A fist struck the table and spun the menu sideways. Lucas eyes darted up to meet the Colonel's yellow glare.

"What?" Lucas wanted to shout it but he didn't dare do that.

"What happened back under the mountain top?" The "mountain top" was the Colonel's nickname for the big top, the place where God's chosen were called. He'd come to that wryly but wasn't in that mood now. "You had a whole speech rehearsed, all about the fight against vegetarian menaces, commie degeneracy, all of that. I was so excited to hear it and you wound it into some mealy-mouthed mutter like you were late for supper. All because that useless pelt of wind came back into your life."

Lucas felt a cold well of disgust rise and put his claws down flat to get up but the Colonel's hand stretched across the diner table to push his shoulder down with force. "You never had a real father so I'll let this lapse of discipline go. I'm going to be what you need, Lucas. And you're going to be what I need in return, what the movement needs."

The Colonel's gaze rose and sought somebody over Lucas's shoulder. His gaze soured and then returned to Lucas.

"I've tried, Colonel. And I thank you for putting faith in me," Lucas muttered. He felt small and hated that feeling more than anything.

"Thanks don't win revolutions. Thanks don't take back the nation, do they?" Lucas detected the scent on his breath of scotch, the very whiskey he'd bought the Colonel for his meeting with the mayor the prior night.

"Hey!" The Colonel shouted over Lucas's shoulder and the wolf turned to follow his gaze to where the bear waitress from before, Lil—Lucas now remembered her name, though not whether somebody had called it out or whether she'd given it—was pouring coffee for another bleary canine patron who sat way in the back.

Standing over him, the bear turned back their way and saw them. Her eyes passed over Lucas amiably enough, but upon seeing the Colonel, she froze and Lucas saw something bitter get buried. She hurried over, pot of coffee held adroitly.

Four or five steps away, Lucas saw what the bear, intent on making haste, could not. A hastily scarfing diner's hat and coat were dumped loosely on the booth next to them and had been sagging floorward. On the hustle, the bear didn't see the coat slip, didn't see the sleeve flop itself onto the polished tile right under one of her descending clawed feet.

She slipped, pitched forward and righted herself after three hard steps. Coffee sloshed from the pot, striking booth side, table, and the left breast of a white seersucker jacket worn by an impatient German shepherd.

Lucas looked back to the Colonel and the German shepherd was livid. He jumped, straightened his coffee-marred jacket, and marched over to the kitchens, hollering to the manager. A fox wandered out, sniffling against the skillet's heat, rubbing dark hands on his apron. The low chatter of the place settled as the Colonel snarled. After nearly a week, most of the small town knew who he was, who his people were.

"What the hell is that clown of a bear doin' servin' newcomers ahead of us that walked in here ten minutes ago and sticking me with a cleaner's bill! You know what kind of schedule I have to keep?"

The fox caught his furious scent and coffee stains, glanced down the diner's aisle where the bear stood with her pot, one hand over her mouth.

Lucas immediately felt her awkwardness and smelled abject terror.

"Colonel Blake…" he spoke up.

"Wait a damn minute."

The fox kept a growl down. Lucas saw the effort. "Colonel. No offense intended but we get pretty busy and I'm sure it was an—"

"You ain't sure of shit. Half the carnies who order here could work these tables quicker and with more deference to your clientelle than that lumbering dolt you've got there. You gonna pay my laundry bill?" The Colonel's voice dropped to a growl. "I suggest you fix things real quick before this place empties out even quicker. You know I can make that happen. Solve a problem."

The fox glanced the bear's way and saw her confusion and he was sad as he beckoned her over and urged her into the back. Another waiter, a scraggly cat, hustled even faster now that the fort was held alone.

The seat groaned as the Colonel's weight dropped into it. "Gotta fix the whole damn world myself. I'm telling you, boy, I can't do it alone. Your useless reprobate of a father turning up made it abundantly clear just how far a carnie can fall and I'll be damned if I see you go that way. Next stop is Boston, the big show."

"I think she was tripped by that coat," Lucas said.

The Colonel glared at him. "You changing the subject? Are you gonna find yourself an excuse for when you trip on stage? It was a whim to bring you on the circuit. Lots of dusty dogs would give anything to get a piece of what I've handed you, so give this everything you have." His eyes were hard. "Otherwise, what good are you to anybody?"

The door to the kitchens opened and the bear moved out quickly, apron gone. Her muzzle was low, a choked sob chased her out under the diner's ringing bell.

"Let's get some damn service," the Colonel muttered.

"I'm not hungry." Lucas rose and the Colonel's eyes followed him up without blinking.

"You gonna work on your speech..." It wasn't a question.

"I need some air first."

Outside the evening air was cold but heavy. October nibbled at Lucas's fur and he heard crying to his left. A phone booth was full of bear.

"I've been let go," he heard her say. "I don't know what to do. I can't..." she said as Lucas melted into the crowd, feeling hollow inside. "Can't bottle up when cork's been lost," was the last thing he heard and thunder rolled in from nowhere, raising countless wandering muzzles to a hazy afternoon sky.

Lucas needed a telephone, but one less public.

The old saloon, O'Holler's, was a few doors down, and nearly empty because too few could afford the three cents for a beer. It was drowned in varnish, cigarette smoke, and sepia photographs of barely smiling bricklayers that only locals recognized. Lucas planted himself in a stool and took a deep breath as he slid his feet upon the brass rail and got the lay of the land. Prohibition had been the law throughout America from when he was seven years old until he'd turned twenty just over two years ago. He'd had a drink or two but never really developed the taste, for which his mother and stepfather had both been grateful.

Not that either of them really had opinions amounting to much. Neither abided his latest life choices or the reasons for them. His oldest disappointment had returned to plague him, the blank slate who'd wandered to the bloodbath of Chicago and from there…

Lucas glanced to a corner and saw a telephone booth, secluded, empty and waiting.

"What can I get you, son?" The old lion behind the bar had a silvery mane bound back as he wiped the bar.

Lucas turned back. "I don't know what I want." Lucas scratched the rail with his claws and rubbed his ear back. "To back way up and avoid a mistake or two."

There was a tingle in the air that lifted his whiskers a bit and he caught the lion's eye. Was the feline's mane standing up just a bit? The electricity in here was different than the coarser currents lurking the streets by the Colonel's tent.

"I might have just the thing," the lion said distractedly, his hands rummaging under the oak top almost without his involvement.

Lucas heard a clasp click and a bottle rose up to be set on the bar. It was dusty and dark like a wine bottle, but glinting in a way that was clearly not affiliated with any nectar of the grape. It had no label. "What's this?"

"What you need," the lion said, as though surprised to find out himself.

Lucas sniffed and caught nothing. "Is it…rum?"

"It's right."

The bottle looked like it had been found in a Civil War footlocker. "Okay," he licked his lower lip. His nerves did need steadying, just a little. Only a little. "How much for a…drum?"

The lion was amused. "A dram. As much as you feel it's worth."

"Fine." Lucas dug in his pocket past a few crumpled bills and fished out two dimes and a nickel. He set them on the counter and the lion snatched one. Nickel or dime, Lucas didn't bother looking.

"That's enough," the lion said.

Lucas didn't want to argue. He wanted as much time to separate him from the tent and all that transpired under it as possible. He needed to make a call. "One please."

A glass was set before him, the cork creaked out, and a finger of the liquid poured.

"Chip some ice?" Lucas asked.

"You won't need it," the lion said clinically. "You do need to drink it in this bar. It's for you only. Don't carry it away."

"It needs to carry me out of this town and away from everything. That's what I'd pray to God for if he was listening."

"God answers all prayers," the lion muttered as Lucas tipped the glass back and drank. It was sweet with a back bite and went down smoother than he could expect.

The lion's expression was blank. "…But sometimes the answer is no."

There wasn't much burn, which surprised Lucas as it was the first drink he'd had in months. A sense of fuzzy detachment came to him, and for a moment he was no son to a failed father nor seeking approval from an angry surrogate who had plans within plans.

"You'd better take that booth over there, the one marked private. It's empty."

"Why?"

"You're decanting things that you've buried a long time. Privacy helps."

Lucas felt light when he rose from the bar and tottered over to the dark corner, past the still-empty telephone booth, realizing he'd sipped strong stuff. The floor under his feet teetered, then a bit more as the rocks out behind the Bradley's farmstead in Virginia threatened to trip him. Laughter tinkled to his right where two half-empty pints sloshed with a coyote couple's emphasis and to his left where Jack the ferret nearly fell out of the tire swing.

Lucas settled down into the bar booth and past that into long meadow grass. "You're gonna crack yer skull," he chided in a reedy cub's voice at Jack as his tail whipped high and head dipped low, feet diving skyward to bring the rope-suspended tractor tire upward on the tree bough with a spin.

Lucas's friend's toes kicked the sky, then curled back down, nearly clipping Rose the beagle from two farms down as she passed. She laughed infectiously. It got a guffaw from Jack on the tire and a whistle from Grint over on the rusting Fordson tractor that was currently a police car in the radio-serial world of mammalian youths. It would remain so until such time as its spark plug was delivered in the mail from Roebucks and it could be restored to tilling fields.

The tractor's steering wheel was stiff in Grint's lean feline hands but its engine was loud with the purr supplied from his throat. Grint did the best engine sounds with his cat-pipes so he always drove while Lucas took shotgun shoulder with the cast-iron Kenton cap gun to take down rumrunners and scofflaws and, on one occasion, Wild Bill Hickock after a picture show in Roanoke that Lucas's mom had taken him to.

Lucas leapt with a scrabble of claws to the Fordson's fender and crouched over Grint, adding a siren sound to his whine of the fast-moving car's engine. He took a capshot into the field at an imaginary running mobster's car, aiming for the tire that would spin them out into the ditch and throw their illicit cargo of rum across the road. Rose ran in front of their police car and made her own gun bangs through her muzzle, ears flapping with the effort, daring them to change course and chase her. She was a cut above the other scofflaws and got away as always.

Dad would catch her, Lucas thought with a toothy smirk. Dad was rounding up a lot of criminals out there in Chicago, which had to be why he'd had to get off the telephone after the frantic call two days ago. Government work made a busy wolf and even though he'd been upset about something, he'd a case to solve.

Mom didn't want to talk about it, but she worried too. Their house two fields away still had all their smells mingling and every meal had a taste of desperation and anxiety added like a spice. Awkward silences at the Cain household were frequent now and—

"Get 'er!" Grint buzzed insistent engine noises to urge Lucas, and the wolf braced his cap gun to track Rose across the grass, firing what was a rifle or a Tommy gun back with invisible bucks of her felonious hands. She passed in front of Jack, who narrowly missed her with the pendulum swing of the tire. The brown-striped weasel looked down the barrel of Lucas's gun and made an "oh" sound as he was shot and slipped oily from the tire and hit the scrub with his shoulder before tucking and rolling.

Lucas felt a buzz of panic as he leapt from the police-commandeered tractor and hurried over to the coiling body on the ground. Jack leapt up and startled him. "You shot me you loony pup!"

Lucas went from startled to relieved with a hot tail wag that fanned Rose as she darted round them both and the ferret gave him chase.

Lucas ran and laughed; a nameless anxiety fell behind.

The world pinwheeled around him, horizon and fallow field and road and disturbed, distant grit. Lucas caught the approach of a car on one spin-round after the ferret and then once more as it passed.

The silhouette out on the road was upright in a familiar shell, a Chevy that bounced on a rut and kept going, the grey fur of the driver's muzzle barely disturbed under a fedora's tilt. The car passed, didn't slow, kept straight. Lucas had the barest moment to recognize that his father, Crawford Cain, defender of Chicago, was at the helm. The wolf's eyes stayed on the road and without a backwards glance at the youths playing on the front lawn of the neighbor's stead.

They were fifteen yards from that road and its settling dust, as impossible to miss as the car had been impossible for Lucas to miss.

His father had seen him. His father had stormed France to save it from evil and swore on the Bible to root out crime in the urban hellscape and promised Lucas he'd be loved and that he'd return. And now, just now, his father had seen him.

But now that car was gone, never slowing, lost from sight beyond a row of trees that were still with indifference.

Rose made chittery sounds of gunfire battle and then went still at his shoulder when he didn't react. A wave passed him over, numb and heavy and inexplicable. Silence descended. Lucas didn't know who asked him what was wrong.

He told them he had to go. And he did go.

His father had seen him.

He stumbled onto his own porch and heard the cap gun clatter uselessly on one of the steps. The air was still tainted with tire dust and that familiar burned oil smell and the faint, oh so faint hint of mature wolf pelt and breath and—

Mom was waiting, tail still. Her eyes held his with sweet sympathy as he took the folded paper from a hand that smelled of something regretful and he unfolded it with shaking hands that were too heavy. The seams were hard to see through the wet blur—

"Wake up dammit," Lucas heard the snapping of claws under his chin and blinked against the saloon's weak light. A dark nose sniffed at him. "You on the sauce, cub?"

Lucas felt a growl rise in his throat as he blinked away a tear he felt with instinctive shame. He sat straight up in the saloon's booth seat, head swimming.

"I said have you been drinking like that heel of a father you—"

Lucas got up on rubbery feet and slipped round the dog, pushing at the Colonel's coffee-stained suit on the way by and not caring. He heard the claws click on the planks as he was followed.

Lucas resented that. Couldn't the fucking dog figure out when to back off?

His own tail was lashing as he glanced back to the bar where the tender stood like a statue, staring his way. The bottle was still upright before him, and afternoon sun caught a glint of something potent roiling within, vigorously shaken. In that quick glance before the bottle was lifted and returned to where it had been sequestered, Lucas noticed through the brief play of light that it was somehow full.

His tail was grabbed and he yelped and span around.

"You don't walk off on me, cub. I've put a lot of faith and time into you!"

"But you don't trust me!" Lucas snarled at him and the G-shep's Stetson nearly slipped from his head. A couple of heads turned their way.

Lucas met his glare with one of his own. "All this time you've held me up like a prop while we move from city to city, making me your gopher while you grab all the accolades for the great mission for the carnivore cause. I'm getting sick of your shadow!"

"You haven't earned any more." The Colonel's voice was low and gravelly with threat.

Lucas took a deep breath and went for broke, slapping that hand away. They were being watched intently now by the few other sleepy drinkers at the bar's corners. He kept his voice down but held the G-shep's gaze. "Then tell me what's in Boston. It's not just the rally. You keep hinting that something big is waiting for us to Benny and Lucy, something bigger than recruitment. So what is it? How can I help? How can I be what you really want if I don't know?"

The Colonel took deep breaths, pushing his lips back down over teeth he wanted to bare. If the Colonel cuffed Lucas, would he hit the him back?

"We took care of that clawrag who sired you. He ain't dead, but he won't be coming round anymore. No more distractions from the cause."

Lucas could read implications in the Colonel's eyes. The dog knew how to make eyes that met his see the long trail of consequences. A twinge of sympathy tried to well its way up within him and he drove away from it steadily. "When can I know where this is all going?"

The smile he drew out of the man he'd followed across two states gave him renewed hope.

***

They both felt it, curling across the dusty median at the small town's outskirt. So much was in motion, close and distant, racing and creeping. "All the spokes moving at once," Grisand muttered as she stared into the Model A's open bonnet and watched the engine's soul make for heaven cloaked in black oil. The cylinders stuttered weakly. "And we're barely gonna limp to the first joint. Goddamn piece-a'-*merde* auto."

"We've got to get deep into Hancock," Baliosi said. "I feel it. The draught there's been given and taken. What's more, there ain't a proposition involved. No favor demanded. It was drank for drink's sake. And yet..."

Grisand made a thoughtful noise, hammered the bonnet shut and dug the folds of her ratty shawl. "Thought I had the tickle. Well, we'll get it. For now, I gotta get onna teller-phone. *L'écureuil roux* is fretting by the beach. Need to shake that tail for help getting this beast looked at."

"You want another neck-nibbler to get involved?"

Grisand rolled eyes and shook whiskers, stamping her tail as she gave the wolf a look-over. "She already is, Bal. Way too many of 'em are. This one's got scratch to lend at least so we can get gettin'. Trail's getting cold."

Another thread pulled taut as Baliosi stared at the overheated car and even though it did little good, she had to pluck it. "A mammal morose draws to the wharf,"

"With danger close and plotters north…"

Across the street at the diner a lone, bedraggled figure shuffled, flies lighting on dark-suited shoulders and lifting off again as the figure peered through a window, searching for somebody. Limping with a sigh, they trudged on past the opening door. A weasel leaving the place took a whiff of the air in the figure's wake and yanked the cap off his own head, shoving it over his nose with a gag.

Grisand turned back to the diner as the dark figure stumbled around its flank and past the garage next door. "Got a nickel for the telephone, Bal? There's one in front of that diner."

A couple coins changed hands between them, cold as blind eyes.

"Get me some pie?"

"It'll be stale. We felt that already."

"Stale pie's still pie," Baliosi frowned.

"Fine."

***

Donovan should have been tired, but he wasn't. Even as the sun beat beyond the drawn curtains of the Royal York Hotel, he was giddy with the sense that all the skulking and hiding of the last decade might truly be at an end. The lynx who'd escorted him through the lobby of the hotel skirted lanes of sunlight as casually as one of his own former workers at Calvert Steel would wind past amber-tinted hissing girders. A gold-leafed elevator took them up to the ninth and down a hall where a beaver maid pushing a service cart ignored them both.

To Donovan's surprise the lynx's room was rather modest, a small taupe-papered suite with a singular poster bed and a petite sitting area, lights kept low and blinds well fastened against the day.

"You were expecting opulence, weren't you? One of the suites kept for royalty or other foreign dignitaries."

"I didn't know what to expect," Donovan replied, and while it was true, he couldn't say he wasn't disappointed.

"You're already finding out that what you owned in breath you were set to lose as each day passed. Reborn, you could literally take it all with you, and yet time makes all you formerly cherished irrelevant. I've learned this." Ferrault took one end of the short couch and undid the button on his jacket. "So, to an extent, have you. A king in the most opulent castle is just an ember burning out while we're gods even when lurking under the mossiest rocks, walking in an eternity they can't even conceive. I've long wanted for very little. Wanting for less is one form of power." The lynx's eyes regarded Donovan thoughtfully. "Who really burnt down your toy castle, was it Mallory or you?"

Donovan felt pinned in place by the question but allowed himself the honesty. "I did."

"If you couldn't have it…"

Donovan didn't want to answer that.

"Come and sit." Ferrault patted the other end of the short couch. "Such a long, torturous trip. You need to relax."

Donovan didn't want to get close to the lynx. In his perfect stillness the cat had a coiled viper's vigor.

"I suppose you would be afraid of me," the lynx said without any relish. "Just as well. Though I saved you in those mountains with the crossbow from that improvised blind of mine, you're asking an important question, 'How much do I blame you?'" Slender marble-furred hands spread to show empty black palms, then returned to his white-slacked lap. "You did work for a worldwide organization that sought to eradicate our kind. You used your intellect, ambition, and chutzpah to craft detection weapons that brought torturous, unrelenting pain by mere proximity, with relief only found by way of the famine of denied needs. Alisandre Mallory brought you into the fold, what, ten years ago? Longer? Do you feel those needs are simple to deny, the dry path easy to take? Were you ever able?"

Donovan didn't answer, feeling the tightness of his ears flattening back. The window blind was behind him, an eyelid from agony. The exit to the room was ten steps past where the lynx lounged, eyes glittering hungrily his way.

"For all I've done for you already I'd really love an answer."

Donovan swallowed. "I wasn't."

Ferrault sighed. "We'd made plans, you know. That edifice filled with your iron shit in Chicago, some trade building, has deep shafts running far under street level."

A knock came to the door and Ferrault turned his head. "Come in."

The door opened and a mink entered. She was slender, silk pelt catching a table lamp's weak light under her laced chiffon dress. The barest outlines of wire-framed knickers were visible under the adornment as she entered. By her comportment and near absence of attire she carried herself as a courtesan for royalty.

"Will your brother be joining us?" Ferrault asked her as she closed the door and began removing her dress.

"He is very tired. With your grace he may need the night to recover." Her dress settled across the bed and she quickly worked the slips and catches of her underthings.

"Of course," Ferrault beckoned. Moments later she was naked and slinking over to the couch where she nestled her soft slender frame against his.

Donovan felt pinned to the spot, standing at the window, arousal not reaching him yet.

Ferrault played with the fur behind her ears and she closed her eyes with an almost catlike purr. "Where was I?" His ears flicked. "Oh yes. We had plans to obtain tainted bars from your burnt-down mansion's fence, have a suitably tight cage constructed."

"That tickles," the mink said with a chuckle.

"Sorry, dear." Ferrault moved to her bare shoulder and collarbone with softer strokes. A bare breast shifted up and down tantalizingly. Donovan caught her scent then. She was mortal. Her heart hammered with anticipation.

Ferrault stroked. "Your machinations made Chicago all but unlivable for us, Donovan, a nexus of culture and sensual exploration locked away forever to us all, much as you intended to do with every center of civilization across this world. Frankly, we wanted recompense." His eyes rose to

Donovan's and the smile was cold. Donovan again judged his distance to escape.

"Once we had you, Donovan, we were going to have our mortal friends, of which we have more than you'd expect"—another stroke—"seal you in that cage of the very agony you'd refined for us, then lower you into one of the foundation pits where just enough room was made for the steel structure of the building to sway and settle over decades, an oubliette of wonderfully just consequences. There you'd be forgotten, in the dark, raving, screaming against your gag."

Ferrault's hand found the mink's breast and squeezed and she breathed deep and shuddered, the steam of life's heat jumping off her now. Ferrault's other hand slipped low and explored playfully as he spoke. "Clerks sipping their morning wine or coffee or whatever drags them through the day would dimly hear the anguished moans every so often, feel the vibrations of something hammering deep in the dark below the city and ask themselves, is that the train again? Or is that the ghost of the lost worker, the suicided stockbroker, the mob-hit snitch? You'd be the seed of a thousand ghost stories. And only we'd know. For the centuries you'd endure...we'd know."

The minx gave a delighted tinkle of laughter and squirmed. Donovan was terrified and aroused and the conflagration of emotions crashed like waves within him. The lynx all but forgot the rabbit standing there, caressing the mink as she twisted athletically and dived her hand past the bent corsage under Ferrault's suit breast, feeling the stillness there.

Ferrault's fangs were starting to extend and he glanced up. "But I changed my mind. Really, Calvert, you're a product of your time and what's hundreds of years of suffering against an honest chance for penance, to prove your commitment to our cause and in servitude reverse your judgement. Care of what I offer you, Donovan, this could be your lucky day!"

The mink was light in the lynx's paws as he bore her up, one hand cupping her buttocks, wiggling as fingers teased under her tail like an inverted pianist. He carried her towards the bed and laid her supine before removing his own jacket.

Donovan didn't realize that he'd backed up against the wall to the window's right side. His pants were tenting and he hated how it made him look.

"Well, Donovan, the picture I painted had an effect I didn't anticipate." Ferrault laughed. "I'll lay it out for you." He bent and suckled briefly on the mink's tit, fingers dancing across her form like a virtuoso, teasing where the fur recessed into darker spaces. "There are members of that snotty hunting club you were a part of, here, now in this hotel. Two Martyres of the Black Well checked in last week to hunt for Nosfurs whom I beckoned lead them here. You and I are going to have that fun I promised. There will be some pain involved, but much more pleasure. The best part is that as none are alive who know that you've ascended to a higher state, we can work off part of the plan you used in New York. I'll lay it all out for you after I've finished." Ferrault's slacks fell to the floor and Donovan saw the lynx's pink erection brushing the bedspread where the mink squirmed, giggling excitedly.

Involuntarily, he stepped forward.

The lynx's gaze pierced him, his fingers rising wet with mink essence to caution Donovan before returning to the task. "Not quite so fast, Don. You'll have the chance to prove yourself but your penance starts now. Get naked if it pleases you, but today you'll learn to like to watch."

Ferrault slipped onto the bed soundlessly, and the mink made beckoning noises, stretching and turning her head just so. The lynx's fangs and cock found their points of sustenance daintily but insistently and Donovan ached at all there was to witness.

Chapter 15

Licked Wounds

"I'll need a minute or two alone." Agent Tomlinson cleaned his glasses and his naked weasel's eyes meeting the mastiff's on watch at the hospital were tired.

"Of course," she said and stepped aside. The G-mammal entered the hospital room.

The skunk was a wheezing mess. He'd seen that Boris Karloff picture *The Mummy* at a bijou about two years ago and the shape under all the gauze brought that back to memory. When the firemammals pulled her from the basement south of Scranton, she'd been too horrible for any cinema: fur burnt away in many places and her nose and lip chewed halfway to the bone. Tomlinson sat in the tiled room with its scrubbed, sympathetic scents and wondered how much pain the morphine allowed her to feel.

Her dose had been limited at his insistence and over the yowling of the feline physician. Tomlinson assured him that he'd be brief. Two eyes glared through the haze his way.

"It's just you and me. I'll get my answers and you can rest." It clearly hurt when she nodded.

"Who was in the house?"

She whispered and he had to lean in close to hear.

"Was she alone? Did you see a goat kid with her?" The crease in her expression told her that she'd seen him. This turned to fury that cracked her lip and made the gauze pink.

"Don't get excited. Stay calm. Did they do this to you?"

Her expression was full of daggers.

"We're marshalling all our resources to find them now. Did you find anything in the house before it burned, anything that told you where they might be now?"

Her expression was disdain and disappointment and he wasn't surprised. The wolf and the doe had clients in their detective work. The officers had confirmed as much. Now most if not all of those records were gone.

Of course, Tomlinson was pretty sure where he could find the wolf.

He raised a coarse paper bag and peeled back its lip to expose the walnut hilt of something tarnished but deadly. "Is this yours?"

Her eyes locked on it and there was a peculiar sense of relief that drifted through all the other smells.

"I'll keep it safe for you, how about that?"

Their eyes locked for a moment to trade even stares.

"We'll need to talk more later, but for now, just get well. You can do that for me, can't you?" He smiled and the skunk didn't smile back.

There was a cold anger in Tomlinson when he finally left the room and he had the pamphlet recovered from the station in his hand again.

Detective Latimer was smoking like a chimney in the waiting room. The fox cop shared a Camel with a cat with a bandaged ear, so he'd made one friend at least. "Skunk give you a better smell to follow?" Latimer asked.

"She confirmed a suspicion or two. My best lead is waiting in Hancock, Maryland. I've got to get down there."

"Want me to notify the locals? They're busy with that American recovery revival thing but—"

"No."

"What should I do with the skunk? Call some buddies of yours in Washington?"

Tomlinson locked eyes with him. "Absolutely not. Leave all that to me. I'm the only channel back to Dee Cee and that's how they want it, got me?"

The fox took a theatrical sigh and stubbed his Camel out in a stand next to the nurse's desk. "You're the boss." For now, his tone added.

Tomlinson was behind the Tudor's wheel and pointed at Hancock minutes later.

***

Crawford smelled himself as he came to and it wasn't good. He saw wet slacks terminating over brown fur before him and the smell through the mire was familiar. "Crawford," Charlie sounded…disappointed. "Damn, Craw, we need to get you gone and fast."

Crawford half expected to be naked and bloody but it was his mortally proportioned, clothed mess that flopped in the shallow water under the reeds and reintroduced him to a dozen hurts. Wet clothes clung to his own frame shamefully. "Lucas?"

"I told you not to—" Charlie bit off a growl and got arms under Crawford to lift him. They teetered to their feet together and splashed out of the pit, Crawford a mess from head to toe and Charlie's long coat speckled with splashes of dirt. Charlie grunted as he helped Crawford pick his way up the ditch opposite the tent under the late-afternoon clouds and make it to the dark Chrysler still idling. The first three steps hurt like hell; pain lanced up under his right rib cage with each wet plant of his right foot. The left knee was already swelling, the kneecap nearly floating on a bath of brine. He tasted copper in his raw mouth like he'd been licking pennies and his left orbital socket hurt with each turn of his eye. Charlie opened the back seat on the driver's side and ushered Crawford in, ignoring his moans and protests before closing him in and taking the driver's seat.

"Lie down. You look like you need to sleep anyway," Charlie mumbled, glancing left and right. It occurred to Crawford without any more exertion rattling his bones that Charlie was angry with him. He couldn't guess why that would be.

So he slipped down and put his head on the floor mat as the car got moving. Each bounce on the seat while the car rolled through the muttering crowds brought a tincture of nausea. The right rib was definitely bruised. Breathing confirmed it wasn't quite broken. His traditional remedy was still in his car and he wondered if the bourbon would be stolen by somebody desperate, going car to car.

He also wondered before he blinked his eyes shut if his son had seen him in that ditch. Seen him and left him.

Maybe so. Fair was fair. He passed out in misery.

He awoke again when they were at a hotel outside the small town, cars darting the lot here and there. This surprised Crawford when he sat up with a bleary groan and found himself one among many. Half the other cars had prone or slumped forms inside. Many of the lost and dispossessed whom the Colonel had beckoned here plainly slept in their cars in and around the town if they had a car to sleep in. Other souls no doubt thumbed it into town with bindles on their backs. He'd felt their anger, a familiar miasma. Speakeasies back in the Windy City had been crammed to the gills with those almost too poor to pay for a drink. They were the first off their stool with the claws and fists when the law rolled in.

In this groggy moment, that was all of America right now, a raided sanctuary whose denizens were ready for a scrap.

Crawford dimly realized he had a dilapidated home waiting with a doe and a kid who were both going to be sore if they woke without a supper to sup on. Were the rats even safe in his car? He knew the windows had been cranked down a bit but…

The hell had he been thinking coming here?

"Take some. You're going to ask," Charlie said in a clipped voice when he hustled a limping Crawford into a room at the end of the row and locked the door behind them. A flask sloshed in his hand.

"Thanks." The first rusty slug moved round Crawford's gums and pinpointed two unhealed splits with pulse-pumping stings. Bed springs bounced as the bed intercepted him.

"Crawford, what in the absolute hell are you doing here?" Charlie pulled a rickety chair from a cheap oak vanity and perched anxiously.

Crawford hadn't been thinking of anything remotely amorous in his condition and realized as Charlie sat by the bureau that he wasn't either. Charlie looked like he wanted to sock him with the bedstand Bible.

"I warned you against coming here, told you we'd have it under control. And that was before you wound up on three states' wanted lists and with charges pending for evading arrest in Scranton."

"That wasn't me." Crawford tipped the flask back, wishing it had started full. He was in turmoil he couldn't unravel and desperately wanted to just quiet the noise. Just for a little bit.

"Who the hell was it then?"

"It was, well, me." He bared his teeth suggestively with a wince, then shrugged with a sniff. Then regretted doing both.

Charlie stared at him long and hard, nostrils on the end of his broad lupine nose fluttering. His next words were clinical when he calmed himself and found them. "Nobody died that I know of."

"I'm glad for that. I was picked up for something I didn't do, Charlie."

"And you couldn't hold it in?"

Crawford should have been angry at that question, but he just didn't have the energy. He took a breath that his rib bit him for. "Full moon, Charlie. You know I can't. There a shower in here? This place has a telephone so it's not too much of a dump."

"Yes," Charlie said, muzzle in his hands.

"Give me ten minutes." He needed twenty, his second-to-last set of clothes in the world piled up in one cream-linoleum corner with agonizing slowness. Raising his right arm higher than his shoulder hurt like hell. The water found more bruises under the fur and he let it. When he came out there were folded clothes on the bed.

"My travel set," Charlie explained. "It'll be tight on you but you won't smell like sweat, blood, and ditch mud."

Crawford finished drying himself off gingerly and noticed in the dresser mirror that Charlie didn't appraise him even once before he struggled into the clothes. He really was mad. "Charlie, thank you for your help. I'm really sorry that I couldn't stay away."

Charlie growled low. "Coming here endangered an operation I had to fight to get rolling, risked your son and yourself all at once. You'd have been better off going anywhere else on Earth."

"I know."

"It was stupid, Craw."

"I know. How did you find me?"

"The report came in from Scranton filed by an agent Tomlinson. Oh, I see from your expression that you've met. Well after you am-scrayed and burnt your own house down—"

"That wasn't me, not the Nosfurs either."

"We'll get back to that. There was a request to have police comb this event for you based on evidence left behind, a request I had to contact local Pee Dee in order to quash as it would damage a sensitive investigation."

"Thank you."

"Thank me?" Charlie growled low and long and Crawford realized he'd never seen his ex-partner this mad.

"Is that flask empty so I can bounce it off your skull? We believe that some local law may be in it with this Colonel bastard, maybe even the mayor's office, and now he might be tipped off. What's more, your past has been canvassed for a lot of irregularities. They know or will know soon enough that we worked together in Chicago. You may have compromised me personally twice over, dammit!"

Crawford found the bottom of the flask and the bottom of his stomach at the same time. He'd erred often in life, stepped carelessly into shit. This gaffe was something truly special.

Charlie paced the room, his tail swiping the bed. "It's a miracle that I found you before local law or Agent Tomlinson did."

"Or whoever you've got watching the Colonel and his men," Crawford muttered, seeing through his own folly just a little further.

Charlie glared his way for a moment, said nothing. He looked like he wanted to say a lot.

"I shouldn't ask when your people are going to move on the Colonel, should I?"

"No, you shouldn't. Crawford, I still don't know how large this group is or how in deep they are with local institutions. The Colonel has a few prominent business backers who like how he leans politically. They've cut a lot of pink slips over the past five years to shore up their fortunes and the anger needs to be directed."

"So, the same people who fired everybody out there want them after veggies instead," Crawford muttered. "Anybody you know?"

"Mostly banks consolidating farm foreclosures all across the Midwest and companies trying to shave off higher bottom lines. Charlatans like the Colonel are lifelines to those in it deep against labor." Charlie sat in the chair again and swallowed. "One example, the destitute carnies drifting West keep finding out that all the slaughterhouse jobs are being deliberately given to vegetarians because they won't steal any cuts off the lines, no matter how many of their own ribs they can count. The few carnies who scrounge up work when they get near the coast are instead chosen to pick berries at pennies on the bushel. Can you imagine what that does to the psyche of any carnie mammal raised on cherry-picked Biblical passages who drifted back from the Great War to this? Who feel cheated? Who are hunting for somebody to blame? This Colonel is pointing their muzzles at easier targets than the bastards who actually cheated them."

"I've met plenty of the type before today."

"That's just the surface of it." Charlie took a needed breath. "The whole thing has my team back in Dee Cee stumped. These goons are being financed by mysterious backers using them to smuggle materials and funds out of America. We've been tracing cells that worked out of Boston, Jersey, and New York, with this one in particular smuggling steel beams and ingots through front companies. There were large payments tracked for shipments of steel, far in excess of what it would ever be worth, clearly money laundering. All that steel originally was strangely forged by just one Chicago-based company. You'll never guess which one."

Crawford wanted to see if he could wedge a question or two about his son into the conversation, Charlie's anger be damned. But something in what he was saying made him perk up. "I don't know…wait, hold on, a Chicago steel company?"

Charlie had gotten his ire down a bit and settled on the bed next to him. "That's right."

"Charlie, was it Calvert Steel?"

"Small world, huh?"

Crawford took a deep breath, letting his senses gather stinks that had sunk into the corners of the room. In several years handling private investigations with Celeste he'd learned to recognize something between a scent and a sensation, the distinctive spoor of a key detail falling into place.

Crawford briefly pondered keeping the truth to himself, but he couldn't lie to Charlie. "Before all this went to hell and our house was torched, Celeste and I were hired to retrieve something from an old safety deposit box in Boston by a…client who had obtained a key and a power of attorney document. The objects were small splinters of iron, like rough-hewn nails. They cause Nosfurs pain just to be near and even annoy my senses a bit."

"What are they?" Charlie said, listening intently, his own analytical wheels turning.

"Well, they're apparently something that was used to make weapons for Nosfur hunters but had other uses as well. What I didn't know at the time was that a Nosfur hired us to do this, one Sandy Mallory. She's a friend of Celeste's you just missed meeting back in Chicago at Celeste's old place. She was a former associate of steel magnate and horrible temp employer Donovan Calvert."

"Dammit."

"It gets even better. My job was supposed to be simple: get the nails, have a dram at Haymarket Square, and get back to Scranton. But that bank got robbed by another party who stole that box before I could obtain it. I never found out who hired them or why. They got the drop on me, clobbered me over the head." Crawford would wince at the memory if it didn't hurt to wince. "I had to…deal with them in order to escape."

Charlie stared at him balefully. Anger had fled, now he was just disdainful. "A dockside murder made the papers because a bulldog they fished from the drink had no jaw."

"I…kinda remember that. They were going to torture me for information."

Charlie said nothing for a long time before getting up again to approach the lamp where the single burning bulb illuminated his muzzle from underneath. Even in the middle of day, what light was available stayed on. "You just aren't cut out for a normal life, are you, Crawford?"

"You're one to ask."

"Your problems are going to be hard to solve and my pull is limited. Tomlinson, for all I know, reports directly to Hoover."

"I kept my head low coming into town for all the good that may have done."

Charlie nodded. "If that Colonel bastard says a word to any law it won't be any at all. I've no doubt they'd kill to collect a reward." Something occurred to him. "You all fled Scranton. Did you bring the suckers?"

"Celeste and Samson miss you too. They're holed up at a second residence we bought in another state. Assuming I get back to them before six-thirty Celeste won't cuss me out."

"However we get you out of town, you need to stay off the board. Away from this fascist group, away from their smugglers, even your son. I mean it."

"I can't stay away from Lucas, Charlie."

That baleful glare again. Crawford loved him but he was getting tired of it.

"Just how happy was he to see you?" Charlie asked.

Crawford shifted in the chair with agitation and managed to tweak two injuries at once. "How much did you see?"

"Nothing. I heard a lupine drifter had the shit beat out of him. Down-on-luck people love sharing harder-luck stories. For reasons I wasn't capable of understanding in my youth I had an absent father, and I can imagine how your cub feels even if he doesn't know why it was necessary for you to stay apart."

"They're going to pull him too deep into this."

Charlie sighed. "You need to let this go and let me take care of it. Go back and all you can do is hurt him, expose our operation, and cause a world of harm, assuming you haven't done all that already. You met him and he said what he said. I understand you're angry, Crawford, but he's an adult who made choices. All I can do is minimize the harm when the things proceed."

The temperature in the room dropped as they traded stranger's gazes. "You wouldn't say something like that if you had children, Charlie. I love you but…goddamn you." His hackles were up. He couldn't help it.

Strangely, Charlie's weren't raising in return. As angry as he'd been at the start, his mate had gotten himself under control rather quickly. "I'm sorry, Crawford."

"I don't doubt it."

Charlie looked away. Crawford saw shame in those eyes through the haze of his own misery and understood that they were both shackled by needy, uncompromising monsters, one hungry and impulsive, the other coldly bureaucratic.

Silence cut the room in two.

"Sandy Mallory had information on the nails," Crawford said abruptly, needing to change the subject. "She might also have some other leads that she hadn't passed us yet. The steel has to be obtained by others who have records right? Maybe she can help you, I dunno, figure more of this out."

"You know where to find her?"

Crawford remembered the exchange even though he'd only dialed their last client once. "I need the telephone."

***

Sandy couldn't rest despite the urgent need to do so. There was too much at stake and she had no idea if Celeste and the others were safe, making it impossible to let herself recover. When her second line for business rang it pulled her directly from the temporary touch of oblivion. She had the phone in her hand in two quick bounds. Only one person should be calling on that line. "Celeste?"

"In a wet cold place both new and old," a voice croaked.

"Lost souls meet and callous truths told..." added another further from the receiver.

Silence.

Sandy furrowed her brow. "Is this the Belle sisters?"

The first voice sighed reluctantly. "Uh...okay, gonna level with you, *rouge*. We need gas and wrench money and we know you have some of the rabbit's moolah left. Is there a Western Union out there on the coast where you are?"

Sandy twitched her tail in confused consternation. "Why do you need money from me? You can see the future—"

"We're out of service at the moment, no pennies in the arcade. Tilt buzzer! But we're followin' a lead that can help us all."

"Help us all? How?"

"I don't know."

"Who is it that can help?"

"Dunno either."

"Well, what do you know other than that you need money?"

"A place. You can be there, or your slinky doe friend can be there, or that strappin' wolf with the hooch tick and the cute brown coifed G-mammal on his arm, but it's gotta be somebody! Cause if nobody goes..."

"What?"

"Dunno that eith—"

"Jesus Merciful Christ." Sandy's tail kinked. "Just tell me where to be and where to send the feckin money."

Baliosi and Grisand argued over their current location from wherever that was and Sandy sighed as they squabbled. "*As ucht Dé*."

They gave her the details for a Western Union office in Hancock, Maryland. Then Grisand told her to hold on a minute more. The sound of flipping pages were like autumn leaves though the phone line and there were noises of assent before the otter repeated what the wolf was reading aloud. "The intersection of Devonshire and Water Street needs you to get yourself there. It's in Boston."

Sandy dragged over the pad and wrote the details down hastily. She could feel an electricity in the air, even hundreds of miles from wherever they were. It was off-putting to say the least. "Why Boston?"

"You need to take another call." Grisand said and disconnected.

Outside the drawn shades the light was bleeding horizontally. It was late in the day and Sandy's heart swelled when the phone she returned to its cradle did ring again as promised. "Celeste!"

"She's fine. Samson too. They're holed up now while I'm further south. Did I wake you?"

Sandy grit her flat teeth. "No. I was quite present."

"Good. I've got an important question. Pertains to the case we were working for you."

The fresh reminder that all the accumulated nails were in shallow pits less than a hundred yards from a burnt-down house being combed by police deepened Sandy's already-active anxiety. "I can't rightly think of anything I've left out."

"Well, you know we might have competition to find those nails and we just might have a lead on who that is."

"Somebody you didn't see off I assume?" Sandy had to be droll. It was the best maintenance for sanity.

"Possibly lots of somebodies, though you wouldn't be happy to meet them. The nails and Donovan's steel are connected right? You told Celeste what that was about but we never went over the details."

"The simplest explanation is that those nails are imbued with special properties and form the cores of the reliquary weapons used by agents of the Martyres of the Black Well. Before he changed sides." Sandy took a moment for a self-satisfied if pained snicker. When she found that bastard… "Donovan developed a process for making them into steel girders for his construction projects, parts of vast detection nets that cause fed Nosfurs pain and reveal our location to whoever holds the other part of the nail, or nails. He'd been refining that part of things when his world came tumbling down."

"Well, some people who my friend in government is following seem to be obtaining Calvert's steel and we don't know where it's going to. I know you made him...well, what matters is, do you know where the rabbit is now?"

***

The day had gone long and Donovan had eventually found the dark in the curve of one of the room's chairs, trying to tune out the smell of mink sex as he blinked through what felt like an instance of restorative darkness. Ferrault stood over him when he opened his eyes again, changed into another shirtless jacket, this time copper pinstriped.

Ferrault cocked an ear. "Dusk waker, good. Sleeping in is so wasteful."

Donovan's eyes darted to the bed where two minks, the female from last night and a male companion, were nestled naked in one another's arms. She was white as snow but her male counterpart was brown to black from ears to toes. Donovan smelled blood on the air and it made him hungry.

"Not yet. Tonight, you prove yourself and you'll be supping well enough. Some old friends of yours from overseas are now checked in."

Donovan sat up, then rose. He realized he'd been in the same clothes for several days now and despite his body's escape from age there were other environmental factors that made them feel positively disgusting on his frame. "You mean, some of my, their order...are here? Now?"

Ferrault stepped back and sat on the bed. The minks made pleasant noises as the mattress behind him shifted. "Specifically, from what little my spies have gathered, it seems to be a seasoned hunter and his, I don't know how you'd say it, apprentice?"

"If he's attending a hunter, learning from him, he'd be an acolyte. I had the position for eleven months in Oxford and then London."

"How very pretentiously important sounding. Important question is, do they both have branding swords?"

"Reliquaries."

The sour look from Ferrault shut Donovan up. "There's as much saintly presence under my testicles as there is in those vicious murder toys of yours. What a disgusting nomenclature."

Donovan said nothing, ears low.

"Well?"

Donovan got himself back on track. "The hunter has a reliquary, but an acolyte is taught to use their intuition and other senses to the best of their ability before they're granted a…weapon that suits their fighting style."

"Such as your old mentor's axe."

Donovan's gaze rose to meet the lynx's. "Christof was never my mentor. The bastard used me and never wanted me in the Order in the first place."

Ferrrault reached out and with the flick of a finger stood one of Donovan's ears erect. "Can't guess why. I'm sure it's a perfectly specist little club you had there."

Donovan didn't want to talk about this. "It was making changes, reluctant though they were. In any case, you want me to deal with them."

"I have questions for the hunter. But getting in close enough without being detected is too difficult and I can't ask my friends to risk their mortal lives for this." He leaned back again and a claw tickled a mink's foot sole-pad making them squirm just a bit.

"You've passed my first two tests for you, Donovan, so I think you're ready."

"Which tests?"

"Resistance to pain with composure. And last night, restraint. I know you were getting excited."

Donovan's eyes roved to the tangle of mink limbs on the bed, two pelts, milky and chocolate, rising and falling with the beating of flush hearts. "Let's just get to it, shall we?"

"But of course, Donovan. And as I said, you know half the plan already, care of that gambit of yours in the Catskills. This time, however, the box won't be full of explosives."

Donovan stood and started pacing. He couldn't help it. "Won't the reliquary presence hurt like hell?"

"For a short time. Pain is as transitory as joy is. As will be yours when you bring them both something else in a smaller box to pique their interest and fool their toys."

There was a burlap satchel on the armoire by the door. A small wooden cigar box sat next to it.

"I have to approach them…directly?"

"Yes. You're known amongst your Nosfur-hunting lodge fellows and could get them up to the room I have ready without too much suspicion.

You only need to be convincing for a minute or two. Most of what happens up here will be up to me."

Donovan remembered the agonies of the Albany train yard and he felt cold.

"Oh, come on, Donovan. Do you know how hard it was to stay still under a blanket in those hills in New York while sunlight soaked through the fabric like lava through porous rock? The first two kills with that crossbow were easy enough, but finishing them all while that pain mounted and mounted..." Ferrault was off his feet and had his arm around Donovan's shoulders in a flash. He was a half foot taller but with his ears suddenly erect Donovan heard him like a whisper within himself. "I know that this won't be too fun for you but I promise there are rewards in store. Carry this off without any hitches and Mercel will be happy to suck your cock."

On the bed where two heads nuzzled, one eye opened under a dark-lifted brow and the lip below it curled happily.

Donovan blinked. "I'd honestly prefer..."

Ferrault's thick fingers squeezed his shoulder. "Don't turn down a wonderful thing on some masculine pretense you've no use for anymore. Myra's best skills are in her hips."

There was a knock at the door.

"Yes," Ferrault called.

A key worked the lock and it swung inward a few inches. Donovan tried to turn but Ferrault held him fast. The visitor spoke from outside. "They're getting drinks at the bar," a male voice crisply reported. "Do we have the name?"

"Ah yes, I forgot. Donovan, you owe me a name as I do recall." Lynx teeth grinned close enough to tickle the rabbit's ear fuzz.

Donovan licked his lips. He'd been mulling over what importance an old alias of Sandy's doe friend could have had but had come up empty. "Marie Laquoix."

"You know what inquiries to make," Ferrault called back. The visitor closed the door behind him.

"Dusk has come. It's now cocktail hour downstairs and your old friends are hopefully thirsty. I know I am." Ferrault let go of Donovan and picked up the cigar box, offering it to him. "The plan is simple. Listen carefully..."

Donovan did so, taking a moment as the lynx spoke to open the cigar box for a peek. What he saw inside nearly made him drop it.

CHAPTER 16

DIRECTIONS GIVEN

"I hear somebody breathing next to you," Sandy said. The light was low outside and she was mostly packed. She wondered if she'd ever return here.

"That's Charlie. He's harmless even with a badge." The grumbling off the line receded.

"Badge?"

"He can be trusted. He's probably been in my life for as long as Celeste has been in yours."

Sandy could laugh. "I highly doubt that."

"Well, look, do you know where Calvert is now?"

"He came here. He left. If I see him again, I'll end him." Certainty was a cold, simple thing.

"So, you don't know where the rest of his shards are?"

He was asking for the government man as much as himself, and that made her more than wary. She could barely trust the were, much less a blind, clanking hand of Uncle Sam. "If he gave me that information, how safe am I giving that to you?"

There was a pause while the wolf on the other end weighed that. "Nobody knows what you are and, well, Charlie and I talked about this long ago. To even try to tell anybody he works with about you or Celeste or Samson would put him in a loony bin pretty quickly. I can promise you the location of the nails would be safe with us. Charlie can even arrange to get the other ones collected."

"You need to swear that to me, Crawford. Even though you know what they could do to Celeste and Samson, the only people I might add who can see you through your own plight in this world…"

"I'm aware, Sandy. By God, I'm all too aware."

"Swear to me that this information goes between you and him only. I don't have the means to get the nails anymore myself. Bruno…"

"Celeste told me. I'm sorry."

She believed his word only because she knew Celeste did. "If I give you of deposit boxes and caches left, you get them and hide them until we can get them all together to destroy them."

"You have my word."

Sandy read the addresses and a couple bank names off the sheet on which Donovan had scrawled before betraying her. As she finished, she noted her own handwriting on the next sheaf of paper below. "There's something else."

"One more address?"

"Yes, but not for Calvert's nails. The Belle sisters called me. They're near Hancock, Maryland."

There was a long silence. "That's…where we're calling from. Why do I think I know who that is?"

"Because they were in Chicago back when we all were. They speak in riddles and limericks mostly…"

There was a long silence on the phone. "Oh. Yeah, we have met."

"They know who you are. And I think they referred to your wolf friend as well. In fact, I was speaking to them on the phone almost immediately before you."

The silence was even longer. "What did they want?"

"They gave me another address. Not for nails. They don't even know what it was for, only that it would be important to all of us."

"I'm listening."

"Intersection of Devonshire and Water Street, Boston, Massachusetts. It's several blocks east of the bank you went to for that nail cache you had to get back from the robbers. They had no idea why the location was important but said it's imperative that somebody gets there." Sandy looked at her open luggage. "And I intend to do just that. I've only one more call to make before I go. Do you know where I can reach Celeste?"

Crawford sighed. "That intersection is also less than a quarter mile from the docks where I was almost finished off by those thugs. There's nothing remarkable about that part of town that I can remember. Why the hell do we need to go back?"

***

"I'm sorry Lil"—the fox's parting words dripped with sympathy—"but they'll clear this place out if they don't get their way. Law ain't doing a damn thing." Hours had passed but the sting stayed fresh in Lillis's mind. She aimlessly wandered through seas of the destitute who'd converged to be fed comforting lies, consumed and then excreted from the tent that the Colonel's savage circus erected. Despite her imposing presence, she was ignored by all around her, anonymous in a town she'd lived in for years.

She'd recommended the only bar in town to patrons on more than one occasion, and realized that, not being a drinker, she couldn't remember the name of it. Its sign was faded enough that she was almost at the door when she read it, O'Holler's Bar. She had two dollars and a well of misery to drain. Maybe just one.

The lion approached when she took a stool, appearing to sniff her with some preternatural sense a barmammal has. "Have you been here before?"

"No," she said, so quietly that she herself barely heard it.

The old lion ruminated on that. "Not sure if you need what I'd usually offer."

She dug out a nickel. "Whatever this gets, please."

He nodded, feeling a hurt that wanted quiet, and moved down the bar.

That was when she heard the shuffle. And caught the smell. Musty, filthy, like a ditch digger pelt-deep in clay and the film of rot that came with it. She felt something at her shoulder and turned to a downturned hat brim with a torn, blackened ribbon.

The black nose underneath quivered and a thin film of mucous dripped. "You need to get to the Tavern," came a strangled whisper.

Lillis wanted to gag at the smell, but had served all manner of customers in her years behind an apron and kept her composure. "I don't work there anymore," she said flatly.

"No. The Bell in Hand. Boston. I had a stake in it from eighty-eight until thirty-one. Then I was cashed out, came back home to take my rest." There was a noisome cough, and something Lillis couldn't make out tumbled down the dark suit and a necktie like rose-flesh dried to ash. She looked down to see dark soil between white feet that were naked.

Naked bone with no pelt or flesh.

Her heart began hammering in her chest and she found herself iced to her stool, startled as a short glass slid before her, whiskey winking as it sloshed. "Enjoy," muttered the lion from down the bar, his attention drawn by another client who in turn didn't look her way. Nobody looked her way. Somehow, no one saw. Conversations carried on, loud and syrupy with libation.

"Best ales out there, at the Bell in Hand I mean," the voice under the hat rasped. "They always need a hand." His own skeletal digits reached out, some bound in shriveled flesh, some stripped down to grey twigs. One hand crossed the other and a tarnished ring was clasped. One tug, then another, and then flesh slid off with it, leaving a sloughed sock of meat like a wet cigar shell on the countertop.

Lillis's breath caught in her throat and she nearly screamed, her voice lost in tight heaves.

"You'll mix many things for many clients, recipes old as this country. You've the skill." The figure coughed again, dislodging something deep and unwanted. "You've forgotten more than you know."

The wraith never raised his head, never showed more than a desiccated nose under that hat brim. The ring it released rolled across the bar in tiny circles that ended with a wobble. "Get there fast before the taps run too cold. They freeze when the taps get too cold. Tell them that Gus is owed a favor. Tell it to Mikkel directly. That ring'll get your ticket. Go now." There was a squelch on the stool as the creature slid away and he raised one hand to lift his hat for only an instant.

Above the muzzle bone's termination where the skull would meet it there was nothing at all.

Lillis frozen spine kept her erect as the figure shuffled away, claws clicking the floorboards and leaving a smear on the door when he opened it and slipped out into Hancock's streets. His suit was parted up the back, the kind slid on and around a bony frame intended to ceaselessly rest. It folded back from the molting pelt like crows' wings and then he was gone.

She downed the whiskey, left her nickel and a few extra cents before clutching the cold ring with a twice-wound napkin and slipping back into the world.

***

Dusk came to the small house and Crawford didn't. Worry dampened the silence. "We need the phone working," Celeste said and Samson could only nod morosely. It had been her own insistence that they install one as soon as they bought the place, and they knew that, used or not, Ma Bell would be happy to take their money. The worn candlestick phone they'd left there had been claimed by a spider or two and it was an even guess as to whether it would pull a current to make the call when they hooked it up.

Silence pervaded the small house as she worked at the kitchen table. "How're you holding up, Samson?"

"Fine." He didn't care that she knew he was lying.

"Thank you again for saving me." She stopped working long enough to hold the goat's gaze. "I'd have been killed if you hadn't intervened."

He looked away. "Least I could do after I brought it all to us in the first place."

"You didn't bring the skunk. That was myself or Crawford bringing back those damned nails."

"I brought the police. I was weak and I fed and—"

"And they attacked you, and you were starving. We settled this."

"I still brought the law to us." The goat wasn't convinced and clicked one hoof on the other as he leaned against the kitchen vanity. "What mistakes have you ever made?"

Celeste sighed. Getting him to accept certain things would take time. They had that. "Where to start counting? I was brought into the world without understanding of what it meant, just as you were, and lost the most important people in my life up until then. Then spent nearly a hundred years living in embittered hedonism, killing often, taking advantage of whomever I could. I collected many regrets before I met Sandy Mallory on the voyage to America." She wound the two wires and screwed the connections shut before setting the telephone down, pressing the earpiece cradle twice and listening for the hum. "Some of the local exchanges are still using loading coils rather than vacuum tubes. I hope we get a good signal. Ah, yes, thank you. No, operator, I'm just checking to make sure this line is working. I haven't used it in some time. Have a good evening."

Celeste put the receiver back. "When we moved here, to New York first, I made a few mistakes more. One of them was failing to see that Sandy had been drawn into Donovan Calvert's cult of Nosfur slaves."

"You said she'd been convinced that she'd been living in sin."

Celeste nodded and sat back in the chair. "It's the question we all ask ourselves, Samson. I know you've asked it too. We have the capacity to cause such pain and sorrow, even unintended—"

"But you don't." Samson said.

"We can manage what we need, Samson. I didn't realize it at first. I'd fallen in with a kind of cult of my own with Torrio's outfit in Chicago. I killed killers for the most part, but even when it became easy, when I became settled into the routine of feeding on mobsters who stepped out of line, I didn't realize that it was a horrid life."

Samson pondered that, arms folded tight in front of him, one hoof lightly clicking the other as though nerves threatened to take him to the roof. "What wasn't a horrid life?" He was asking himself as much as her. "With nearly a hundred and fifty years to think on it, what do you want? I mean really want?"

"Surprisingly, the same things every mortal wants. Safety, security, freedom from pain and the means to live without causing it. And love. I've wanted a quiet life long denied me. For you and me it's hard just as it's hard for Crawford in his own way. But it is possible, Samson. It's possible."

The goat met her gaze then. Twenty-five years of experience leadened his gaze. "Is it?"

The telephone rang just then and Celeste snatched it up barely a second before Samson. "Crawford?"

"No," Sandy said. "But I did get your new exchange from him. Slept in, did you?"

Celeste gripped the candlestick telephone worriedly. "I could only wish. Is Crawford okay?"

"I believe so. He's in Hancock, Maryland."

Of course. "We're all supposed to be laying low. How many police departments is he going to run afoul of in this half of the country?"

"Many to choose from," Sandy said, unable to insert any humor in her voice. "But that's not important now. I have to go to Boston."

Celeste's ears stood up and so did Samson's. "What's in Boston?"

"An intersection in the North End, near, I'm told, where your lupine friend met some unsavory types. What's important is who presented me with this information. The Belles are back."

"The sisters? Did they come to you?"

"No, they had me wire them some car repair money to Hancock. Where Crawford is."

Outside darkness had fallen completely now, and with it came an ethereal glow. Samson went to a blind and peered out of it. "Sun's gone. Moon's out now. No clouds," he muttered and Celeste immediately realized what that meant. Even with it close to full... "Do you know where Crawford is now? It's very important that we know."

"Motel on the outskirts of Hancock last we spoke. He's not alone."

That might have been very bad news. There was something else she wanted to ask Sandy, something that had been important. With all that was in the wind, she couldn't remember now. "We need to get to him. Did he tell you where they are staying?"

"He didn't. But Celeste, there's one of those carnie-first rah-rah rallies happening there. You and Samson would stick out like sore thumbs."

Celeste looked back to Samson again. "We wouldn't be looking for any trouble but if it found us there would be a lot more sore appendages than thumbs."

The glint in Samson's returned gaze was unsettling to say the least.

***

The bar off the main lobby of the Royal York was a brassy, upbraided affair, as well appointed as the library above. Donovan had wondered how he would find the pair he was looking for and realized soon enough that he'd only need to find discomfort and move in till it worsened. They'd worked that into the plan, of course.

He knew neither Martyre but could guess who fit the bill amongst the thin smattering of patrons from their bearing. The pair were both dressed in conservatively muted colors, tightly fitted for alley skulking; not hunting at the moment but ready to at any time. Both were also hatless. The stocky bulldog with the British accent had his back to Donovan as he slowly approached, snifter waving in his canine hand with the slightest sniff of crème de cacao and cognac. The dark-furred young fox across from him was ramrod-straight and attentive, a small tumbler of water before him. Acolytes were forbidden from drinking until they'd gained knight status, but this fox, as had Donovan himself, would likely drink off the job. The things he'd seen in that first year after joining the Order...

"Telephony from handling in London says we're still on our own, as it should be. More on foot in America it would appear," the bulldog said and sipped his Alexander. The dark fox just nodded over his water, tail still behind him.

Donovan took another few steps. Unless he'd left his reliquary elsewhere the dog had to sense him now. The urge to find a shadow and bind it for safety was palpable and he wrestled it down. He needed to get this part over with and readied himself for the discomfort to come. It found him at six paces and grew to a burning sensation at four. He held the cigar box before him and let the reliquary that the bulldog would hopefully have on his person tingle its way through the alcohol fuzzing his distracted head. It was a sloppy showing, Donovan had to admit.

The fox saw him standing there as the bulldog's hand went to the throb under his coat. He set the drink down and shot his gaze back at Donovan.

Donovan took a deep breath with useless lungs as he'd practiced so often. "Oculus vigiliae nunquam cludit." The eye of vigilance never closes.

The bulldog and fox stared at him as though seeing a wraith. Then the fox piped up. "Manus Dei semper praeparata est." The hand of God is ever prepared.

Donovan was loath to admit it, but Ferrault was right. After so long outside the fold, the trappings of it all sounded pretentious as hell. "Do you know who I am?" Donovan asked, his voice clipped to hide his discomfort.

They looked at one another, then at the rabbit. The fox seemed clueless but the bulldog would have seen the lists of the dead and the missing, Martyres lost to the cause over centuries. "Are you...Calvert? Donovan Calvert?"

Donovan kept ears back and gaze steely. The box was heavier in his hands as pins and needles pierced. "I've been...on long-term assignment... reporting directly to Von Haften. It's slow going, but I've rooted out more vermin here."

"Long-term assignment? You've been missing for over ten years!" He nearly spilled his drink on the lacquered oak table.

"Sequestered. My work has been quite involved."

The fox looked from bulldog to rabbit and back again while the bulldog in turn fingered the object under his coat. His soft eyes went flinty. "Involved you say. Get close to them, did you?"

Donovan read his expression and forced a smile. "Quite. I have secured a guest as a matter of fact, working the creature over for information. When I learned you'd arrived I thought I'd surface, ask for you to—"

"I have to confess," the bulldog growled, "I'm finding this rather spontaneous appearance of a member we'd long assumed lost at a hotel in Canada a bit peculiar."

Donovan knew what was going through the mammal's mind. Nosfurs turned up in places like this all too often, but never, ever preyed in public. Nor did the Martyres engage where all could see. This was a venue for stalking, assessing, maintaining careful distance lest the reliquary that picked the Nosfur quarry out alert it in turn. That was a skill in and of itself, another reason acolytes had to earn their tools.

That it had taken less than two yards before he'd even been sensed told Donovan this Martyre had gone to seed.

And now, head fogged by a drink in the field, the dog was confused as to how to act.

"You're getting the tell," Donovan said with a smile. "That's because I brought you a little welcome gift, care of my pet upstairs."

Discomfort became pain as he stepped closer and worked the cigar box lid, playing off his clear discomfort with a limp, an injury taken in a pitched battle. "I did make a mess taking him into my custody and now he's sequestered quite well."

He tipped the box as he opened the lid. The fox had leaned forward and then pushed back. The bulldog nearly spilled the dregs of his drink.

The light brown lynx's hand was severed inches below the wrist and already carried a scent of decay. Immortality didn't linger with anything materially parted from preternatural owners. Donovan closed the lid again and stepped back, not as far as he wanted, but enough to let the hunters overcome their surprise. "I'd been informed that agents would be coming here but I didn't get your names," Donovan said with a pained smile, managing to keep his fangs from projecting during the brief flash of flush teeth.

Thankfully the steak being carved two tables over wasn't too bloody.

The bulldog's ears were back and forward. "Madrey Sinclair and Vincent." Acolytes were only ever introduced by singular names, family names suspended until such time as they completed final trials and took the vows. The bulldog's mouth closed and he said no more.

Donovan didn't want to stand at four paces forever. "You've many questions no doubt and I have many of my own. If you help me with interrogating our friend on the ninth floor, well…" Donovan looked to the brown fox. "Have you taken your first yet?"

Ears went back nervously. "I…no."

"Well, this one will need a send-off when we're done. And then, from your attire, I'd assume you have hunting to do."

The bulldog nodded sagely as he slugged the last of his drink and straightened the reliquary in his jacket as he rose, eyes searching Donovan's. "You took one down within this hotel?" He glanced down to Donovan's weeks-old but scentless suit, hastily brushed out an hour ago. The longer everyone delayed, the more irregularities mounted.

"Yes." Donovan slid the cigar box under one arm, tapping it. "And this fragment your tool felt isn't the only thing removed. I'll provide more details on the way up. He'll be trying to…regroup about now."

"Push pin?" Code for impalement.

"Tight faucet." Donovan replied, slang used to indicate when a neck was garrotted or severed most of the way from the trunk, keeping the subject conscious but with so little contact with the body below that they were immobile. "But I must say, not as tight as I'd like."

That got everybody moving, giddy with excitement. Walking together, the pain came more forcefully; not the agony of Albany, but enough that Donovan winced as they moved together to the gold-plated elevator off the lobby with its deco veneer. Donovan kept the box between himself and the reliquary the bulldog bore as he selected the ninth floor and the badger attendant dutifully ran them up with agonizing slowness.

Sinclair didn't speak again until they disembarked. The hall was empty of witnesses. "Why would you bring such a souvenir down with you? It's not too crowded in that bar but what if it had been seen?"

Honesty turned a couple degrees made the best lies. "We hadn't been formally introduced yet and I needed to get you up here while my quarry was still contained. The hand's proximity to your reliquary gave you more proof than anything I could tell you. We weren't provided with business cards a decade ago when I went underground and I doubt that's changed."

The bulldog made a thoughtful noise that the fox duplicated, probably unconsciously, and Donovan felt what passed for butterflies in a body that only breathed through deliberate fakery. So recently in life these fellows were his compatriots, part of a brotherhood he'd been scorned for joining by some, but he'd been a brother nonetheless. And now, for what he'd become, they would butcher him right here on the ninth floor of this Canadian hotel.

So, betraying them was not his fault. Not his choice. God damn you, Sandy.

"What's that?"

He'd muttered the thought under his breath. "I'm just worried that the gag isn't secured properly. I don't want the bastard screaming for help."

"We shouldn't leave them long to do so," the bulldog said and cocked an ear. "So perhaps you should lead the way."

"This way," Donovan said, pain now progressing to agony as he tried to stay a few steps ahead. Despite his best efforts, his mind strayed into the fate Ferrault had pondered for him, lowered into the dark within his own steel prison, no sight, no smell, only unrelenting pain.

Donovan fought back panic as he weighed options. Could he betray Ferrault, help the hunters take him down and get back into the Martyres' good graces in some way? Be made a spy for the Martyres if he could somehow prove his devotion again after all these years?

As hearts as anxious as he was beat behind him, he realized through his hunger for what had to be the thousandth time that such was a fantasy. The voices of both Von Haften lions sounded off in his head as he moved from crystal sconce to crystal sconce in the hotel's cold hall. The rabbit was a fool who'd tried to make a place in the world for monstrous vermin, and as vermin in Martyres' eyes he would be expediently extinguished.

They reached the room, and Calvert felt Sinclair's reliquary like a burning brand at his back, the cigar box and its severed hand a useless prop from this juncture.

"Let me introduce you to a new friend," Donovan tried to sound enthusiastic but it came in a grunt. "The bastard nearly broke my ribs laying him low," he added for effect.

The key worked the lock over a sign requesting no disturbances and a mate to Ferrault's small room was revealed. Poster bed, mirrored armoire, small wash station and toilette through a small door. There were two small sitting chairs and a table that had been shoved to one side for the tall pine box that leaned upright next to the window, its quarry within naked and bound. The lynx's eyes bulged and his fangs were fully extended over a leather gag, head held in place by a cross-board that cut off circulation to his neck as it was nearly severed. The bare chest was bloody with its last meal having leaked from a rent throat down a leather-strapped chest, arms tied to the side and right arm behind him. The paws flexed and clawed the bottom of the box it was made to stand in.

The Martyres had such boxes, used to transport both decapitated and staked Nosfurs across borders for autopsies, or in rare instances, still-active, wriggling captures for experimentation and training. Much of the information they'd gleaned was through direct dissection, which their scholars refused to call vivisection. The dispatched vermin were, of course, not really alive.

And Ferrault knew enough of all this to have a near replica built.

Or was it. The back of the upright coffin was stained dark with blood that was old, layered, aged like the wine of suffering.

Speaking of which: "He's quite well contained. I was mostly worried about the gag coming off and some maid being drawn in here. This would look like an erotic gambit gone wrong to the uninitiated."

Sinclair and Vincent traded impressed looks. "You've had a great catch. He looks like a formidable animal," Sinclair said appraisingly as he passed Donovan and approached. He drew a wince from the rabbit as the reliquary the bulldog drew, a long dagger that was a typical hunter's choice, nearly brushed his suit and threw fire up and down his right side. Donovan stumbled back and excused himself, meeting the fox's curious eyes.

"Allow me to get the door. We'll need to keep things quiet." Donovan drew the latch before standing before it.

Sinclair lifted his blade and ran it across the lynx's chest, drawing a line of fire that singed the cat. He cried through the gag, then growled.

"Lot of fight left in this one, isn't there?" Donovan could feel the smile in Sinclair's voice as he stepped even closer, bringing the blade up past the neck-slat to the cat's nose.

Ferrault's eyes went down, then up, judging distance. His hiss of pain became pained laughter in that moment, lips upward in a smile.

Sinclair growled. "Don't think you won't suffer, you spawn of—"

The twin belts binding the lynx's trunk and arms fell away as his right arm, complete with intact clawed hand, thrust out and up and grabbed the bulldog's shoulder, breaking it with a single squeeze. The left arm batted Sinclair's right and the dagger was bounced across the bed to clatter to the carpet.

"He's loose, my God," Vincent shouted and drew a pistol.

The decision came in an instant, without any real deliberation. Donovan took two steps, brought up his elbow and boxed the fox's left ear. The young vulpine cried out as he went down, hand with the gun nearly limp. In moments like these Donovan forgot the preternatural strength his curse had given him. No, he realized anew, his gift. Blood ran from the fox's ear and from a laceration in his temple as Donovan spun him around to seize the small automatic, free it from the amateur hunter's grasp, and then pistol whip his nose with it. Vincent was on his knees with a cry.

Ferrault meanwhile stepped forward and spat out the loose gag, the loose plank of wood with its neck-shaped divot slipping free to clatter on the carpet. The bulldog tried to kick the lynx. Ferrault's reach was much longer than the squat hunter's, who would never have allowed such proximity in a fair fight. But to the gurgling dog that was moot.

"You have the whelp?" Ferrault asked.

Even having exposed his nature to Christof in New York, he'd done so with a life-long adversary. It hurt Donovan to answer, to have the two Martyres whom he'd led to their deaths hear him. "Yes."

Ferrault spun around and thrust the bulldog in the box, nearly crushing his throat in the process. Weapon gone, no place to feint to, the bulldog could only sputter and thrash, his blunt claws desperately trying to scratch furrows in the lynx's lanky arm. Strong as he was, the Nosfur was all the stronger. "I suppose we don't have so much time, so I'll have to ask you just a few questions."

"Fuck yersel—" The bulldog wheezed as Ferrault punched the dog's broad stomach with his left fist and Sinclair upchucked brandy and liquor on the lynx's bare forearm.

Ferrault ignored the mess. "I'll make a little deal with you, not for yourself because you're such an upright, stout man who'd accept any fate life hands to you, but for the runt you're siring." Ferrault turned for a moment and met the upward gaze of the young fox who bled and cowered. Donovan realized dimly that Vincent wasn't really Martyre material. Not that that would matter now.

"If you answer the questions I have then I'll be merciful and not tear the fox's hide from his pretty flesh while you watch from that box. Does that suit you?" The bulldog made an agonized noise as his body was ground against the wood wall behind him. "Let's try this. I've been trying to draw your attention for a long while, but they've only sent you two. With so many of you on the continent, why so few up here? Hate the cold?"

With pressure eased off the bulldog's throat he was able to blurt, "I'll tell you nothing."

"That's going to cost your fox an ear to start. Take an ear, Donovan."

Donovan's gaze met Sinclair's over the lynx's shoulder and the rabbit realized from the look of utter despair what the bulldog saw.

With flowing blood filling the air, Donovan's fangs had erupted at last.

"Calvert, the real Calvert, gave us victory," the bulldog wheezed, broken shoulder spasming, teeth bared in a bloody, brandy-soaked smile of defiance. "We gained a way to defeat you. The route for salvation is leaving Boston. And you're too late to stop it."

"What's in Boston?" Ferrault pulled him back from the box, nose to nose. "Tell me or the tod gets skinned while you watch." Spoken like a butcher choosing hock or haunch.

"I wasn't told!" This time the cried response had tears. "Vincent doesn't even know what I'm talking about. We only know the assignment handed to us: vermin removal. I only know that whatever they have planned is the means to end you all." There was the feeblest sense of victory in that voice, Donovan realized. Any bargaining chips had been spent. The bulldog was trying to meet Donovan's gaze again but through the haze of hunger he couldn't meet the weight of those judging eyes.

"We're going to get a disturbance complaint so I should really say farewell," Ferrault said apologetically. On the other side of the room's taupe wallpaper, a cacophony of noise came at that moment. A phonograph screamed horns through the thin walls to a ragtime roll. Commensurate with that, twin familiar mink moans were comically loud as a bedpost began clipping the plaster.

"Those delightful kits," Ferrault laughed. "Well then." He bodily shoved the bulldog back in the box and folded his claws together in prayer before jutting them forward, piercing through cloth and pelt and what lay underneath with a single stab. The bulldog's eyes rolled back in his head as the lynx's hands twisted inside him finding the bony obstructions of the rib cage just above the profusely bleeding cavity. "Donovan," Ferrault muttered, unable to keep a giggle out of his voice. "If that's your only clean suit then perhaps you should powder your nose."

Donovan grabbed the fox, shoved the wretch into the bathroom and hurried in after him as the bulldog's moan became a whine, then a shriek terminating in what resembled the obliteration of wet celery. The room's now-unseen lone bulb had suffused the room in a yellow glow and abruptly cast everything beyond the bathroom door in muddy maroon.

Vincent cried, tears flowing freely as he slid down the side of the bathtub with his own gun set by Donovan on the vanity out of reach.

"How could you?" the fox whined as the jazz bleeding in from next door fuzzed the world through Donovan's growing hunger. "You were one of the best of us. I learned about what you did here. I was proud of you."

Donovan leaned forward, trying to find a calming word, a touch of sympathy. But in the moment he didn't feel it. He didn't know if pity was a thing he ever really knew when it would do any good. All he knew for certain was right in front of him. He leaned into the fox's ear like a lover and gathered the blood flooding the acolyte's temple on his tongue, suffering deep and sweet.

Chapter 17

Snag or Two

Crawford growled. "Can you please try again?"

"I'm sorry sir. The line is unavailable or in use."

Crawford hung up. He set the upright phone down and felt another twinge from his abused body, this time in a more generalized location from where his injuries ranged. That gave him pause. "I should have gone back with the damn rats and hooked the phone up, left the doe and kid a note. Son of a bitch, I didn't think anything through."

Charlie diplomatically didn't comment and stopped pacing. "Still can't reach them?"

"They might be resting too far from the telephone. Charlie...what time is it? Is it past five o'clock?"

Charlie's ears went back, his tone incredulous. "How long do you think you were passed out in that ditch, Crawford?"

"Couldn't have been more than ten minutes." Crawford marched to the window and parted the blinds. Deep dusk settled outside.

"It was a lot longer than that. Craw, it's nearly six-thirty."

"Why didn't you—" Crawford snapped his muzzle shut. Even battered to within a yard of his life, why hadn't he thought to ask. "I feel it coming on."

"It?"

"Yes, it."

"Oh. Should we lock you in here?"

Crawford hunched forward as his spine ached. "Look at what this place is made of, Charlie, there won't *be* a here. You need to drive me down the road, take my clothes. There's plenty of forest for me to run around in." He wheezed. "I still hurt so I don't think I can get into too much trouble if I stay out of town."

Charlie had his hat in his hand and wrung it like a chicken neck. "What the hell am I supposed to do then?"

Crawford could smell his mix of anger and worry like a hanging sweat stain. Nails were digging the carpet because he was on the verge of sprouting them further. The room was too small, too closed in. It stunk of the cigarettes of a million strangers and the mattress under the neat sheets had the mildew dampness of soaked guilt. "You need to keep calling the house. They'll be up soon and getting the phone plugged in." If it wasn't he was in trouble.

His son was in this town. All the more reason that he had to be out of it.

That was banished from his head as it had to be. "Get them here fast as you can. All they need is an address. Second…"

Somebody had something meaty and fried outside that Crawford could fight them for. He was stronger than— "Oh right, hamburger lunchbox."

"What?" Charlie had taken a step back.

"Get some raw hamburger and fill a lunchbox. Celeste might need it. Raw or slightly cooked, doesn't matter."

"Oh-kay."

"You're driving. North." Crawford shook his muzzle. It hurt to talk. "Now."

Minutes later they were tearing north, Charlie passing slower cars that could only be seen by their headlamps spreading the night apart. The hand that landed on Charlie's shoulder from behind was a bony monstrosity and Crawford, feeling playful, could smell just the tiniest bit of urine let loose as his packmate's soapy-smelling move-den jerked to the curb.

His own wrappings were behind him, piled like rocks. Brown wolf with the powdery fear scent had wrappings still on him as Crawford scratched the door to be let out and his mate left the iron prison, opened the door, and let him out.

Crawford leapt on him and his mate squealed as he went down and now wasn't right for mounting because he had many hurts so he lapped brown's nose with a great panting tongue and caught a different scent that was earthy and interesting. It hurt when he bounded but he wanted to smell all that fecund green.

***

Not a minute after disconnecting from Sandy, the telephone rang again. "It's Crawford's friend, Charles," Celeste confirmed for Samson after answering.

"You did get that phone working," Charles's voice squawked through the earpiece, out of breath.

"I was speaking with Sandy on it." Celeste felt time ticking by. "Is Crawford with you? We're leaving to search for him."

"Too late, I had to take him up the road to make sure he was out of town. He was urgent about it for good reason."

Kept the last of his wits, Celeste thought idly. "So, he's changed."

"Yes," Charles muttered with a sigh. "Slobbered on me and hit the bushes a mile or so north of the hotel. I'm sorry. I should have done something to keep him—"

"He wasn't going to help you solve a crossword, Charles. On his best nights he nibbles saplings."

"I know, it's just…he's been hurt. It's a long story. And it's Charlie," Charlie said.

"You did exactly what you needed to do. We have a map with us. Tell me the address of the hotel. I'll go to intercept him and try to stay out of that town."

"Please do. It's…hostile out right now."

Celeste wondered if their house outside Scranton was still smouldering. "You don't say."

Charlie scrabbled for something. "I've got that address here. I'd drive up to get you—"

"No need. I know which way to go and I'm quite fast. If you want to help, I'll need you to get a room for me. If it takes till dawn to find him, I'll need to have a roof to rest under. You understand."

"I think I do. Okay, the hotel is Starlight Trails on Seventy going north. Just outside Hancock, Maryland. I'll get another room for you if I can."

"Please do. I'll find him." Celeste hung up.

"We'll find him," Samson said flatly.

"You should stay here in case Sandy or Charlie calls."

"What would be the point of that? I can't telephone you, can I?"

"Samson, it's dangerous. If Crawford is near Hancock while all those angry carnivores are, then they'll be looking for blood and pointed at those who look like us. A haberdashery was burned to the ground a few towns from here and a panda family was nearly killed."

Samson had closed the door and now planted both hooves directly in front of it, teeth grinding. "I read papers. And I see news reels between picture shows. I get out more than you do these days."

Celeste's ears brushed back in exasperation. "And that's—"

"The problem? That's what you're going to say, right, Celeste? Because I caused all this in the first place?"

"I wasn't going to say that at all, Samson. I don't want to risk anyone else getting hurt and that includes you."

"Crawford needs both of us. But you're assuming I'll make it worse, aren't you? Even though I handled myself with those cats in Scranton you think I'm in danger."

"Samson…"

"And you think I'll go too far."

Celeste wanted to choose her words more carefully, but his disposition since the cats in Scranton had been too difficult to ignore. "The thought had crossed my mind, Samson."

Rather than being hurt, he cocked his head and his stare went from defiant to coldly proud. "You know why I did it, don't you? Why I really fought those cats instead of running? Because for all I can do, all my strength and my speed, I'm supposed to act like I'm powerless, as I have my whole life. I was born a veggie in a carnie's world, made into a doll-sized tool. Just a little stick of dynamite that was supposed to blow up in Chicago and be nobody's problem anymore."

"You were never that."

"Only because Crawford refused to kill me. And for a while I wondered if he made a mistake, but I know now he didn't. Because I'm not powerless." Samson showed his teeth, fangs recessed but ready. "I cheated fate. I can do so much with the gifts I've been treating like circus tricks for these past dozen years while we hid and played house and cleaned gutters and did taxes. I was robbed of so much." His lips slowly pulled back, fangs parting as slow as petals seeking a long-forgotten sun. "Not anymore. I'm done with being ashamed of what I can do."

Celeste took a few steps forward and put her hand carefully on the goat kid's small shoulder. Bundled energy collected there despite the absence of breath moving through him, indignation honed to a potent point.

She saw so much of herself in that want for vengeance. How could she not? She had fed of every class in France, fled to the British Isles, prowled London, then Ireland before meeting the first of her kind that wasn't a passing predator in competition. Sandy had loved her until the betrayal in New York, after which fate had transplanted them both to Chicago. Celeste had made such an effective murderer for the mob there, content upon a pile of made-mammal's corpses.

So many bloody lessons, betrayals, punishing expressions of power, each ending in loneliness. Celeste's smile couldn't hide the bitter weight of history. "The power that we have, to cause immeasurable harm, is all they would define us by, the Martyres, or anyone else who discovers us. Power corrupts so easily, makes presumptions of supremacy so seductive. That was my very first lesson in Paris, before I was even turned."

Samson listened, but he was clearly impatient. "And if they seek to cause Crawford harm, which it sounds to me like they already have, then that power to harm right back is exactly what we need, isn't it?" It was barely a question.

Celeste met Samson's gaze with all the kindness she could muster. "That can't be our first choice."

Samson said nothing for a time. "Alright. Well then. Should we find Crawford before we don't have a choice at all?"

"We should."

Map in hand, they left the house and merged with the dark. Their area for the search was nearly ninety miles away, but they had the power to cover that distance rapidly. The shadows were endless linked corridors that defied space and even time in a sense. From the hollow of a tree to the lee of a bridge to a thick cluster of pines, they darted near the roads where the occasional pass of a car's headlamps would break the chain of shadow's communion and insert them on mortal terra firma for an instant. But keeping close to the roads helped them orient. They reached the hotel in just over an hour and studied the smattering of dilapidated automobiles huddling around it, then backtracked up the road Charlie had told Celeste about, breaking shadow and cover every so often to gather scent.

Their noses sorted the spoor of night-things that barely registered their presence. It didn't take long to catch the drift of Crawford's most common nocturnal calling card, hot, coppery, and recent. Fear scent drifted with it.

The farm they crossed in an eyeblink found the feral cattle dumb and coalescing protectively by a rooster-red barn, far from the darker smears dragged across the grazing meadow and through the rent, gored demarcation of wire.

"Not so wounded after all," Celeste muttered as they kept high and moved in.

"I've got his scent. Definitely him." Samson said, balancing effortlessly on a branch too narrow for Celeste. "There's just a bit of his blood in the air…" He turned dark eyes her way. "Have you ever wondered…"

Celeste's lip curled. "I know you're joking, but to be clear, Samson, I've read someplace that were blood would likely kill us if we tried it. A curse of that kind changes your physical form in every way with the moon, while our gift all but freezes us in time when the blood slows. Imagine a body compelled to simultaneously shift and remain static by irreconcilable forces."

"Might hurt," Samson said flatly. "That reminds me…" He trailed off as they heard a sound southwest of where they perched, low and guttural. They bound shadows another few dozen paces, held still, moved again. "You've noticed his knuckle," Samson muttered more quietly. "The finger he lost, it's slowly growing back."

They bound new shadows, sniffed the next copse of trees. "To what extent Crawford's recuperative powers work is a mystery. The only other were I knew of died pretty quickly and pretty violently." Celeste's voice dropped to quiet, waving her finger across her lips to suggest Samson do the same.

They came across a massive glistening rib cage curling up from a blossom of red in the shadows. Celeste had peered into a few slaughterhouse kitchens in her time and could discern some of what was missing. "He took some of it away. When the farmer comes looking, this is where the trail will end. He has some wits for a feral."

"Good for us, I suppose," Samson agreed. "No shotgun-happy farmer to deal with."

"To avoid."

They moved on, the scent of blood winding them west and back towards the road. The moon was being overtaken by cloud cover but its departure wouldn't let Crawford's sapient aspect draw him back right away.

They caught the sound then, the whisper of pelt against leaves and twigs, passing fast. His scent came then. Pelt oil. Earth. Canine saliva. Blood. And the tiniest telltale tincture of whiskey.

"Let's tire him out." Celeste picked a shadow and bound through it to an intersection with the wolf's path. It was easy to overshoot him for how often he went nose to ground to sniff.

"Crawford, it's me," Celeste called out. A great head panting through cutlery jaws rose. Dark, glittery eyes were curious over a fluttering nose. "You're very far from home tonight," she added.

Angrily or playfully, they were never entirely sure, the werewolf clutched earth and launched the doe's way. She slipped from the shadow for a single instance, let him see and smell the deer before him, then she bound another shadow a few feet away and transported herself to the next one as wolf muzzle pushed its way past the dark spot that she'd conquered and struck the small tree with his shoulder. He cried out—Celeste did remember that Charlie had said he was wounded—and rolled away with a snarl.

"Barrrrnie Gooogel, with the goo-goo-googly eyes," Samson sang from a shadow behind him. The wolf spun, snapped air, and bound into the bushes Samson vacated. The feral wolf stumbled as Samson was already two shadows higher up the tree.

"He's hurt. Let's try to get him someplace where he can't make it worse."

Crawford had already rested back on his haunches and craned his thick neck to stretch a kink out. His ears swivelled to follow the deliberate commotion of Nosfurs leading him off to a wide thicket. Celeste caught the wobbly way he loped and when the meager traces of remaining moon caught his glassy eyes she could see he was hurt. In an open, untilled field shadows were sparse, but the safety of deeper forest was kept extremely close. Dodge and feint, glimpses presented. It had to dizzy whatever sentient kernel of Crawford consciously remained and they kept the game up for an hour, then two.

Celeste's prior encounter with a were before Crawford had mostly come care of the hideously violated corpses in its wake. For the Nosfur pair whose scents he knew he was like a drunken relative being kept out of fisticuffs at the local tavern, most of the time.

Crawford hadn't gotten them the sustenance they needed this time and they were famished as a result. They'd discuss that along with all his other lapses of judgement later.

He was tiring out. Chasing shadows swallowing or disgorging goats and does was becoming exhausting. He eventually settled down in a thicket to rest. Celeste and Samson drew close as his trunk's rib cage surrendered its depth and his limbs lost their distension, fingers regaining their slender tool-working aspects. He sniffed his own maleness once and then finished his return to mortal, modern mammality with a labored sigh.

Celeste shook her head. "Always the last thing he checks. We'd best get him back to the hotel."

Crawford was shorter than Celeste by several inches but weighed considerably more. She checked the horizon through the ample trees for the faintest ribbon of morning gold. "Watch his head."

Celeste hefted the wolf carefully, leveraging herself as his mass exceeded hers and could easily topple them both. In a firemammal's rescue-carry he was legs first with tail drifting over his own rear end while Samson kept close behind the snoring muzzle down Celeste's back, making sure his head didn't bounce and collide with anything. A long hour trudging south ended in a stretch of hotel windows overlooking boxy automobiles in rank and file. Samson hurried across, moving as best as he could out of the motor hotel's lamplight before knocking on the right door. Another wolf answered, fur brown under his rumpled suit and smoking like a chimney. Goat and wolf talked and they left that room with a bundle under the brown wolf's arm to walk three doors down to another at the end. Charlie handed the goat a key and then Samson turned back to the dark, nodding once in Celeste's direction.

She closed the distance quickly, pausing briefly between cars to check other rooms' windows for nocturnal onlookers. Seeing none, she hurried to the door and past the waiting wolf in a rumpled suit with her own grey-furred naked cargo, dropping him bouncily on a stiff starched bed.

With goat and doe inside, Charlie closed the door, but not before turning the lights on. "You're fortunate half the people collected in this town are too broke to afford a room right now. He okay?" Charlie asked breathlessly, setting folded clothes on the same bed.

"As well as he ever is. He fed." Celeste responded.

Charlie nodded. "You said you needed cover for daytime, correct?" He waved at the room in general. "The drapes are pretty thick."

"Thank you." Celeste took the key that Samson passed over. "Dawn's too close to get home. We'll need to be moving as soon as night falls, but not back there. We have to head for Boston."

"Alright. I'll put a don't disturb sign on the door."

Celeste gave the door a hard glance, wondering if they might need to put a chair under it in case the sign was ignored. "We should keep Crawford with us. The chances of another turn tonight are slim, but not unheard of."

Charlie sighed. "I understand. If he wakes before you do whatever it is you do during sun-up, let him know I'll be back to check on him. I have to leave the hotel, government hush-hush stuff."

"We will, Mister G-mammal," Samson piped up, looking between the two beds appraisingly.

***

The fox's body rested on the small suite's short couch, head tipped back while the arm of the naked, gore-smeared lynx was wrapped around him in a comradely fashion. The same blood and material that spattered the lynx from knees to chin was also all over the floor and speckled the lid of the mercifully closed box that now held different cargo.

Donovan sat in another chair that had been across the room and wasn't a horrid mess. He'd only sipped of the fox's living nectar, and at the moment was simply numb.

Ferrault smiled bloody teeth. "It's a pity you haven't been in town very long. Street Lawrence Market is just east down Front Street. Most wonderful bacon sandwiches there I'm told."

"We can't have any," Donovan muttered, looking at nothing.

"Not on an otherwise empty stomach, no." Ferrault smeared blood on the fox's lap when he patted it. "But our friend's not finished and still warm. You can get that heart of yours moving a bit more."

"No. Thank you."

Ferrault got up and hefted the fox, Vincent had been his name, like a ragdoll. Donovan hoped he could forget that name soon. Ferrault moved the standing coffin-box lid aside and Donovan had only the most cursory glance of the abattoir inside before Ferrault pushed the dead fox in and forced the lid closed fully, taking a moment to fasten four iron screw clamps. He returned to the couch and patted the empty space next to him. "It's relatively dry here," Ferrault said. There was a genteel insistence in his tone that brooked no debate.

Donovan reluctantly rose and moved to sit next to the fouled lynx, eyes on the closed box.

"It's not the dead hunters that has you bothered, is it?" Ferrault mused. "I'm thinking you mourn the final loss of your prior place in your perceived order of things."

Donovan closed his eyes, wished for the oblivion of day. "That happened a dozen years ago."

"But the truth pinned you down tonight. I know you've thought about somehow going back to them. It's in those eyes of yours. Hope smothered by shame. Despite all the years of abuse their higher-ups heaped on you, you crave the structure and the discipline of a hierarchy to serve."

Donovan wanted to laugh but it strangled in his throat. He'd worked tirelessly to upset the Martyres' hierarchy from within, change the mission of the Order entirely. But even as he mused on the means he'd tried, his iron gambit wasn't something he wanted to dredge up again in Ferrault's presence.

The lynx snickered. "Even with your rebellious tendencies, you craved validation by those who decried you all those years." He made a thoughtful noise. "The fox was a bit put out when you turned on him, wasn't he?"

Donovan felt the lynx's closeness as an offensive thing. "Let's leave him out of this."

Ferrault folded his legs and leaned back. "Let me tell you a little story about a free monarch and his favorite slave." He smiled deeply at the stir of a fond memory. "Circumstance connected them, but fate bound them both.

They adored one another, making love on their villa's many hills. Off to war, back to sabbatical, the emperor toiled. Always the slave waited, toiling in his own limited yet important scope. Their relationship was closer than marriage, more intimate than prayer, and kept secret enough. For the ruling class had their toys, but always toys they were. Not these two." Ferrault ran fingers through the crusted gore on his chest and smiled with reflective bliss. "They frolicked often, taking roles manly and womanly in the sense that their day and age saw such things and as some still do. Responsibilities of the realm fled among the estate's flora and warm bodies pressed together under a sun's kiss rendered forgotten every verbal spar of royal office, every exhaustion of tilled soil. One day the stranger came."

Ferrault regarded the room's distant mauve wall, at the remnants of life that adhered there. "Monotheistic mutterings of gods and devils weren't far off from germinating, but this was still a time when any god getting his feet muddy among the mortals could be either a boon or a blight depending on their whims and tastes. The same went for those who were their messengers, their seers or oracles. The pair assumed that it was a trickster who brought forth the offering of eternal life on one cool autumn night, their frolicking spied upon, the guards at the estate's periphery evaded. But she had seemingly come from far above. Or perhaps below. It was a challenge presented that enthralled them like two kits before a magician: live forever in each other, never to part, never to love another. Become one heart that beat with the rush of all other life and see eternity in each other's eyes.

"Readily, in all innocence, they accepted. For what is any heart both low or high in worldly stature when laid bare, but fearing inevitable loneliness? They felt complete only in each other. Herbs were bestowed, and they nibbled bitter essence before the next essential step was whispered with loving assurance. The tongue is the root of all truths and lies and they bit one another's and drew a kiss and drank. And drank. And drank. The pain was glorious in the sharing. Master and servant transcended the flow of their own lives as their hearts stopped altogether. A pass through oblivion was both instant and eternal. They awoke to the night, Donovan. And it's possible that, if the visitor were a god, they were the very first mortals to do so."

"The first Nosfurs," Donovan whispered.

"The name Nosfurratu came so much later. They were above titles now, borne to night and free of mortality's cage. And in the dark they loved. And they hunted. And they loved. And they culled. And they loved." Ferrault stopped talking for a moment, his eyes closed tight as he fought to hold an image.

There was a knock at the door and Ferrault rose. He opened it a crack and then a bit more. Donovan caught a brown-furred hand on the frame with a white shirt cuff. Whoever it was could clearly see that Ferrault was both naked and bedecked in gore but didn't react. They whispered low and while Donovan couldn't make out the visitor's words clearly he could discern an impatience.

"You know what inquiries to make. We have confirmed our destination now," Ferrault told them grandly. "We're heading to Boston."

Fingers drummed on the frame. The question asked was once again indistinct.

"I've not forgotten what you've done for me and your time is coming. Go, please ask the twins to start packing."

Dismissed, the door to the suite was closed again and Ferrault returned to the couch. "Some of us are a bit impatient," Ferrault snickered.

"Who was that?" Donovan asked. "Do I know them?"

"No, you don't. Where was I? Yes. Centuries passed and two entwined lives blended in worlds not their own, history and culture rolling relentlessly onward until such time as they began to feel mutually…disaffected. First they took one another for granted, then familiarity's creeping contempt found them both in small rusty morsels that grew and grew, and they spent more and more time apart, yearning for a world they'd left behind that no longer existed, each new land they stalked taking them further from their history, each language and custom learned burying their shared past deeper, and with it, the stations and classes they'd once been stamped by like inks fading from terracotta. Despair sought them out, for they didn't know where the march of time would take them, and they quarrelled more and more. Then one day…"

Ferrault stopped talking and choked as though drawing breath. He smiled through a pain that had been studied like a votive object.

"The end itself is transitory and what comes after it guiltlessly final. In cowardly fashion regrets are bequeathed in full to whoever remains."

He regained his composure with effort and spoke so low it became a whisper. "Funeral pyres are both sacred and profane, the disposition of Viking kings and plague victims and condemned witches. Fire is ever so greedy. Thatch huts are ever so acquiescent. The pair lived alone, suspected of nothing by those who feared life-stealing wraiths on the periphery of their terrifying worlds. That fucking fire didn't start itself." Ferrault looked Donovan in the eye now, naked and bloody and stripped bare past that. "When night fell once again and the ashes were sifted, the only one the lone Nosfur had ever known was mostly bones, some gristle, and on the blank besooted bark of a face, the trace of a grateful smile. And so...the companion persisted alone."

Donovan waited but the lynx had finished speaking, lost in contemplation. "Which of them...ended? Was it the emperor or the slave?"

Ferrault didn't even look at him, just shook his head. "You adorable fool, you missed the point entirely. I don't remember if I was a king among kings or the lowly slave who loved one. It's irrelevant. The only way to endure is to let go of it all. Time unmoors us from any age's pretensions. Rich or poor, powerful or weak, we leave it all behind, everything we once considered important. Learn it however you have to because you're worth no more to this ancient world than the sweaty beasts who poured your steel for fifty cents an hour."

"Sixty."

Ferrault laughed. "I took notice that you packed no bags when leaving your chalet behind. I respect a clean break, even from one who knows they're on the run. How much money do you have?"

"I, uh," Donovan reached carefully into his breast pocket and removed a thin billfold. "I have about sixty or seventy dollars."

"Twenty should do."

Donovan looked into the billfold's recesses and then up again at the lynx's insistent patience. He carefully extricated a twenty and Ferrault lifted himself from the gored couch as he took it. He went to the bed, folded it carefully and smeared a bit of bloody grease away from the pillow before setting the bill down for housekeeping.

He walked past the rabbit again and Donovan had an eyeful of the lynx's blood-speckled, swaying maleness before he disappeared into the bathroom and began running the tap. He leaned back out. "Go tell Myra and Mercel to have the crate collected. Then they can calm you down. You need it. A private carriage will take us all south."

***

"We're getting out to Boston, tonight." The Colonel was anxious.

Lucas sensed it even as he tried to keep his emotions in check. He'd heard from Lucy what the Colonel's crew had done with his drunkard father and was careful as hell about going back to check the ditch where they'd left him. It had been empty and Lucas didn't know if he should feel relieved or further disappointed. Or vindicated. "What is it?"

The Colonel stopped at the hotel room window next to Lucas and glanced down at the hive activity of the downtrodden moving in and out of the dimly lit bar across the street below, trading nickels for numb swallows of escape. Lucas still couldn't account for the vivid memory that seized him after he'd tried to quiet his own roiling mind with a drink. Of course, his father had ruined that from wherever he'd slunk off to.

The Colonel's teeth wiggled a cigarette as he took a chair. "One of ours reported a problem. Brother with the law says we might have inward trouble that needs dealing with."

That got Lucas's attention. "What kind, Colonel?"

The German shepherd took off his white Stetson, gazed inside it as though seeking some insight before setting it on his lap. "You looking to get married, Lucas? Do your duty to wolf kind?"

The question caught Lucas off guard. "I haven't had time to—"

"You have a sweetheart back in Delaware?"

"Virginia, sir."

The colonel growled one of his mirthless chuckles. "I figured you for a coastal. Don't mind it. Do you have a to-be Missus Lucas in your life whom you'll be fruitful and multiply with?"

"Well, there was this dog back in—"

"You mean wolf, dontcha?" His eyes pinned Lucas where he stood.

"No, sir, she was, uh, half collie."

"Half," the Colonel said flatly. "Half..."

"Yes, sir."

"Do you know how breeds came about? The pedigrees and bloodlines of which I am a part? Dignity and discernment. Station and standards. We have breeds because under God's stewarding staff we figured true kind from false kind, and monarchs and holy men further refined these distinctions by rule of law. Sometimes veggies got in the tent, with the French and the Spanish and others. But carnies have always taken the thrones. Purebred ones. I will never dilute, never compromise. I catch a fox sacking with a cat on my payroll, I fire the bastard without hesitation. You're young, and forthrightness may keep some stupid offa you. But never doubt that your responsibilities only start with me."

Lucas felt small in the moment and for a brief instant he had to fight his own hackles from going up. He'd been upbraided, but in this were lessons regarding this man whom he'd come so far to learn from.

The Colonel looked outside again. "We need to get on the road before dawn. Go see how they're doing with striking the tent."

Annoyed that the Colonel was keeping his counsel inner again, Lucas shuffled to the door. He opened it upon a sleek male fossa with a hand raised to knock. The visitor was bedecked in a charcoal three-piece suit with a white cotton shirt. The homburg on his head was cream in color. Lucas had seen the face before but couldn't place him. The fossa scrutinzed the wolf as if he were a curious obstruction and stepped forward, nearly shoving Lucas out of the way. "Colonel," he rumbled. "We need a word."

The Colonel had backers whom Lucas had never met and he was certain this was one of them. He stepped out and around the fossa's path and found himself in the hall. The door closed with finality upon his muzzle. Confused, Lucas took the stairs to street level where he was anonymous in the crowd. Carnivores, bothered and restless, roved about, many having no place to wander too far beyond curb-staggered automobiles where feet up on wheels and dashes twitched with snores.

He crossed the street to pass O'Holler's Bar. The field with the collapsing tent was only two blocks and a left turn away. The door of the bar opened to indistinct grumbles and an old otter in a worn shawl and younger wolf with scarves winding around her like a maypole poured out into the street. "Well, if we're still missing somethin' from the crate then what is it?" the otter complained.

"I don't know, I packed one of everything," the wolf grumbled. Something smooth glinted under one arm.

"Then we're missing one of something, so you should know what—"

Lucas stopped to avoid a collision but the smaller femme wolf all but bumped into him. Her layered accoutrements smelled like a spice rack had burned, sweet and bitter at once. Her distracted eyes fixed immediately to his. "You know where you're going?" she asked. It was genuine curiosity, not an admonishment.

"Vaguely," he muttered.

"You're walking a path that's hard but sure."

"And pain's a companion to whom you're in—you know what," the otter huffed. "Ferget it." Her face screwed into a whiskered knot and she kept on.

The young grey wolf—or was she actually old?—shifted the bottle in her arms and the dark contents shimmered in the weak light. Lucas had seen it before. "Where are you going, Lucas?"

"Boston."

"And where are you going to find your answers?" She reached out and took his hand. It was soft, but firm, and he didn't want to let go.

"Uh…Boston."

A spark leapt between them and he felt a momentary gust of sensation from tail to teeth that passed as quick as it came.

"That's where it is," the wolf said, eyes bright. "I knew it."

Lucas didn't want to move a muscle. The world had quieted around them both. She leaned in and her voice tickled his ear. "Go make a phone call." The wolf released him and tottered after the otter who was two dark storefronts down and winding a Ford to life.

Lucas watched them go, forgotten but feeling as though countless eyes were on his back as he made his way into the bar. Only a few stragglers were left drinking their last pennies into a quieter oblivion. Make a phone call. Yes. The Colonel was with the fossa with the purse strings and the rest were packing the tent away.

It was time.

The lion wasn't on the taps. A ferret had replaced him, boredly counting down till he could sweep the few inebriates left into the street. The telephone booth was empty and Lucas made sure he heard nothing at all when he closed its dusty-paned door. Nobody sat close, nobody glanced his way.

Dime down, Ma Bell present. "I need eff eee four six two six please."

Connection was fast. "Carl's Lumber," a tired voice muttered. "We're closed."

"Barney knows I'm calling."

A long moment passed. "Getting him now. Wait. We have to redirect you to another line."

Lucas was confused. "They aren't…?"

"Switching over," the lumber salesman said resolutely. There was the silence leading into a ring and it was answered after three rings by a panting voice that sounded as if it had run a marathon. "Yes?"

"Scranton station. I'm alone. It's me, Agent Rothscub."

Lucas could almost hear the other wolf's heart hammering through the phone.

"How alone?"

Lucas peered through the dirty booth glass and regarded the closest muzzle drifting over a half-downed beer, uncertain how to make it the rest of the way. "Alone."

"What the hell are you doing? You got yourself on stage with those bastards?"

Lucas's own pulse started racing. Deep down he'd anticipated a response like this. Charlie Rothscub was overly protective of his agents; Lucas had sensed that in him from the moment he'd joined the outfit. "You took me onto your detail, assigned me to observe and I'm observing. The Colonel met me and I got in his graces—"

"How the hell did you do that?"

"I got close during the early meet and greet. He had family that let him down. Or he let them down more likely. I was angry, made an impassioned speech about deadbeat fathers and the ruination of America and it sounded good to him. He had me speak to his inner circle, liked how they responded. Found the youth of America wasn't represented enough. That was my way in."

"You did all this in a week without reporting back?"

"A month. It took a month, hanging on, getting chummy. I reported in twice during that."

Agent Rothscub's sigh was weary and exasperated. "But you never told me—"

"Now I'm figuring out his whole outfit. There's only been one snag so far, but I handled it." Walking away from his father hadn't been that difficult. The wood frame of the booth was cold under Lucas's dark palm and he welcomed it.

"You know just how much danger you're in, don't you?" Rothscub kept his voice low, as though others might be near. "These people aren't the pimps you cut your teeth on in Pittsburgh, Marsten. They truly believe everything they're doing, moreso if the doing is violent."

"Some are just lost and hurting and angry for it. Some are taking advantage of those who are. And sure, they're all violent, but not towards me." He thought of the fossa entering the Colonel's room again. He'd seen him in some tradespaper...some kind of big shot. "I can handle myself. You knew that or you wouldn't have advanced me to field work. I'm not gonna run away from something important and leave you in the lurch." The unspoken example crawling around town somewhere remained unspoken and Lucas wondered for a moment if his father might not be nursing his wounds mere feet away in the dark of one of the bar's corners, a ghost refusing to banish itself from those it haunted.

"Things were complicated back then..." Charlie wanted to say so much more and didn't. That gave Lucas a bit of pause.

"They're complicated now. The Colonel has financial backing from a few sources, but one of them came to see him just now. A fossa. Dark brown, lighter throat, eyes black, grey speckle on left nostril. Gold rings on wedding and small fingers, left hand. Don't know who he is but the Colonel wouldn't just lay the carpet down to anybody who wasn't giving him something he really wanted. It's more than just a larger-than-average donation. This one's got the Colonel's ear and he slipped through the back where he wasn't seen."

Charlie was quiet a long time. "Don't dig into this. We can handle those inquiries from afar. You're in enough danger as it is. Once this speaker gig is off in Chicago, you'll need to melt away."

"No."

"Say your Mom is sick or anything you need to and leave those people."

"I'm in deeper than anybody else has managed. You know that. I disappear and they'll know something's up and you'll never get another nose into this den again."

"And I know what they'd do to a snitch."

"Can't be a snitch if you were their enemy from the start."

"Lucas, for God's sake, from their perspective that's worse. You know that, right? Where are you even calling me from?"

"Payphone in the back of the local bar. I can see I'm out of earshot of everybody."

"Dammit if I'd known you were going to get this deep into this thing I'd have requisitioned you a radio."

"I'm rooming with two others on the Colonel's posse. Where the hell would I hide that?" Charlie was sounding more like a worried father than a section chief and Lucas felt rankled by that. "I can find out who's backing them. Just give me time. I need to see this through for more reasons than you know."

"Because you think he didn't. You think he couldn't." Charlie said flatly. "He'd…"

"Don't."

"He'd worry about you."

Lucas let the subtle noise of the bar wash over him and washed back into the memory of cops and robbers and dust trails of abandonment. He'd been so close to putting it behind him. One well pour at this shitty, stale bar… "Twelve years too late if he did. To hell with my father. Next time I call I'll have names, plans. You saw the pamphlets they put me on. The big rally is in Boston."

The crackle of the line sounded like doubt. But it was doubt defeated by the pragmatism of duty. "Be careful, Agent Marsten."

"I have to go, I'll be missed."

***

It was true. He'd be missed.

Crawford was snoring a few walls away, dreaming what Charlie could only assume were blasted patterns of civilized worries and self-reflective regrets. A hand on his shoulder could rouse him from that. A few frank, honest words could help him understand.

It had all been Charlie's fault of course. The family name-change of Crawford's ex-wife Kamila had come to him through something innocuous, the admission from Crawford that she'd been moving on and he was happy for her. And then the recruitment rolls had a familiar name on the '32 roster and he'd kept tabs on the graduate out of Virginia who'd filled out the team busting pelt-peddlers out of Pennsylvania.

Forming his own unit, Charlie found the fresh agent who'd cuffed law-breakers in Pittsburgh on the Fed office shooting range where targets were punched by the decisive snap of .32's. Charlie saw more decisive snaps in the young agent's mind when he laid out the simplest of assignments.

It would have been simplest for somebody without a fang to sharpen, a need for family retribution in Lucas's drive that Charlie failed to properly decipher. But the fledgling cub with a legacy to burn behind him said yes as though he'd waited a century to be asked. And Charlie had thought he was doing his former partner a favor by letting his son leap for the moon.

Now here they all were.

Charlie returned to his own room after stepping out for two hard-drawn cigarettes by the hotel's office. He didn't really like how the room smelled after burning too many chimneys inside and he had so many choices to turn over, some made and some yet to be made before Crawford and the Nosfurs woke up.

Entering his own room once again, he noticed what he'd missed from outside: the lights were off. He could have sworn he'd left them on after disconnecting with his agent, but it instinctively made sense to kill illumination when a doe and goat were carrying a naked wolf into the second room he'd rented. He'd long worried about too many eyes on him, long before a speakeasy raid in Chicago showed him there were worse things than vice cops in the world.

He slipped in with the door opened behind him, unwilling to close it and plunge himself into absolute darkness. Two hard breaths into the deep, still shadows of the room and he turned the lamp on before slipping off his suit jacket. Charlie turned to toss it on the bed and nearly jumped at the presence in the chair behind the lot-facing window.

The brown-furred weasel stared levelly at him over circular spectacles. He wore a dark, tight-fitting suit with a flat blue-grey tie. "Hello Agent... is it Rothscub?"

"Who the hell are you and how did you get in here?"

The weasel said nothing for a time, considering things. "I'm from Washington too," he said at last. "Tomlinson. I'm working an investigation involving a foreign national and several homicides out in New York."

Charlie waited for his heart to stop hammering. "I've heard of you. What part of your investigation involves sneaking into somebody's hotel room the next state over?"

The weasel smiled a little smile. "I follow my work wherever it takes me. The vast fraternity I'm part of would have it no less."

"I'd be happy to help you with any part of your case that crossed my desk but I don't know of any out-of-state murders. I'm on different work."

"Different work." Tomlinson's mouth smiled but his eyes didn't.

Charlie knew the man's name but nothing else about him, including how long he'd been in here. "So, who are you looking for?"

The space between them was cold. "I was looking for a wolf named Crawford Cain, who is more than a wolf as I'm sure you know."

Charlie froze. Countless things the weasel could know about him and Crawford relay-raced in his head.

The weasel chuckled at something distasteful. "Interestingly enough, Cain was just a surprising discovery found on my little odyssey through this part of America. It's nice when your pull in a shiny new Federal Bureau lets you select your own assignments. My fraternity and I were always after somebody else. Them...and any bastards who they'd drawn in as accomplices. Until I saw them, I'd never suspect it would be another employee of Uncle Sam."

"I don't know what you're talking about..." Charlie trailed off as the weasel raised an automatic the wolf hadn't seen.

No smiles now. "We have names for slime like you where I'm originally from," Tomlinson said with venom. "But I doubt you'd know enough Latin to understand them."

Chapter 18

No Sides

"The hell are you talking about?" Charlie's heart pounded as Tomlinson stood up, passed the nickel-plated pistol from one hand to another, and rooted inside his jacket.

The weasel drew a wicked silver dagger and deftly spun it. "What am I talking about? How about, Agent Rothscub, you and I talk about my wife. She'd been following leads through several states, whispers of a wolf and doe working as private investigators who relocated every few years. Funny enough that I'd split off to track what turned out to be the same thread. One of the founding members of my order was—"

"What fucking order, Tomlinson? You're an agent of the Bureau." Charlie yelped as the dagger flicked out and nicked his chin.

"Don't you dare scream," Tomlinson hissed. "You call out and the minutes we have till somebody comes will be the longest and last of your life." He took a deep breath. "The name left in a coat pocket was that of your old partner on the Chicago Prohee racket but I didn't know that yet. The name had come up. Those funny mismatched doe and wolf PIs again. My wife, Dierdre, followed a redirected cheque payment to Scranton from an old address we'd kept tabs on and a reported triple murder of some cats had a name on a witness report taken by a Scranton beat cop. Too coincidental. So, we worked as we always do, separate but in tandem. I got the wolf down to the station where I confirmed what he was"—Tomlinson waved the dagger—"And my wife came to the house to confirm what the doe was." He sighed. "Then it all went wrong. A dagger in the back in the dark should have finished off your were drunkard partner but I was stuck in a cluster of clutzes over by the fuse box. And my wife, well, a Nosfur engaged in daylight has ways to be expunged, but she didn't know there were two of the monsters. The fire"—he swallowed with deep bitterness—"retired her from active duty as a hunter in the Order. She was so close to achieving council rank, a truly rare thing for an omnivore."

"What the hell does any of this have to do with me? And what's a Noss fur?" The appeal to ignorance was weak. But biding time was all Charlie had. His gun was atop his suitcase in the far corner, settled uselessly atop a new bath towel.

"That's where the fun starts. You were already endangering our operation chasing Rutland Blake with whomever you have planted among these reprobates wandering around. And we're frankly not done with him yet. But to find out that you, an agent for the highest security apparatus in the country, was in thrall to them? My God, you stupid dog, you think that power or sex or whatever the doe promised you isn't going to land your soul in damnation when you shuffle off?"

"The doe is not doing that for me."

Tomlinson took a deep breath. "However svelte they may look, a mammal with so little to smell is just goddamn disgusting."

"I agree," Charlie said, finding that his throat was getting a little tight. Anxiety was climbing but he didn't want it to show. The cut stung but he ignored it.

The blade was down but the gun was up. "Oh, you'll agree to a lot before you're done here. So, what was it? What brought you to accept Satan's kiss in order to betray your country?"

Charlie wanted to laugh but didn't dare. Something about the likelihood that death was imminent was strangely liberating in an idiotic way. His legs felt a bit wobbly and he couldn't resist leaning back against the dresser. "You think I betrayed my country? Didn't you just admit you're working with Colonel Blake?"

"Using him, Rothscub, almost the way the Nosfurs are using you. And I've seen that you know exactly what a Nosfur is. Or perhaps you call them vampires like those idiots wasting nickels at the bijous."

"Means nothing to me. What does is the Blake connection. I know that people he has working under him are being used to gather steel from the Calvert mills that closed down a decade ago. Too much money trading hands for that to be simple embezzlement, isn't it?"

"You're almost intelligent looking when you get something right. Or half-right. Others gather the steel. The shepherd is just the means to get it to Germany. That steel is important in ways you will never understand."

"Because it hurts...vampires, I suppose?"

"It violently does just that. The rabbit Calvert had a useful idea but it was conceived with flawed intent. His betters in the Martyres are finding different ways to employ it in considerably wider applications. And the catalyst for what's coming is brewing right now."

"What catalyst is that?" Charlie coughed and it hurt. Was he having a panic attack?

Tomlison's smile returned, sadly confident. "What always results from a world in economic ruin and easy blame to place. War."

***

Crawford woke with a start in the dark and smelled traces of doe and goat. But he wasn't at home, either home. The walls were too close and the wallpaper was inoffensively ugly. He'd seen it all too recently. "Charlie?"

"He left this room for us, to get through the day," came Celeste's voice. "Dawn is in less than an hour. He left clothes for you. You'll need to rest."

A test of his own muscles confirmed he was still wounded. "Hurts like hell. Where is he?"

"He would have checked out by now. He has to keep an eye on his operation." She said the word with marked indifference. Next to her sitting form in the dark, Samson's small shape was ramrod-straight on the bed, like a tin soldier in its box.

"Did I do anything..." Crawford muttered.

"No murdered thinking mammals. No attempted sex with anything living or otherwise, some dead livestock."

Crawford vaguely remembered mooing and the chewy texture of organs, gritty and coppery. He pushed that aside. "I have, uh..." Thoughts were like leaves he raked together. "My car is around here someplace not too far. I might still have dinner in it for you if they didn't escape."

"Good. I'm starving," Samson said, not a muscle moved.

"Dawn is coming soon and we need to get to Boston."

Boston? Yes, that had come up at some point. A drink would knock the kinks out and Crawford couldn't help feel bad about that. His son was out there somewhere…

"Okay. I'll get dressed, go find my Chevy and get the curtains up. You two can deadnap in the back and I'll get us on the road."

Celeste nodded. "Better be fast. You know where we are."

His ribs hurt at the memory of angry carnivore claws kicking him over and over. "I do."

He dressed hastily and staggered out, closing the door behind him carefully. Dawn was half an hour away at most, he could feel the fuzz of it. Smells crossed his nose, much of it already familiar: the mix of unwashed pelts, burned engine oil, and the distant tang of whiskey-infused vomit that he didn't want to track down. He crossed the lot past haphazardly parked jalopies and rust-flanked sedans, finding only two straight-parked cars to move between. It was during a slide past the Ford Tudor on his left that his nose caught something familiar that stilled him. The window was cracked an inch to let air through and he smelled the distinct taste of weasel that most wolves' noses wouldn't have been able to extricate.

It was a scent he'd been in close quarters with all too recently. Working his nose at the window's top he managed to peer into the car. It was spotlessly clean but carried under the weasel scent the tiniest whiff of skunk. He closed his eyes and let sense memory take him back.

It was indeed the weasel who'd interrogated him in Scranton. Crawford ducked instinctively and slowly ran his gaze along the other vehicles in the lot and the rooms behind them. He came across something else he recognized, scent unrequired, out before one of the rooms.

Charlie's car was still there.

***

"We're not at war." Charlie's knees buckled at that moment and he had to lean hard on the dresser. "And if we were, why are you using fascist sympathizers to smuggle steel to Germany?"

"Because we can't simply ship the next hundred girders to Germany in the same way we did with the prior hundred to England. Not now that hostilities are brewing anyway."

Charlie blinked. "But...if you suspect a war why would you supply both sides with that steel? Who are you backing if a war breaks out?"

Tomlinson adjusted his glasses. "You mean which country?"

"The Martyres of Blackball or..."

Tomlinson gave him a droll look. "Well, we do strive to be invisible. My stupid Nosfur-lackey American friend, we back nobody." He waved the gun in a quick circle before keeping its dark eye on Charlie. "Wars are effective solutions to depressions and collective national shames, tonics to restore economies just like this one. And they're inevitable. We don't back any winner between socialists and fascists because we couldn't give a god-damn who thinks they run this circus. Factories we already own are ready to produce engines and munitions as demanded. Bunkers, bridges, and mortar shells will be imbued with the steel as needed, whatever best suits our needs for spreading its effects if war rages." Tomlinson sighed, pushed up his glasses with his blade and shrugged. "And if war doesn't break out, well, the rabbit's original plan could still work. Frigates or Ferris wheels, it doesn't matter. We're going to save the world from evil and be amply compensated, as we deserve to."

"What..." Charlie's voice struggled as though he were trying to breathe cement. His limbs gave out and his slipped down to the carpet, lower body so numb that he had no idea if his tail were under him or to the side. It was torture to keep his head up.

Tomlinson cocked his head in a wolf-like manner, amused. "Yes, Charlie? What's on your mind? Have you wondered why I've been telling you all this so freely? Distracting you with worthless truths?" He was enjoying himself now. "Does that cut I gave you still sting?"

Charlie's heart tried to hammer with panic and couldn't, as though it were lubricated with sand.

"Relax. That's not going to be what kills you. You're going to end your life extremely winded and quite unable to scream. And before I get out with the dawn to deal with your hellspawn down the row where they'll be pinned down, you'll want plenty of opportunities to do so."

Charlie fought hard for the four words he could dredge from himself. "What do you want?"

Tomlinson crouched low so they were eye to eye, the gun put away and the dagger slowly drawn. "I want to know the names of your informants watching Colonel Blake's tent-revival agitators. One phone call from you or them endangers what's been a very simple operation for us. The Martyres will have their righteous vengeance appeased with the two pairs of fangs, and on of were canines sent back to Europe by courier mail." Tomlinson pushed up his glasses, licking his muzzle's upper jaw thoughtfully as his tail twitched behind him. "And once it's all done, I think I just might put in for promotion with Edgar. That is, after your body is discovered."

Tomlinson's round, wide-spaced ears perked a split second before the room's window exploded inward. Grey-furred fury in a tattered dress shirt and slacks hurtled through the blown drapes and slammed into the weasel. Tomlinson rolled with the bulk atop him and transferred the furred missile's weight to the far plaster wall. Charlie felt broken glass pepper his legs but was unable to do much more than twitch as Agent Tomlinson swept with his dagger, missing the wolf's forearm widely before changing hands to draw his pistol again.

Charlie forced himself to bundle all the locomotive power he could gather as Crawford rose, halfway into were form and crouched again to charge. With a last burst of energy, Charlie swept a leg against the weasel's shin and the mustelid stumbled, the gun hand dipping low to stop his tumble and then coming loose from his grip as Crawford charged. The were shoved Tomlinson back through the broken window.

Charlie closed his eyes as the scuffle continued outside and tried to concentrate in order to move his limbs. Breathing was almost a full-time job and Charlie realized that he could feel the glass tumble off him as he fell on his side and struggled to push his limbs forward. It took an eternity while outside grunts and growls sounded between cars rocking with impact. Shuffling, wormlike, Charlie began to move himself towards the room's open door, compacting himself and then stretching again, a move of his whole body that thwarted the numbness in his extremities.

Was this permanent? If he wasn't tortured to death by a bent Bureau agent, would he never hold Crawford or anyone ever again? Would he ever do anything?

Worries banished as he stopped and started, some in agonized thrashes, some in exhausting stretches. He made it two feet, then three, the tall window's jagged frame gradually widening as his blurry vision saw past it.

The lot wasn't crammed with cars and he caught glimpses of Crawford darting over, clothes torn and tireless despite his accumulated wounds. A swung dagger pulled a yelp from the massive wolf but they kept on. Lights from rooms at the motel dimly illuminated the nearest cars as guests were waking up.

They were far from the lot's meager lamplight now, and in the space between two rugged Fords, Crawford's silhouette fell to his knees.

Triumphant, the weasel regrouped. His dagger dropped and he raised his glinting automatic that he'd drawn from somewhere low as he approached and took a direct bead on Crawford's head.

Charlie wanted to cry out and the weasel turned once, his lower body obscured by a car's fender, and saw Charlie prone beyond billowing drapes. Tomlinson gave a cold wink his way.

And failed to notice a stir behind him.

The shadows burying a wood-panelled pickup behind him shifted and moved and grew a slender cervine arm. It wrapped around the weasel like a cracked whip and clutched him, a doe muzzle and fangs rising over his shoulder.

There was a gasp from the weasel's throat as he brought the other arm back to shoot the Nosfur in the head, but a second smaller arm erupted from another shadow, gripped it in steel, and pulled it back.

Arms pinned, he squirmed and pitched forward, pulling both Nosfurs down to the gravel with him. Low, among the cars, Charlie just barely had line of sight with his head weakly lifted as high as he could manage. Behind them all, Crawford slid down another car's front grille much as Charlie had fallen himself. The were clutched a bleeding arm.

Despite all his worry for Crawford it was Tomlinson's gaze who caught his own, all confidence shed and his glasses fallen in the dust, leaving naked fear plain in the wide mustelid eyes that met Charlie's. He resembled a damned soul on the Sistine Chapel wall as two pairs of fangs found either shoulder with python precision, sinking in almost simultaneously. Their black-pooled eyes were bottomless shafts of hunger. The weasel gasped with his own blood flecking both cheeks as he was dragged back across the gravel, through the indifferent sentries of other rusty cars and into the dark thicket bordering the hotel lot. There his silhouette joined the two who stole him away to inescapable darkness.

Charlie closed his eyes, saw another weasel he'd known named Spettle in a speakeasy basement so far and yet so near, fed upon by darkness itself. He abruptly opened them again, his pelt damp with pure panic.

"Keep it down out there. Some people need sleep, ya jackasses!" came a call from down the row. Another door opened and some cat in night clothes wandered out into sight, glanced left and right before grumbling and shutting their door once again. So much readiness for violence had come to this unsuspecting town, and those uninvolved were sick of it.

Out in the lot, Crawford muttered from a car's shadow something half howl and half curse as though he were just another drunk. He rose and teetered on limbs that regained normal proportion as he stumbled through the half-dark back to Charlie's room. He growled a question and then his smaller mouth repeated it. "Charlie…you okay?"

Charlie couldn't answer as his stinking, bleeding mate lifted him, grunting with enough pain for both of them. Crawford dragged Charlie up and settled him back to the bed. Charlie managed just three gasps. "Lights on. All."

***

Dawn lifted everything but Lucas's spirits as he looked down at the scrawled speech on his lap in the charter bus's seat and saw only words that didn't want comity with one another. He looked up and saw the other close members of the Colonel's entourage all trying not to look at him. They all had demonstrated their thoughtless loyalty in ways that Lucas had noted very carefully, most often intimidation and keeping the new hangers-on in line, of which there were many.

Lucas's contribution to keep his precarious position was this very speech, the youthful face of the Colonel's party. The shepherd in question had demanded Lucas cram more into his speech about socialism and the evils of single females and pansies, more links in the endless chain of non-conformist grievances to ensure the anger machine would never be sated. Lucas didn't even know the man cared about those things, but he realized the fossa who'd visited likely called a few shots. The poor needed targets to blame.

And Lucas was expected to be the voice of all this. Bloviating about absent fathers and lost destinies was one thing, but the call to violence was getting too apparent. At some point, his participation was going to cross the bridge to instigation and burn everything behind it. Nerves started to mount.

The young wolf kept quiet all the way to Boston, his mind running back over all he'd seen, the server bear fired from the diner, the raccoon threatened. Desperation wore a million faces, and Lucas knew the time was nigh for the Colonel's reckoning.

***

Lillis stared out the bus window to Boston, seeing all and nothing at once. Her whole known life was behind her now. The bus itself felt still, as though the whole of creation were moving below and around it. Whatever awaited her in the Bell in Hand Tavern, her tears were fully spent and she knew a page was turning. She couldn't for the life of her figure out why the unknown was so viscerally exciting but she fought for calm.

She couldn't make herself wear the dead mammal's ring, but it weighed heavy in her pocket. She was afraid to even touch it. Deep inside herself, something undefinable couldn't be bottled up.

***

Sandy Mallory cursed herself as the hot shawl about her head began to slip back. She couldn't wait another night and her impulsive nature was already haunting her.

She'd done this so often while under Donovan's sway, moving through the day covered in so many layers of clothes that she felt like a Hallow's Eve ghost. She would have been glad for Bruno's company, driving or not.

The absence of her only friend outside of Celeste still hurt, but his mortality had made that an eventual certainty, one she'd pondered on occasion. So she drove and the punishing heat that bled past the curtains and shawl gaps kept her from ruminating. For that she was strangely grateful. Pain could be recruited to center oneself. Back in Ireland that had been her earliest lesson.

Sandy rounded a bend and came to a wider stretch, slowly coming up on a large lorry covered in flapping tarps, its boxy cargo weighing the bed low. She gunned the engine to catch up, pulled alongside to pass, and the molten sun that assaulted every inch of her through her deep coverings nearly ran her off the road. Breeze opened a gap in the overlayed tarps on the flatbed's back. Iron girders were rigid underneath and she pulled the car over with supreme effort, doubling over as the truck kept on and the pain she'd presumed was the sun's alone slowly receded.

She knew what they were and instinctively, where they were going. "Move your narrow arse, Celeste."

Sandy took side roads the rest of the way, paying extra for a marmoset gas-bar attendant to top up her tank with haste. Boston beckoned.

***

"We'll arrive in six hours," Mercel told Ferrault, who watched the mink's tightly slacked behind rock with the train car as he left the sequestered cabin.

"Why is this trip taking so long?" Donovan muttered, nerves finding him now that he'd fed off Myra a bit. He knew he needed to stay on Ferrault's good side if he was to keep enjoying her company, but he was inescapably anxious.

"Because," Ferrault replied flatly. "Somebody tainted the direct route for us. Did you manage to forget?""

Donovan wanted to curse himself. "I'm…"

"Don't be sorry. Be useful." Ferrault was back in his customary bohemian half-dress again, a gentlemammal's jacket with naked chest underneath. He'd eschewed the corsage this time. "This trip is as important for you as the rest of us. I already arranged for an introduction with yourself and Sandy to reacquaint you."

Myra was sleeping in the long couch under one drawn shade, her sheer slip rolling with each rock of the train carriage. Ferrault reached out and drew a claw across her cheek as he glanced at Calvert. "You're going to recruit the squirrel for us."

Donovan sat upright, feeling himself grow colder than customary once again. "That would…I'm afraid that would be complicated."

283

Ferrault's gaze met his with wordless reprobation.

"We didn't get along when last we met," Donovan added.

"She gave you Celeste's alias, didn't she?"

"Yes, she did." How to approach this with delicacy… "But her manservant became a bit of a problem and I was forced to dispatch him."

Ferrault stopped toying with Myra. "Why was that, Donovan?"

Outside any wall of this train was light and pain without escape. They could all overpower him, toss him into fire. His mind worked frantically fast. "He threatened to expose me, call contacts in the Martyres and tell them where I was. He was one of mine originally and we didn't part on the best of terms."

"One of yours. I see." The tone hadn't changed. Ferrault sat back. "Well, if you can't recruit her voluntarily then you'll have to bring her to us by other means." He looked at Donovan directly and his smile held a million unspoken promises Donovan wouldn't want kept. "By any means. Is that clear? And as soon as possible. A stage in my long-term plans depends on it."

"But we aren't going to Atlantic City."

"Alisandre isn't there," Ferrault said. "She's following the same path we all are."

***

Celeste and Samson ensured that the weasel's body was stripped and left deep in the foliage for ferals to find before returning to the room at dawn's first crack. Samson watched through drawn curtains as sunlight's glint cleared car tops and light's discomfort mounted.

Celeste sat on the bed. "We need to rest, Samson, head to Boston as soon as it's dark. Possibly sooner if Crawford gets the car ready."

"You saw him too."

"Who?" Celeste said. With life running through her veins as it was through his, the doe didn't want rest either.

"The wolf. The other wolf that Crawford loves," Samson said, turning to see that Celeste's eyes were still dark. Always that hunger, so rarely sated. "He was more terrified of us than the weasel we rescued him from."

"You know what happened in Chicago. He nearly died in Bucky Cavali's speak. His experience could easily have him more comfortable with the idea of eradicating us than most. And yet..."

Samson said nothing for a long time, then took the other bed and resumed his stillness. He let himself fall away as Celeste did, thinking of Charlie's rictus of terror and where he'd seen it so recently before.

***

Crawford got the innkeep calmed down and the old tiger chuffed as she stepped back into the office, scrutinizing the cheque Crawford had written from Charlie's book under better light. The old mammal was built to wrap a tractor round the average tenant like a tin shawl, and it was doubtless that the broken window down the row was going to cost her some business.

Crawford played it both careful and assertive at the same time, a common disposition in his PI work. He flashed Charlie's Federal badge at the squinting gopher seated at the desk and promised with apologies that any additional damage that may turn up upon leaving would be covered by the government.

"Can't wait till every last one of you have gone," the gopher still at the desk growled and Crawford raised an ear as the tiger returned and approved the cheque with a shallow nod.

The gopher pointed a muzzle out at a dim glow far beyond the hotel lot that was not the sun, but something closer and fiercer. "A riot broke out by the train tracks after that bastard's bus left, took alla donations and didn't give one dime to all the people they lured here. Townsfolk are sick of this travelling brute circus and what they've heaped on us. Good people been hurt. The Fed ain't doin' a damn thing so a thing got to be done." He was unapologetically resolute and Crawford left the office feeling a sense of calm satisfaction to go with his many aches and pains, even though the gopher had looked to want to spit in his face.

Maybe if this place wouldn't roll over to the Colonel's thugs then the world wasn't going to hell after all.

That gave him a renewed sense of purpose. Cryptic witch-games be damned, his son was bound for Boston. So, Crawford would follow.

He returned to the room and checked Charlie, who breathed slowly and whispered that he would be okay.

"God, I was worried that you were gonna choke."

"No. Can breathe, just weak," Charlie muttered blankly. Whatever the weasel had given him had been a low dose for interrogation purposes and was slowly wearing off. "Tomlinson was one…of those Nosfur hunters. He had poison on his blade."

Didn't that beat all. "Either what the bastard had wore off before he cut me too, or poisons just don't work on me."

"Did you drink a lot? Before?" Charlie coughed. "After?"

"Doesn't matter. Don't talk now. You're almost as much a mess as I am. Fill me in later."

Crawford wrapped another towel around the slowing bleed on his arm. He'd tell Charlie about the cheque he'd already filled out when the shock wouldn't cause him to swallow his own tongue. He held Charlie close, relieved as Charlie's arm weakly and clumsily patted at his and they fell into the entwined slumber of the injured and the drugged in the fully lit room. Charlie had wanted to say more but drifted off anyway. Crawford, exhausted, went under but didn't dream.

When Crawford came out of a coma-like well, Charlie was gone. A note sat next to a small pile of fins and sawbucks. "Tried hard, couldn't wake you. Forgive me, had to get to Boston, Omni Parker House. The weasel worked with the Colonel, moving steel to Germany. Can trust no one. When we talk again I need to tell you about what Lucas is into."

That got Crawford wide awake. Outside it was late morning and the place had that hungover dreariness left in the wake of a departed carnival, complete with the distant smell of burnt burlap. Crawford wasn't hungry but desperately wanted a coffee or a whiskey or both. Instead, he found his car.

It had been ransacked. The rats were gone, probably bit the thief good, and so was his pint of bourbon, which would have hurt his feelings under less dire circumstances. The gas hadn't been siphoned so he chugged it to life and got it back to the hotel, slipping into the dark room slowly with gratitude that the sun was over the roof and not at his back to lash the figures inside. "We've gotta haul it," he barked unceremoniously, and the Nosfurs sat upright with sour expressions.

"Car prepared?" Celeste raised a brow.

"Yes. Breakfast got away, sorry."

"We're fed," Samson said.

"Oh. Right."

With the draperies locked down like a darkroom about the car's rear they wandered out under sheets like eyeless ghosts, hurrying against the burn that penetrated the fabric. Once they were in the car, Crawford tossed the sheets back in the room, tossed another dollar on the dresser, settled up finally with the gopher who was glad to see the back of him, and they were off.

***

The Colonel wanted the speeches on Sunday evening, but the Emerson Colonial Theatre had been booked solid with acts, and he hadn't provided too many details about the proceedings during the two hours they had the place on Monday. Fortunately for the Colonel's needs, the Depression had taken a large bite out of the theatre business during the past six years and what kept the playhouses afloat kept them afloat. The Colonel's people made sure that none of the workers handling lighting or usher duties for his rally were vegetarian or any sympathetic types. That had taken some discouragement to ensure but a payoff to the owner had soothed any nerves.

Up in his hotel room where Lucas waited anxiously for directions, the Colonel called the number his contact had given him but the weasel back in Scranton didn't pick up at the appointed time. Strange. Lucas kept hat in hand and tail still.

"Get a bottle of whiskey, boy. Good stuff. Practice that speech. I've got business elsewhere for now."

"I want to go with you! Isn't it time for—"

The Colonel growled. "Keep yer tongue! You got a stage on which you're either seizing your destiny or discarding it. The Emerson's gonna have our biggest crowd yet. You don't stir them up tonight you'll be back on the farm with your mother wondering what destiny smells like."

Lucas was silent for a long time, chastened, ears falling back and then going up again.

"Get the crew up here in the next hour. We need to lay out the game plan in advance," the Colonel added shortly.

"All…alright," Lucas said. Something in the way the Colonel held his gaze for another few seconds, as though he were weighing it, didn't sit right.

Lucas went back into the empty hall and held back a moment. The Colonel called an exchange again, no answer. He then rang a different exchange that was international. "It's me. I can't reach my guy. Are you sure we can still go ahead?"

Lucas couldn't hear the response but the Colonel's voice caught. "The stage will be set on time for Monday night. Looking forward to seeing my Ark come in."

Lucas was quiet but excited as he slipped away.

***

Out on the Atlantic waters, the distant strip of Massachusetts was indistinguishable from the rest of America's eastern shores. The prow of a steel cargo hauler cut each wave between itself and Boston decisively, approach timed to avoid the United States Coast Guard, which was being drawn by distraction further south. The crew had been hired for discretion, their ulterior motives hidden from the silver-furred fox who smoked on the bow, nervously minding the time.

***

The day lengthened and the sun set with many souls converging. The bus pulled in at South Station and disgorged a handful of mammals, Lillis being the most imposing and yet most hesitant. Her modest cracked-leather suitcase creaked as she hefted it after getting a direction pointed by the lanky dog in a bus driver's uniform. She made her way north, brick-building facades to her left and the wooden frontages and planks of the dockside carrying over the Atlantic's brine. She came across a small Hooverville on the dock's verge, crates and car hulks squatted near where iron fences imposingly stood unattended, opening every few days to offer a handful of dockhand jobs to the hundreds who would clamour for work. The most desperate among them filled the adjacent empty lots with the little they had, their cubs running circles around drum fires as their elders stewed within themselves. Dusty cobbles were clicked by the claws on her feet as Lillis passed and she felt a moment of irresistible guilt. If a job did indeed wait for her, it was more than these people had.

The horn of a large truck startled her as one of the Kleiber cabs that occasionally had pulled up to Furdy's diner in Hancock with a hungry mammal at the wheel hurried by. This one drew a large, tarped load that kept its body low to the wheels. It made a turn half a block in front of her and disappeared down a wharf-pointing alley. Ears in the Hooverville went up and then down again.

Lillis kept on, getting directions from an elderly marmot trudging nowhere who had her turn left on Pearl Street and follow it through red-bricked industrial buildings, some bricks so old that they had originally been ballast on ships from England before America was even an idea.

Pearl met Water Street and Lillis turned left, coming into Boston's faster beating heart. She felt a chill wind as she crossed Devonshire as though an ownerless breath through the city's heart sought a word. A moment later she turned right on Washington and then left into Pie Alley.

There she found the Bell in Hand, modestly appointed with signage of a brown-furred fist in profile holding up a crier's bell. Lillis took a deep breath, put her hand around the ring that had been provided as her passport to whatever waited, and went in.

Ten minutes later within the cozy colonial frame of the tavern she found out that someone had just quit. Soon after that she'd spoken to the owner, shown the ring, told of Gus's favor. When the calico owner recovered from a near faint, Lillis knew instinctively that she had the job.

As she poured her first pint, she could have sworn she saw the crow-bent shape of Gus once again in the corner of her eye, a wraithlike reflection in the taps. Whispers under the amiable chatter of weary Bostonians mounted and Lillis felt a preternatural calm as she lost herself in her work.

CHAPTER 19

INTERSECTIONS

The trio stopped twice for gas and a hastily fried Reuben sandwich for Crawford that he barely chewed. The Nosfurs had drunk well enough on Martyre weasel and were still deliberating on what Charlie had written for Crawford. The dead agent had been in cahoots with the thugs heading to Boston. Donovan Calvert's steel was trading hands and was important to some sketchy European plan. That was all they had so far. The Nosfurs took rest and the wolf took the wheel.

The over-ten-hour trip was uneventful for Crawford, who every so often checked on the still bodies behind him, Celeste on the floor and Samson on the seat. He drove slowly and carefully and was saddle-sore as the sun dropped around Springfield, Massachusetts. The Nosfurs were suddenly staring over his shoulder, startling him.

"You look like hell and you're making us a bit hungry," Celeste said. "Once again."

"Making you…"

"Your wounds didn't fully close, and you bled a bit on the steering wheel while the sun was out."

"Can I drive?" Samson piped up, hopefully.

Crawford and Celeste said nothing for a moment. Celeste assumed diplomacy. "We can't be stopped by police, Samson. I'll take over at the wheel."

"Of course we can't," Samson said dully. "Are you worried that I'll tell them I drank the blood of a federal agent?"

Crawford shrugged into the long silence. "I ate a crooked cop twelve years ago."

The silence became much, much longer.

"I didn't tell you this?"

"No." Celeste leaned forward. Both Samson's ears and hers spread wide. "I don't think you did."

He was sure he had. "He was going to kill me. Got instructions to do so from Al Capone if I remember correctly."

Samson nodded. "That's alright then."

"Samson," Celeste said.

"We just did it. Probably before this is all done, we'll do it again."

The silence that time was somehow more uncomfortable.

"I'm going to drive. Crawford, get some rest," Celeste instructed.

"Alright. I'll admit, I'm kinda tired."

Boston was only a couple hours away and night had fallen as they pulled over and switched positions. Crawford rested his muzzle on the dash from the passenger seat and blinked two hours away. He dreamed of his son, and he dreamed of the dead thugs he'd left on the dock the last time he was where they were heading. In the portentous gauze of anxious dreams they were all one and the same, his son's face on mutilated bodies, floating across Boston harbour in multitudes.

***

Lucas was two hours to curtain call on a threadbare speech, and his nerves were frayed for far more important reasons. The table in the Colonel's hotel room was packed with his innermost circle and smelled of stale anxiety. Ben was elbows on the table, mustelid whiskers dancing, while Lucy the cat was simultaneously still and sinewy with coiled impatience under her pageboy cap. Larry the bobcat sipped something noxious, Walt the black bear from Wisconsin cracked knuckles in boredom, Sam the wolverine from "out West" stared into the table, and Clara the husky watched everybody else balefully. The curly-furred mutt, Clyde, scratched himself through a dirty shirt as he sat and closed the circle.

Outside, brick and haze hinted at Boston's storied presence. Inside—

"We need to go over a thing or two." The Colonel didn't sit. He stalked the periphery of the seated like he was either protecting something special or sorting it for deficiencies. "I've been keeping an eye on things and I've got concerns."

He let silence carry tension for a moment as gazes were traded.

"I get alla the papers, particularly the coastals because, well, you know your enemy by their lies and there have been very many lies told about this odyssey. What's more, they know details about who I talk to and who I dine with in private that they ought not to have a damn clue about. That's 'cause somebody talked."

The temperature fell a few degrees in that moment and Lucas's fell a few further than that.

Walt took a rumbling breath. "What got said, boss?"

"Too much." The Colonel stopped at the window and found something outside it fascinating. "Far, far too much."

He turned back. "Lucas."

He didn't hear his name at first, but when fourteen eyes at the table locked on his he realized he was on the spot. He fought the urge to tremble. Ten paces to the door. How fast could he—

"You went back to your room last night around, what, nine or so?"

Lucas swallowed. React naturally, he'd been taught. A man cornered would be nervous and to not be nervous was even more suspicious. "I did, Colonel."

"And when you did, who among your bunkies was there?"

He was rooming with three others. "Uh…Lucy was. She was in bed already."

"Tired out from booting veggies outa town," Walt rumbled, seemingly ignorant of the cool tone of the room. "You tuck her out any further, boy?"

Lucy hissed at him as the table laughed nervously. "I wouldn't let any dog get a piece o—"

"Stop messing around!" the Colonel barked. "So, it was you and Lucy. The others were out."

"Uh, yes," Lucas said. The Colonel's diatribe about interspecies mixing came to the fore in his panicked mind and he wondered if he was going to have to defend his honor and Lucy's at the same time. Not that he liked her or her cruel streak but—

"Clyde." The Colonel didn't shout but the clipped tone of his voice almost sounded like one. "Get up."

The curly-furred dog rose slowly, chair sounding almost plaintive as it squealed on the floorboards. "Uh, yeah, Colonel?" Every eye found him now.

"Come round here and tell me where you were last night after the tent was broke down in Hancock."

Clyde rose and shuffled round behind Lucas and three others to meet the Colonel, muzzle down, tail still. "Well…"

"Tell me, Clyde. Did you meet a certain raccoon reporter from the New York Times for drinks?"

Ears went up around the table, but one pair went up an instant sooner.

"I didn't sir," Clyde answered with certainty, and both his and the Colonel's grips dropped on the shoulders of the last remaining bunkie Lucas had settled with in Hancock. Sam the wolverine from some damn place out West would have jumped if he could get out of his chair.

"They had a word with one of ours, got more than a few juicy details, didn't they, Sam?" the Colonel growled. The rest of those present got the gist of the situation and rose all at once, chairs screeching back on that pocked wooden floor. Lucas rose with them instinctively.

"What?" The wolverine took deep, throat-shuddering breaths. "I didn't hurt the cause!" The white band round his brow shrank as his brows went up, eyes wide.

"When you told them about how we convinced the local constabulary to look the other way while we worked? And fingered two of the officers involved?"

"I named nobody!"

"The reporter did. She also asked you about a friend and benefactor out West-a-here with some Red problems to solve and you, like a fool, laughed and nodded, didn't you! Didn't you?"

Lucas stood where he was but others moved round the table to flank Sam, hackles up, claws out.

"So?" Sam panted wafts of confusion and fear that carried the musky residue of ashen leaves. "So what?"

"So, four of the others we were hoping to onboard backed out after the hotsheet fell offa the truck, Sam! I told alla you, no press! Not without my personal say-so! You did us all dirty with that move! Dirty!" The Colonel took hand from shoulder and cuffed the wolverine, hard. With a backwards thumb and snap of his fingers, Blake was behind him and dragged his chair back while Lucy's hand fell on the shoulder the Colonel had let go of. The wolverine was gasping now.

"I tolerate mistakes to a point!" The Colonel's growl buried any magnanimous traces. "But this is a war of inches. And your stupid drunkard stunt cost us several inches, Sam!"

Sam was surrounded now. Lucas saw the exit was blocked as the Colonel's people smelled blood in the air and closed in. He fought down the desire to intervene and kept his mouth shut.

"I'm sorry! I'm sorry! It won't happen again!"

Colonel Blake drew something pearl-handled from his coat pocket out of which he unfolded a length of burnished, sharpened steel. "Oh, I know it won't, Sam. Because you're paying those inches back, voluntarily. Six by my reckoning. Maybe eight if the act is a bit sloppy."

"No, please." He was gasping for air now.

"Tie his tail off to stop any mess," the Colonel intoned. "I don't need to see it, let him keep it. Every lesson deserves a souvenir." He went nose to nose with Sam, eyes cold. "Unless he resists. Then I want the whole damn thing. Go."

Hands were off Sam and he teetered to his feet, searching for sympathy among the gazes. When his eyes fell on Lucas, he recognized terror in the wolf's return gaze and the wolverine's eyes pleaded for help, any intercession the new kid could provide.

Instinctively, Lucas turned away, shame biling his throat. Sam was ushered out and three went with him.

That left Lucy, Ben, and Clara. The females had both been propositioned by Sam and didn't like him very much at all. Ben seemed indifferent and Lucas tried to copy his mannerisms, wondering if he'd hear what went on two doors down.

"You can be sure," the Colonel sighed bitterly, "that if the press knows lots then any law enforcement, local or federal knows more. Never assume they're our side. Enemies are all around us."

Lucas's heart thrummed as his nod came as readily as anyone else's. He was running out of time with too many names to get wind of. The Colonel's outfit was still a spider whose long legs reached into shadows.

An hour later, as if in another world, Lucas was in the thick of it all.

The Emerson was packed to the rafters, a vast assortment of the disgruntled and dispossessed who'd barely ever afford a ticket to a show in this place with the boxes and upper balconies filled with the well-to-do backers and hangers-on of the movement. He was sure he recognized the round-eared silhouette of the fossa who'd visited the Colonel in Hancock, but the man's shape amongst a few other homburgs and a top hat was all he could make out. Lucas instead watched the Colonel work the crowd like a well-tuned instrument. Applause and whoops were punctuated by flat palms thrown up, palms vertical, claws a-prow. Lucas kept panic at bay as the moments ticked down to his own time on stage and he took deep breaths. Everything had led to this. He was either going to earn the Colonel's trust today, or it would all be over and he'd be running for his life if lucky. He'd know soon enough what his future entailed.

"The future will leave no room for us, lest we come to it as conquerors! Our time is now!" The Colonel's tail lashed as his arms stretched wide and clutched for the rafters and cheers rained down upon him. He threw up the Ark's prow salute and left the stage with tail and muzzle high, trading a single look with Lucas as he passed.

The time had come.

Lucas took the stage, feeling the hot spots on the varnished stage floor where klieg lights flooded in from all angles. He felt the heat of those lights like a thousand bodies packed angrily against his and wondered if Sam had struggled at all when his tail had been clipped. Lucas hadn't seen him since.

"We come here to save something more important than ourselves," Lucas began, needing a moment to collect himself. "This nation has failed us but we cannot fail it, not what it represents, nor…"

In the featureless glare, the recently exhumed image came unbidden of a rusting tractor, crowded by the smells of careless, unburdened children. Far beyond that, on a horizon he didn't want to see, a plume of dust followed a Chevrolet far and away, the silhouette of its driver pointing at a future without a family, without a son. Anger returned like rank fuel. He could get through this. Just once more. All he'd memorized burned away and he let it. "This nation was, for so long to me, a father. One I thought I could trust in and could be trusted in return. But it was a faithless relationship, one that saw us all abandoned to the whims of a careless world, seeking worth in institutions that didn't see any worth in us. And we failed to see the real enemy…"

Again, he trailed off. He was supposed to mention communism at this point, unionist plagues spreading Hoovervilles of the dispossessed across the American landscape like boils on a dying body, but the metaphor was weak, its causes made so nebulous and so ill-defined that the words could be pointed at any target at all. At the back of the room, in the lush pill boxes, dim shapes of the wealthy glared down on him and he could make them out now that his eyes were adjusting. Among them the fossa was resplendent in a darker suit bearing a brandy snifter from the benefactor's private lounge bar.

Lucas found a different thread to follow. "The real enemy, my friends, is those who would seek to lead us but fail to instill any trust in exchange for what is freely given by its children. I've seen so many men wounded in a war that I was too young to fight, so many discarded by industry that is too hungry to give back—"

"And what is it hungry for, soldier?" A familiar voice boomed from behind him. The German shepherd was a dozen feet away, but Lucas could feel the urgency on his breath.

What was he doing? All this way, all this trust earned with his own blood and sweat, and Lucas was risking losing all by wandering off script. Eyes bored into the back of him.

"It's hungry for the cheap labor of the weak and the slovenly!" the Colonel continued. "The lesser creatures who drag at the keel of God's miraculous Ark that bore this country and threaten to engulf us all with sin and depravity and sloth!"

Whoops rose up to this accusation, confused at first but then enthusiastic at the comfort of familiar enemies and easy enmities. Lucas was losing the room. His voice cracked when he called out. "We must fight to regain America before it slips away from us. The time is now to fight for what we really believe in! Our enemies seek to divide us, make us find blame in one another while the real enemy encroaches upon us!"

A stomp came behind him. "And that enemy comes with flat teeth, empty smiles, and open hands ready to steal from us all through the poison of the New Deal!" The Colonel roared. "Are you all ready to take this nation back?"

Feet pounded the auditorium and were joined by frenzied snarls. A few battered hats took to the spotlight beams and tumbled back down. The Colonel must have signaled someone because the klieg light left Lucas entirely and fell upon the German shepherd, letting Lucas see the auditorium again. The downtrodden stamped and howled while, deep in the back, high and disaffected, the benefactors holding the Colonel's purse strings regarded the stage as though a middling amusement was fizzling before them. Some were already wandering out, including the fossa.

"Lucas Marsten, everybody! Next up, my friends, learn some political sciences in support of our noble cause from Doctor Koffler of the International Alphaics Institute!" The Colonel's tone was that of a carnival barker pointing at a circus exhibit, drolly bringing attention back to the centre ring as he backed out of it.

Lucas followed to find him waiting. An older dachshund in spectacles and a ruler-straight tie put his shoulders back and marched out like a military cadet as they left.

The Colonel scrutinized him like an entomologist finding something interesting in a corner. "You made a mistake drifting off out there," he said levelly. "Improvising…is not for you, Lucas."

How many inches in the Colonel's war had that cost? Lucas took a moment to let the words sink in as cheers for Doctor Koffler washed back over both of them. His hackles went up despite his best efforts and he thought of Sam being meekly dragged away for penance.

Like hell that was going to happen to him. "You cut me off! I was getting around to what you wanted to say. But I had things I needed to say along with them. Dammit, if you just want a ventriloquist puppet without a mind of his own you could have just had one made. I have to show what I'm feeling for this to mean a damn thing, Colonel. Why don't you trust me?"

The hand that fell on his shoulder hurt when it squeezed and the eyes finding Lucas's were both pained and yet had that ever-present glint of menace. The Colonel came to a decision. "Alright, then. Tonight you're going to see what the real stakes are. Just maybe that will help you find the resolve you seem to be struggling with."

The meaning of what the Colonel was saying settled in and Lucas felt his heart skip a beat. "I'm ready to—"

A claw quieted him. "Because if you can't demonstrate that resolve tonight, I'll really, truly have no use for you." The Colonel said it with all the sympathy he could muster, which wasn't much at all. "There's a bar a few blocks from here up Pie Alley. Bell in Hand. The boys are going for a drink now that this phase is over before we meet friends at the pier. Follow Walt, he'll know where to go. I'll see you there."

The Colonel patted the young wolf hard enough to rock him as the doctor's voice drifted back to them with droning, authoritative declarations about defective diets and brain shapes.

The Colonel nodded approvingly from the wings as the dachshund wagged a finger out on the stage. He met Lucas's expectant gaze again. "I need to place a call to the wife, then get out there for the closing remarks. Go get yerself calmed down," the Colonel instructed and walked past the young wolf as though forgetting he was there.

***

The hotel room was much nicer than the flop in Hancock but Charlie didn't give a damn. He shoved a five in the bellhop's white glove and saw her off. Michael picked up in three rings at his own staging area several blocks away and for once Charlie didn't wonder what that luxurious tail was doing. "We're ready," Michael said.

"We'll need a patrol on the docks, fast but discreet. North End, South End, get a car to Dorchester. We're looking for girders of steel. The steel. It's happening soon."

Michael was puzzled. "The steel purchases aren't just money laundering fakery? How do you know that?"

"New information came to light. I can't go into it now, Mike. The source..." Charlie tried not to think of Tomlinson being dragged into the dark and swallowed to keep his dry throat working. It was midday. Nothing could sneak up on him now. "The source is in the wind. We need to get everybody prepped for a raid."

"Shouldn't I call Dee Cee and get more claws on the bricks down here?"

"No!" Next door, cutlery clattered at how loud Charlie shouted. "I'm sorry, Mike. We're on our own. My authority. The six of us will handle this. We may have...uh...we may be compromised." Charlie regretted saying that word, a word with a thousand questions and protocols behind it. He was as truthful as he could be. "Somebody might have informed them."

"Do you mean...?"

"I have people I can still trust, Mike." Charlie wondered where Crawford was at that moment and knew that, with the information the Nosfurs had, he was likely breaking speed limits with two vampires in the trunk. Not that Charlie would ever call them that to their faces. His mind's eye fixated on his would-be murderer's fate again and he pondered just for a second what Tomlinson's last moments had been like.

Charlie forced the anxiety down. Instead, he thought about Crawford and Crawford's son, right in the middle of all this. The promise he'd kept to his agent on the inside was going to cost them all if Lucas couldn't extricate himself at the right time.

He wanted a drink and a cigarette. "I have to take care of a few things but will come to meet you shortly. Break out the Thompsons, get the trucks ready. We roll in clean and a show of force should put the Colonel's men to heel."

"On it, boss."

Charlie remembered the last time he'd fired a Tommy gun in fear and hoped that, God willing, sneaking around was most of it. Assuming God wasn't forsaking this whole mess.

***

Donovan disembarked with the others at Boston's South Station and was somehow unsurprised to find that two cars awaited them all, isolated within a garage on the station's vast flank. Ferrault left the covered track the train car had berthed and crossed the early evening threshold as casually as whoever owned the place. Donovan and one of the minks followed. The brown mink, Mercel, opened one of the town car's doors and Ferrault entered. Donovan put his foot on the sideboard and the lynx's right hand pressed coolly on his chest. "You have other work to do." Ferrault pointed at the second car, looking strangely annoyed, as though the rabbit hadn't surmised his desires.

"What do you need me to do?"

"I told you that you needed to secure a friend's help."

Sandy Mallory. "I don't know how to—"

"You did it for a living. You obtained her. Do so again. A mutual friend you're travelling with will assist."

"What precisely do you want with her?"

Ferrault chuckled. "I've spent far longer than you've been alive gathering friends from all parts of the world for my needs. Relationships with me are promises traded, Donovan. You want power. Others want restitution from past wrongs. I find ways to give everyone who joins me what they want."

The lynx released his chest, patted his white cheek, and closed the door. Immediately the garage door sealing in the two sequestered town cars began to open, and Donovan urgently scurried to the open door of the other car. Dregs of dust crept into the garage as the lynx's chauffeured car drove out. The engine was only turning over as Donovan closed the door to the second car and sat at the flank of a dark brown suit whose owner was much taller and of more slender stature.

"I know who you are," a nasal voice said as its owner leaned out of the shadow it was playfully binding. "And I know what Ferrault wants of you. Help me get what I want tonight and I can help you get what you want, a way into Ferrault's graces. And perhaps much more."

***

The place was both stuffy and cozy in that way of some well-travelled establishments that kept up through the worst of the Depression, but Lucas felt lonely in the crowd. The Colonel's retinue surrounded him, sipping the same ale that he did, and he wondered if the fuzz of the beer made them as numb as he was. The Colonel's weasel muscle, Benny, was at his left, joking about how fox musk made a vixen's trap easy to find in the dark. Sex jokes, explicit or derogatory, were the primary outlet for the Colonel's crew, and they kept laughing at things like the parts on rabbits that were the floppiest or how ungulate whores had it the hardest with hooves because they broke their own teeth in back seats. Lucas didn't have any zingers to share but always made sure to laugh along lest the feeling that he didn't belong circulate.

Even Sam was there, nursing a drink in silence, eyes distant and sitting upright so his shorter, bandaged tail wouldn't brush anything. When he laughed at other jokes it was pained and mechanical.

If things went the wrong way tonight, Lucas knew he'd be far worse off.

So, he let himself get just a bit numb. The first ale soaked through him and Lucas was partway into the second, which he'd predetermined to be his last, before the cotton-wad bluntness of intoxication struck him. It was a pronounced juxtaposition from the whiskey—was it whiskey?—that he'd had at O'Holler's that had dragged such a vivid memory out of the murk into cutting, crystalline clarity. The beer of the Bell in Hand blunted him as one would want, took inhibitions down and made the world that was falling down around him just a bit inconsequential.

Halfway through the second he thought he should stop but one of the Colonel's inner circle shouted out, "Round three is on me!"

A third beer. Lucas nodded dully as a large ursine waitress lumbered over and took orders over his shoulder.

As she was doing so, a chair was turned and the Colonel settled into it. "The boat comes in within the next three hours. All the steel's ready. And what will be offloaded, well…" The Colonel showed every tooth. "We'll be amply supplied by early next morning, let me tell you."

"Bars?" Clyde was excited enough to nearly drool in his beer.

"That and more." He caught the server's attention. "The ale's good here, right?"

The bear looked his way and nodded. "It's the best in Boston."

"Then…" The Colonel trailed off, studying the bear for just a moment, his nose and eyes both working. "Bring me a pint of that," he said without emotion.

The bear took more orders of the same from around the table and trundled off.

The Colonel was suddenly quiet as was the rest of the table, seeing he'd figured something out. Lucas watched her go and realized what the Colonel was on to.

"I know that bear," the Colonel said, teeth clicking together. "She was in Hancock a day or two ago. That diner, Furdy's it was called."

Muzzles turned to the table the bear had moved on to, then back. "You sure, Colonel?" Lucy asked, beer foam on the cat's whiskers.

"Sure as God knew top deck of nautical salvation from bottom," the Colonel muttered gravely, eyes gleaming cold. "We got us a spy."

"What ya want done, boss?" Walt rumbled.

The Colonel blew air out one side of his muzzle as he deliberated. "Blood is stronger than steel. And we're trading one for the empowering of the other. Tonight's too important. Lucas?"

Hearing his own name nearly made him jump. "Colonel?"

The Colonel laid down a couple sawbucks. "You, Benny, Walt, and Skippy are coming to the docks with me. Go settle the bill. Rest of you…" The Colonel leaned in. The three thus far unnamed, Clara and Clyde who'd roughed up Lucas's drunken father, and Lucy, who'd leaned hardest on the raccoon shopkeep back in Hancock, leaned forward with him.

His voice dropped even as his expression remained jovial. "Nurse your libations and leave when that bear does. No way random chance had her follow us all the way here. There's just no way." He narrowed his gaze. "Make it an accident. Or a robbery. Be creative, but be fast and thorough."

Despite the urgency for discretion, every muzzle at the table turned back to see the bear girl filling ales for them at the bar. She paused to move bottles around, lifting one magnum of hooch that she realized had lost its cork. The bear stared into it, unblinking, lost in thought for a moment and failing to see all the beady glances of ill intent aimed her way.

Lucas froze to the spot, weighing what he'd just heard.

***

Samson glared at the road ahead with grudging eyes. Dark had fallen fully and he'd pushed the Chevy's curtains away without tying them off. The car looked like it needed a pelt-cut with the curtains fluttering, not that he cared. "We're close enough to town that you could let me drive. Plenty of states have little kids running errands with cars. Tractors even."

"We can't risk attention here, Samson." Celeste was frustratingly patient as Crawford snored next to her, muzzle bobbing. "We're close now."

"And what will I do when close is here?" Sarcasm dripped.

The outskirts of Boston became the center of it soon enough. Brick rose and Celeste remembered the few parts of Chicago that climbed the banks of Lake Michigan in stories by the dozen. No edifice shot as high in this city on the Atlantic's salty banks.

"We'll need your help to scout around. There's a corner that Sandy was told we have to arrive at, though we don't know why."

"Then why are we even going? Didn't you want the sisters dead? They were the cause of the mistake we buried in Chicago."

"They were. And I wouldn't mind seeing them laid low. But if they have Sandy concerned, then so am I."

"Sandy...who you slapped in the face when—"

"If you don't want to get involved then you don't need to," Celeste snapped. "I'm sorry for all you've gone through but there are larger things than your worries or mine or Crawford's. Trying to simply stay out of fate's way, or the sisters' twisting of it, hasn't ever worked. I'm tired of hiding."

"Right, that's my job." Samson fumed for a moment, staring at the back of the doe's head as she kept the Chevrolet moving with a tightly knuckled grip on the wheel. He wanted to say that Celeste was walking into a trap, that Crawford was going to get himself killed if they let him go after his son again, which, judging by the pamphlet he'd been clutching, was exactly what he was doing. The wolf couldn't even get through the day without getting into drink and risking everything.

The last few years came into stark relief for Samson in that moment, bouncing powerlessly, small and ineffectual as always, in the back seat of a car falling apart on a ride into almost certain death or possible exposure to the world. Everything he did or thought felt pointless. And his only moment of clarity, of actual usefulness, was a fleeting moment that had come in what felt another lifetime, in an alley in Scranton, where those who presumed themselves predators had learned the hardest lesson.

"You should let me out a few blocks from, what, Water and Devonshire, right?"

"Very good, Samson."

Her tone made his stubby horns hurt as though he butted something. "I do pay attention sometimes."

Celeste was quiet a moment. "I wasn't trying to be patronizing."

"Let me out so I can look around. Nobody would suspect that I'd be any trouble. And if I run into any..."

"Samson..."

"I'll lead them away and go to the hotel that Crawford's Federal friend mentioned. Please start trusting me," Samson grunted.

Celeste didn't reply. The bones of old Boston climbed to tenements worn and crumbling. A fog dampened the light, casting the lanes with their buzzing snatches of nightlife in dreamlike gloom. Celeste pulled over and let Samson out.

Crawford jerked awake in the front seat as the doe pulled away, and Samson enjoyed a moment of peace and the sensation of freedom before he got moving.

***

"You've done well tonight," Mikkel said. Strangely Lillis had worked for the calico for nearly two hours before she'd even confirmed her new boss's name, such was the pace at which she dived into work. She'd handled several dozen tables in the space of a few hours, the Bell being a bustling place by any standards she'd ever known. The smells, heat, the electricity of mammalian buzz as repasts sizzled and brews flowed at Lillis's deft handling invigorated something deep within that reminded her of the quintessential essences of life. She'd collected more tips than a week back in Hancock to boot.

It was as she cashed out the coins and bills that were to be rendered unto the calico Caesar that a familiar presence touched her senses again. Among all the tables she'd waited, she'd caught a whiff of the familiar. A German shepherd in a white suit and hat moved past her as though she wasn't there with a younger wolf in tow. His eyes met hers for just an instant and she remembered someone like him from Hancock, a few kind words from a clutch of casual abuse had mended one crack in a horrible day that had worsened regardless.

If he recognized her, he said nothing, but the look he gave her was... worried. The shepherd and the wolf were out the door at the suited shepherd's beckoning and then a minute later so was she.

She felt something off as she left Pie Alley and turned right, the canine and lupine already lost in the sparse crowd. She trudged east towards the clutch of hotels that she'd vaguely remembered spotting earlier. Hopefully she could find a place to rent longer term in a few days.

***

Two blocks after dropping Samson off, Celeste pulled over and asked for directions. A tipsy buffalo pointed and she returned to the car. "I was right. Water and Devonshire are just two blocks from here."

Crawford awoke looking like hell and clawed at his own muzzle as though trying to get insects off it. He'd made too many transitions in the past few days and that always made him itchy and ornery. "So, what, we should circle in? We don't even know what we're looking for and I need to get to Charlie."

Celeste scanned the street ahead, feeling something off. "You know where Charlie's hotel is. I can go to the intersection while you…" She had only glanced at the car haphazardly straddling the curb ahead, but as squabbling resolved from the mutterings of a city at night, she'd picked out voices and made out silhouettes, one of them slapping a car bonnet.

Crawford's nose worked but he didn't see what she did. "What is it?"

Celeste showed teeth. "An answer, perhaps." She turned off the Chevy's engine and handed the key to Crawford. "Go find that hotel."

Crawford tried to follow her gaze but the otter swearing at the car was unrecognizable to him. Celeste was glad for that. "Where are you going?" Crawford asked.

"Charles—sorry, Charlie—will need your help. You should find him." Celeste moved quickly. A few moments later she was standing over an otter's shoulder as the hag banged on a Ford's shell.

"Dis *merde voiture* ain't worth a cold damn," Grisand was growling. Across the car's bonnet, a younger wolf with a wart and a distant expression did a double take as her eyes met Celeste's.

"*La voiture n'est pas ton problème,*" Celeste whispered icily into Grisand 's ear. "*La loutre est en faute, j'en suis sûr.*"

The Belle sister turned and her expression soured. "Shoulda known the squirrel would blab to her *suceur-de-sang ami.*"

Celeste glanced around for witnesses. Smatterings of mammals migrated in small preoccupied groups. Boston wouldn't crawl with barflies on a Monday night, or she wouldn't expect it to. "You knew full well she would. You probably used her to draw me here."

"We have no threads to pull with you," Baliosi muttered disdainfully as the wolf peered over the car bonnet. "Or anyone for that matter. Leguna's passed on. We're blind to the sight now."

The one-eyed coyote had looked on her last leg in Chicago. Too bad. Time hadn't cut into her enmity for the witches one bit, not after how they'd used her. She kept her arms at her side but wondered how much throttling it would take to render the otter or the wolf unconscious. "I don't believe that you're here to sample the salty air. Who are you toying with in this city?"

"You soft in de head?" Grisand snorted. "We toy with nobody. The completion of things as they oughta be needs help sometimes. And you're with better kin now than bootleggers, ain't ya?"

"My life is none of your business, and your help killed more mammals in three nights than I'd been responsible for in a year."

"Other lives, other threads. Things went as they were supposin' to."

The Chevy drove past and Crawford leaned far enough over to the passenger side that his nose fogged the glass. 'You alright?' Crawford asked with his brows.

Celeste nodded his way and pointed in the general direction of the center of town where Charlie's hotel was. He nodded and pulled away.

Grisand didn't look back his way, shrugged. "There goes one now. We can't see what's happening, only that it's happening."

"You're just trying to save yourself—"

Baliosi tentatively moved round the front of the Ford, clearly cautious before Celeste but braving her anyway. "No. Something needs you, needs him, needs us. We need a working car at Water and Devonshire in case we need to leave quickly and you're holding us up."

"From what?"

Wolf and otter growled simultaneously with exasperation. "We don't know!"

"That's not good enough."

Baliosi and Grisand traded looks and Celeste could see their hearts racing. Grisand swallowed as she looked into Celeste's darkened eyes and her own widened as something occurred to her. "Boston never came up in the sight in all our time after Leguna left us until the broken chain just rattled the intersection out at us a day ago, signifying nothing at all even though it's so close I can feel it. But now, in this moment, I remember that this time and place was almost certainly stirred up before. But not the place itself—"

306

"More damn riddles…"

"No," Baliosi barked, putting her hand on Grisand's rounded shoulder. "I know what she's getting at. Leguna's last glimpse with us, before the cancer stole her…the draught was taken, memories bottled at a bar in New Orleans, old ones, deep and precious. The imbiber wanted to know when you'd meet us again, you specifically. He gave your name. We knew it would be by the sea, in a greater calamity's hail with the scents of—"

"Salt and ale," Grisand muttered.

"…but that was all," Baliosi stammered. "The drinker would give us no name of his own. He was of your kind. And old, so old."

"A Nosfur? What did he look like? What species was he?"

Baliosi opened her mouth to answer but was startled by a scream that cut the night from two blocks away.

CHAPTER 20

CORKS

Lillis was a block from Pie Alley when she realized she'd turned too soon. The hotel she'd seen was south, not east, and Boston's winding cobbled streets were disorienting. She turned back to retrace her steps and almost ran right into a large dog with curly fur, a dirt-darkened shirt, and denim slacks. He had a nose that seemed crooked, as though broken. Even with her own size, Lillis was almost eye level with the wiry-looking mutt. "Excuse me," she said and stepped around him.

A cat with a tawny pelt under her pageboy cap and bony shoulders under checked flannel was there to block her.

Claws scuffed the pavement and another dog was behind her.

The October air got colder. "How can I help you?" Lillis swallowed.

"Long way from Hancock, innit?" the curly-furred dog asked with a yellow-toothed smile.

"Han…" She'd seen them before. At work not half an hour ago. And now that her memory was jogging: "You were at Furdy's."

"And you were there, big girl, getting the Colonel's suit ruined."

"Who?" But of course, Lillis immediately remembered the German shepherd who'd turned the whole town against itself and gotten her fired to boot. That *had* been him at the Bell.

"Don't play dumb," the dog at her back growled. Lillis didn't turn to look but knew it was a third stalker, tone low with portent. "The Colonel has enemies in all directions, veggie sympathizers, commie rag-writers." The voice dropped lower. "Even goddamn Feds."

"Which one are you?" the cat hissed with lagered breath.

"Feds?" Lillis peered past them to the cold, empty end of the alley, then glanced back the way she'd come. Street signs crossing one another read "Water" and "Devonshire", and no other souls were in sight. The space tightened as the trio closed in. "Please leave me be."

A whispery metallic click was barely audible. "We're gonna leave you, alright," the curly-furred dog promised, gaze empty. Steel glinted in one knobby hand.

Lillis's breath caught and the dog froze.

A creased dollar bill fluttered down between them, pinwheeling in the heavy air as the thick-muzzled husky behind Lillis came into view. The dollar settled on the cobbles and all eyes darted up to the darkness above.

Another dollar fluttered down, slipping off the curly-furred dog's shoulder as something indistinct moved above.

"Thought I'd share the wealth," a voice teased in a light Irish lilt, then came again, elsewhere, unrooted. "It was the cat's, but I don't need much of it myself."

A red-furred squirrel in a dark cloak slipped into their presence, the alley behind her deep and vacant. She plucked one more bill from a ratty fold and let it flutter to the ground, touching the husky's toes. She stepped back. "I'm feeling generous. How are you feeling, children?"

The cat's gaze narrowed and she patted herself down. "Peanut has my wallet!"

The squirrel, a young waif barely in her twenties, skipped away down the street. Another bill descended like an autumn leaf. "I'm done with my generosity. I think I'll keep what's left."

"Thieving veggie mick!" The cat charged past Lillis and the red squirrel darted back. To Lillis's surprise, the dark of a building's flank drank her up as though the squirrel were liquid. The cat skittered to a stop, gaze darting and nose hunting as she snarled.

Slender red-furred hands wrapped the cat from behind and Lillis caught the flash of wide eyes, dark as the night around them. A blunt muzzle opened wide and Lillis caught an instance of something wrong with the squirrel's teeth before the cat was bodily lifted off her feet and out of sight. A thin cry came from impenetrable darkness a moment later.

Lillis's heart nearly stopped as the scream came a second time, far higher in the shadows above them. She shut her eyes and felt herself shoved, stumbling but not falling.

She opened them as the cat's body bounced on the cobbles before her, limbs ragged, the throat spread and scarlet.

The husky brandished a pistol.

The curly-furred dog with the knife studied the dead cat for a moment. His tail coiled behind him and then between his legs as he dropped the weapon and ran with a keening cry.

"Clyde, you coward!" the husky called back and tracked the gun over the darkness.

"What happened?" Lillis called out and met the husky's gaze, who tightened her muzzle and turned the gun's cold eye on the bear.

"Won't matter to you," she growled and cocked the weapon.

The gun disappeared. An empty hand dangled limp, fingers bent at angles nature didn't favor.

The husky gasped, trying to draw breath, eyes wide. The arms that embraced her from behind were slower, more insistent. They were tawny-furred, fingers slender but nails thicker, those of a cervine. Lillis's eyes widened as the outline of a doe's head rose behind the husky, ears eagerly forward, features hard to discern but the black orbs in place of mammalian eyes were pitiless, just like the squirrel's. The husky was dragged back into the dark with the broken hand clutching feebly against the deer's grip. Shadows swallowed them both.

Lillis took wracking breaths, heart thudding as silence fell around her, the cat's body still, the dog fled, the husky stolen away. Of the squirrel and doe, assuming they had been real, there was no sign.

Scuffs on the pavement sounded as two figures turned the corner of Water and Devonshire. Lillis crouched, her large frame impossible to conceal and yet desperate to be unseen.

Those that approached were preternaturally calm, their shapes lupine and lutrine. The female wolf and otter wore haphazardly layered garments, garish and bohemian. They smelled of sweetness and corruption and smiled oily smiles.

"You outta der woods, honey bear?" the otter asked. Lillis broke down and started to sob.

***

Sandy was on the rooftop, watching the moon's silvery filaments peer under the glide of clouds. Everything was so beautiful with life singing inside her. A light touch of hooves next to her, as though delivered by a breeze, brought company.

Celeste had a drink of her own. "Fancy meeting you here," the doe said warmly through a bloody smile. She held a squat canine's limp shape, eyes empty and aimless. "This one was going to shoot that bear. Share a drink with me?"

Sandy was already tipsy but recognized the husky who'd brandished the gun. "Enchanted."

"*Enchanté*," Celeste corrected amiably and they imbibed together, letting the husky settle to the rooftop once full. Down below a bear would have questions that they regrettably couldn't return to answer. Alive and frightened was a far better state of being than her attackers had intended.

"So, we were to prevent a murder…" Sandy mused. "Is that what this was?"

Heady with blood, Celeste cocked an ear. "By my arithmetic we didn't quite do that."

"Well…" Sandy shrugged. "You have to admit that a would-be murderer tastes better than rat."

Celeste rolled her eyes. "Anything tastes better than rat. Sorry that only the big cities have enough on hand to compensate."

"Feral rats or murderers?"

"Second one."

"You've been reading the wrong newspapers, dear. Cities just cram the worst closer together."

Celeste shrugged. "I'm certain those carnies targeted that bear, followed her down that alley."

Sandy licked her teeth, sharp and buck. "Want to ask why?"

"I'd like to. But I don't want that bear getting another look at me." Celeste licked her lips clean. "On another matter, did you have anybody looking for me recently? The sisters, specifically?"

"No, why?"

Celeste sighed. "It doesn't matter now. Sorry that this reunion has to be so fleeting. I've got to get after Crawford. His son is in some dire business and might wind up in jail tonight or worse."

Sandy gazed into Celeste's eyes, seeing the soul within black pools that mortals presumed impenetrable and alien. Her ears were forward and the slenderness of her frame, the smooth lay of her fur… "Do you have to go right away?"

Celeste frowned and even her disappointment was beautiful. "Had we more time…"

"Soon enough," whispered Sandy, close enough to smell the scent of life on her. In a hundred years or so, enough life would pass Celeste's lips to make the last white spots of her youth fade from her delicate flanks. So many moments and yet each would need to be cherished all the same. "We'll have all the time we could ever want." They kissed, lips warm and hands entwined. They could settle on this roof right here with only the moon as witness.

But, responsibilities. "Go help your were sort his problems out," Sandy whispered as they parted. "I'll get a room somewhere with thick drapes and just maybe a strapping bellhop who could be coaxed to lose a memory or two…"

"Sandy."

"Okay, then. Another pet rat. After."

The doe smiled and kissed her quick once again before slipping back into the nearest shadow. Sandy felt her slip to the next and then the next till she was gone from sense and sight.

She sat with the dead mugger, wondering a moment if there was anything left. The husky was gone. Sandy knew that she'd been granted more mercy than bullets and blades would have provided the ursine below.

"Alisandre."

The call that caught her ear was distant, from a rooftop at least two buildings away. She'd not gone by Alisandre in over fifty years.

Her tail twitched as she picked apart the shadows with eyes and the flood of the wind. The scent was all too faint, but unmistakably lapine.

A distant shadow in a chimney's lee bled a form and the white rabbit in a creased, worn suit met her gaze implacably, ears back and nose quivering nervously. Donovan managed a weak smile. His Oxford accent measured out his words like a Savile Row tailor seeking a best fit. "I've had time to reflect on recent events, and well…it's quite possible that I may owe you an apology."

Sandy was still as the moment settled in like a cold weather front. Her fangs were already out, smile thin on her lips. Squirrel legs were strong and could propel her in a leap several times her own length. An immortal Nosfur had far more on tap.

Her body met his in an instant and chimney brick fractured behind the concussive delivery of the rabbit's body.

He didn't cry out. They grappled, clawed hands and feet seeking purchase as they rolled across the roof. Sandy snarled as she scrabbled and the rabbit was almost soundless in return. All too quickly they broke apart, regained footing and stood erect on loosened tar shingles.

"You killed Bruno! He was finally free of you and innocent!"

"Not innocent. He made mistakes and so did I. I'm sorry, Sandy." Donovan's nose twitched again and Sandy wanted to bite it off. "I was too hasty."

"I won't be! I'll take a week to kill you if I can, you peg-eared bastard!"

"I've come to say I'm sorry."

"Not goddamn yet, you aren't!"

She crouched to leap. If she could hurl him to the pavement below—

"I loved you."

She froze, blinking. The words he spoke made no sense.

"When you were under my sway, back in Chicago, I did love you."

"*Mallacht Dé ort!*"

"It's true!" Donovan swallowed, stepping back, keeping distance. "As a Martyre of the Black Well I was forbidden from taking anything further."

"I was a toy to show off to that lion you fecked!"

"Never! I didn't confess my heart during our time together because, Sandy, I...I was a coward."

"In all this, just one whiff of honesty. The devil can cut off your head and make work of your neck."

His hand spread on his chest. "I'd deserve it. For all I've done, I can't fault your hate."

She crouched for the next charge. "In some luck then, aren't ye?"

"If you knew I loved you then you wouldn't have sworn off the vein for its own sake. And if you'd loved me in return..."

Sandy wanted him dead. But she wanted a hell for him to go to even more. The long black of oblivion just might have to do. "You knew I did.

You knew all along! And you took advantage of it. Every day you strung my heart along as my limbs and tail shriveled and all the pain mounted like piling rocks. Made it easy, didn't it, seeing starvation shrink me to a wee hag?"

Donovan swallowed, a mortal mammalian gesture that he didn't resist as he closed his eyes and opened them again. "Yes. As much as it pained me, seeing you age did just that. I owe you so much. Honesty is the first step."

"First step to what? Do you actually think you're going to steal forgiveness from me after all you've done?"

"After all we've done, Alisandre."

"Don't you call me that!"

Donovan shook his head. "You helped me make others become like you out of guilt." His eyes trailed over to the now-distant husky's corpse, two rooftops distant. "I didn't appreciate how potent that could be even as I used it to thwart the others in my order. But I understand now. I understand how relentless that thirst is. And I understand how much stronger you were than I ever was."

"You mean how easily I played into your folly," Sandy rumbled. She wanted to kill him. But to drag this much honesty out of him, while she had the chance…

"Perhaps. But I've come to implore you, even after the revenge you spent a year taking back in that mansion on the Gold Coast, I beg you. Even if you can't forgive me yet, allow me to prove myself to you. I'm alone, Sandy. It's been so long. And we can still benefit each other. We can rekindle what I was too afraid for us to have when my heart still beat and my ambition owned me."

Rekindle, what? Love? She could spit in his eye if she had the saliva. A doe whose heart she'd torn in two for this greedy charlatan was now heading into uncertain danger. Better Donovan be put out of her life tonight and forever than strung along as he deserved.

"No. You can feck right off and kiss the devil's—"

A steely grip wrapped round her and bodily lifted her from the rooftop, her feet kicking for purchase.

"This *salope* is wasting our time! You know what to do!" The snapping voice was nasal, infuriated. Sandy thrashed in the embrace.

Donovan's ears drooped past his shoulders. "We were—"

"You're worse at finding sympathy for your affections than even I was and that's truly saying something. Stop fucking around and do it! You can find comfort up this tree rat's skirt later for all I care!"

Sandy bucked and squirmed but was held fast as Donovan reluctantly hopped over to another shadow and withdrew something in a deep burlap bag that made him hiss with its sting. He leapt to where she bucked and opened the drawstring as his other hand dipped within. Sandy felt immediate discomfort that increased to pain as tongs within the burlap were withdrawn and the container was allowed to slip to the roof, revealing a ring of steel bearing a smaller inner ring of more polished metal that glinted in a sickly way. The ring was hinged, opened like a claw.

The Nosfur holding Sandy—for what else could he be?—hissed through unseen fangs as Donovan's grip on the tongs wavered. Then he thrust the burning object with its inner sliver of reliquary steel forward, slipping it round her neck and causing her blinding agony as the Nosfur holding her released her. Donovan closed the ring with a snap.

He dropped her to the slanted rooftop and she nearly tumbled to the edge. Only a merciless grab of her ankle prevented her from a tumble to the street.

"I have her," the nasal voice said. "It's done. You know where to take her and get reacquainted as you'd like. Now it's my turn to settle my affairs."

Through the crippling agony wracking Sandy's throat, jaw, and shoulders, she could hear her captor's malicious glee.

***

Samson could have bound shadows up high but decided against it. As diminutive as he appeared, he wasn't the least bit interested in concealing himself as he wound through alleys and side streets, coming gradually closer to the corner of Devonshire and Water.

He obtained directions from some passing gophers, skittish, packed together and quaintly worried at such a young ungulate out alone. Samson thanked them indifferently for their concerns and kept on. He was about two blocks distant from the all-important place and with his senses as open as he could keep them. Then he heard a scream in the distance. It was female, feline sounding.

He tested the air, deciding which fork in the road to take ahead, when a shadow just on the periphery of his vision was disturbed.

Deep black rippled with the sense of transition, then another shadow played with the light it drank and was gone.

Would Celeste's friend Sandy play games with him? He didn't think that likely.

He waited, tempted to bind a shadow of his own, but decided otherwise.

Another trick of light, flitting at a corner beyond a streetlamp's glow. He approached, then hesitated. The way to Water Street was left. A door opened to the street just down at the right, and some mustelid was leaning past it, gaze meeting Samson's with intense curiosity as a shadow beyond the door was disturbed and then seemingly abandoned.

"Samson," the mustelid said to him, drawing his attention from whatever had fled further on. The mustelid raised one hand, showing the underside of the wrist, index finger beckoning. Within the abode the mustelid stood before in a liminal fashion, the breathy current of many conversations bled out.

Samson pondered his next move. Someone had to be at Water and Devonshire for, well, something.

But Celeste and Crawford were likely there already. More than likely the unfamiliar scream, definitely not one of theirs, had resulted from their own handiwork.

Much as he was loath to admit it, he was certain they didn't need him.

Samson approached, checking other shadows for movement, detecting none. The dark-furred mustelid had stepped within, leaving the door open. The rumble of noise was further refined by the clinking of glass and metal, the shifting of furniture. Indistinct boasts met indistinct peals of laughter. The tingling scents of food and beer flowed out. With them came the dander and musk of dozens of species, vegetarian and carnivorous both.

This place was public, full of witnesses. Whoever knew his identity wouldn't be able to make any drastic moves. Not here.

He tentatively stepped inside.

Ales, lagers, mammal sweat, and a patina of grime layered the clearly working-class social space. Tables around which mammals gathered were dimly lit by mixed electric wall lamps and sparse candles. Tails switched back and forth behind scattered chairs and stools where veggies and carnies cavorted, mutteringly sober or blitzed-drunk. It was the perfect microcosm of the city Samson imagined beyond its walls.

Samson spotted the mink again, standing amongst the bustle and staring straight at the young goat. The mink propped up a chauffer cap and muttered into the ear of a white-furred mink in scanty dress who nodded smilingly. They tittered something too low to hear and parted. The dark mink melted into the crowd.

The white mink walked slowly, eyes on the goat kid, and Samson followed her into a part of the establishment that opened up with a high-raised ceiling and a surrounding mezzanine balcony on three sides. Brickwork climbing a wall had a darkened fireplace at its base, and before it one table with two chairs held a single waiting patron to whom the white mink leaned over to whisper a word before stepping away. A lynx lounged there, ornate dinner jacket over bare-furred vest and a red thin-petaled flower at one breast, a freesia. Samson remembered helping plant several ahead of winter at their prior home, now ashes back in Scranton.

Pale grey eyes held Samson's own, expectant, patient, and implacable.

The seat at the table's opposite side from the lynx was the only empty one in the establishment. Samson dragged it back and sat.

The lynx flicked his tufted ears back. Then forward. "Samson. I'm so pleased to meet you."

Samson met his even gaze and kept his senses to his surroundings. "You know me?"

"I know all of you," the lynx said, his accent slight and unplaceable. "For as long as you have been alive and more than alive. Tell me, how did you come to keep your Scottish affect? Do you recall the people you were of before you went to that school in Chicago? Noah's Ark I think it was called? No, plank. Noah's Plank. Dull name."

Samson blinked. "It was. How do you know about me?"

"I've learned much, but as you can guess, not all."

Samson listened to the tingle of conversation around them for a moment before answering. "One parent died, the other was broke. I was left with an uncle who didn't take to me. I learned English until I was eight and enough Gaelic to know when I was in trouble. By the time I was sent to the orphanage in Chicago, I knew lots of Gaelic."

The lynx listened intently and sallow sadness set into his eyes and ears. "And so that which should have tied you to a place and a people was instead used to instill you with fear. Is this uncle still alive?"

Samson found the question odd. "I don't know." He noticed then that the lynx's chest didn't rise and fall. At that moment he knew.

"So many cruelties…I'm pleased to see you endured, Samson."

"Why does any of this interest you?"

He smiled then. And Samson saw the carnivore's fangs grow percep-tibly longer. The dark flitted within the whites of the lynx's eyes like the shadow of a passing car and was gone.

"I seek others most like myself, torn from a world having designs for me that I've rejected, social shackles, decreed intolerance, and interspecies cultural enmity. You know intimately what I'm talking about."

Samson didn't like that topic. "What do you know about my life after Noah's Plank? If, as you're telling me, you've been watching?"

The lynx smiled again and despite himself Samson felt its warmth. "I know of your found family, truly a fascinating thing. I stayed away because I'm ever so proud of all of you, including Celeste."

Celeste had spoken of her past back when Samson had been newly turned and terrified by his circumstances. Some of it, anyway. "You know her."

"I made her. She is of me as so many are." The lynx sighed, a theatrical effect with no breath to draw. "And it hurt when she left me. I had grand designs for her, to free her of all the world's pains, as they now fall on you."

"What falls on me, or her, or anyone for that matter?"

"Besides relegation to your status and place, as"—he started counting claws—"a vegetarian, a kid, a monster out of God's sight? A tool others wanted to dispose of?"

Samson froze.

The lynx slid a hand across the table, his claws not touching the goat but open to accept his in return. "I know what was intended for you, and by extension for us all by the Martyres of the Black Well, those carnie-club, bloated, pseudo-aristocrats, grasping at their inbred pedigrees and nepotisms. The one who saw to your turning was upset that war burnt her pointless lineage to the ground. Most of the rest in the mix are a greedy, worthless orgy of old and new money falling to common malaise and looking for a jolly-good time killing freaks of nature like you or me. Samson, I know why you're angry and I cherish the purity of it as the essential struggle of us all. You didn't ask to be what you are any more than I did, but you have a right to live and see your potential fulfilled."

The smattering of conversation carried over them both and Samson weighed the words carefully. "Just what potential is supposed to be found in a four-foot runt whom everybody wants seen and not heard?"

The lynx's expression transitioned in that moment. The last traces of sympathy slipped away and what replaced it was potent with pride. "Oh, Samson, you think yourself a cast-off mistake, but you are in simple fact the most graciously blessed of us all. You know that life is not eternal for us. We who follow the vein's tributaries through other's brief lives take single steps of our own forward with each nourishing kiss. And yet our passage is spread upon breadths of time that the follies of mammals, their empires, and their philosophies will never endure to see.

"We can live thousands of years if careful enough, watch nations rise and fall. But you, Samson, turned so very young…you have the potential to surpass all current understandings of life and culture within worlds we can't yet dream of. This Depression. This New Deal. This angry, squabbling thirst for vengeance. It will all pass and you will forget it all. Doors will open to you that none living now can comprehend. And I want to help you, Samson. You can't be relegated to case-filing spouse-beaters and tax cheats. I've not seen into your whole life, but what I've seen has to disappoint us both. Much raced through that mind of yours while you painted the upper floor of that house in the dark last May. No surprise that you should seek better lives through illusions of light cast upon silk."

Samson realized what he meant. "It wasn't the motion pictures that meant most to me."

"I know. Yet you returned again and again to peer over the shoulders of all those other voyeurs, seeking validation in real people seeking validation in fakeries."

Samson sighed, studying eyes before him that had been on him for a very long time. "They imagine a better version of themselves. Don't you? It's the most natural want to have…" He trailed off, memories flooded with failed battles for self-discipline and Celeste's resulting chastisements. His very self-worth, his need to surpass his arrested, childish state, was a problem Celeste and Crawford had to consistently navigate while struggling to pay bills and maintain their anonymity.

So, he'd learned to restrain himself and his strength, appear harmless and ineffectual, invisible. How incredibly, furiously sick of it he'd become over just a dozen short years with who knew how many centuries to go.

The lynx read his mind. "You have been fortunate, Samson. But that won't see you through the rest of existence. I want to help you as I've helped so many, to seize your full potential and free yourself of the last of your dependencies and restraints. Celeste has been good to you, as has the were. But this is only a liminal stage. I know that house you painted burned down. You were found—"

"And it was my fault."

"Celeste may let you think that, Crawford too. But what they fail to understand is that you three weren't made to persist as ghosts of a family with a mortgage. You're a pioneer in a new world to come, forced into violence in Scranton...and I've learned why. I not only forgive you, I applaud you."

The lynx dropped his voice low to a whisper and Samson heard him clearly. "Let me show you powers we can harness that you've not dreamed of. You have come far with your friends but they can only hold you back now despite themselves. And the tighter they cling to you, Samson, the more urgent your desire to escape. You know this."

It occurred to Samson at that moment that as the lynx's voice dropped lower he could hear him more and more clearly because the surrounding chatter and merriment of the nameless tavern had lulled, quieted, and now gone silent. Not a chair or utensil scraped. He felt countless pairs of eyes, around and above, settle expectantly upon him. For each and every one here had all been waiting.

"Love is letting the chained go free. So, I implore you, Samson, free them and be free of them." The lynx took his hand and it was cool as autumn. "I am Ferrault. I am not the first of us, nor the last. But I have seen the fall of empires, heard the final rattles of despots, and I can save the least of our disinherited from the very worst of our many enemies. All I ask is that you join me. See what we truly are and what we can truly be. Let me help you see."

Silence held court, countless unseen gazes patient. Samson felt the moment pass like the changing of a season. He loved Celeste and Crawford both. But he had to explore the possibility that he needed more than they could give him. He had to understand what was being offered at the very least. "Okay. Show me."

The chatter rose again in the nameless tavern, cheer enlivening every voice as Ferrault rose and took Samson's hand, turning him to look back into the hopeful smiles of fawning, excited mammals around and above. Ferrault guided him through. The mink pair had returned, tails moving together as metronomes. A squirrel dressed as a train porter scampered up a wooden rafter and clinked a beer stein with a cat at the balcony, sharing a laugh. Another lynx, mortal and tawnier in color, gave Samson a cloudy grin from a table bearing many empty whiskey glasses and gazed lovingly up at Ferrault with grateful tears in his eyes. The lynx's good left hand proudly massaged the bandaged stump of a right arm amputated near the wrist.

Cheer followed Ferrault and his new friend out into the cool dark of the Boston night. Samson was uncertain, but giddy with excitement.

***

"Who are you?" Lillis asked in the shadow of Water and Devonshire, heart pounding as the wolf and otter traded looks.

"Take a minute to get your bearings. Still got yer wallet?"

The wolf gave the otter a look. "We've come a long way. So have you," said the wolf, only a little older than Lillis was, but carrying herself as older still.

The otter sighed, testing the air with her nose, gaze drawn inward. "Well, bear-friend, long stories bore so we worked out a short one."

Lillis looked to the cat's dropped and bleeding corpse that the pair who had approached were studiously avoiding. "A short what? Why do I remember what's happening now? I've never seen any of you before and yet this is happening...again? What was the squirrel—"

"Somebody we don't owe any money to if they ask," the otter cut in. "That's not important. What's important is what you already do know, what you need to be reminded..." The otter spat on the pavement. "Our circle, Baliosi's and mine and…well, ours have travelled the world for as long as there's been one. We've crossed deserts on sedan chairs, been dragged through swamps in chains, been confidants, confessors, our favors begged by the powerful, heads spat on by the pious. Our lives have come and gone in gilded palaces of the ruthless and tied to smoking stakes in crumbling villages of the mad. Our whisperings turn the ears of kings from Denmark to Memphis."

Lillis squinted. "There's a king in Memphis? I don't understand."

Baliosi shrugged. "That's down the road a piece, don't know what it means yet. You're holding on to more than a few morsels yourself, sister."

"Sis…" The word was a strange taste on her tongue. "I have…my name…"

"Was a breath in an empty room," the otter said. "All your life. You were never an orphan but felt like one because you've never found yourself. A father walked out. A mother walked inward as the dust came and kept her pain from you at loneliness's cost. We know your name. I'm Grisand."

"It's Lillis…"

"Belle." The otter put one hand on her shoulder and the wolf touched her elbow and an invisible bolt of electricity found Lillis through both the grinding earth under her feet and the dark sky hissing the stars' silent chorus above. The smell of growing and dying things emitted from every follicle in their pelts and the clothes they wore. Their fur was singed with time's ashes. She'd known them all her life and had by bad fortune been kept a stranger. Till now.

"You're Lillis Belle."

Lillis was terrified as confounding sensations knitted into glimpses that she'd long spotted in a million bubbling coffee pots and rippling rain puddles, whispering tree boughs and angry train whistles. "I'm scared! What is this? What does it mean?"

Baliosi smiled. "Let it tell you as it tells us. It's ever present and looking for criers. Just open up! It's an endless verse and you know it." She closed her eyes, released the bear's elbow, and took her meaty hand. "A father seeks, a son conceals,"

Grisand took Lillis's other hand. "The lost doe fears what heart reveals,"

Lillis spoke without thought, unable to contain it. "And timeless hands hook souls in tow,"

Baliosi nodded. "To bring old orders ruined and low,"

Grisand looked to the sky, "And anger and rage exact high cost,"

Lillis shivered. "Can't bottle up when cork's been lost." The release was a heavy millstone finally dropped into endless dark. She gasped, a drowner learning the first strokes of a swim. "It can't mean what I think it does."

Baliosi's eyes were bright. "You'll find that it means much until it's happened and can mean nothing else."

Lillis looked down at the dead cat again. "Am I in more danger?"

Grisand sighed. "You've got your toe dipped in all of it as we do, catching it coming and going by. But you can't control it. Accepting that is the hardest part."

Baliosi put an arm around the bear and drew herself into an embrace with the larger mammal. "We have the secrets south of here, a font of experience and wisdom long gathered that we need to show you. But it's dangerous to go out tonight. We'll need to steer clear till the morning. Bit of a mess brewing right now. We can only stand back."

Grisand nodded sagely. "You can take us both for a drink before you quit, after the dust settles. We've got a ride waiting to get us to Kansas though it might need a kick or two to get going."

Lillis took a centering breath. "Um, yes. It's certainly worth a visit. Bell has the best ale in town. I think."

The joy Lillis took from their paired smiles was equally comforting and maddening. She'd known those very smiles long before she'd known her own and there was serenity in remembering what always was.

"Lead on, sister," Baliosi said, and Lillis did.

CHAPTER 21

THE IRON ARK

Crawford second-guessed himself and second-guessed himself again as night ticked by and the North End of Boston came to life. If Charlie knew that his son was in danger then Crawford needed to get to the hotel and find him. But with himself on who knew how many state or federal wanted lists, Crawford would need his head examined if he showed up where any number of federal agents would be happy to arrest him. His likeness was circulated, scent rubbing from the Scranton Police Station might have even made it to Washington for the best noses to draw into memory before it faded. If they ever made a camera for mammal scents...

The question of the missing agent who'd come to kill Celeste and Samson was a whole other matter entirely that he couldn't help Charlie solve, not now anyway.

So, Crawford was, in essence, stuck. The Omni Parker House hotel was close, but so was the Emerson Theatre Hall, where the last of the carnivore-first bunk on the Colonel's pamphlets had been set. Crawford could go find the Colonel's friends and get his ass kicked there too.

With the hot edge of the curse flowing through him he'd need to make a decision before anxiety made deliberation moot. Charlie had asked for forgiveness in the letter he'd left and the implication that Lucas might be in the firing line for real was far too chilling to wait on. So, Crawford took the Chevy over by the Omni Parker hotel and caught a flurry of activity out front as he carefully drove past.

Back in their Prohibition days, speakeasy and warehouse raids were messily staged affairs that risked encounters with ignorant public or mobsters out taking night air. Speed was the only leg up those outfits ever had.

Wherever the Colonel was hanging out and whatever plans Charlie's outfit sought to interrupt, Crawford realized when he saw the two black trucks chugging in wait that it was close and soon. The suits on the milling mammals were dark, the hustle into the cars quick enough to rock them on their springs, and then Charlie himself appeared, finishing a cigarette, and stubbing it out hurriedly under his foot pad. To anyone not in the know, they looked like a wedding party running disastrously late. Crawford's preternatural nose caught the scent of gun oil.

"Damn it, Charlie. You're going to take in the whole damn group on smuggling charges, aren't you?"

They could only be converging at one place, a place near where he'd already been and made messes. The desire to change burgeoned, greedy and anxious, but after two changes in the last evening, he was able to tamp it down more easily.

He ditched the car two blocks from the dock and used a fire ladder to get to a roof vantage. As he felt the change line up to take him, worry bit relentlessly. If it came down to seeing his son hurt or seeing Charlie thwarted, he'd have no choice at all.

***

Lucas fought the verge of panic as he bounced in the car's back seat. He'd heard what the Colonel intended for the waitress but it hadn't really settled in until after the crew left that the Colonel was literally going to have a murder committed for his cause. The final line had been crossed.

"I need to get out for a minute and—"

"We're on a schedule," the Colonel said, tugging the white sleeves of his suit over his dark wrists. Lucas began counting the seconds. He could demand to be let out. But would he be?

"There are things beyond your control to prevent..." He remembered those words, seemingly a million years ago. "Sometimes you can't intervene, you can only contend."

Recrimination stabbed him in the gut. Why, why hadn't he said something back at the Bell in Hand?

Because he'd come too far and committed himself to seeing this through. Lucas settled into the seat feeling heavier than the world.

There was a glimpse of pale fire from the car's left side as a Hooverville drifted past, the destitute keeping heads down and shoulders hunched, the main gates to the docks avoided entirely. The Colonel spared a brief glance, unfolding his leg and accidentally kicking the black bag at his feet. It rang with the disturbance of hundreds of donated nickels, dimes, and quarters among too few dollar bills to matter. The real money was in the trunk, Lucas knew.

The Colonel's car turned the next corner down a narrow alley, through a smaller gate manned by high-collared toughs and the worn planks of the Boston Harbor docks shuddered under them. Rumbling slowed as the car cut speed. It came into the shadow of a large warehouse, massive dock-side doors yawning on a long track facing the open waters not twenty feet further.

An immense silent shape was sliding forth, steel prow coldly wet. Figures milled on its deck, throwing lines to the waiting hands of carnivores who scurried from the dark of the warehouse.

Lucas turned his head, saw cigarette embers drop to bounce on concrete off in the dark. The familiar shapes of the Colonel's inner circle, and a few more hangers-on he'd picked up, got to work. A truck's rear bed backed out from the dark, climbed over by carnivores with high excited tails. They threw back the flatbed's tarp to expose stacked rows of steel building-frame girders, some old and flecked with rust, but all bound in multiples on pallets.

The Colonel got out and Lucas followed along with two others. Taking it all in, Lucas traced the German shepherd's upward gaze to the bow of the boat where a silver-furred fox in a dark suit as finely tailored as the Colonel's own and a mariner's hat glanced downward, hands in deep pockets.

A gangplank was dropped with speed and a dockside suspension crane on rails chugged to oily life. The fox was as slow and casual in his movements as the Colonel was. Lucas looked back and forth along the dock but could find nothing looking like an office or anything that might conceal a telephone. He forced guilt deep down and followed Colonel Blake over to the gangplank's base as a winch lowered a hook behind him and the first stacked pallet of girders was wound with ropes.

"Lucy," the German shepherd showed all his teeth.

"That would be Lucien," said the fox. His accent was an upper-class British that Lucas couldn't pin down.

"Your people need to empty their hold before we can fill it, correct?"

The grey fox didn't answer, pulled a long brown-stemmed smoke pipe from his pocket that he put in his mouth, then drew a small envelope from which he pinched a tincture of tobacco into the pipe in his dark lips, then a bit more. He carefully put the envelope back, then brought out a small wood-handled tamper that he used to press the tobacco down. Putting this away, he drew in some air, let his ears rise with satisfaction, withdrew a box of matches, lit one, applied it to the pipe, and drew in. He took two or three puffs, then let the smoke roll out through his thin nose. A full minute passed during the ritual. "There are a few useless odds and ends that we need to have as decoys just in case we were boarded."

The fox waved an indifferent hand high in the air, and at the top of the plank four impatient-looking dogs looked at the Colonel, then the fox's back, then disappeared for a moment. The fox wandered over to the truck's bed. Behind him the gangplank bowed as a long-crated box was carried down by dogs muttering in German to one another.

The Colonel watched the box coming down with interest, then noticed Lucas at his shoulder. "What, you think you were brought here to spectate? Go help with the girders!"

Lucas nearly bolted at the command, hurrying over to the truck where a stack was already aloft, lifted by crane to the boat where guide ropes kept it from spinning. He climbed up, took a fruitless look around from the higher vantage for an office that may have a telephone, and then began pulling the rest of the tarp off. The pipe-smoking fox approached the steel, studying it intently before placing a hand on one girder and drawing a deep breath. Lucas studied him as the fox's shoulders settled back, expression taking on a distant, meditative expression. His ears went back as the transcendence became disgust. "My God, some are right here, in this very corner of the bloody city." A hand went into the suit lapel and fingered something within. The fox's wrinkling muzzle rose then and met the young wolf's confused stare. "What the hell are you looking at? Get to your bloody work!"

The chugging crane's line slackened within the boat, then the hook rose from its hold again to swing back to the flatbed. At the base of the boat's gangplank four long crates were deposited on the dock with two more descending. Fascinated, Lucas watched the fox return to where the

Colonel waited. The vulpine dug something out of his other lapel, a folded envelope that he passed to the Colonel who opened it and leafed through a fat stack of bills.

"Pleasure doing business," the Colonel said and then sighed. "Lucas! You're a steering wheel on a steer up there. C'mere! Open one of these crates."

The fox, hackles up with agitation since touching the girder, took a glance at the offloaded crates. "I was told there's nothing of any use in these. They're old cookware, bait for coast guard inspections. Nothing more."

The German shiphands standing by traded flat, muzzle-down looks as Lucas went over and took a crowbar sitting by a tool-stack pulled from the Colonel's car. His heart raced as he sensed something in the air that was quickening everyone else's pulse. The Colonel laughed. "Actually, Lucy, your shipment coming in had more to worry 'bout from the coasties than what's going out."

Lucas worked the bar under a lid as the Colonel returned the fox's prior favor and made him wait while Lucas worked. Inside the crate, on a bed of straw, lengths of dark steel and walnut-stocked machinery glinted in the uneven sodium dock lights. The Colonel stepped forward and hefted one for inspection. "Emm Gee Thirty, Swiss-made for Germany to get round the injustice of Versailles. Eight hundred rounds per minute, thirty per magazine. Ninety of these and a few dozen Model Twenty-four potato mashers makes for a good start. Lucas, Verity, and Freddy, get a count."

Lucas was frozen to the spot for a moment as implications hit. Guns. Grenades. A good start.

He kept calm and began opening the next crate as others took crowbars and got to work. How many in the Colonel's inner circle had known about this? Were his backers at the final rally involved? Possibilities reeled with the need to break away. He knew Charlie's outfit was watching, assembling to intercept and break up some money-laundering hoopla.

They had no idea what was waiting for them.

The fox's ears were so low they seemed to be trying to touch his toes. "What the bloody hell are munitions doing here?" the fox shouted, then forced himself down to a growl, eyes checking the shadows. "Our arrangement was for the steel. I don't want any part of what you do with your recompense."

The Colonel's gaze narrowed. "I need what I need and you were already bringing a boat. Our German friends like good business and so do we. Wouldn't your old dog Oswald Mosely approve?"

The fox's nose had gone white. "You mistake me for someone politically motivated, Mister Blake. Mosely isn't my dog, and I've no affiliations with this business. Our arrangement was a temporary convenience to facilitate movement of my steel. I'm not here to facilitate you getting killed agitating against your damned government."

The Colonel stared at the fox and blinked implacably as another crate was brought to the gangplank and another steel pallet was hoisted. "Well, that's too bad. A mammal without a cause is no mammal at all." He peeled off bills and counted before passing the dividend to a waiting German terrier. "I can count on you to keep your limey mouth shut, of course. You float your iron back quietly and we'll do the same with ours. Everybody makes out okay."

The terrier took his pay and jerked his muzzle up and back. "*Es gibt noch sechs weitere Kristen.*"

Another concentrated before speaking in broken English. "Six more boxes, good stuff."

Lucien bitterly muttered something best unheard before turning to the terrier. "When those beams are loaded, we're leaving immediately, Captain." The fox's glare promised a further word upon heaving to. The returned expression suggested his ire didn't mean a damn thing.

"My boys and girls can hurry that along," the Colonel chuckled with naked amusement. He waved his arm in a gesture that included Lucas and two others. "Get on the boat, help 'em get the goods off."

Lucas hopped to it. The British fox was clearly a means to an end who'd considered the Colonel the same and yet there could be other conspirators aboard. More importantly, there might be a radio aboard that he could slip away to use.

He dutifully went up the narrow gangplank, teetering above the drink, and a German dog that followed laughed at him.

On the deck another bundle of girders lowered shakily into the hold. Lucas was ushered down a narrow stair by another of the German shiphands who pointed at a stack of boxes in the back half of a hold being quickly filled by girder stacks. By the time he and the deckhand had dragged a long crate up the narrow stairs to the top deck, another pallet of girders had been moved. He nearly slipped on the gangplank carrying the front end down and the curse in German behind him was pitying. He had to get away.

But the crew dogged him as he felt time tick down. Four crates later, the flatbed was all but empty, just one pallet left on the truck. Why this steel was even being loaded, Lucas had no idea. Mills in America had all but closed from disuse. What the hell was happening in Germany?

They were on the fourth of six boxes without any chance for Lucas to get away when it all went to hell.

"Boss!" a cat keeping watch back by the Colonel's car yowled.

All eyes on the high and low went to a figure racing down the dock towards them all, stumbling and gibbering with naked fear. Lucas recognized Clyde, the dog sent to kill the bear waitress. The curly-furred dog looked as though he'd pissed himself.

"Monsters! They were waiting for us! Oh gawwd, Colonel, veggies sent by the devil!"

The Colonel's retort was something that Lucas didn't catch. Light suddenly flooded the dock from two separate sources and a voice echoed with force close by. "This is the Bureau of Investigation! The Federal Bureau of...Put your hands up! You're all under arrest!"

Down below, the silver Brit fox drew a long silvery blade from his jacket, racing up the boat plank in six light bounds. The crew handling both crates and steel beams dropped their tools and scattered. The Colonel was still holding on to one of the contraband machine guns. He dived for one of the crates, drew a curved ammo magazine, and hurried for the boat's gangplank.

***

Word came back from one of the four pairs of eyes watching Boston's battery of docks, a gamble Charlie was relieved to see come to fruition. "We're on the move," he growled, heart racing all the way down to the hotel's lobby.

He'd done all this before, in Chicago. "Good hunting," somebody said in the dank of memory as he nestled into the back of the rolling truck and accepted a Thompson and straight magazine.

Only Charlie truly knew why the steel was important to the people smuggling it, a secret he had to keep from the whole crew bouncing with him. They'd think him insane if he fessed up. He had to remember that.

Halfway to the muster point, Charlie caught sight over the back gate that they were being followed. The rickety Chevrolet was familiar, as was the shape of the grey-furred driver.

"You handsome moron," he muttered, and wanted that wolf in his arms just then. There would be a reckoning for what was all too likely to pass despite his best efforts, even if Crawford's kid got clear when things went down.

The staging area was two docks further south where the night wind wouldn't blow their scents over and Charlie's unit kept their voices low. The last two members—it was actually eight including Michael and himself—came together. "We observe only as long as necessary to get everybody in one place, then we move in and arrest. The Colonel is the primary muzzle we need to fix. That and his contact making the drop. We have two minutes to get into place, you six from the north, two south keeping out of the line of fire and picking off those who try to flee. Michael, you and Atburn will really have to huff it."

Atburn was a cheetah who gave the lemur to his right a once-over and rolled his eyes.

"We'll make it." Michael ignored the glance with a sigh.

"Get the Colonel and whoever's captaining that boat." Charlie counted six Thompsons, common Bureau issue since the Pretty Kitty Floyd affair in Kansas City, and two Winchester .351 self-loaders for the sharpshooters who'd hang back to pick off resistance. "Whoever refuses your order to stand down is fair game. You go home tonight if it's you or them. You clear?"

Every muzzle nodded. Nostrils flared. "All enemies foreign and domestic. You know the before and after. Get moving."

Charlie counted every heartbeat on the hustle round the warehouse, his blood chilling every time he moved through shadow. The steel hurts them all. They'd be anywhere but here, he rationalized. Knowing Celeste would help Crawford and he her in return wasn't necessarily a comfort.

A minute later they caught the grinding chug of a dock crane. Charlie slowed their progress with a gesture and tested a door to the warehouse carefully, covered by one of the others. An agent slipped inside, then reached back out with a beckoning claw. They filed in fast and spread out, the agents with the Springfields creeping upstairs to second-story gangplanks. Charlie dimly recognized a couple of whiskey barrels among the waiting manifest. Federal prohibition had ended in thirty-three but the past poked a claw back at him anyway. He'd want a drink after all this.

Creeping forward, the team spread, Thompsons low and night vision acclimated to the dusty dark. Charlie made out the wide doors on the warehouse's flank and the prow of a cargo ship beyond the bed of a large truck. A gangplank on the boat had carnivores bearing a crate down. Two more were hefting another up top. He couldn't precisely see what the crane was lowering into the hold but the components on the pallet were angular and heavy-looking.

It had to be the steel.

His eyes moved from one roving body to the next, seeking a familiar lupine shape. "Ready..." he muttered, knowing that his order was being relayed from agent to agent, all spread out and still. "Pick your targets."

Colonel Blake stalked in his white suit next to an array of long wooden boxes, all opened. The German shepherd held a long weapon with a serrated shroud around a long barrel. Was that what Charlie thought it was?

"Boss!" Somebody hissed. Just beyond the yawning mouth of the warehouse a cat stepped into view, pistol out.

Beyond the walls another voice was screaming, drawing everyone's attention.

Somebody had been spotted by a sentry.

Or they weren't. But everybody on the dock would have a weapon in hand momentarily.

This was it. He didn't have a bullhorn with him but didn't need one. "This is the Bureau of Investigation!" Charlie barked, then remembered the new name was now official. God dammit. "The Federal Bureau of...Put your hands up! You're all under arrest!"

Hell opened in a split second.

Mammals on the dock dived for cover while some other hands dived into jackets. The Colonel scattered crate straw as he hefted the rifle and scooped up a curved magazine from a neighbor while the grey fox with him inexplicably drew a short wicked sword and ran for the gangplank, claws scrabbling.

The first shot was fired by one of Charlie's people with a Winchester in the warehouse rafters and a weasel on the flatbed spun and fell out of sight, dropped revolver bouncing after him.

Of the dozen or so mammals on the dock two of them went down, tails tucked, and put their hands over their muzzles. All others dashed for cover, some taking pot shots, one of them nearly colliding with a curly-furred dog who ran screaming bloody murder through the fray, slipping once and hurtling for the darkness of the harbour beyond.

Charlie's own people returned fire, Tommy guns stamped the night, some met by pings on boat or flatbed steel and one drawing a thin scream from another of the Colonel's crew.

On the gangplank, two shiphands stumbled at the bottom end at the sound and feel of close gunfire as the fox with the long knife darted past, thick tail a kite. One cat muzzle-planted onto the dock, dropping the crate, which cracked and spilled long arms onto the planks behind him. The dog who had the back end lost footing, slipped, and spilled down into the drink out of sight. Colonel Blake immediately filled the gangplank space they vacated, bearing the long weapon before him and slapping a curved magazine home as he hurtled upwards after the silver fox. There was another shiphand up above watching the grey fox and the German shepherd Charlie's people had come for. The observer was a lupine, ears back and low. He was too far away to be sure, but Charlie could have sworn it was Lucas Marsten.

"We need to stop that boat from leaving!"

Nobody heard him as gunfire was traded. The Colonel's men, seemingly unaware that he was abandoning them, fought almost to a mammal.

Near the bow, a dock line dropped, cut at the source.

Charlie's men were all but pinned, unable to advance, and with the Colonel's loyalists pinned down in turn. Charlie raised his Thompson and fired, the gun clutzy at this distance but still grazing the hip of one Doberman who stumbled and fired upward.

Charlie heard one of his own whom he didn't know scream. Then he heard the slam and strain of metal once again above him.

"What the hell is that!" One of his sharpshooters on the Winchesters, likely Brumley, hollered as something hurtled forward in the high dark, leaping across the crate stacks and onto the borne-aloft pallet of steel being transferred by Blake's men. The crane chugged against the patter of rounds hitting its iron hide and the pilot, who couldn't see from their vantage that its load had increased, kept to task. The heavy tray of steel barely rocked as a bulky indistinct shape crouched upon it. Charlie alone knew what it was.

"Hope enough of you is in there, Craw," was all he could say before the hulking shape leapt from the pallet to the highest perch of the rolling boat, tattered clothes rent. On the boat, another line cut away.

"Advance!" Charlie shouted and took the initiative. He fired at the concentration of Blake's goons he could fix on, dumped the empty magazine, and pressed thirty more rounds home before leaving cover. Down at the warehouse entrance a lanky shape staggered and fell from a shot from further down the dock. Michael and Atburn were flanking.

A gun was thrown and another of Blake's mammals hit the deck and yowled surrender. "Where's the Colonel?" The terrified cougar flattened his ears against his head as he wailed. He couldn't have been older than eighteen. "He promised us he'd lead us!"

Charlie's team moved forward, potting at those who hadn't yet figured to surrender. The Colonel's remaining few threw their weapons or ran like hell.

On the boat behind it all, two last lines dropped, the thrum of the engines hammered as the cargo hauler backed away, the gangplank dragged to the water's edge and then dropped.

"Fucker's getting away," somebody growled. The Colonel was aboard along with most of the crew and Charlie squinted to make out the name stencilled on its prow: *Flood's Grace*.

"Anybody who names boats read any other damn chapter in the Bible?" He growled.

The dock had at least eight mammals lying prone, most alive, some wounded. Charlie was sure two were dead. He heard German curses coming out of at least one mouth. The real quarry was getting away. "We've got contraband here but we still have to intercept that boat. Get back to the wireless and signal the coast guard with the name *Flood's Grace*."

The agent he'd addressed ran.

Michael met up with him, the ringtail huffing almost painfully while the cheetah at his elbow rolled his eyes. "We didn't get anybody on the boat before it cut and ran."

The *Flood's Grace* had nearly cleared the end of the dock and was turning hard to port in the bay, countless yards from the federal agents on shore, its remaining crew smartly huddled from sight.

Charlie knew the truth. "We do have somebody. Our man is aboard. They're in trouble."

***

Opening her senses had been the key to her survival for as long as Celeste had been a Nosfur. Care of eighteenth-century French revolutionaries she'd been cautious before even that.

Sandy had already dealt with the sisters' problem, the diminutive squirrel enjoying herself. Celeste for her part had business to attend to first. Tires squealed, and towards the smell of saltwater, she caught echoes from the first of many gunshots. Chicago's clumsy violent games were being played all over again and Crawford was heading straight for them.

The wolf was close enough to mortality that a bullet could end his life. If the change found him, he'd be in a state where he might not be conscious of that.

Priorities chosen, Celeste closed in on the docks, staying high, binding shadows, but only made it to within a block before the discomfort arrived. A hundred yards closer, with the commotion close enough to hear, pain stopped her dead.

The reliquary steel was here, incredible concentrations of it. Her most recent meal was turning to molten agony in her veins.

She got clear, cursing. She was as powerless to help Crawford as she was to stop him.

And of course, there was Samson. He would hear the sound and be on his way, assuming he wasn't waiting at Water and Devonshire. Hopefully he'd stay clear of the bodies of the female bear's attackers.

Still, she had to be sure. She doubled back to a building overlooking the alley once more. The dead cat was being checked for life by a police-mammal with two other ungulates holding back and staying quiet. Samson would be nowhere near that now.

She circled, binding shadows, leaping, binding again. None of the surrounding alleys or rooftops bore evidence of a wandering goat kid. She took to the street near a more open area of town, close to the docks and its assorted Hoovervilles but far enough from the bramble of pain collected there. She took the bricked street near a massive, darkened hall balustraded by steel and glass. This in turn faced bricked colonial structures that had clearly squatted for a long time, perhaps longer than this city had been standing.

"You felt it too, didn't you?" A shadow spoke with a nasal voice, transatlantic in accent. The Nosfur within bound another shadow further away, closer to a sign indicating that Celeste's hooves walked Market Street.

Celeste searched her memory for that voice, familiar in a way she couldn't place. Of the dozens of Nosfurs she'd encountered in her travels, some were hospitable and curious, some quite the opposite. "What did I feel?" Passing mortals wouldn't hear her mutter but she was sure her interlocutor would.

She kept in sight of the few wandering nightgoers passing by, but few were curious. It was late. People with short, tidy lives had places to be.

"It's happening again," the male voice answered from a shadow on the next roof. "Just as it did before. Down by those docks. Somebody's pain for somebody's righteous cause. As far as you've run to escape it, there it is once again. Aren't you sick of it?"

A shape too dark to reveal a silhouette approached. The upward glint of weak light from windows or lamps above allowed a slender, long-limbed frame to trade shadows. Celeste caught the briefest glimpse but didn't follow. She'd be led nowhere.

She kept walking west; a structure was identified as Faneuil Hall by a sign near its drawn first-story awnings. The route was opening up and there were plenty of avenues for escape. She replied evenly, "I've had enough dealing with riddle speakers for one night. It's tiring. Whoever you are, be plain."

"Oh, come on, Celeste. It's been so long but you would understand what's happening here far better than any of *ces animaux qui se promènent dans cette ville.* A world away and I've learned there are, truly, no worlds away."

Celeste froze. The closest shadow in the lee of the bricked hall ahead bled a form.

"Not for me," he said, one hoof clicking in the brick. "Not for you, or your squirrel friend, or your goat kid. Not even your pet werewolf." The other hoof joined it, brown breeches above the hocks impeccably pressed as the shadow surrendered narrow hips, a chestnut-dark jacket over a cream silk shirt wrapped round a slender frame.

"Here we meet again in a time and place where freedom has become a fanciful cry for a vicious few who would strip it from everyone else. Every tyrant wears a liberator's dress. It's the only costume they know."

Recognition dawned. Celeste took a step back.

The shadow relinquished its cargo entirely and the elk stood level with her, antlers spread and yet short, his eyes dark and hard above a broad nose that drew in her scent. "The true tragedy is that love is supposed to be the answer to calamitous times, the one grace that binds us and saves us all." He smiled a cold smile and fangs crept low. "But not for me."

The open square of the Boston marketplace joined with the open air of the Place de la Révolution in Celeste's worst memory. The stench of countless dead clawed forward through time.

The elk saw her recognition and was pleased. "I loved you more than the world. And in return for all I sacrificed, you made my heart a blackened thing that would never know peace, didn't you?"

"Pierre," Celeste replied, her blood-flushed heart hammering. She felt her own fangs coming to the fore.

CHAPTER 22

CHOICES

"You do love them, don't you?" The lynx lounged in a high-backed chair across from Samson in the drawing room overlooking a slumbering street. As in all cities, so close to the thrum of its night life, and yet so far.

In the distance Samson heard what may have been fireworks, drifting in through a window that the lynx had let him open. Samson had said the parlour-style room with its plush furnishings was a bit warm, but really he wanted to keep an avenue for quick departure if needed. "If you mean my friends, then yes," he replied.

Ferrault smiled a kindly smile. "Crawford and Celeste have been detectives for some time, I'm told. Surprisingly successful despite this Depression."

"Sometimes." Samson gauged what to ask next. He'd wondered for so long what life was like for the few others of their kind out there. A thousand answers to a thousand questions sat across from him. But he was sure he knew who this really was. "You suggested it before, but you…are you the lynx who turned her?" He tried to keep the accusation out of his voice but faltered.

"Yes," the lynx replied, without reluctance, proud. "I saved her. Despite that we had a bit of a falling out. She'd forgotten something that wasn't so important in the grand scheme and sadly didn't know what she really wanted when she remembered. We curse ourselves with the things we can't let go of." Ferrault shrugged. "So it goes. I made other friends."

The lynx rose and didn't react to Samson sitting forward in his own chair, ready to bolt for that open window. A few steps took Ferrault to a corner where something tall was covered in coarse linen. Ferrault tugged and pulled the sheet free from an oval vanity mirror. "Take a moment and do what that picture-show Nosfur can never do. Look at yourself, really look at yourself."

He gave ample space as Samson stepped toward the scrawny goat kid scrutinizing him disapprovingly in return.

"You're not seeing. You're only doubting, always doubting. Look."

Samson did so again. The goat in the mirror was as angry as always with its small horns and gangly limbs.

"You look for everything wrong with that reflection and see nothing of what is wondrous. The astounding powers you have the capacity to accumulate will open doors the rest of us can only dream of. It pains me that, for all the affection your guardians have for you, they never helped you mount the path to your full potential. To the contrary, for what they presume to be your own good, they've held you back."

The goat kid in the mirror said nothing, listening. Doubt was so palpable he was surprised not to see it perched birdlike on his own shoulders.

"I know what you're going through, hard as that is to believe. The hardest truth to confront is that your caretakers can only see in you what they've lost elsewhere. The wolf, his estranged son. And Celeste…her lost sister."

Samson could say nothing, for what Ferrault said made sense. The doe and the wolf were as isolated as he was, cut off from any normal lives in a world in ruin. Always a drawn curtain, always a stolen shadow, always to stay unseen.

And look where it had gotten them.

"To be perfectly clear, Samson, it's not my suggestion that you should leave them forever. I could never ask you to do that. What I can do, and what I offer," Ferrault waved a hand beckoningly and the door behind him swung open. The lady mink from the tavern strolled in, white-furred, demurely dressed, and with kindly warm eyes that pulled Samson away from the mirror and towards her.

"…is a way to get what you truly want." Ferrault finished.

The white mink was not alone. Peering from behind her, a shorter, more diminutive ermine whose fur was a cloudy grey poked a nose into the room. Whiskers quivered as she sampled the air. Taking another step, Samson could see that while the older mink was in her mid to late thirties, the younger mink in the faded blue blouse and long skirt was a young adult, not yet twenty. The minks traded glances and the older one spoke, coaxing gently. "You're ready," she whispered barely loud enough for Samson to hear and stroked the youth's slender chin gracefully. "I'm so proud of you."

The young mink met Samson's gaze and he saw excitement, trepidation, the unmistakable hint of checked fear.

Ferrault smiled. "You can advance your age without starvation, Samson, without pain and impossible yearning. And you don't even need to always take lives to do so. We've a covenant, Samson, my friends and me. We care for one another."

The young mink smoothed her dress and approached Samson, her eyes drifting to the chair he'd rested in and sat to one side. Instinctively, he joined her, hearing her pulse. It was smooth and regular within her warm frame and sped slightly as she registered his attention. It wasn't the panicked rapids within the weasel on the Maryland border or the cats in the Scranton alley. It was the calm certainty of life that he felt as she sat next to him. As his fangs descended and he felt her warm body against his that current of vitality sped only a little faster.

The older mink sidled over to stand behind Ferrault, who reached back, took her hand, and clasped it in tight affection as they both regarded the twin tableaus of youth before them.

"Accept this gift Samson, given willingly. Delilah understands what we must do to survive, as does her elder sister. Their family has been with me for two generations, through famine and feast. We honor their contributions with our gratitude and love and the promise of greater prosperity. And we employ restraint as often as our condition allows. I know you have experience in this, Samson."

The smell of Delilah flooded over him and what he felt was unabashed, relentless hunger. But nothing else. He'd been in the world for twenty-five years, even longer than she, but her warmth, while comforting, spoke only of sustenance. There was something undefinable that should accompany this proximity. A mystery had folded bodies together in the cinemas and on the promenades where he'd been a stranger, perpetually confused. The body he lived in had no concept of what it meant.

The hunger was all he had.

She sensed the turn of his head and her heart beat faster as Delilah tilted her head back. And away. Her throat's fur glinted in the weak electric light of the room. Out the window, the distant unseen fireworks had gotten louder, staccato. He found it easy to ignore.

"Accept, Samson. She is ready." The lynx's and mink's hands gripped tighter, their gazes expectant.

Samson twisted and his teeth found their way home and Delilah gasped, first with a wince of pain and then a throttling shiver of excitement as they both leaned back and life flowed and Samson received.

Immediately something was different. The minute sparks of life from the rodents Crawford had fetched had been dull but sustaining. The flood of panicked nectar from the mammals who'd tried to kill Samson or his friends had been much more than sustaining, rich and heady and flooding the body with an exuberance that was undefinably superior.

Delilah's lifeblood was something so much more. His heart began pounding as the nectar flowed through him, burning his core with a vitality that felt like a missing part restored, an essential sense of completion. Senses sharpened. He could smell the sawdust in the cut planks that composed the room, feel eddies of air from currents warping sails out past Boston's docks, and hear the rings of brass accompanying each stamp of gunfire out where salty air carried the drifting scents of even more liberated, wasted blood.

"Samson," Ferrault said calmly.

Samson dimly heard him as Delilah's hands found his frame and gripped his shoulder and back. He drew more copper ambrosia and felt as though he'd drift off the earth itself.

"Not too much," Ferrault chided.

Delilah's hand was between them now, pushing away.

Celeste's voice was in his head at that moment, echoing Ferrault's. "We need to restrain ourselves," it whispered.

With a gasp matched by the mink's Samson opened his jaws and pushed himself away. His body felt as though it were made of starstuff, winking, shining eternal, and he stood up, teetering as the mink settled back and took deep breaths. The older mink spoke something enthusiastic to Delilah that Samson couldn't hear. Only Ferrault's voice penetrated. "Now look at what the mirror gives you, Samson. Place your future within it."

As distant guns shot and other city sounds collected, Samson smelled the world flow in and regarded himself in the mirror once more. The young buck goat stood maturely in the tight clothes of a child, horns swept back over proud forward ears. He stood stock still as his true aspect receded and reappeared once more with the tide of his heart's leased life. Had he any tears to release, he would have cried them.

"What you see is no illusion. It's the future you can make for yourself, Samson. If you can let go of what holds you back."

Samson watched the image fade one last time, leaving the goat kid behind, no longer sullen, no longer trapped in forever's amber. A way forward was clear.

Ferrault was at his shoulder and Samson turned to see Delilah and the older mink shuffling out, the younger mink leaning weakly against the older. Delilah turned back, soft eyes over a warm, grateful smile. Then they were gone.

"You need to see the world as it can be, Samson," Ferrault said excitedly. "No time like the present…Let's take a walk."

***

"How are you here?" Celeste couldn't accept what her senses told her. "I put you out of your misery."

Pierre took another step, his dark eyes narrowed. "I would have been glad to leave a world that still had you in it. After all I did to—"

"How are you here!" Celeste hissed. An otter couple across the square looked quizzically their way and sensing trouble, moved faster.

"A lynx came, asked a wretch in stocks what he had left in the world. On the verge of starvation, I told him only love. Only love, Celeste." He snorted as though the pain of any laughter would finish him.

She said nothing, certain she spoke to a ghost. Had the sisters somehow drugged her again?

Pierre flared his nostrils. "Ferrault promised I could live forever if I agreed to let love go. I thought him a madman taunting the condemned and agreed if only for a morsel of sustenance. The bread was bitter and I mourned as I partook. I thought you had been killed, perhaps even worse. After all I did for you, all for nought."

"You betrayed my family! You had them killed!"

Pierre took a step again, antlers forward. Celeste didn't step back. She didn't care how public this was. If he dared to touch her…

"I did no such thing! They were grist for the revolution as we all were. You knew this. I could only save one of you and had to negotiate with all I had for even that broken promise. You never saw the scars, Celeste, saw what they took from me at hot iron's touch before they turned me out, followed me, and forced my hand."

"You should have led them away!"

"They would have found you regardless. They maintained lists, spies, informants everywhere!"

"And you expanded those ranks."

"I became beholden, promised so much worse if I gave them nothing. So, we bargained. And they betrayed me, leaving me pilloried in public to starve, to watch!" Pierre rubbed his neck as though chasing an irredeemable itch. "Much later, when the stink of La Place became unbearable, there was one bargain more. I ate the black bread Ferrault provided, certain it was a last meal. Then you came. You, for whom I dared to cheat fate, you came and made sure all the love I ever felt was for nought."

"*Ma mère, mon père, ma sœur*! My whole world on pikes! And you actually thought for an instant that I'd go with you? Live and love you and forget them?"

Pierre bared his teeth and his fangs were long indeed. He didn't care who saw. "Love makes for hard choices. Brands and blows make them stronger. They would have killed you all if I hadn't played the advocate, told them you could be turned from the monarchy's lingering sway or whatever the hell *merde* I can't remember feeding them. *Of course* I wanted your whole family safe, but that was never in the cards, Celeste. Nor apparently was there any chance that you would understand the sacrifice I made for you."

She wished she could spit. "If you thought for a second that I'd have let them kill my family…"

"You had no more choice than I did, than did my own father who was one of the first to die. And what did I learn from Ferrault after you assaulted your savior and left? You forgot her yourself. I was there, alive with my neck craned behind the flies, watching them push the fawn up on a stool so they could—"

Celeste lashed out to strike him and he feinted back, deflecting her arm with a block of his palm. She lashed again and he danced back. "Stop, Celeste! Again, I had no choice. That's what you fail to understand. It wasn't I who betrayed you, it was you who betrayed me!"

"Go straight to hell!" she hissed. She could tear him in half and dash venison like a bloody witch's mark across the threshold of Faneuil Hall.

"No! I made the impossible choice for you. All for you! And I've borne the scar of your last violent kiss, your callous, hateful dismissal, for well over a century. It burned in me, Celeste. And now, at long last, the impossible choice has circled round to burn you too."

"What the hell are you talking about? I'm going to twist those fucking antlers off and bury them in your eye sockets."

Pierre smiled then, fangs glinting with slick vengeance under pitiless flints. "You won't touch a strand upon me, Celeste. Otherwise, the choice you have to make, the one I will force you to make, is rescinded. We have both of them, your squirrel lover and your goat cherub. And if you don't choose, as I was forced to choose, well, we'll simply destroy them both."

***

He struck the deck with all four claws and smelled iron tang, fish-stink, and mammal-fear. Up high on the swaying mountain, the others could not see him, stumbling in their webs of fabric and soot stink as they threw licks of fire at one another. Blood made him hungry but the snaps of fire brought anxiety.

A scurry came to his left flank. A thick dog rounded on him from a niche unseen and its tail fear-curled. It made noises that sounded like challenge even as it fright-pissed and snapped its fire wide.

The fire was remembered, and unwelcome.

The wolf reacted, lashing with a hand that broke something, and the canine made a terrible sound as it slammed a rigid outcropping and tumbled over. Water splashed and the wolf growled as it went back and forth; anxious, rankled, sorting smells through the noise below.

One canine in tight white fur raised a larger stick than the others and spat fire that hurt to hear. Down below a hillock of cover exploded in splinters like a tree chewed by a creature invisible. A mammal screamed unseen. Many others scrambled for the drifting mass upon which the wolf above it all crouched, unnoticed by most of the creatures trying earnestly to kill one another. The ground beneath him thrummed and hummed and banged and it was making him mad.

The lights and stinks of the land slid away, and with it, pops and snaps of fire faded from the mammals on land. The dark-skulled dog in the white filigree of what the wolf remembered were clothes, barked challenges over the lances of fire that hammered every few seconds. Hot brass pebbles skipped about him.

Smells drifted up, mostly the ashen metallic spoor of the fire, but it was crowded by others. Crawford—for there was the vague awareness of self bleeding outward—felt the awareness of another, one whose scent touched the stirred gruel of memory. In the faint glow of the moon's sheen, the glint of straight silvery shapes were visible in the deep dark. The wolf that was kin was down there.

Down he had to go. Claws found difficult purchase where iron succeeded wood. Other mammals scrambled and another smell crowded Crawford's burning nostrils, heady and rank. Fox musk.

He reached the widest expanse of the island in motion, everything rocking steadily now, and starry eyes twinkled from shapes falling quickly behind. The fox scent grew stronger, the breeze scrambling the distinctions of upwind or downwind.

A scrabble of claws alerted the senses a second before iron tried to bite him, thudding against something impenetrable that made a loud ringing sound. The fox spat sounds of disdain and swung its tool again. Sense memory brought back another cavern of steel, another swung iron tooth, the scream of a lioness rather than a fox. The mudded mind was clearing. The screamed sounds "were bastard" had a meaning and that meaning wasn't playful. Crawford growled and spun and swiped. The silver fox rolled and swiped in turn. Crawford's short finger hurt, nerves tingling with past lessons. The steel could hurt. The steel could kill.

The fox shouted, but not at Crawford, who growled and crouched for a leap. At the distant edge the dog in white spun and showed all his teeth

345

before speaking words that were profane and fearful and mostly foreign to Crawford's turmoil of a mind. The burning stick of fire rose. The fox screamed something terrible as it dived away and Crawford didn't know why he knew to do the same as the white-spun dog's black branch spat angry light. Wood splintered. Metal pinged and punctured. Crawford felt the sting of a hot nettle graze him and the fox shouted the only understandable word again and again that instinct sorted from the mire within.

"Stop! Stop! Stop!" This was followed by more colorful growling chatter as the branch's licks of fire ended in clicks leaving only the sounds of other mammals panicking and the thrumming of primordial forces under their feet. The lights of the land curved, fell away some more.

Crawford was furious but equally confused. Dominance needed to be asserted but he didn't know how. That scent regrouped and renewed, a part of him yet not a part, tinged by fear.

The dog in white called down to the dark for something and Crawford craned to glance at where the familiar scent originated.

A familiar face looked up, squinted, tried to make out his in return. Grey fur, the same color eyes tied to a smell that was an extension of self: worrying, fearful, endangered. Crawford knew and felt and understood this force within at once.

There was a name. Son. There was another name that he heard from the white dog above, calling downward even as it stared at Crawford, plaintive in words that connected to meaning. "Lucas! Get another mag for the thirty! There's a huge goddamn feral up here! Bring it now!"

Crawford felt the shadows beckon and instinctively crept back from the weak reach of buzzing lights, still able to see below. The young wolf dropped whatever he'd been trying to drag, as the canine who'd had the other end had already fled. The wolf clutched at something that he swung down upon one wooden—they were crates—breaking it like an egg. Sifting the broken planks, the younger wolf found straw and small eggs of steel. He raised the axe again over the other crate close by.

Crawford barely heard the second strike as the moonlight glinted off the steel swinging his way. His shoulder was grazed as he darted back, feinted, and charged with a renewed fury. The fox was rounding for another swing of his own implement when Crawford struck the vulpine's mid-section with just enough force to hurl the silver-furred vulpine backwards, a cindery stink on the fox's breath as his back collided with the rail.

The fox pinwheeled his limbs, stuck out his feet to try to keep more mass away from the pit beyond. The silvery blade clattered on the deck. Crawford grabbed the fox's kicking leg to drag him back but the squirming vulpine thrashed to avoid him and tipped over instead. The fox screeched as he tumbled into the pit below, striking the unyielding rigid shapes piled in the dark with a sickening crunch and wet gasp.

The young wolf below gaped at the twisted limbs of the fox twitching between the pallets with a shudder, and then back up again at the shape moving above for only an instant before spreading straw frantically to extract something black and curved within.

Crawford smelled the familiar smell and peered below before slipping over the rail and letting himself drop twice his own height to scrabble for purchase on something unyielding. Feet stung as though he'd dropped onto burning nettles and he leapt from the piles of what his regrouping mind told him was iron to the deck below.

The shorter wolf, fur arching in fear, began backing away, scent spreading.

His son. Crawford's son.

Somebody shouted something, but it couldn't be understood even with a mind recollecting. German, Crawford vaguely remembered as a loud snap sounded off from a portal by the door, then another. Crawford dropped back to fours, hissing at the discomforting closeness of the straight prone branches of—steel, they were girders of steel—and rushed the door as the implement in a surprised cat's grasp clicked and clicked again.

There was the briefest moment for the cat to feel terror and try to turn. Crawford swept his massive arm, claws closing over a shoulder, jaws closing over a skull. There was a crunch and the gurgle of a closed mouth within Crawford's own. He thrashed the feline twice before tossing it end over end to strike something and slide down bloody and limp. Somewhere beyond the portal the cat had tried to duck into, other Germanic voices cursed and receded.

Behind him, steel thundered as something else came down and he caught a glimpse of the dog in white, descending to the far side of the piled metal, sputtering oaths, down towards…

"Lucas." The word escaped Crawford's distended jaws as he fought for conscious control. Crawford's claws touched one of the girders as he righted himself and pulled back from the shock of contact. A glance at his palm for the invisible burn saw the limb shrinking, the claws losing proportion. Crawford stood straighter and ignored it, feeling a sense of awareness that came with worry and shame.

How much had they all seen? How much had Lucas seen?

He took stock of himself. He was bare-chested, yet another pair of borrowed trousers shorn to the point where modesty was all but gone. He felt his spine try to align itself against the accumulated abuse as he rounded a pallet of rust-flaked Calvert Steel girders. As always, his voice was a syrupy thing that needed to be reclaimed and he had to wrestle out every word. "Lucas. Lucas it's me. Don't panic, just please listen to me—"

Something struck his shoulder blades hard enough to rattle his spine. He went down, muzzle nearly breaking on the salty deck of the ship's hold. Starbursts of pain raced through his nose and back.

The dog who'd leapt on his back tucked and rolled to a standing position in the corner of Crawford's eye, brushing at his crumpled suit. "Magazine, Lucas!" the German shepherd shouted.

Crawford pushed himself off the deck with an aggravated grunt, wounds complaining for equal attention. He grabbed for the hot barrel of what he recognized was a depleted machine gun. It burned his hand as he dragged it from the Colonel's loose fumbling grasp and Crawford swung it into darkness over the pallets of girders. Its stock cracked when it struck the wall and disappeared from view.

"You!" Crawford shouted as the white-suited German shepherd stared him down. "You messed with my son's head, you thug bastard!"

The Colonel stood in a boxer's stance, but didn't advance as he reached into his lapel, drawing a blue-steel forty-five that Crawford immediately rushed to claim. The shepherd was ready this time and grappled him for it, teeth bared, growled hate plain. Crawford gave up trying to get the gun as he dragged the struggling German shepherd towards himself and batted the hand against the stack of girders. The auto flew from their grasp and skittered along the deck to be scooped up by a young wolf's uncertain, shaking paw as Lucas rounded the corner and saw them both.

Lucas raised the weapon. "Stop!"

The Colonel and Crawford froze, still in one another's grasp.

The young wolf bared his own teeth. "Dad! For fuck's sake. You've ruined everything! You have no idea what you're interfering with!"

Lucas's eyes bored into him and Crawford felt himself shrink.

The Colonel thrashed out of Crawford's grasp. "You know what you have to do!"

Lucas met Crawford's eyes, his true eyes, and his son's eyes were cold as Lucas checked the safety on the Colonel's gun. He'd seen what his father had become. Fear was naked on him.

Lucas took sharp hard breaths as he aimed for Crawford's head.

***

"Choose?"

"Yes. One of them. Only one. Who's most important to you, Celeste? I know whom my world revolved around and you broke my heart for it. Now it's time that you finally understand how painful that betrayal was." Pierre's glare was unblinking, his indignation so strong that his fangs ground noisliy. "No escape, no mercy, only a choice and all the guilt in the world to follow you for it."

"There won't be any guilt at all when I finish you."

Pierre laughed, disdain in its purest language. "Oh, Celeste. I've learned what you've become. Do you honestly think that violence wasn't the first and only impulse I expected you to surrender to? This was foreseen, and for that reason we're being observed. We've been extremely busy making new friends. If you move against me, both the goat and the squirrel are gone and I'll ensure that their heads are mounted where you'll find them, maybe not today or tomorrow, but in years' time when you think that grief has been spent." He smiled wide and toothily at the thought. "The only choice before you is to demonstrate which of the two is more important to you. As I had to bare my own heart, so will you."

She'd held Sandy not an hour ago, let Samson off only a half hour before that. Both held firm and present in her mind as she took a step forward. Her gaze promised enough that Pierre's backward step back was involuntary.

"I'm not helpless in stocks this time, *ma chèrie*. Even should you overpower me, one hair harmed destroys both of them. It's time to settle accounts, Celeste. I gave you my love, now I give you my pain. All of it."

Celeste closed her eyes, feeling heartbeats around her, close and far. Pierre's brood could be fed Nosfur, or mortal spies moving in plain sight. Or he could be lying, playing some sick gambit for sympathy. "I don't believe you."

"You don't believe what, Celeste? That the goat was seen leaving your car, wandering dejected down a back alley? Or that Sandy shared a tender moment with you on a rooftop so close to here? Do you instead think I would merely know these things, let those close to the one who betrayed me go, and then make a gamble out of this confrontation?"

He slipped something from his jacket that he allowed the wind to tease. Black and silken, Celeste made out the tiniest glimpse of what seemed to be Sandy's silk undergarments. Pierre snickered. "I took no trophy from the kid, of course. Such was never a proclivity of mine. I can only promise that, for him or for her, the end will be quick. Far quicker than the suffering I endured. I generously grant them that." He shook the torn silk with a manic fist. "But not you."

Celeste couldn't speak, bound in the shadow of her worst fears. She could imagine what else had been taken along with Sandy's modesty. The spectre of Pierre's cruel hands on her body...

"No." She'd already lost Sandy once, granted by fate a glimpse at a second chance. She fought the lead space growing inside her down. Celeste wouldn't weep, wouldn't keen. "You bastard, no."

"Choose."

Sandy's scent, the way her teeth glinted when she smiled, that coquettish twinkle in eyes that always kept secrets. Celeste held that image she'd known so long...and then steadied herself by setting it aside. She instead focused on Samson, innocent, wayward Samson, drawn to Celeste as a little brother, a confidant, a kindred soul she had accepted as her own. She'd vowed not to fail him, not to abandon him. He was of her people now and she of his. What little good she could do in the world, she would find through helping him.

And Sandy...

Pierre watched her strangle into despair's grasp, his ears fluttering excitedly and predatory with vindication. "I certainly don't want to rush you, Celeste. In fact, the more time this takes, the more I'll savor—"

"Samson," Celeste said, voice breaking when the name left her lips. "Return him. Now."

Pierre's cocked his head, confused. "You…just like that? That's it? You let your squirrel lover go to destruction with so little consideration? How can you? Are you really so cold?"

Celeste parted her fangs and felt the world go dark about them both. "Cold? You foolish blind bastard," she hissed. "If you truly knew either of them or had any understanding of what real love or sacrifice ever meant it would have been perfectly obvious. I know that, given the choice, Sandy would have made this very decision with no hesitation, Samson's life spared in exchange for hers. That's why."

"You can't be—"

"The very essence of her that makes her who she is, belies how she cherishes so much above herself, her life given to noble causes. Some have exploited her for ignoble aims, bastards all of them, but she has always sought a measure of justice for the innocent. Even when violence was her only weapon, Alisandre Mallory strove to employ it to moral purpose. That is why I choose as I do. She would never have tolerated being rescued at the cost of Samson's stolen life. It would be the most sordid of bargains for which she would never have forgiven me, any more than I forgive you for Lavert."

Pierre was confused, opened his mouth to say more and closed it.

Celeste took another step forward, defiant. "Do you know why you aren't relishing my pain in reaching this decision, Pierre? Why you get nothing of the satisfaction you're expecting in this sick-minded scenario you've crafted? It's because, for all you hoped to gain from my suffering, you realize that I not only have at least two lives who mean everything to me, but that they mean more to me than my own life. You could never imagine that, Pierre, never understand what love is or ever was."

"You make absolutely no sense," he whispered, snorting his nostrils. Something inexplicable to him overtook malice. He took another step back and nearly stumbled.

Celeste advanced, fighting back a sob. "Your triumph is empty because you never had me to lose. Even though you told yourself you wanted me, you never, ever considered in your whole mortal life what I would want. It never occurred that *ma mère ou mon père* could be so inseparably important to me, much less *ma sœur*. You chose the solitary object of your affection apart from all else and that's why I know you didn't suffer long for all your martyr's pretentions. I was a trophy you were due when the revolution came calling, nothing more. Only your loss or gain was any consideration and as such it was never really love. I sincerely doubt you've ever felt that even once in this life or the last one."

Celeste couldn't weep but she could lay her pain bare regardless and when she did she could see the recognition cut Pierre deep. "That empty space that left France within me didn't bear your name for long. A century later, I found love. I found love and for another kind of love I'll surrender it." She saw Sandy's smile in herself, that wide Irish beam in a sunless place and said goodbye. And she let the wilting stag see that. And despite all he wanted, it hurt him even worse. "You're blind in your self-pity, Pierre, bound in hate's contortions, and that's why you will never find love yourself. Hate only pushes us in one direction, but love moves us in many at once."

"Damn you." Pierre's curse was a tiny empty thing.

Celeste drew herself up, weeping dryly. "Bring Samson to me before your enablers find out just how little honor you ever had."

About them both, shadows and mortals alike bore witness.

Chapter 23

Du bist ein Werwolf!

Mike had brought the truck around and even though the ringtail was wheezing enough to have a heart attack the radio inside was brought to life and working. Agents secured the arrested with difficulty and heard every curse to their mothers ever devised but Charlie didn't give a damn.

The most important asset and target in the whole hemisphere was chugging out of port, its stern lights a shrinking curse. "What do you mean Coast Guard's not in place! What the hell are they doing off Nantucket Island? We phoned this in"—Charlie looked at the watch on his hairy wrist and couldn't believe it had only been thirty minutes since they'd fired the first shot—"an hour ago! Get them the hell back up here to intercept *Flood's Grace*, repeat, that's *Flood's Grace*. False registry painted on a foreign ship. What?" Charlie listened while he was squawked back at. "I don't know boats! It's a merchant hauler, grey steamer with one coal stack. Probably can't go too damn fast, heading out to the Atlantic. Why would I know where?" He heard one of the cursing dogs on the dock as a muzzle was wrestled on to keep him from biting ankles. "German. It's likely heading for Germany."

They would do what they could do. Charlie acknowledged, signaled over, and went to the dock's edge around the contraband rifles and grenades to where the last felon was being fished from the drink. The ship's lights were ghosts receding into the night.

***

Lucas's gun arm wavered but stayed high.

"Kill 'im," the Colonel barked. "You saw whatever the hell he was!"

Lucas squinted. "I don't know what I saw…"

"Just shoot, Lucas!"

Crawford closed his eyes and opened them again. This was as good a place for his curse to end as any and his son was as good a hand to finish it. He merely found his gaze and held it. "It's just us, Lucas. Everybody on the shore is—"

"Shut up!" Lucas shouted at Crawford. "The fox is dead, Colonel."

The Colonel's eyes went from Lucas to the gun to Crawford and back to the limp grey-furred ragdoll several yards away. "Yeah, looks to be. You know what you have to do next. Don't stall on me, boy."

"You just couldn't stay out of my life, could you?" Lucas said bitterly, holding the gun with one hand while the other unbuttoned the thin, nearly fur-tight jacket he was wearing. "You ruined my childhood and came back to ruin this too. My future, the destiny I fought for!"

"Lucas," Crawford was already tripping over what he wanted to say. He focused on the dark pit at the end of that gun and wondered if he would see it light up. "This was never the way. You know why…"

"Lucien's dead," Lucas said to the Colonel.

"You already said that." The Colonel was annoyed. "Now end this berserking bastard so we can get a launch to the shore down coast. All my money's in the car and the dirty Fed bastards are gonna—"

"What was Lucien's last name? You said before he had offices in London, but who was he?" Lucas let the gun waver, then held it fast.

"The hell does it matter?"

"Tell me! He obviously got compromised, or how the hell else did they know where we were?"

"Limey's name was Prennick. Lucien Prennick. You gonna mail his vixen and cubs a condolence card? Lucas, this is it, life or death. You wanted into the rebellion, then damn well get in by killing the sack of shit who abandoned you! Now!"

Lucas reached into his jacket and wrestled something free. Something metallic bounced on the deck but Crawford couldn't take his eye off the forty-five pointing at him until he saw the black leather square Lucas drew turn over, saw a familiar shape in golden relief: an eagle over a shield embossed in blind, sword-borne liberty.

Lucas turned the gun on the Colonel, his eyes hard as he found his voice. "Between that and all your other high-roller friends that took too damn long."

The Colonel's jaw dropped. "What are you doing?"

Lucas took a breath. "Rutland Grummel Blake…I'm an agent with the Federal Bureau of Investigation. You are under arrest for multiple violations of the nineteen thirty-four National Firearms Act, conspiracy to commit insurrection against the lawful government of the United States—"

"No."

"Conspiracy to commit murder on two confirmed counts."

The Colonel backed from the badge like a hot poker. "No!"

"Embezzlement and lending material aid to a foreign power." Lucas kicked and the cuffs that had landed on the deck below him bounced against the Colonel's claws. "Put them on." He glared at Crawford and Crawford wondered if he was hallucinating. "You know how they work when you're sober enough. Fix him with the bracelets."

Crawford's voice was hard to find again. "Son, I—"

The Colonel's wasn't. "You mange-hide snitch little shit! I brought you to greatness! I would have made you a king."

"Don't play me for the same sucker you played everyone else," Lucas snarled, and jabbed out with the gun quick enough to make the German shepherd trip back against the girders. "You left them behind without a thought, every starving, desperate mook you led around by the nose while you roused them up and robbed them blind. The money is the only thing on that dock that you even care about."

"How dare—"

"Shut up, Blake. I swallowed bile every second I had to beg your favor. Thank the patience of the real chief I work with that I kept myself from putting a bullet in your miserable back…"

Lucas trailed off and Crawford absorbed all that was happening, shock giving way to disbelief. Lucas was the informant. Every deflection and warning Charlie had fed him in hotel rooms and moving cars in the past week suddenly fell into relief and Crawford felt cold.

"Don't lose your head now, Cain," Lucas said the last name he'd let go of with a hard indifference that cut through all else. "Get the cuffs on this bastard and stay with him while I deal with the few crew left."

The Colonel regained his posture and spat. "You can't turn this boat, you don't know who's left or where they are. You're in it deep now, both of ya!"

"No, we're not," Crawford muttered. "Keep the gun on him." He darted to a corner.

"What the hell are you doing? I said put the cuffs on…" Crawford was back in a moment with the Colonel's machine gun. "You had magazines for this." He saw a curved black object and dipped to pick it up, drove it home, drew the bolt back. "We can take the bridge before we get too far out to sea and—"

They all perked to the grind of metal on metal, a door swinging round to bang the hull. Round one pile of the girders that Crawford felt shift him between itchy and painfully burning, a thin dog in mechanic's overalls wandered forth, both hands high above himself. In one hand was a narrow stick of wood that terminated in a node of metal. At the base of that stick, trembling fingers gripped a small while ball tied to a thin rope disappearing into the wooden rod.

Crawford had seen potato mashers in France and what they could do to pelt, flesh, and bone. He lowered the muzzle. "Put it down, fella," he said.

The dog gibbered out one side of his chattering muzzle. "*Ich habe gesehen, was du bist! Du bist ein Werwolf!*"

"I'm…Lucas. We have a bit of a problem."

"*Du hast meinen Bruder Heinrich getötet!*"

Lucas had the gun on the dog but knew a grenade when he saw one. "Federal Bureau of Investigation, put it down!"

The Colonel dived for the rifle Crawford bore, seizing it by the receiver. Lucas couldn't put his own gun down to help so he tentatively stepped back. "Put it down! Blake, let it go! It's over!"

The Colonel pressed his body against Crawford's own and they were eye to eye for a moment, growls matched. The German kept shouting with the grenade over his head as the Colonel got both hands on the gun, feeling the flex of hands over the weapon's surface that were beginning to grow in proportion. Crawford didn't care who saw him now. If the Colonel took the rifle, Lucas was as dead as he was.

They struggled, they spun. The Colonel's finger found the trigger.

The stamp of the rifle was deafening as it cut loose, spinning with them to stitch rounds in the wall up and down, ping off the steel, and catch the German machinist on the shoulder and chest, blossoms of red nearly sawing his arm away. He fell dead and the fuse cord left the grenade that he'd dropped and rolled behind the cover of steel.

Crawford forcefully pointed the gun upward, letting the last few rounds punch the clouds far above the hold. When it clicked empty he let the gun go and swept his claws wide in one blinding quick motion, scraping the right side of the Colonel's face halfway to the bone.

The scream was delightful and Crawford knew his other self was hungry.

"Grenades!" Lucas shouted behind him.

"Steel'll cover—"

"Lots of them!"

Fogged memory from the last change snapped back: Lucas, using an axe to break open crates. One of them had steel eggs aplenty.

They bolted, four paces, five. There were two solid stacks of steel girders between themselves and the ruin of the contraband grenade cache when countless simultaneous explosions filled the opposite side of the hold with powdery light, rattling the girders on their pallets.

Crawford's ears rang sore and his son shouted something unintelligible as the opposite bulkhead rivets popped, a flange of torn hull buckled inward, and water sprayed in.

The hold tipped, steel starting to slide towards the tortured hull joint, and the last of the hold's weak light faded out, casting them in darkness.

Panic found Crawford in the murk. The change came anew and despite the pain he didn't fight it. Freezing water clutched their feet as tortured metal roared. The ship listed another few degrees in the space of a few seconds. "Hold on!" Crawford screamed through ravening jaws his son couldn't see. Crawford's night vision made his son out. Immense claws, all but bleeding from the resurgent change, grasped at the slippery steel wall of the hold, found purchase at a seam and dug.

His other hand scooped up the soaked wolf struggling to keep footing as the opposite hold wall gave way completely and all became Biblical flood. He drew the younger wolf closer, drawing them both up against the torrent, one hand and two claws working to drag them up, drag them over. The boat was quartered to port now and Crawford realized that, for the first time ever, he was now fully changed while fully conscious, every sense and every conscious awareness present. His son grasped him, gasping for air as gravity pulled the submerging girders to the perforated side of the hull, tearing the mortal wound wider. A fire had started in the engine room, painting Hell's pigments through the dying ship's portholes.

He perched on the starboard side rail for a moment, registered distant muffled screams from below and caught a sliver of moon through the cloudy expanse above. He howled, and then, with his son in his arms, he leapt.

The shock of the ocean's encompassing grip parted his son from him, only for a moment. Fire blossomed from the dying ship above the curtain of frozen death and he opened his eyes to make out the cub in front of him, weightless, painless, an adolescent unencumbered by time, still loved, still nurtured.

Crawford blinked hard, grabbed his only son and broke surface with a wet snarl. Lucas reached out, instinctively clutching his coarse pelt with wracking shivers as Crawford fixed on the lights stretched out where smells and scents that he knew intimately came from. He swam against the chill that stabbed right to his center, finding his place in the current, and didn't let his aching limbs stop.

***

The lights of the city moved for Samson in ways he couldn't describe, stars trapped on Earth for him alone. Currents of life buzzing in his veins had brought him to euphoria before, but this was a different level of transcendence that paradoxically calmed and invigorated him simultaneously. Every fear and insecurity fled like phantoms, doubts parted like clouds, and he felt as though the bricks of Boston itself were cells in some great breathing beast with a story it was desperate to share. "What was that you said?"

The lynx spoke from over Samson's shoulder as he followed but it was as though his words came from within the goat's own head. "There are manifestations of our very reality that we dance upon without having the merest understanding," Ferrault said breathily. He'd drunk himself and his heart beat in tandem with Samson's. "The shadows we bind aren't merely puddles to skip in, but liminal spaces, doorways and windows to other aspects of existence that none have dared explore." He took a deep draw of the carried salt of the ocean. Samson felt compelled to do the same. Water-tortured oak, muddily rusted iron, spent powder. Fresh blood. Something close and violent had left its spoor. "None but myself have seen beyond," Ferrault added proudly.

Beyond the streetlamps and thin moonlight rays, shadows shifted, shadows whispered. Or perhaps Samson's fired imagination conjured it.

"I've spent centuries studying the assumed limits of our reality, seeing the shadows for what they are, reflections not of light's absence but the encroachment of something beyond. All the world is churning, struggling calamity but the answers to so much can be found in the deep stillness, the spaces between the material."

"I feel it." Samson looked up to streetlight-dampened stars and the black velvet spreading far and thick between them. "I've always felt something but I never knew where or what it was."

"It's much the same for me, for my whole existence since circumstance left me alone for so long. You can help me, Samson, and I can help you. There are discoveries to be made…and I have a plan."

"A plan for what?"

There was a change in the air just then, a distant flash blipped off distant clouds that appeared in the dark and disappeared as quickly. A sound rolled in from somewhere, low and booming.

"That's not thunder," Samson said, ears perked and nose questing.

Ferrault cocked his own ears. "That's folly. Come, let's get to the waters. That aggravating ache from the docks seems to have faded at last."

***

Pierre glared back at Celeste as she trailed him through Boston's main thoroughfare. "You'll have your goat kid soon."

"I don't trust you! You'll bring him here, now! I don't doubt that you've caused him all sorts of harm."

Pierre rounded on Celeste and they nearly butted heads. "I keep my word, Celeste. Better you have him around, intact, to remind you of what you have lost, just as your skulking and fucking your way through the world will perpetually remind me of—"

Celeste had his rack by the hands and her fangs returned to the place where she'd tried to kill a traitor and instead birthed a monster. Bucky Cavali in Chicago hadn't been the first after all.

Pierre froze in anticipation and his words came with a tincture of panic that made him sound like he breathed again. "I already told you, if I'm harmed…"

Celeste showed her teeth. "Oh, I won't harm you today. We have to keep our respective promises, don't we, Pierre? All these eyes seeing our truths for what they are? But don't think that this will square a debt. This is not the end of things, nor will it ever be forgiven or forgotten. We both have all the time in the world. Know that."

She released him and a far-off boom muttered against the sky, veining a cloud over the waters with flashes of light.

She ignored it with supreme effort. "Take me to him."

Pierre's bow was so obsequious as to be the grossest insult and he turned to saunter from the square.

***

Two wet wolves floundered onto a meager strip of shore south of the docks. Crawford was exhausted. For what he prayed to God was the last time for at least a few weeks, his muscles unclenched and his limbs shrank, whole body raw as he winced. He stared into claw-scarred sands as his vision swam and caught the shuffle of wolf's claws as his son backed up several steps. There were none of the shadows of the boat's mid-deck to melt into and cast doubt. He knew as he regained himself that Lucas had seen everything.

To hell with it. Crawford rolled onto his back and panted into the night sky. A wolf's head blocked out some of it with trepidation. "Dad… what are you?"

"Hurt and hungry." Humor wasn't appropriate here. "I'm…a were."

"I don't know what that means." His son looked ready to bolt.

"Twelve years later, neither do I. I might be the only one." It hurt to say it, but when he tried to raise himself off the pebbly sand it ached like hell and his son took another step back. Out of the drink the October air was cool on their dripping hides. The flames of the sinking wreck had extinguished far out, the Iron Ark on its way to the bottom. Rushing surf and night birds calling were all that was left.

"You should go get a blanket back on the dockside and dry off." Crawford realized who would ultimately give one to his son and a dark space filled inside. "While we've got a minute...why did he recruit you?"

Lucas stood on the cusp of turning to flee or charging forward to shout. His mouth worked around a lot chewed up in his mind. "He?"

"Agent Rothscub. It was him, right? My old partner from Chicago?"

Lucas flicked an ear in confusion. "If you mean the Bureau, I got myself in, had to use a fake name until Charlie recognized my smell from somewhere and found me out."

"Fake name?"

Lucas started pacing and a bit of sand kicked onto Crawford's bare-furred arm that he ignored. "I had to. After all, my dad was a deserter from law enforcement. Knowing that made it easy when you—" Lucas stopped and faced the city; his tail lashed. "You didn't explain *any* of this to me, you were just *gone.*"

Crawford faced the sky. He tried to find the right thing to say up there and couldn't. He sighed. "I had to be."

"Why? You son of a bitch, Mom told me you left us because you were too affected by what happened in the war, and that sorry note you left was boilerplate. You had to know what that would do to me, so goddammit tell me why!"

Hundreds of city dwellers who had heard the boat's explosion rumble the bay would be crowding the shores soon enough, seeking a show that was already over. For the moment the secluded inlet had just the two of them, and even if there were better, dryer places for this conversation, they needed to have it out. Lucas didn't deserve to wait any longer.

Crawford forced himself to sit and raised his left hand. It hurt like hell just to make it peek out again, tempt the change to the edge but not succumb, but he did it anyway. Claws grew, knuckles distended and fingers lengthened. Then they slipped back and he gasped. "That's why. It all started after a bite that followed a speak raid. I killed a man who tried to kill me in Chicago, then another. I barely remember either one. Then I met…people who explained it all."

Lucas was furious and Crawford couldn't tell if his cheeks were still wet or getting there. "All this time I thought I lost you to booze and cowardice. So did everybody else. Friends, family, everyone. Do you know how shameful that is?"

Crawford swallowed and it was a hard lump of truth. "Yes. But I'd have hurt you so much worse if I'd stayed. When the change got bad…that was it. There was no way to hold this back. And for that reason, I had to hurt you once. Just once. It was the hardest thing I've ever done."

Lucas stared at him, bitterly coiled from nose to tail with recrimination. "I wanted to be you," Lucas said bitterly, vowels spreading as their shared Virginian accent firmed up the way Crawford's did when his own ire was up. "And when you left and hollowed out my life, I needed to be a better you, one who wouldn't run away. I had to make Mother proud and put you behind me. That's what this was." Lucas jabbed a claw at the bay.

Crawford forced himself to stand and the world heaved. Every muscle screamed at him and he was tired of their complaints. "Yes," he nodded, and forced a smile. "And you did that." He caught his breath. "You've saved lives, Lucas. Lots of them."

They were quiet. The ocean rolled. The city murmured.

Lucas met his gaze. "Agent Rothscub understood how important this was to me, and why. I fought like hell to get on his detail…"

Mention of Charlie pulled at Crawford in a way that hurt, but that would wait. "The Bureau is damn lucky to have you."

Lucas hunted for the right question, wiping away tears. "How often does it…"

"A few times a month, tied to moon, uh, things. Sometimes I need to make it happen."

"Does it hurt?"

"More than a bit but less than too much."

Lucas glanced down then up. "And are you always, uh, naked after?"

Crawford had learned to ignore breezes with experience, realizing now his last pair of slacks were gone. "I have clothes put out for me usually." His hands covered up what he hoped the low light didn't expose too much.

Lucas studiously looked up shore. "I don't know what to make of all this. Everything in the world has changed now. Literally everything."

Crawford thought of Celeste and Samson, somewhere close or far, and decided to leave that subject for now. He saw his son was still dripping. "Can I borrow your jacket?"

"You need to cover up lower than that."

Crawford coughed and instinctively reached to tip a fedora that he'd lost somewhere. "I was going to wrap it like a kilt till I get something else." Waves lapped at the shore and his own scent blew back his way. "I'll launder it, I promise."

Lucas slipped his wet jacket off and passed it over without looking at his father, his expression wearily confused. "I need to get back and call things in."

Charlie would be where he was going, as they'd clearly outnumbered the stragglers left on the dock when the boat had fled.

Crawford was far too tired to change again. For that Charlie should be thankful.

"Oh no," Lucas muttered as the approached the dock. "With all that's happening, I actually forgot!" He hurried up the strand to the nearest dockside building and Crawford grunted as he followed after.

***

Ferrault found his way to the docks along with the goat kid and they saw the conflagration in the distance. A hull's prow raised in prayer, painted by flames at a central breakpoint. Water roiled and the flames were slowly extinguished as water claimed the doomed ship and its sickly light.

"It's beautiful," Samson said. The essence flowing through his veins had spread now, the purest nectar of Delilah's offering. The dose Ferrault bid she consume had been small, not enough to poison the girl, but enough to paint the light of life in the goat kid's eyes and open his mind to endless possibilities.

And wants that inhibition would no longer shame or suppress. Samson could at last see the possibilities ahead.

They stood quiet sentinel on the sands, waves caressing shoreline again and again. It almost surprised Ferrault when one tall crest delivered sputtering cargo.

The bloody and torn suit worn by the German shepherd had been white at some point and reminded Ferrault of the vestments favored by the rabbit Calvert, who was off helping Pierre with whatever vengeful nonsense. The dog before them both scrabbled at sand and threw up seawater, a flap of pelt on one side of his face dangling wet, revealing bone. A glint of light collected the intact side of his features and Ferrault thought he recognized the dog from some newspaper somewhere.

The scent of blood came thick off the dog's hide and Ferrault turned his gaze to Samson. Time for the youth to fly.

The lynx sensed a close shadow nestled in a brick warehouse abutment and bound it before the German shepherd registered the goat's presence.

The dog teetered to his feet coughed up more water. His arm was bleeding along with his face and the ruined side of his muzzle exposed grimacing teeth. "The fuck you staring at?" he asked deliriously in a dialect that Ferrault assumed was affected Georgian.

Samson gazed up at him as he approached, placid and unafraid. "Were you on the ship that…exploded?"

Eyes clouded, then hardened, the shepherd half-aware at best. "That's none of your goddamned business." He slurred his growl. "Go fetch a doctor. Now!"

Samson's body was like a statue without any breath to draw. "I know you, saw you in a movie house news reel. You left all those pamphlets in Hancock." Samson was amused by whatever he remembered from there. "You made a lot of people angry. Not sure what that ever got you."

The German shepherd grunted and stood shakily taller, wounds bleeding freely. "It's getting me my nation back!" He staggered a step towards Samson. The kid was unmoving, a pillar.

"You dare crowd my shores, fill my factories? Hop a steamer back to haggisville and screw ferals you worthless little shit. I'm hurt! Get me! A doctor! Now—" the dog coughed noisily on Samson, eyes a murderous rage without sense.

Ferrault was riveted. This was the perfect initiation, all things considered. He projected his voice just enough that the kid alone could hear him. "Samson, remember what I told you when I introduced you to young Delilah. You won't always need to take lives to fulfill yourself." He couldn't keep the smile out of his voice. "Not always."

"Dammit, go git help!" The German shepherd growled anew and wound back on teetering legs to strike the goat kid.

His swinging arm was intercepted as though Samson had waited a lifetime for it and Ferrault was sorry he couldn't see the look on Samson's face when the kid snapped the wrist like balsa wood.

The German shepherd's voice was gone as it tried to go one register higher in a scream and broke instead. He fell to his knees, wet claws kicking the strand, arm a spasming hook. The dog's eyes met the goat's and Ferrault was treated to Colonel Blake seeing the pits of midnight that were a Nosfur's ready for the feast.

Samson clutched the dog vice-like with both hands and parted fangs that punctured fabric and furred flesh. The already-decimated suit on the struggling dog striped red once more down one breast. The dog shuddered, gasping.

A half dozen yards away seaweed collected at the base of dockside pillars, the darkness under the planks waiting patiently. Samson dragged the struggling German shepherd into that darkness and Ferrault parted from his shadow to get a better look as dog's feet kicked feebly at the last thread of distant light before being swallowed from mortal sight.

Ferrault could hear and see enough.

Samson didn't draw things out but didn't hold back either. The kid was quite thorough.

CHAPTER 24

RECKONINGS TO COME

Crawford and Lucas hurried north around the dock entrance where Hooverville denizens were uneasy at all the law rushing in. Crawford ignored screw-eared looks from mammals armed and cuffed alike as they got close. Boston's finest had arrived to process arrests and Charlie looked up from the radio off the back deck of one of the trucks they'd brought round.

Far offshore, the last sputters of the dead ship were long gone, its cargo now spread a quarter mile from land. Crawford realized dimly that nobody ignorant of what the steel represented would ever bother to dive for it. Donovan Calvert's legacy was where it belonged.

Crawford tried to ignore the eyes roving over his own near nakedness as Lucas hurried through the crowd. Lucas skidded with scrabbling claws to meet Charlie who clapped a hand on Lucas's shoulder and sighed with relief. Crawford glared at the rushed exchange, wiping a myriad of feelings from his face and ears. PI observational powers he'd nurtured for the past decade took over. Only Charlie and one or two others reacted to Lucas wading through the cleanup. The rest of the team were nonplussed and staring at the naked wet wolf using a jacket as a kilt.

The whole team knew his son on sight. That made things better in most ways but worse in at least one.

"You hanging on there, fella?" A fox cop pushed up her cap and gave Crawford a cock-eared lookover. The glance down tried not to be too appraising. Crawford shrugged as he passed. "I got mugged. Too many of you all screwing around down here."

Charlie looked over Lucas's shoulder—that was Agent Marsten's shoulder—and caught Crawford's gaze. Charlie took another deep breath and put the radio squawker back on the suitcase-sized machine, giving

Crawford's son a few more platitudes and attaboys before Lucas whispered something urgent-seeming to him and stepped away.

Crawford wandered round bits of strewn crating and guns.

"He's good," Charlie muttered to the two agents stepping forward to intercept. "Let's get him some pants. Size thirty-four waist by the looks of him."

Playing the stranger. Smart little move on Charlie's part, one he was getting far too good at.

Charlie got back on the radio right away as Crawford approached. "This is Agent Rothscub, all cars notice. Get any available officers over to the Bell in Hand Tavern and start fanning out. Agent Marsten says a brown bear in her early thirties who's a material witness is in immediate danger." The radio squawked back and Lucas sighed anxiously before hurrying back to get the crew caught up.

Crawford stopped with his and Charlie's noses a foot apart and Charlie cupped his ears forward to hear Crawford's cold mutter intended only for him. "Would your entire team like to know, descriptively so, what sounds you make when your ass gets worked over?"

Charlie kept his expression from caving in at Crawford's stewing anger, but his eyes said he understood.

"Then we should talk in private. Right goddamn now."

Charlie cleared his throat. "Mike, get notes from Agent Marsten. Might be a deposition later."

A ring-tailed lemur in a tight suit tipped a hat. "Do you know what happened to Blake?" That was to Lucas with a short glance to Crawford.

Lucas sighed. "We think he went down with the ship. If he didn't, the steel's at the bottom. So are the rest of the guns. Money's in his car. He's got nothing but a waiting arrest warrant."

Charlie nodded. "We've already got police at his hotel. Take over for a minute, Mike."

Charlie led Crawford into the warehouse where more splintered wood hinted at trajectories in a firefight Crawford could still smell. Smeared blood on the dock just outside had no immediately discernible owner. It didn't look like a lot, Crawford hoped.

Around a set of crates was a small office with a couple filing cabinets through a grimy window. Charlie checked the handle. It was locked. "We're out of earshot," he said reluctantly.

"You son of a bitch!" Crawford shouted and it may have echoed across the rafters. He didn't care. "You used my *son* as an informant in a god-damn…whatever the hell all this was!"

"You need to understand—"

"He almost died, Charlie! My son almost—"

"Hold it there, Craw." Spread claws warded him off. Charlie cleared his throat again. "You need to understand some things. When he came to me for a better job in the Bureau he was already making a name for himself, had his badge for a year before I even met him. I didn't know I was putting him in any danger when I signed him on to be an observer. An observer, Crawford, that was all."

"You should have goddamn told me!"

"He didn't want that. He found out who I was through connections he'd made and knew I worked out of the same Prohibition office in Chicago as you at the same time. I didn't lie when I told him we worked together but told him it was complicated." Charlie took another breath. "I gave him a simple stakeout job to build his credentials—"

"Simple. Stakeout."

"Yes, Crawford, you ass. Simple! Go to a rally or two, get info from way in the back, shout 'damn the commies and veggies' once, shake a fist for good measure and get back to me. But he's ambitious to a fault. He met the Colonel, got his ear, played the part like it was a picture audition, and by the time he reported in, well, I suppose Blake saw Lucas was useful in that malleable wanna-please lost-kid sort of way."

"You'd fucking know, wouldn't you?"

"Dammit, Crawford, that's not fair! He's his own man with his own ambitions and he wanted only one thing from me to do this job. That you not know. That you *not know*. He was trying to get out from your shadow, put you behind him exactly the way you wanted him to."

"Charlie, he was in danger. My son was in real danger from the worst of people and I could have helped him."

"That so?" Charlie's brown-flecked eyes bored into Crawford's and hardened. The diplomatic Charlie Crawford had known so long receded and someone furious stepped in. "How? How did you try to help, once you found out he was on that lecture ticket? Which I found out about at the same time you did, by the way. You endangered more than the operation, Crawford. Lucas went all in to sell himself as being for their cause. Had they found out after that who he really was, what he really was, they'd have killed him."

"So why didn't you call it off, Charlie?"

Charlie looked away. "There was no backing out from the role he'd taken on. And he'd taken on a responsibility that meant everything to him. His country needed him, still needs him, in fact. Don't you get it, Crawford? It's exactly what we talked about. Lucas is trying to actually make the world something we can call better. How many cops taking hush from Torrio's crew while we were in the Windy City did it take to jade you and me? Most days it felt like we were just cashing a check. When I think of quitting all this, it's people up and coming in the Bureau, like Lucas, who quite literally keep me going. Take some damn pride knowing your son did that. Not for me. For everybody those smuggled guns were going to be pointed at."

Silence between them carried the drifting sounds of agents on the move outside, Lucas among them. Crawford tried to pick out his son's voice but couldn't.

Charlie groaned. "And now Lucas has to be complicit in another dangerous lie, doesn't he?"

"What the hell does that mean?" Crawford's head hurt. Everything hurt, but Charlie's anger cut him worse. He'd been the one who lied, endangered his son…

"I can guess where your latest set of clothes went, Crawford. Did he see you change? Did he see you kill anybody?"

Crawford opened his mouth to answer and snapped it shut.

"That would be a yes. So, your son, despite all you told me you wanted, knows what you are. He knows what's in you. That was another thing I was trying to avoid in having you meet under stressful circumstances, Crawford, despite wanting to tell you every damn time we spoke. I worried like hell about that. And now he's going to have to keep your secret in depositions where lies are literally treason. Did anybody on that boat live?"

Crawford felt his anger cool and freeze over. The tone of Charlie's voice told Crawford what he meant. And how he meant it. "I remember…finishing one or two. I didn't see any survivors in the water when the ship blew."

"A long way offshore in the dead of night. You both made it so it stands to reason that somebody might wash up downstream spitting guppies. If so, and if they saw, we three will need to have it straight that they're crazy. Nuthouse, sleeveless-jacket loony. It'll be an easy sell for traitors to the country." Charlie's eyes were hard and it hurt him to say what he said next. "We might even have to make sure they don't talk at all. You know what that means, don't you?"

Crawford felt the wind leave him. All he'd tried to do, everyone he'd tried to protect, and to this… "Yeah."

"How's it feel to be thrust into an impossible place, Crawford?" Charlie fumed, his own claws flexing as though he was holding back a change of his own. "No choice but to handle what comes to you and lie to those you love just to protect them. Think it might tire you out after a while?"

Crawford's eyes were wet. He still felt the ember of betrayal, at being pushed out of something critical to all he held dear, but above it all he felt empty, defeated. "Fuck you, Charlie."

He turned and stormed out.

***

Pierre led Celeste westward to a massive expanse with its elms and pines arrayed across the rolling mall. The Boston Commons was America's oldest parkland and Celeste knew fragments of its history. She would have loved to wander it with Sandy arm in arm but forced herself to remain calm and contained for Samson's sake. She'd made her choice.

"They used to have whipping posts and stocks here for pirates and other criminals, didn't they?" she muttered bitterly and Pierre ignored her, his expression an unconvincing mask of triumph that failed to bury his unfulfillment.

The presences that Celeste had sensed near Faneuil Hall were more plainly in attendance here as they followed the wide byways past wooden benches dimly illuminated by the buzz of electric tungsten lamps. One or two Nosfurs bound shadows out past the flowerbeds. Mortals out to take the evening air openly watched her as the two deer took a left turn off Tremont Street and passed a wrought-iron fountain. After the first dozen pairs of eyes were counted Celeste realized that those Pierre associated with may literally be legion.

A beat cop dog with short grey fur gave the two ungulates a once-over but let the vegetarians go unchallenged. Shadows were close enough that his life would have been endangered had he done so.

"Where's Samson?"

There was no answer.

Celeste turned and Pierre was gone, shadows interspacing park details around her for what seemed like a mile in all directions. "Pierre?" Wind disturbed vegetation. Mammals on her periphery stalked around, ignoring her. "Pierre!"

The area of the park she turned in was nondescript, a grassy rolling area with only a small plaque in the ground, copper oxidized in mossy emerald. The top line demarking the place Pierre had abandoned her read: "SITE OF THE GREAT ELM".

"Celeste?"

A shadow released Samson from the cover of a slimmer tree not ten yards away and the goat wandered over, confused. Celeste nearly felt her still heart skip as he approached. "Samson." She caught her voice and tried to keep emotions contained. Countless hidden spies no doubt sorted her slimmest hope from her pain like buzzards looking for ripest flesh. "Are you safe?"

He tottered over dreamily and Celeste caught sight of his clothes. The shirt he wore was smeared with blood, a feast finished messily. She smelled wet dog and terror-stink and something else on the goat's aura that was sickly familiar. Samson didn't walk into her embrace, but rather wandered up to the plaque, glanced at it as if it contained something of interest, then regarded her stonily. He blinked at her question. "I'm alright," he said defensively, as though unsure why she'd ask.

"Do you know what made that elm great? The one reflected on in the plaque?" The voice was at her shoulder and far away at once and she knew it immediately. Ferrault let her see him coming. His feet were light on the grass, his suit jacket and blade-pleat trousers grey. His bare milky chest played with the moonlight over the jacket's yawning vee and the white lily peering from his breast pocket caught its glint. His eyes, the same piercing gaze that held a mortal doe's in a revolutionary cell over a century past, took her in and his tufted ears were piqued and ever attentive. "The tree that fell here in eighteen seventy-six was used to hang many of the criminals you told Pierre about. Robbers, thieves, apostates. So many lives passed the veil right here in the oldest Eden America ever curated. A country is only as good as the bones it's built on, after all."

Celeste met his gaze, remembering their last encounter in the shadow of her dead parents and sibling, Pierre in stocks. Slapping Ferrault then had been just one of a thousand violent casual acts to come.

And just maybe the only one that was ever justified. "You killed her."

"Her?" Ferrault cocked an ear, confused. "I killed no one. Who are you referring to? I've heard about—"

"You killed Sandy!" Celeste hissed and her fangs went low. "If not then bring her and show me."

"I've no idea who you're talking about, Celeste. Samson has been taking the night air with me and he's recently dined," he recalled with amusement. "Twice in fact."

"Sandy's dead?" Samson asked Celeste, blinking. He seemed confused, unfocused. "I haven't seen her at all tonight."

Celeste jabbed a finger at the lynx. "You had Pierre, your lickspittle thug, offer me one life to be returned, Samson's or Sandy's. I was told that the other would be killed!" She took a step towards Ferrault and was shocked to see Samson hurry to step between them.

"Celeste! I'm not in any danger. I never was. I was careful, worried at first, but Ferrault showed me things I can't describe," Samson raised his hands to the sky and there was relief in his voice. "There's another way forward for us. I've seen it. We don't have to hide all the time."

"What the hell are you talking about?" Celeste felt panic rise as she looked into Samson's placid gaze and didn't recognize what lay inside.

Samson reached out his hand and took hers, squeezing it. Dog blood crusted it and his gaze seemed as blissful and disaffected as Ferrault's. "We can be more than what we are, you, Sandy, and me, wherever she is right now. Possibly even Crawford."

"Possibly even him." Ferrault made a thoughtful noise.

"Sandy's dead! Samson, your teacher and my friend is gone! They told me they would kill her or you and I had to choose which—"

"I never said any such thing," Ferrault said, eyes widening with shock. "I've wanted you back at my side for years, Celeste. Why would I kill your squirrel?" His eyes were hurt and yet Celeste saw what stirred behind them. His smile was a cold empty thing. "What purpose would that ever serve of mine?"

Celeste squeezed Samson's bloody hand again with both of hers and pulled. "We need to get out of Boston, now!"

She pulled and Samson's hooves dug into the Common's lawn. They dragged nearly two feet of soil up before he shook off her grip. "No!"

Celeste met his gaze and saw the anger return that had been bubbling back since the embers of Scranton. "Samson, you don't understand how much danger we're in. We have to get as far from here as we can."

"From danger?" Samson scoffed and stamped a hoof, his placid demeanor crumbled. "Really? To where?" Samson ground his teeth together. His fangs, recently bloodied, came and receded. "Our last home burned down when the Martyres came. The one before that had to be abandoned because we thought they were close. We're not safe anywhere."

"You don't know him." She pointed a finger at a disdainfully disappointed lynx. "He can't be trusted, Samson."

"You don't know him either! France was lifetimes ago!" His brogue crept in and he bowed his stubbed horns. "You've not the first clue what any of them really want or what our destiny should be. I'm tired of running away from everything, painting useless throwaway houses in weed-infested dead ends."

Celeste tried to keep calm, searched Samson's gaze for understanding, but there was an almost instinctive obstinance, that same anger that had crept into every gesture since Scranton and too often before. "Samson, please listen. Come with me and we'll talk about this. But not here, not where they're all watching us."

Samson sighed and hurt crept into his eyes. "That's the thing. That's what I'm trying to tell you. They care about us, Celeste. They have friends for us, Ferrault and all the rest. I've met them. I'm actually wanted here. Do you know how long I've desperately needed that? I've already taken steps to fixing things." He gestured to the smeared crimson on his shirt and Celeste froze.

"Samson, whose blood is that?"

"Somebody who damn well deserved it."

"Samson…"

"It was easy to fix him, good fun even. Just like the cats in that alley. I'm using my power for what it's meant for, not watching the world turn from a basement. We actually have the chance to make things better and Ferrault has a plan!"

She glared at Ferrault. "I don't know what nonsense you fed him but I want Sandy back! Give her back to me!"

"I can't give you what I don't have." Ferrault genuinely looked confused. "I never did."

"Then make Pierre give her back!" Celeste saw more shapes at the periphery of the meager lamplight now. A few Nosfur-disturbed shadows, a larger flock of mortals, silent and expectant.

"I don't know who that is, Celeste. In fact, if I recall correctly whom you're referring to, you killed him yourself quite a long time ago, in the Place de la Révolution. You drained him dry and then you struck me." He closed his eyes and beneficently banished the memory. "If someone claiming that name did approach you with a threat of some sort, well, I'd think you may have been played the fool."

The pity that leaked from behind Ferrault's sympathetic smile was glass through the heart. Celeste was sure of it, Ferrault knew. As for Sandy, dead, not dead, but very likely suffering or made to have suffered.

No closure without knowledge, no release without acceptance. Her worthless elk paramour had another wound to draw even deeper from wherever he'd fled to.

"Celeste," Samson tugged on her sleeve and dragged her gaze back. "Please," he said low. "Let me look for her. If somebody really does have her, I'll find out. Ferrault can help us."

"No," she whispered, voice cracking. She'd given her love to so few, and now she was on the verge of losing them both. "Samson, please listen very carefully, you can't go with them. They've lied to me already. They're lying to you right now."

"No. I'm resourceful, Celeste," Samson said soothingly, and for a moment she could hear the full weight of his twenty-five years of existence: yearning, wanting, but unwavering nonetheless. "I'll find out what we need to know and—"

"They won't let you go, Samson." Desperation was a wild thing that chased her heels with teeth. Samson was being toyed with, his anxieties stoked, groomed with his own fragile pride. "They'll needle their way into you, like the rabbit did with Sandy, making you doubt yourself, making you let go of everything you've ever felt dear. I can't let you go." Celeste felt the panic rise with her own plaintive cry. "You have to come with me!"

Confusion clouded Samson's face, a well of doubt dredged up from the depths. His lip quivered under shrinking fangs as he saw the earnest demand in her eyes.

Then his expression twisted with a growling contempt. He struck her, knocking Celeste back on her haunches. "I hate you!" His hiss broke in a sob. "Everything I've done, everything I've tried so hard to prove to you, but you never had any faith in me at all!" He backed away, fists shaking. "Just a clueless infant whom you'll never respect, a stand-in for your sister." He grit his teeth in sorrow. "I'm through living as a fucking keepsake doll to keep you and your guilt apart! I never want to see you again!" He spun, racing deep and far across the grass, through the boughs and into the refuge of shadows.

Celeste was numbed as she fell to her knees, gazing off into the long dark. The October cold settled over her as moments passed and Samson didn't return. Shadows were legion here, hundreds if not thousands of sanctuaries occupied by those who'd proudly thwart her search.

A voice drifted from somewhere close. "If I could only have tears to bottle," Pierre muttered gaily, fading away. Something trickled on a breeze in her direction, littering the grass.

Celeste closed her eyes and cried and when she finally opened them again, all were gone save Ferrault. He stood beneficently, his gaze a tableau of contemptuous pity. Samson was his. He barely needed hide his triumph now. "Celeste, you poor soul. I've seen that clapboard dollhouse of domesticity and I'd have burned it down myself to save you if fate hadn't intervened. So much worse that you tried to trap Samson in that lie with you, haunting a world that wants none of us. I wish you'd learned my first lesson. But after all this time, after all your experiences, you still haven't learned to let go of the mortal anchors that hold you down. I'm so very sorry for you."

He turned and melted away, leaving Celeste to stare numbly into the dark. A frail wind tumbled detritus that caressed her knee and she collected the silken fabric that smelled faintly of squirrel.

Her fangs erupted anew and Celeste keened like a dying thing.

Chapter 25

Swears

Sandy hurt. The collar had been taken away but the manacles were tight. It didn't surprise her too much to discover upon regaining awareness that she was naked. She felt the cool air of the dank room on her nipples and privates where she lay, her hands bound above her as she sat against brickwork.

"I'm at a quandary," Donovan said from somewhere nearby.

"Spike through the eyeball will solve all problems," she suggested helpfully.

"I have an order to carry out…" He heaved an exaggerated sigh. Nosfurs usually relinquished breath-emoting in their first year. Here the idiot was a dozen of them later. "I had instructions regarding you from Ferrault that were challenging enough. New ones came from that elk that kisses his arse."

"Whichever told you to let me go was right." Sandy opened an eye and saw him staring at her from a rickety wooden chair. Once, long ago, she'd have yearned for his eyes on her body. Now it was slimy and distasteful, like the lechery of a barber who would certainly trim too close down low. His attempt at appearing modest while stealing glances was downright pathetic.

The room around them both had brick walls and a damp planked celling, certainly underground, likely still in Boston. Ocean salt touched her nose faintly.

"Ferrault wanted me to gain your forgiveness in order to be welcome in his…group. Or so he told me before passing your…acquisition on to Pierre."

There was mild pain from the collar, which rested on a bench at the room's opposite corner. Donovan kept far from it of course and she knew that he'd expend a little pain to put it back on if she was too sharp with him. "And…?"

"And the elk, Pierre, wants your head in a bag. Or your tail. He was a bit indifferent."

"One has me dead and the other maimed so I'm sure not."

"He's a vicious bastard." Donovan crossed his legs, glanced at her breasts, glanced away. "I rather like Ferrault's original request, but the fact is, I can't be sure you can ever forgive me."

Honesty came far too easily, even when it was ill-advised. "You can be sure I wouldn't. Which of you perverted swine decided I'd be bare-arsed?"

"That was Pierre. And I'll confess that after the months you kept me that way in my own house it initially felt…just. After, well, I'm not sure what he wanted your clothes for."

"He a sniffer?"

"Quite possibly. Not sure if that's a French predilection."

Sandy rolled her eyes. "That's not—Forget that. Wanting my forgiveness as you say you do, you didn't put up much resistance in my favor."

He stood and glanced her way once more before pacing. He had a new suit on, darker, a bit loose fitting, off the rack. The rabbit looked like a scolded accountant. "I wasn't in a position to refuse. And yet, I can't confess enough just how difficult it would be to cut your head off and give it to the elk as instructed."

"Unless the elk lied to you and this Ferrault cat wants no such thing. Delivering my head helps Ferrault resolve to put yours in another sack. The elk wouldn't have any competition for the puma's favors."

"Lynx."

"Like I give a feck."

Donovan nodded dejectedly. "Their wishes notwithstanding, I don't want to kill you, Sandy. In spite of everything, you see what kind of trouble I'm in."

"Yes. *You're* in it quite a bit," she replied evenly as she shook her manacles. It only made him glance down at her chest again and she rolled her eyes. "I would make a strong case for not killing me."

"I don't want to do that anyway," he said in a small voice quite unlike the one she'd known in all their time together.

"That's good. Fact of it is, I'm all that's between you and things far worse than destruction."

He was dubious, but miserable enough to listen. "Is that so?"

"It's more than so." Sandy's legs were getting as stiff as her arms so she brought them up close to her, hiding her breasts, but providing more of a glimpse of her sex. At least he didn't look down at that. Then he did that exactly. Pervert. "Let me tell you a little about the last twelve years. I looked for your nails but found so much more. I'm afraid you aren't going to like where this is going."

His wilted gaze had a spark of fear in it. Sandy didn't mind that one damn bit. "You, Donovan Calvert, are a legend. In all the worst ways. If Ferrault told you that you're not loved among our kind, he didn't seek that information out. Nor did I. Every one of us on this side of the Atlantic knows why downtown Chicago is a torture chamber along with many haunts all around the country, everywhere your steel wound up when your company went tits up."

Donovan returned to the chair and fell into it like a string-cut marionette. "So, you're saying I should flee to England."

"Nosfurs know how telegrams work, Donovan. Telephones too. You'd have to find a map to the farthest corner of the earth to find a place where they don't want to impale you on a shipmast. Won't give that too long either."

"Dammit, you helped me do it all!"

"As an unwilling slave, which I emphasize when making new acquaintances near Chicago." She jingled the manacles again. "And you've kept to tradition."

She enjoyed seeing reality crush his last delusion of supremacy or even independence. The room shrunk around him as his ears wrapped back and she caught his eye by letting one leg slip down. "I'm chained to this wall, Don, but face facts. You're chained to this very world, a prisoner every place you go. The lynx may favor you for a time but somebody is going to have to fall when one of his schemes comes asunder and you're everyone's favorite place to pin a dart. We both know it."

Donovan began hyperventilating at that moment. Nothing went in or out but he stared into space as he imitated a boat-bottomed trout. It was frankly embarrassing. "I don't know what to do," he said at last.

"Serve me," Sandy said.

"What?"

"Let me go and fecking serve me!"

"I can't let you go! They expect me to kill you."

"And then your usefulness ends if you ever had any." Sandy pressed. "If he has other Nosfurs around then they'll be whispering every chance they get for you to die. So stop! Think! You want forgiveness from me as I'm the only one who can save you from all of them out there in the world. T'ain't coming while I'm chained naked to a wall, Donovan."

Silence fell as he worked through variables. "They want a part of you sent to Celeste, to prove you're lost and gone. A tail will be proof enough."

"You may as well kill me. I can't keep balance without—"

"I can obtain one if I have to. Either a red one, or another I can dye."

"How…" She shut her mouth. He was coming around. Sandy could feel it and hope was a line she'd grasp. "I have to get free, find Celeste."

"They'll be watching her. Ferrault doesn't care that much but that elk wants to see her mourn you. He's rather sick and obsessed."

"Coming from you…So, if I'm presumed dead I can slip out and search surreptitiously. I'll need to find her."

"Only if you can do so without being detected. If you even reach out to a single one of our kind who you know and it gets back to Ferrault—"

"I can help you escape whatever Ferrault wants of you. Hell, we both already know that you'd go badly when he's done with you."

He was up and pacing again. Annoyingly, he reminded her of herself with that. "That has occurred to me," he muttered. "Too frequently."

"Sooo…" She jangled her bonds again.

"I'll get you new clothes."

"And then?"

"What…" Donovan stopped and leaned against one wall as though holding the place up. "What do you want me to do to regain your devotion? We'll have to run, Sandy, both of us, from everyone. If they discover I've not killed you as instructed…they may finish both of us."

"Get right acquainted with this. You aren't getting my devotion. Ever. You may get me to not kill you. First you'll take me to somewhere they can't find."

"I have, already. I rented this place under an assumed name." A tincture of anger crept in as he froze. "And if we're putting up terms then let me be clear in return. If you turn me in, to any of our kind out there, I'll make sure with my last dying…sound, that they know that you were a full partner in all we did in Chicago. You tied them down while the sun—"

"One of us regrets all the hurt we caused." Sandy gazed daggers at him. "The other only regrets getting caught." Sandy thought then of Celeste, presuming Sandy lost, mourning. She didn't want to do that to her again, even though she realized that Celeste would be on the run herself. It could take weeks, months, or even longer to find a doe who didn't want to be found, which Celeste would no doubt want after her life burning down. "I've sinned against everyone I ever cared for but found my way to penance. If you're truly sorry for all you've made me suffer, for all of us you've made suffer, you'll do something else for me to really prove that you are turning over a new leaf, that you really value my forgiveness. Or anyone's for that matter."

Donovan swallowed his useless throat and went to her, sitting cross-legged on the dusty floor. His eyes met hers and by not trying to ogle the delectable parts she knew he was at least serious in his own head. "Name it."

"Back in Atlantic City I have a camera in my flat. Make whatever excuses you must to get out there. You're going to get that camera, drive north to where the beachline ends, look for a strand where the sand is hilly and an upright plank of wood stands with a letter 'B' etched in it."

"Yes?"

"Get Bruno out of that sand and give him a proper burial. Take photographs to prove it. Once you've interred him properly come back to me. And we'll talk."

Donovan's face fell anew and his mouth worked to put together the right words. "Are you serious?"

"As a heart that can henceforth not be attacked. You owe it to Bruno no less than me. I'll hide here, plan our escape from this coterie of beasts you're tied up with. When you and I bust our way out from Ferrault's long shadow we'll be on the run then. You'll need my help to avoid the barrel and the stones."

"The what?" He was terrified and the sight was great to see.

"I met with a lot of angry Nosfurs while tracking down your nails. I told you that. Well, there are ways to deal with Nosfurs who cheat or harm other Nosfurs and it involves barrels sealed shut with just enough stones to sink. Alternatively there's the saw-log split-leg slide, for those who want things done quicker with mill gear at hand. The living boiler still with the copper tube to the gullet was a bit fanciful sounding, but the marmot who narrated that one over a cow's blood snifter was sure that he could get—"

"Alright! Damn it all, Sandy. Anything! We'll have to hurry. My time is as short as yours, I think."

Sandy smiled. "Do you have the key to these manacles?"

"The elk does."

"Well," Sandy said. "The feel you've been looking to cop is going to be in an elk's pocket then, isn't it? That or you'd better get a decent hammer. However long I'm here, I'm not staying on this feckin' wall."

Donovan Calvert closed his eyes and ran fingers up his ears, a rabbit salve against the onset of headaches that did less now that he was clinically unalive. "I'm honestly hoping that you and I can rekindle some of what we lost in Chicago after we get free of all this."

"No," Sandy said with cold amusement. "But we won't kill each other. That'll be grand enough."

***

The police search ended back at the Bell in Hand, where they learned that the bear waitress had returned an hour after leaving, alive, seemingly disquieted but calm. She'd bought two other mammals pints with her tips, and then quit. So, service for the celebrating off-duty cops and straggling nocturnals was slow.

Crawford sat across a table from Lucas, the two of them looking past one another. Crawford had a whiskey in front of him and Lucas had a beer losing its foam. Crawford could see that his son's anger had been salved for now, but the spectres of abandonment had weighed him for so long and healing the damage of over a decade would take a long while. Crawford had barely known his own father before pneumonia killed him, his mother following a year after his marriage to Kamila. Looking back, he knew that having a loved one taken was far less painful than what Lucas had gone through.

Now that his son knew why, there was the chance at least for something to be regained. "You probably need to hear it from me least of anybody, but you really kept to the role. You honestly had me convinced that you...that you believed in what they were selling."

Lucas's gaze touched his and Crawford felt the storm that had driven Lucas to the badge and its dangers. "I cracked once or twice. On top of trying to get word out about the bear, I almost lost it all on stage," Lucas said.

"The rally?"

Lucas nodded. "Tonight, before the dock meet I tripped through the speech I'd written to impress the Colonel and stared past all those angry faces at the calm ones, right at the back, the wigs who put up Blake's money. I almost gave it all up in front of hundreds."

Crawford watched his son ponder darker possibilities and put a hand on his. "It took a Herculean effort to play along as far as you did, facing all of that down, especially while playing to both the mob and Blake's pursestring holders at the same time."

Lucas chuffed. "Not one of the real instigators will ever pay a price for it. We don't even have Blake."

"You've a long career ahead of you. One battle at a time, right?" Crawford smiled and sipped his bourbon.

Lucas needed to change the subject. "I've been thinking about Mother...you should call her."

Crawford met his son's gaze for just a moment and saw the frankness in it. It touched him even though he disagreed. "She moved on. That was for the best."

Lucas sighed and sipped his lager. "You come up when we talk sometimes. Whatever you said on that last visit...she didn't feel the same about letting you go."

"I was at least partly honest about why I left," Crawford said. "The drinking pushed the worst of what I was feeling up and away, even if just for a little while."

"And did that ever make you happy?" Lucas seemed afraid of the answer.

Crawford looked down into his bourbon's sepia glaze. "No. It can't ever do that. It can only make you feel numb in the way you're most comfortable with. After the war, I felt I needed to be numb." He had no idea how to unravel what he said next. "Chicago certainly didn't help."

Lucas thought on that, picked his next words carefully. "Does my mother know about…"

"Not that." The same mental arithmetic that made Crawford's nature—his first one—a concern in every circle he'd moved in from the war onward started up in earnest. How much to tell, how honest to be. Lies, even the ones he needed, hurt. "I wasn't entirely loyal to your mother while I was in the war. And I found out that I had other…needs."

Lucas thought and his eyebrow raised a bit. "Like the brickhouse dames who work the howitzers and landships in the pictures I've seen? I didn't really think much on it but with the body that, uh, condition gives you I could see a couple bears catch your eye." Lucas shrugged, neither approving nor judgemental. He'd grown up far too fast and it hurt Crawford a bit to see not one trace of boyish naivete holding on.

Lucas met his gaze as a battalion of answers tripped through Crawford's sore head, each more potent with truth than the last.

They both had toes in law enforcement and the carnivores' club. And it would always drag its hooks into how one saw the world. Pansies, limp-wrists, faggots…

"Maybe bears." Crawford gritted his teeth and his ears went low in shame at the lie. What Lucas knew was already too much to handle. And if he figured out that Crawford had bedded his boss…The wall came up, smelling of cheap May-heat perfume. "The point is, I stepped out. I begged her not to tell you. It wouldn't have changed anything anyway. It was my other…matter, that truly kept me away. I'm serious about how badly I could have hurt you. Even with better control now, and help…" Crawford realized that Lucas's mother now had one truth about him and his son had the other and he didn't know how to resolve that.

"Help from whom?"

Crawford knew things would have to go in this direction and even now he wasn't sure how much to say. Secrets burying other secrets. Lucas needed to know about this. "What I have isn't the only thing, well, out there." Crawford waved a hand around and Lucas glanced from his beer to the sparser corners of the tavern where taps were pulled, a kitten fiddler counted coins in her battered case, and deep shadows collected. It occurred to Crawford that he didn't know where Celeste or Samson were just then and that one of the shadows at the inn's musty corners could be holding somebody he knew. Or someone he didn't.

"What other things?" Lucas was intrigued and Crawford could see that his fur was rising a bit. How to put this...

"You see *Dracula?*"

"With the Romanian cat guy who became a bat and drank blood?"

"That picture, yeah."

"That's...real?"

"No. Not exactly." Introducing him to Celeste or Samson would be interesting. "They aren't evil agents of Satan or any of that bushwah. I've met a few and...live with two of them. Just as friends," he added quickly.

Lucas raised his ears. "Are they here?"

"I've not seen Celeste or Samson in hours. Not worried yet as they'd have stayed away from the steel on the docks."

"The steel Blake was selling?"

"That's a long story. But you need to hear it."

Lucas was intrigued now. He'd barely touched his beer and nearly knocked it over when he leaned Crawford's way. "Just tell me first, if there are Draculas out there and they aren't all friends, how much danger are we all in?"

He'd asked himself this very question every day for the last twelve years and had to confess, "From...them? I don't know. I learned that most just want to live their lives, getting by in circumstances that try the best of us. Some even want to make the world a bit better."

"For whom?" Lucas asked.

***

Boston had been a successful outing but Ferrault was ready to put it behind him. The plan would keep him in America, but further west where he had prospects.

Samson had been sequestered and Delilah was with him, comforting him as she knew best. Such dedicated family were more than Ferrault knew he himself deserved. Samson would need that in turn to realize his full potential.

Hooves clicked as Pierre approached and Ferrault didn't turn from the window overlooking the bay. He missed the Royal York in Toronto. Such a tidily kept little world that he couldn't return to now. The papers were far too dramatic about the state of Room 916. "Yes."

"We lost track of her."

"Celeste, you mean?"

"She may be scouring the city for her squirrel."

"You saw to Alisandre?"

The pause sought the most agreeable lie but Ferrault didn't mind. "I'm sure the rabbit did his job. He fears you and hates her. I was told we'll have a tail." So performatively differential. That was Pierre.

"You mean you'll have a tail, you sick bugger." Ferrault turned and gave the elk a baleful look. "How goes the other work?"

"We're moving on Scranton at this moment. I just got off the telephone with our friends there."

"Keep it tidy. The law will likely have moved on now that they've picked the scene clean. We'll know we've found what we seek when the pain starts."

"Of course." Pierre nodded shallowly.

"And the other business?"

"Ah, the name that Celeste provided? That proved very fruitful. We've found a recent registry, twelve years old. I can have the right location within a month or even less."

"No hurry." Ferrault smiled, close-lipped.

Pierre was rooted to the spot. "No? I would have thought you'd want to have this resolved quickly. The state of—"

"I can very well imagine the state. And I can imagine how much more amicable that state will be if we're patient."

The room went down a few degrees in temperature. Pierre didn't have much empathy, but he did understand what the consequences of waiting too long would be. "Amicable? But your plan—"

"Involves Samson most prominently, and we have him already. I'll need time to work on him, decant him like a fine wine, help him see purpose, and through purpose, resolve. As for the other player we need, well, the longer we wait, the more malleable the material to work with will be. We have to time things very precisely to set our liberation in motion. Trust me."

Pierre met his gaze and saw that he was serious. "How long?"

"Not long at all. Perhaps another decade. Maybe more."

Pierre shuddered and opened his mouth to retort, but Ferrault's placid gaze silenced him. "Patience is the virtue we are free to benefit from above all other creatures crawling on this earth. I gave you the revenge you sought and you had your fun. You simply need to do a night's work when the time comes that will benefit us all. Be ready."

Pierre nodded and said no more.

***

A day after the raid, Charlie sat alone in his room at the Omni Parker House in Boston at a narrow desk, staring at a dossier that had just been couriered. Photos peeked out but he didn't want to look at them now. He wouldn't be sad to leave this place behind him, was getting sick of hotels in general. The telephone rang on schedule. "A Douglas Grenwall is coming up to see you."

"Thank you." Charlie hung up. An hour prior, Hoover had congratulated him for defeating the communist menace, and to no surprise J. Edgar was taking credit for the operation that wound up giving the team a slight pay bump and a little time off. Edgar hadn't seemed to give a damn that the insurrectionists were actually fascists or that hundreds if not thousands of bamboozled poor and destitute spread Colonel Blake's poison across the nation. Somebody had had the director's ear all too quickly.

There was a knock at the door.

"It's unlocked."

The door opened under a gloved hand that receded, and a puma backed into the hall as the fossa entered. The fossa's homburg was in his hand, eyes studiously soft and supplicatory over a hard mouth. The door closed behind him with the slowness of an apologetic whisper.

"I have come, Agent Rothscub, to congratulate you personally on the capture of Colonel Blake's posse and restoration of order to Boston."

"Why, thank you," Charlie said evenly and didn't get up.

The fossa noticed and wrinkled his nose. "I do hope that you will continue to show my good friend Edgar how we handle communist infiltrators with the same rigor—"

"They weren't communists, Mister Grenwall. I've been debriefed extensively on the Colonel's motivations for what he did and what he sought to recruit for—"

"And yet, as we both see, he betrayed this government by arming for insurrection against it." The fossa had grit in his voice. "He lied to me about the reasons for his funding as he did his other benefactors from all over this country. Such a thing would surely make him a radical."

Charlie had a poured drink that he lifted off the desk, set it down, and let it slosh to punctuate a thought. "Interesting choice of words, Mr. Grenwall, all over the nation you say."

The fossa read the edge in Charlie's voice and showed a bit of teeth, just a bit. His nose rose, just a bit. The dominance was funny considering Charlie outmassed him by about twenty pounds. "And why would that be an interesting observation, Agent?"

"Special Agent." Charlie wiggled his eyebrows. "Well…" Charlie stood then, and wandered past the fossa who had to step just slightly out of his way to let Charlie see the mirror. There were shadows behind Charlie that framed him as he glared at his own reflection for the briefest instant. "We have the names and identities of quite a few who attended yesterday's rally at the Emerson. Everybody who stood at the back and everyone who mounted that stage has a name and a face. Did you stick around for Doctor Koffler's pitch? A year ago he was settling a lawsuit for ligament-healing creams with leather-polish bases, and yet for three nights with Blake he was talking about vegetarian brain masses."

"Some colorful characters came to entertain the rabble." Grenwall shrugged. "I'm not any authority on their scientific qualifications. What of it?"

"Colorful characters had a lot of the segregationist-leaning well-to-do pretty excited, and the one thing that unites most of them is that they all maintain business interests in cities and states that the Colonel's travelling circus crossed. All except yourself. You are the operator and owner of over two thousand acres of fruit orchards in the Salinas Valley of California.

Considering that the Colonel wasn't the only hate-rally act in circulation, it's strange that you picked his to finance."

Grenwall was uncomfortable now. "He presented himself as a patriot whom I met in the course of business out this way. I was lied to like all the others."

"And yet you followed him through all six stops in parts of the country where dust storms rendered the land not worth a damn. That's why, care of my many eyes, we had your name first, and had plenty of time to do some digging on you."

The fossa drew himself up and was openly baring his teeth now. Charlie could smell the man's hostility loading the room.

"I came up to congratulate you, and for this you're casting aspersions and—"

"I'll be more direct then. Have a seat, won't you?" Charlie returned to the desk chair and pointed at the bed's edge. Grenwall disdained it with a tail lash and a lowering of his dark ring-shaped ears.

Charlie folded his leg. "You've got no European connections that I'm aware of and I doubt you speak any Latin. Call it a hunch that you aren't connected to that particular scam of Blake's."

"What does Latin have to do with a goddamn thing?"

"Nothing. Boring story. Here's the one that's good." Charlie knocked back the whiskey and wondered if he'd regret that soon. "Your name turns up on a lot of California wires and papers that the Bureau reads and I wonder: Why would somebody who has a literal labor revolt going on out where Roosevelt's triple-A subsidies are scaling back crops to raise prices be all the way out East following these anger rallies when you're accused of both underpaying workers and raising prices simultaneously out on your own turf? Is that because, just maybe, nobody would be expected to know who the hell you even are out here?"

"My movements are none of your concern!" Grenwall barked. The door opened behind him and the puma leaned in only to be shooed back out. The door closed more quickly but oh so softly.

Charlie grinned, feeling just a little looser even as his heart quickened. "Did it disappoint you to learn that the Colonel was seeking two paydays at once? He was moving steel offshore while moving untraceable weapons on shore through the same conduit. The guns he collected are impressive, half a city armoury's worth, but not enough to mount any major assault on a federal building. It would be perfect if, for sake of argument, they were used to violently suppress a revolt of unarmed farmers who are starving while picking peaches at pennies on a crate. Deed done by out-of-town agents who faded away. You could try to pin it on anyone you wanted. No weapons purchases under the firearms act would be traced back to you."

The fossa hissed and took three stomping steps towards Charlie's desk and Charlie, tired, fed up, and now nursing cold loneliness, was more than ready. He rose, grabbed the rich mammal by his ample lapels and put him against the wall with a growl.

"How dare you?" Grenwall spat. "Do you know that I could have you fired? Or worse? You're literally nobody."

Charlie felt a smile light his lips. The weight of Douglas Grenwall's presumptions were as insubstantial as a feather, and all at once he felt inexplicably powerful as he truly realized that for the first time.

"Shut up, Douglas. You picked the wrong friends. Not just Blake, who exposed you six ways from Sunday for his own greed, but my own boss. If Edgar gets even a sniff of what this really is, he won't risk the damage it could do to his Bureau or his precious career, he'll throw you to the waves. What choice would he have? Roosevelt's White House is riding him to cut down crime in America, people are still destitute, and everybody hates livelihood-thieving opportunists like you with a passion." Charlie twisted the fossa's tie and the man swallowed. "Yes, Grenwall, I'm little people, but so is everybody I put my faith in. Doesn't matter how the winds shift, there will always be people like me who see you and your ilk for what you really are and this nation literally can't function without us. You can't purge this government of us if you pull every string you know or spend every cent you have. If you want to see how things can go you just goddamn try it."

"You can't—"

Charlie leaned in close and he could smell something buttery on the fossa's breath that made him want to gag. He held his gaze with pitiless eyes. "Go back to that expensive house you own in San Lorenzo overlooking the river with those French windows facing west over those miles of rolling hills to the ocean. My people told me everything a working mammal's sweat can buy for a privileged man like you. Go back and look down on all those angry people lured there with the promise of work who you had fighting over scraps before they became too much of a problem. Put your head down on that soft pillow and wonder how long you'd have after you hear glass breaking. We know reporters everywhere, Douglas Grenwall, making nickels digging for scoops like sea clams. Every tent that gets pitched in this nation with angry mammals beckoned underneath will have one of ours among them, seeking your muzzle out. Are we perfectly clear, sir?" He let the fossa go.

Without a word, Grenwall took two teetering steps, opened the door himself, and departed without a backwards glance, leaving the hall visible in ghostly silence.

Charlie closed it away, returned to his desk, and gazed curiously at the empty whiskey glass resting there. The bottle of Ballantine's waited by the folder sent to him by Michael earlier, which he opened. He poured again, feeling his hand shake with spent ire as he pored over the images sent back from Scranton, Pennsylvania wondering what the hell they could mean.

"How'd that make you feel?" The voice came from the room's corner. "Confronting him in that way?"

His hackles leapt up and the room got cold.

"It wasn't my intention to startle you." The voice bled from one shadow in a corner. It grew fingers, hooves, and a black dress that was tight to a sinewy cervine shape. Even when he recognized Celeste stepping out from an impossible crevice of dark into the meager light, he fought to regain his breath.

"Don't ever do that again. Did Crawford send you?"

"No. He's catching up with his son. That's not why I'm here." Celeste made nary a sound on the carpet as she approached the desk and the bottle of whiskey standing sentry there. Her expression was haggard, her emotions withdrawn. "I need a word."

"And I need to speak with you." Charlie recovered fast. He didn't need his gun but he knew to an inch how far it was from his grasp. Blake's people had borne the brunt of suspicion for Agent Tomlinson's disappearance, but Charlie would never forget what he'd seen. Celeste was a killer, always would be.

"I asked how it made you feel," Celeste repeated.

"Right," Charlie answered. "It felt right."

She considered saying something that she instead kept to herself.

Charlie smoothed his brow fur. "I sent people to your burned house outside Scranton." He picked up the stack of photographs couriered to him by car and turned them round. "You should see these."

Celeste met his gaze, then glanced down and shuffled the prints, studying each one. Holes had been dug, holes that were empty.

"Was this your people?" she asked worriedly.

"No. Several holes turned up like this and the mail was taken. The bottom photo has something we just don't understand."

Celeste went through the photographs of the remains of her destroyed home and emotion was kept out of the doe's expression until the last. She set it down with deliberate stillness. In the last photograph a stack of iron fence posts lain as scrap next to the house had been disturbed. Three of them were stood upright in the ground in a short row. Two of the spike-headed poles were tall, while the last of the three had been driven further into the ground to make it over a foot shorter than the others. Emotions played across her face that Charlie was afraid to decipher. Anger wasn't hard to pick out.

"Can you tell me who took your nails?"

Celeste looked up, expression purged neutral with effort. "Someone who will have those nails destroyed or lost but is most certainly not your friend. Or mine. That's what I've come to speak with you about."

Charlie scratched behind an ear. "I've nothing to drink that you'd want, but please do have a seat."

Celeste turned to the window. "I have a confession to make, but it's information that would be useful to you." She took a moment to steel herself. "From the year nineteen-twenty to nineteen twenty-three I worked on a freelance basis for Johnny Torrio's outfit in Chicago, Illinois. In that capacity, I killed seventeen mobsters, three corrupt officials, and two informants as an assassin for hire. I was very good at that job, Agent Rothscub. I tidied up many loose ends very efficiently."

Charlie's palms felt sweaty on the desk. "Why are you telling me all this? Are you turning yourself in?"

"No. I will admit nothing on record and sign no confessions. I come to you because with those skills, and some freelance investigative work during intervening years, we can help each other."

"How so?"

"You've already had exposure to one enemy to American interests that you didn't see coming. The Martyres of the Black Well shared to some extent what their goals are."

"Wipe your kind out."

"With prejudice and no regard for collateral damage, as you've no doubt learned. I read the Boston Post today, saw the guns and the pictures they took of those dragged away. I've seen their like before."

"The Colonel's people who we arrested."

Celeste nodded. "I understand lost people pointed at power and freed from restraint very well. I'm sorry to say they and your rich fossa swindler aren't your only problem."

The room got colder. Charlie swallowed. "Go on."

"Others of my kind with far less scruples than I have banded together for…something. A plan of some sort. They took the life of someone dear to me and led another down a path to some cause that I'm certain will endanger his existence, him and the rest of us. I have to learn more and stop them. I don't have the means to do this alone with the resources I have."

"So…what are you proposing, Celeste?"

She glanced in the mirror between the shadows, didn't find anything interesting there, and glanced beyond it to the glints of street life outside. She weighed something heavy within herself. "I tried to live a quiet secluded life, keep a home, stay invisible. It didn't work. Not for any of us. All I ever wanted in life was taken, what I held dear turned against me. And something is coming. We have mutual enemies." She looked haunted as she glanced higher out the hotel room's window at nothing at all. "At this point fighting is all I know how to do. So, I intend to do that."

She turned and met his gaze evenly. "For what he tried to do and for whom he tried to hurt, do you want the fossa to die tonight?"

Charlie stared at her and she back. "No," he heard himself say without even thinking for a moment.

Her ears fluttered and then settled, gaze remaining implacable. "Good. If you'd answered too easily in the affirmative, I'd have known right away that power too easily corrupts you too." She lowered herself into the armchair in the corner so they were eye to eye, her stature putting her gaze just above his.

393

"What if I'd answered with *difficulty* in the affirmative?" Charlie asked her.

Celeste only smiled in reply and the cold twinkle in her eye illuminated something Charlie hadn't really internalized before. She was beautiful, deadly beautiful by the standards of any mammal who was attracted to her sex, and Charlie could intuit that her tools of persuasion were no less formidable than her capacity for violence. Just how long had she even been in this room, anyway?

"So, you're proposing working with me? With the government?" he asked more carefully.

She nodded slowly. "With you. From what I've seen, your government's wants are fickle to say the least."

"I can't argue that."

She leaned forward. "We both know," she said, "that such would have to be a clandestine arrangement. You can't tell your people in Washington any of this."

She was right. Charlie had imagined countless ways to broach the subject of creatures in the dark living for centuries and drinking blood for sustenance. Always his rational mind's eye concluded with wan smiles followed by sedatives in a padded room. Sadly, keeping his lights on every night had never been the work of a paranoiac. He was barely further along the curve than anyone else in Hoover's shiny new outfit.

He nodded. "I have some pull, and I can deputize agents. The less paperwork the better. That approval was gained on...improvised circumstances."

"Such as hunting embedded fascists? I don't discount their danger for a second and I'm happy to help deal with that problem on the side."

Charlie met her gaze and let himself be scared of what he saw there. "My boss has it in for communists, mostly."

It was eerie that she didn't sigh. "Can't hurt him with what he can't know."

Charlie took a deep breath. "First Nosfur undercover agent for the United States of America. We'll never be able to write that milestone in anything," he muttered as he stood up. He didn't want to drink anymore.

He opened the hotel bedside drawer. The Gideons had been by. He removed the Bible and walked to where the Nosfur doe waited patiently.

"Can you swear on one of these?"

What he saw in her eyes wasn't patient at all. Slow burgeoning anger was sequestered. "God and I do get along on the very rare occasion, Agent Rothscub. So, I can swear on anything you like." Her ear cocked at that moment as something caught her attention. "But perhaps we should handle oaths later."

"Something wrong?"

Her nose worked. "No, I don't think so." She shook her head ruefully and her demeanor admitted a trace of pained amusement. "You might as well have a waiting bench outside your door."

The knock came right away, hard and insistent.

Celeste rose. "I'll follow your fossa quarry out, make sure he gets where he's going, and take stock of whom he sees. We'll work on minor payroll details later." She slid open the window and admitted a breeze that ruffled her tight dress. They were four floors up and Charlie knew there was nothing outside. "I regret I can't close this from the outside," she added.

"How did you even get in?" Charlie asked, but without even touching the ledge, she slipped from sight.

The knock came again, more insistent.

Grenwall was feeling chagrined and coming up for another round. Or perhaps his puma servant or even one of Blake's stragglers. Taunting the fossa had felt good, but as he checked the pipe on his forty-five it occurred to him that he might have opened himself up too wide to the rich bastard.

He unlatched the door and kept his muzzle back as he opened it.

Another wolf's nose caught his scent. Crawford looked tired, sore, and still a bit angry. "The kid joined his detail to celebrate," he growled. "You alone?"

Charlie blinked and loosened his grip on the gun. "Pretty sure."

Crawford shouldered his way in. Charlie got out of his way and the grey wolf elbowed the door shut behind him. The rumpled clothes looked like they'd been shot onto his body from a cannon and bourbon on his breath traced a stronger scent.

"Did you come to fight some—"

"Shut up," Crawford demanded. "You feel ready to apolo—"

"Shut up," Charlie replied, dumped his mag, ejected the round, and tossed the open gun on his luggage.

Night city sounds came in through the open window, growls went out. Gazes agreed, words were useless after all.

They grabbed for each other's muzzle at the same time, first in hard-play cuffs, then their teeth clicked as muzzles locked together. Claws found shoulders, pulled, then tore. Buttons peppered wallpaper. They bounced onto the bed, slacks kicking free, shirts flayed open. Slain fabric spread underneath them both. Teeth and tongues worked one another over, and when Crawford hissed at a hurt, he pulled a momentarily reluctant Charlie closer to explore elsewhere.

Charlie did, nosing, pulling hurt needy scents apart as he moved south. Soon enough the brown wolf moved past the lean belly to lap at the grey wolf's salty scrotum and trace his straightening shaft with a slide against his jaw. Crawford spread himself and shivered against the cold footboard of the hotel's bed as heat rose. Charlie parted his lips and got to work, sucking his cock clean of countless layered scents, some of it blood. Charlie felt the fire rise inside of himself before one last lap, rising to drag the wolf toward him by this thighs.

"What're you—" Crawford nearly hummed.

"I thought we told each other to shut up," Charlie growled and slicked his own shaft with his own cock's dew before pressing an equally slick finger between grey-furred buttocks, winding within. Crawford's gasp was bright with surprise and need at once. Charlie lined himself up, grabbed Crawford's spread legs, and moved his hands up thighs and shins to the grey wolf's ankles as he slid hot past the tightness and started fucking, his hips a quickening piston, muzzle panting wide. The rough pads on the bottom of Crawford's wide feet spread under his kneading thumbs and he rode harder and faster.

"I'm going over the falls," Crawford grunted, eyes crossing.

"Not yet. In me. You hold it till you get it in me you feral bastard." Charlie came then, Crawford's erect dick leaking down before him. He pulled out fast, still ejaculating onto the other wolf's pelt and restrained himself from granting Crawford another lick that would finish him off. Instead, he threw himself on his side, making them both bounce on the bed. Crawford spooned him.

"I'm not slick." Crawford grabbed himself. "It'll hurt."

"Let it." Charlie grabbed his own flank, spread the buttock and cold and heat mixed where the wet cock found him. He had to have it now. "For crying out loud, Craw."

So, Crawford did as ordered. A starburst of pain and flaring heat settled into the rhythmic dance of Crawford's hips against his. The movement hurt less and less with each thrust and the balance of bliss and soreness was pure and welcome. Charlie hadn't come down from his own ejaculation before heat flooded him. Crawford's hiss was a sizzle of hot steel and their hips slowed to rest.

They breathed. Outside Boston honked and muttered.

"Still mad?" Charlie asked.

"Ask later," Crawford said indifferently. He played with Charlie's ear for a moment, flattening it against his skull, letting it pop high again. "Why were you so on edge when I knocked?"

It didn't matter. Just the furred hands holding him were all he wanted to think about. But think he did.

"I just told a wealthy cheating con artist who tried to hurt a lot of people what I really am. What lots of us are if he ever stops to think about it."

"A good lay?"

Charlie couldn't help but smile. He didn't have Crawford's fangs or Celeste's but he didn't need them. "One of a great many people you don't dare try and walk over." In the moment Charlie was both nervous and exhilarated, a different sort of spark lit within. He was carrying a torch forward into the dark that had plagued his dreams every night and a way out was ahead. He let Crawford's strong warm hands grip his own tightly and feared nothing at all.

***

In the heart of Kansas, the very center of America, bottles and urns were kept and tended in mine shafts long drained of mineral wealth and filled anew with something far more precious.

Joys and pains were anchors as the sisters sat in their circle and sifted.

"The science-borne sun brings a war to end," Baliosi Belle breathed in the center of their carefully curated world.

"And the coldest peace our fears will tend," Grisand coughed. The years were catching up and the otter knew her days were short.

"The empire out West, will seek no rest..." Lillis sighed. "Sorry girls. Still having trouble finding the groove."

"You don't need to rush anything," Baliosi said calmly. "It took me years to hold it all together. The threads of fate don't ever knit from just one end. You have to feel along till you find it."

"I've found that it's all beautiful even when it's not accurate," offered a passing beaver who smiled with fangs astride his bucked teeth and turned a couple bottles on the shelf before trundling off into the dark.

"Thanks, Joachim!" Baliosi and Grisand said at once. "He's a sweetie," Grisand added and coughed again.

Lillis waited till the beaver, who she'd been told was a previously enslaved Nosfurratu, went on his way. "I just don't want to let you both down."

"You can't!" Baliosi said with a wolfish smile. "You'll feel the eddies at the pace that's set for you, and you'll see what you're supposed to see. You just need to practice letting go to hold on."

"Get yous to Carnegie Hall," Grisand muttered with a laugh that hurt her. "Let's try again. There's no wrong where you're telling it. You'll be spoken through as we all are, chère."

They settled in, and the saved whispers from behind a thousand corks and wax stoppers all around them cried and thanked and begged and prayed. The eddy came and they surrendered to it as the candlelight danced on breath wheezing up through the earth's lungs.

"A kingdom west where wheels ever turn," Balisoi remembered.

"But only fortunes move, advanced or spurned," Grisand saw.

"Leads a path to the place where yearning sates," Lillis felt her fur stand up as the current rushed in.

"The lost man who's a boy seeks to bend all fates."

"To dire plans laid plain for the doe's loving pain,"

"And the wolf who finds new familial vein,"

"The capital stamp of the foe pointed out,"

"Won't stop the mammal who'd twist and who'd shout,"

"In the place where hope leads the lost souls with their pleads,"

"Waits the fool…" The line cut and sputtered. The candlelight stood upright. The sisters stopped to breathe.

"What was that?" Lillis gasped. "I felt…ecstasy and suffering in a soul that didn't know one from the other anymore." The bear shivered and stress-shed strands of fur slipped off her neck, down her caftan, and onto the rocky floor.

Grisand and Baliosi were silent, sifting their own frayed strands and finding something familiar they didn't like, something they themselves, as fate's hand, had been a part of all too recently.

"I knew that was going to come around again," Baliosi said bitterly.

Grisand remembered. "Oh yeah." She sighed like a broken rattle. "That asshole…"

EPILOGUE

"THEN I HEARD THE JUDGE MAKE HIS DECISION..."

He should have turned the radio off to save power drawn by the headlamps, but Patsy Cline was alright company. He worked slowly but thoroughly, uncertain how long this would take. The derelict yard next to the decades-old tenements was all scrub and bits of brick, forever locked in deed to an owner who couldn't be reached to buy the land where another apartment would have stood otherwise. Legalese had tied progress. For now.

Pierre didn't sweat, didn't tire. His weariness was borne of impatience and worry at what he'd find. The detritus of things past had blown across the uneven scruff. Crumpled cigarette packs mixed with sodden takeout burger packages, all excreta of a careless world.

His tool came to stiffer resistance, and he had to go slower. An hour passed, spreading, sifting, and then his nose caught what he'd known he'd revile. A sepulchral stink rose as he unearthed the first layer of soil spread through with rot.

Back at the car, he got the trowel and the vial. He worked with more care. Dawn was hours away. The lights of the car dimmed so he shut them and the radio off, ending some moaning Midwest dirge by George Jones. As a French mammal, culture relentlessly absorbed him, even that which Pierre didn't care for. Such was the perpetual curse he had to suffer.

In silence, he worked with meager light coming from a close billboard lamp. He caught the scraggle of what had once been russet, now rotted to near black. His trowel scraped back dirt from teeth. He opened the vial then, let the iron nectar of life descend. A drop hit the shrivelled remains of a nose and dripped down to what few teeth were visible. He dumped it all and waited.

Movement.

He worked faster. It didn't matter if it hurt. Hurt was proof of vitality.

And hurt it did. A grizzled muzzle shot up from its prison and coughed a loathsome slurry of insects and bile up onto the slope. The creature gurgled as pipes long blocked were cleared. Eyes opened, festooned with filth, and roved up to the lone light source against the North Chicago sky.

On a billboard rendered in pastels, a dapper otter leaned possessively over the mint-green broad nose of a Chevrolet Fleetline, the silhouette of a patient paramour in a paisley scarf smiling beatifically inside. Best-selling car in America, the advert declared to eyes that hadn't spoken the language of light in decades.

The fox screamed, thrashing mindlessly, and Pierre knew there was much work ahead. Ferrault had better be happy.

"So, you're Bucky," the elk said as he went back for the shovel. "You've clearly met my ex-fiancée, Celeste."

The fox disgorged more filth and bile and gargled at the heavens.

"Yes," Pierre agreed and had to laugh despite it all. "She's just the fucking worst."

Acknowledgments

This novel was outlined while writing the back half of *The Dry Spell* in 2021 and written from about April of 2023 until August of the same year. All the while history went the way it's been going while animals in another reality went the way they did back in the dust bowl of the mid-1930s when things were rough, to say the least. A corner of Europe fell under the sway of bitter, narcissistic madmen, while on this side of the Atlantic, people suffered both the ecological ruin of the Dust Bowl and the gambling debts of financial speculators, both disenfranchising millions. Calamity finds blame long before workable solutions. And blame is the feeding trough of con artists and autocrats. Many of us knew that.

Nature makes no one a monster, even in the worst of circumstances. Very deliberate choices do. This run of furry-history-fantasy-critter yarns are about that if anything. I hate that this ninety-year-old chapter in history is somewhat topical now and became more so while spooling out, but I know that despite everything it did pass. We've read this stanza in history's rhyme before. Once again, we fight to choose who writes the next verse and, in the process, leave no one behind.

Thanks very much to FurPlanet for having me around for another round, and to all the critters that keep the Badger and Fox's lifeblood flowing. Thanks also to my beta-reading /editing team of NightEyes DaySpring, Utunu, Domus, and Ty. Special extra thanks to Utunu and Ty for the extensive copy edits required in order to get this ship to launch. And finally, for my mate Kim, who heard me mutter arcane dialogue aloud as I clattered these keys and has called nobody to drag me away. Thus far.

About the Author

Ryan Loup-Glissant, (AKA Slip-Wolf) has been writing and publishing furry science-fiction, horror and fantasy for 15 years from various haunts in the West Greater Toronto Area and Niagara Wine Region. The Dry Spell is his first novel after a long affair with short fiction.

He's travelled extensively, loves reading history and fiction of all types and is obsessed with crashing genres into each other at unsafe speeds. When not doing this, he does relatively safer things on motorcycles.

ALSO BY RYAN LOUP-GLISSANT

Novels (as **Ryan Loup-Glissant**)

With **FurPlanet**

The Dry Spell

Short Fiction (as **Slip-Wolf**)

In Print with **FurPlanet** and in e-book form with **Bad Dog Books**:

Relics, Rabbits and Tuscan Reds – *ROAR Volume 6*
Kypris' Kiss – *ROAR Volume 8*
Ashes – *FANG Volume 6*
His Palace – *FANG Volume 7*
Heavenly Flesh – *FANG Volume 8*
I Went Back 50 years and killed the Vicious Tyrant Adon Howlitz and All of You are Welcome – *FANG Volume 9*
Waters – *FANG Volume 10*
Smokey and The Jay bird – *CLAW Volume 1*
Every Breath Closer – *Inhuman Acts: a Collection of Noir*
Sighs for the Labyrinth – *Dungeon Grind*
Chain Link – *Will of the Alpha 2*
Mustard Mulato – *Will of the Alpha 3*
A Melody in Seduction's Arsenal – *Gods with Fur*
Lime Tiger – *Dogs of War 2*
The Oroborous Plate – *Bleak Horizons*
Vanilupus and Other People's Wits Take on the Inhospitable World – *Tales From The Guild: World Tour*

In Print with **SofaWolf Press:**

Jewels of Remorse – *Heat Issue 11*
Unfading – *Heat Issue 12*
Skyleaper – *Heat Issue 13*
West – *Heat Issue 14*
American Heat – *Heat Issue 16*

In print with **Weasel Press:**

Due – *Knotted Volume 1* (Also available as an e-book with Bad Dog Books)
Paint the Square Cut Sky – *Fragments of Life's Heart Anthology* (available as an e-book with Bad Dog Books)

www.ingramcontent.com/pod-product-compliance
Lightning Source LLC
Chambersburg PA
CBHW071147020726
47502CB00002B/307